CW01642862

TH

THOMAS HEALD

WWW.THOMASHEALD.COM

THOMAS HEALD

HUNTER GATHERER

First published in paperback by
Michael Terence Publishing in 2025.
www.mtp.agency

ISBN 9781800949461

Cover image (AI)
Michael Terence Publishing

Michael Terence
Publishing

For my darling wife Margaret,
forever in my thoughts…

MEET ADAM FOX

Born:
North Yorkshire.

Physical description:
6ft 4in height, 14 stone 3 pounds, slim figure, clean-shaven, black hair, smartly dressed.

Education:
Grammer school, university degree, police college.

Employment:
South Yorkshire & Derbyshire police constabulary.

Personal profile:
Married to Dr. Vivian Flemming, one daughter Scarlett, no hobbies, goes to the gym twice a week to maintain his fitness, likes music, in particular The Beatles.

MEET VIVIAN FLEMING

Born:
Lincolnshire.

Physical description:
5ft 8in height, 11 stone 4 pounds, slim figure, long blond hair, casual dresser.

Education:
Lincolnshire Grammar School, Sheffield University, Nottingham Medical School.

Employment:
General Practitioner Edgewater Medical Centre, Derbyshire.

Personal profile:
Married to Adam Fox, one daughter Scarlett, hobbies, healthy eating, gardening, and socialising, with a keen interest in clinical innovation and patient care.

Dear Reader

This book is by a brand-new writer. Thomas Heald introduces some new characters with clear-cut and intensive storylines. Based in and around the Derbyshire and Nottinghamshire boundaries, the stories focus on two main individuals, Detective Inspector Adam Fox and his GP wife, Dr Vivian Flemming, who through personal tragedy, have relocated to this beautiful part of England.

Hunter Gatherer is the debut book from Thomas Heald, achieving a lifetime ambition of writing what I believe will be a best-selling novel.

Creating new individuals from scratch is always demanding. I do hope that you allow both Adam and Viv to become familiar with you as they have with me over the last two years.

Thanks, and enjoy the read.

– Thomas Heald

"I will hurt you for this. I don't know how yet but give me time. A day will come when you think yourself safe and happy, and suddenly your joy will turn to ashes in your mouth, and you'll know the debt is paid."

– George R.R. Martin

Prologue

AS I LIE IN BED, THE HORRORS build up in my body, and I struggle to let them loose. My heart is pounding in my chest and my pulse, hammering in my ears. I wake up with nightmares that continue to come and go. It's always been the same, these recurring visions that have plagued me all these years. As the morning light drifts through the partially opened curtains, waking me fully after months of torment, anguish, and distress I finally make the decision. This was the day I was going to start to put my scheme in place, bringing comfort from flashbacks of the past.

Beginning unhurried and over time, selectively, my plan will ensure that they all suffer as I and my friends had suffered for all those years.

Showering, hoping once again that this would wash the images away, which it never did, I get dressed in the second-hand clothes that I'd purchased many months ago, which will be burned later in the day.

I make my way down the carpeted stairs, looking at the family portraits hanging on the wall, and into the kitchen, which remains untidy from the Chinese I'd ordered and eaten the night before, opening the leaded window to let the smell of stale food and red wine drift away.

Sitting at the solid oak table and drinking hot, strong coffee I run through in my mind what is my execution plan, all of them need to bear what I and many others endured, they deserve to experience pain, and *yes,* it will hurt, it's intended to.

Maybe not all of them right now. I'd got to be careful and protect my identity, but I've plenty of time on my hands, it might take months, probably years, there's no hurry. 'I've plenty of time.'

Checking I'd got all the equipment I needed and closing the door to the house, I walk down the gravel path, cutting a red rose from a standard bush at the side of me, a smile on my face and turning back, I wave to someone who hasn't been there for years.

What I started that day still haunts me all this time later and remains a permanent reminder of the sadistic and horrific actions that I'm now taking.

The first person I'd hunted down always took the same walking route to the pub, every Sunday morning come rain or shine, without fail, a person of habit no doubt, so it wasn't too difficult to arrange where to meet up.

I don't think he knew that I lived just outside the village, why would he, it was so long ago, so when I contacted him and asked if he could meet me near the entrance to the wooded area about a hundred yards from the pub and shielded from prying eyes, I was initially amazed that he accepted.

Interestingly to him, it didn't seem to come as a surprise, although there did appear to be an air of confusion and then caution in his voice, as we hadn't seen each other for some time.

The car started on the second turn, checking my watch, I'd plenty of time to kill I thought, and putting it into first gear, I made my way to the meeting point we'd pre-arranged, somewhere quiet, and at the time, hopefully, relatively isolated, where no one would see us together.

The journey didn't take as long as I thought, although it was Sunday morning, a day of rest for some.

I was already there when he arrived, he was dressed differently than what I remembered or expected, baggy grey stained trousers and a loose-fitting cardigan, the smell of smoke still on his clothes, his long grey, unwashed hair blowing in the wind.

Despite his appearance, I recognised him immediately, how could I forget, but he couldn't bring me to mind at first, just my name when I telephoned him out of the blue. Why would he, it was a long time ago, a time that I wanted to try and erase from my memory but couldn't.

That made what I'd intentionally prepared to do all the more satisfying.

'Hello,' he said, with a slight look of puzzlement, as if there'd been some misunderstanding about why we were meeting.

'Your call surprised me… After all these years, it must be, honestly speaking, I can't truly remember.'

'I remember it well,' I replied, 'but it's a period I'd prefer to forget.'

He looked directly into my eyes, unsure what that meant or what to say.

Slightly nervously he replied, 'Well, it's good to see you again I suppose, didn't know you lived locally?'

'Lived in Derbyshire most of my life, good times and some not so good, you'd know a lot about that,' I said under my breath so he couldn't hear.

'If you don't mind me saying, this is an odd place to meet, the local pub in the village would have been better. I go there most Sundays as they do a great lunch.'

Hesitating slightly, I replied,

'Here's fine. I'm fine.'

Standing there with him in front of me brought it all back into focus, a period in my life that I wanted to forget, but couldn't, it was like a cancer, eating away at me, and like all cancers, it had to be removed.

I'd hidden the hammer behind my back, tucking it into the waistband of my blue denim jeans, so it was initially out of sight. I moved my right arm and grabbed the handle lifting the hammer above me.

The first blow struck the right side of his head, a look of shock in his eyes, as blood began to trickle down from his ear rising into his nostril as he desperately tried to take a deep breath. His mouth opened, showing yellowed teeth from constant smoking. Trying to say something, but nothing came out, just a gurgling sound followed by blood and spit.

He fell onto his knees in front of me, as I lifted my hand and struck him a second time, on the top of his head, exposing the white and grey matter of the brain. Falling on his side, his body started to shake uncontrollably. Kneeling, grazing my knee on a sharp piece of stone, as I raised the hammer, a third blow to his face crushing those yellowing teeth back into his throat. That wasn't planned, but it did mean that identifying the body would be more difficult. I took out the kitchen knife from my black bag, together with the cigarette lighter. It didn't take long for the blade to turn white, heat moving up the handle. Very slowly, taking each of his hands, I burn his fingertips, ensuring that identification would be increasingly difficult. The smell of burning flesh rose into my nostrils. That would buy me time I thought, time, which seems to have stood still.

As the body lay there, I waited to make sure he was dead, looking around to check that there was no one in sight, it does attract visitors from time to time.

Once I knew all was clear, I laid the body out, legs together and arms by his side. His long grey hair dampened the soil absorbing the remnants oozing from his skull.

I noticed a signet ring on his little finger and removed it over the burnt skin, it was inscribed with the initial A, which I placed in the bag together with all the other items and closed the zip.

I get to my feet, stepping back to check my handiwork, my heart was pounding, not from remorse but from the satisfaction of what taking revenge felt like.

Finally, I sprinkle rose petals over the body, letting the wind take them in all directions, and lastly removing and throwing the pair of gardening gloves that I'd worn well into the overgrown bushes.

I head back to my car the way I'd come, blood beginning to soak into the knee of my jeans. Opening the boot, I throw the bag inside, before driving off, a feeling of fulfilment moving through my body.

One

THE SUNLIGHT MADE MY EYES squint as I climbed the well-trodden wooden steps up to the brightly lit courtroom, turning once and then again until I reached the top. This was the day that everything would change forever, after months in detention, I was finally realising that my life was never going to be the same again. Holding the wooden bar in front of me, I notice dirt under some of my fingernails from gardening.

Adjusting to the bright lights, I looked around the room, my face reflecting at me in the protective glass of the dock. Seated right opposite. I count twelve people of different ages, eight men and four women.

Feeling the tensions rising in my body, I swallow hard to try and keep my composure. It was impossible to understand what the jury was thinking, there was no reaction when they saw me standing there in front of them. Just blank faces that theoretically held my future in their hands.

Moments later a large polished wooden door opened at the front of the court, and everyone stood as the judge entered and took his seat under a large image of the UK Government Crest.

'All stand,' said the court clerk.

Dressed in an outfit of red and white, with a black belt around his waist, the judge opened his laptop, removed his glasses, and looked up.

Two Prison Officers stood at my side, one glanced at me as the court clerk looked over towards the dock.

'Will the defendant please stand?.'

Holding onto the banister in front of me, I stand up, my legs feeling like lead weights were tied to them.

'Will the foreman please stand, have you reached a verdict of which you've all agreed?'

All eyes were on the foreman as he casually rose from his seat. A middle-aged man, around fifty years of age, who'd together with the other jurors, had been discussing my fate.

He stood up, cleared his throat, and spoke.

'Yes.'

The court clerk purposely looked up at the judge,

'Do you the jury, find the defendant Daniel Ashby guilty or not guilty of murder?'

Seconds passed in silence, as the man glanced over to face me, the accused.

'Guilty,' delivered the foreman.

Two

THE DARK GREY HEAVY METAL DOOR opened for what was hopefully the final time, shedding further light into the prison cell. 'Move to the back wall,' said the prison officer with a serious look and a stern voice.

'Now, step forward Ashby and follow me.'

Walking down the prison corridor, Daniel thought the smell of cleaning fluids, unwashed bodies, and over-boiled food, would never leave his nostrils, as clapping from some of the inmates echoed with shouts of 'Good luck, Danny, watch you back out there' and 'Best of luck mate' bellowed around the tall grey walls.

The twelve-foot by eight-foot prison cell had been the home to Daniel Ashby for the last fourteen years, following his sentence at Nottingham Crown Court, in the East Midlands. The jury at his trial had found him guilty of the slaying and the murder of Arthur Richardson. He was sentenced to twenty-four years in a maximum-security prison. Danny, as he became known would never bring himself to admit the crime he was convicted of. He knew he was innocent, and if he'd admitted his guilt his sentence would have reduced.

Although he'd been locked up all that time, he'd never forget the day of his sentence. His Right Honourable Justin-Courtney looked sternly at him over his half-rimmed glasses and asked him to stand.

Daniel did as he was told, looking around the courtroom for his mum and dad, his mum had promised to be there, but she wasn't sure about her husband. Members of the public had formed a line outside the court to make sure they'd get a seat to hear the verdict.

Daniel continued to look around the courtroom, but he couldn't see his parents among all the staring faces.

'Daniel Ashby, you have been found guilty of first-degree murder of Arthur Richardson, have you anything to say?'

The prosecution had already presented the case against the defence, emphasising some of the critical points, which in their mind, was why the jury would come to the right decision.

His defence lawyer, a slim, well-dressed woman who'd represented Daniel from the first day of his arrest, stood up, checking her notes for the final time.

'Your Honour, my client continues to claim his innocence, and due to his age, I request the most lenient sentence to be passed. Daniel Ashby has never been in trouble with the police and runs his own successful landscaping and gardening business. He's popular with his customers, having done work for some of them for several years. He is well-liked in the village where he lives with his mother and father. He categorically denies any involvement in this shocking crime and is determined to prove his innocence, no matter the outcome.'

Judge Justin-Courtney sat and reviewed his notes, repositioned himself in his highchair and spoke.

'Daniel Ashby, you have been found guilty of the manslaughter of Arthur Richardson, this was a heartless and cruel act from someone as young as yourself. Taking everything into consideration, including the comments from your solicitor, I sentence you to twenty-four years in a maximum-security prison, with a minimum sentence of fourteen years, take him down.'

There was a silence in the courtroom as members of the public began to digest both the verdict and the sentence, some beginning to stand and make their way towards the exit at the back of the courtroom, some of them looking around for Mary Ashby, Daniel's mother.

She sat at the back trying to avoid eye contact, a lonely figure, with tears in her eyes, and a dishevelled look on her face, as her only son was taken away.

Three

IT WAS AN OVERCAST DAY in Nottingham as crowds gathered outside the imposing Crown Court.

Family and friends of Arthur Richardson, together with local photographers, stood waiting for Daniel Ashby to leave and join the other inmates in the white security vehicle, commonly known as the Court Bus, transporting all of them to prison.

The same two prison officers who'd been with him in court accompanied him to the awaiting vehicle, protecting him from several people who moved forward, shouting abuse.

'Rot in hell,' shouted one young woman, as cameras began to click, trying desperately to catch a glimpse of Daniel for the local papers.

He climbed the steps and entered, a strong smell of disinfectant hitting his nostrils.

'Move towards the last door on the right,' said one of the prison officers. Daniel slowly walked down the vehicle, passing numbered doors on both his right, and left, reaching door number eight.

With it securely locked, the engine roared into action, flashes like lightning continued through the small opaque window, as the last remaining journalists ran alongside, trying to capture that final, all-important shot.

It didn't take long to arrive at the prison, with Danny and five other inmates exiting the security van, high stone walls giving a fearsome impression of darkness.

A tall stocky prison officer with a clipboard stood at the exit to the vehicle, all six men were immediately checked in and escorted to a reception area, if you could call it that.

Time seemed to stand still, as Danny was interviewed and assessed, prison rules explained, which was followed by a strip search by one of the male officers. He was assigned a prison number; his photograph was taken together with his fingerprints.

Finally, several hours later, he was shown to his cell, closing the metal door, locking him in for the night. He sat on the side of the single bed, all alone for the first time he could ever remember.

Wakefield prison is classed as a category A jail, one of the oldest institutions in the country, housing hundreds of murderers and sexual predators, and one of the toughest prisons in the UK.

In the early days and weeks, Danny had to become accustomed to witnessing drug taking. Vulnerable inmates were being punished for not doing as they were told. And regular fighting broke out between prisoners.

He was told to keep his distance. Not to get involved. He did as he was told.

Being only twenty-two when he was sentenced, his time in prison for such a young man was to prove difficult and potentially, dangerous.

His solicitor had explained that if he'd been a few years younger, he'd have ended up in a Youth Offenders Institute. But he wasn't and he didn't.

Four

PRESENT DAY

DERBYSHIRE, UNITED KINGDOM. THE DO NOT CROSS blue and white plastic tape swayed gently in the wind, moving in and out like a heavy sea. Having been tied from several branches by one of the young, uniformed officers on duty.

He was wet, cold and by the look on his face, wasn't enjoying this part of the job, all he was doing was following orders, not to let any unauthorised people cross the taped line.

It had rained throughout the night, leaving pools of water and sodden ground underfoot, small twigs cracking underneath fallen brown rotting leaves, and mist rising as the early morning began to warm up.

Detective Inspector Adam Fox, known to his close friends and colleagues as 'The Man,' parked his metallic black Audi A4 about 10 yards from the cordoned area. Blue flashing lights bounced off the leafy trees, giving a ghostly look everywhere.

He took a quick drink from a water bottle, flicked the boot release, exited his car, and walked round to the back, taking out a pair of size 10 black wellingtons, donning a pair of blue latex gloves and wrapping a face mask around his wrist.

He looked down at his feet, telling himself. 'Wellingtons looked ridiculous with suit trousers.'

DI Fox was part of the Serious Crime Unit for the East Midlands force. The SCU had responsibility for the Derbyshire County boundaries, covering the main city of Derby and the surrounding geographical areas stretching from Glossop in the North to Swadlincote to the South. Famous for its ever-changing landscape, rolling hills and dramatic peaks, Derbyshire is one of the most picturesque counties in the country.

It was still raining slightly, droplets catching his eyelids as he made his way down towards the young officer, his fluorescent jacket making him stand out in the semi-darkness. He checked the time on his watch, 07.27 a.m. whilst still early in the morning, Adam was surprised to see a handful of onlookers.

Two dog walkers in their raincoats, an early jogger getting their exercise and someone standing much closer, dressed in a long dark-coloured coat, and wearing what looked like a black and white baseball cap, the peak hiding their face.

They were holding something in their hand, it could have been a notebook or a mobile phone, clearly trying to assess what was taking place, making notes or taking photographs.

The officer, PC D1026 on his lapel, asked for identification, which Adam provided by showing the officer his warrant card. The young man proceeded to record D I Adam Fox in the logbook.

Most police officers sympathise with anyone being on duty at a crime scene, it was one of the shittiest roles you could encounter. As the young officer closed the logbook, Adam asked him in an empathetic manner, 'How much longer do you have to go young man?'

The police officer looked at his watch, 'About another four hours sir, but it might be longer if the relief doesn't turn up.'

'I remember my first time doing crime scene duty, it sounds to some people outside the force, quite exciting, but once you're here it's no fun is it?'

'No fun at all sir. But you've got to start somewhere, and since junior school, all I've ever wanted to be is a police constable, my parents wanted me to go into teaching, like my old man, but it wasn't for me sir. So, I'm happy to start at the bottom and work my way up, that's my plan, and it's interesting to experience a crime scene like this and absorb what's going on sir.'

'Well good luck, we need dedicated officers like yourself, so if I can help in any way now or in the future, just ask for me at Police HQ, my name is Detective Inspector Adam Fox, but you've recorded that already.'

Adam had checked the names of the people there when he signed in, three names on the sheet. Odd, he thought, how come they got here so soon?

He quickly glances back, checking the car is remotely locked, noticing that the figure in the black coat has disappeared.

Lifting the tape himself, he made his way down the path, trying to avoid mud attaching itself to the bottom of his wellingtons, and into the wooded area, noticing his boss a short distance away.

Detective Superintendent Tom Vickers walked over and shook hands, feeling cold to the touch. Although Adam had been in post for almost six months, his boss still greeted him with a handshake; he often wondered if that would ever change.

'Hi Adam, good to see you,' he said, 'Sorry for the call and dragging you away on your day off, but this looks like a nasty one, female I understand, not sure of age at this point, found in the woods by two ramblers.'

'Not a problem sir,' my wife's on call over the weekend, so it's fine.'

'How is Vivian? Has she settled into the new job, it's a great medical centre apparently, with an excellent care team. You know what they say, new job, new house, new baby.'

All DCI Vickers was trying to do was lighten the moment. But embarrassed the minute he'd said it.

'I'm sorry Adam, that was a real crap thing to say. I don't know what I was thinking, *I am sorry*.'

'Actually, we're doing okay. Viv has settled well into the GP Practice, and I was ready for a new change, being honest, I stayed in the South Yorkshire division for too long. And with that official inquiry still hanging over the force, it was the right time to move, it's good for both of us.'

The two of them made their way further along the path towards the bright lights, as the rain intensified, noticing the white tent, illuminated in the distance. Neither of them said a word, the silence giving an eerie feeling as they headed towards the crime scene, not fully knowing what lay ahead.

The victim *was* a woman, possibly in her mid-sixties, she was fully dressed in dark black trousers, a light grey loose-fitting top and laced-up trainers, which looked brand new but covered in mud.

The skin on her face was pale grey. With blue eyes, wrinkled at the edges, and pale lipstick covering her mouth, which was wide open. That wasn't what startled the two men, looking more closely, they both saw two vertical open wounds on the woman's forehead, it resembled the look of a Roman number two that had been purposely inscribed into the bloodied skin.

The Forensic Pathologist was already hard at work, on her hands and knees, examining the corpse. Her assistant, purposely kept a distance from the body, not saying a word, just walking around, taking numerous photographs of the crime scene, the camera and flash recording every single detail as it went off.

Adam noticed there was no tread on the Forensic Pathologist's black trainers she had on her feet. What stories they could tell.

Tom Vickers did the introductions.

'Alex, meet Rachel Munroe, *Dr Rachel Munroe*... Rachel, this is our new DI, Adam Fox, he's transferred down from South Yorkshire Division.'

She stood up, wiped her gloved hands down her overalls and shook Adam's hand firmly. Dr Rachel Munroe was in her late thirties, around five feet nine, with what looked like short black fringe held in place by the white hooded Tyvek over suit she was wearing, the floodlights almost giving her an angelic look.

They all stood there for a few minutes, balancing on the stainless-steel supports already in position to avoid further contamination. Several numbered evidence markers scattered around like little yellow tents, as they tried to take in what they saw in front of them.

Moments passed before the first question came from Detective Inspector Fox.

'How long do you think she's been here, and what do you think is the cause of death?'

She took a deep breath.

'Difficult to accurately say right now, but in my experience, I'd estimate a timeline between twelve and eighteen hours. I'll know more once I get her back to the morgue. But on examining the body, it looks like the victim was attached with a hammer or similar object, looking at the damage to the frontal bone of her skull. That's not what she died of however, it's clear from the obvious bruising around her neck that she's been strangled.'

She took out a handkerchief and blew her nose.

'On closer examination, I'd say with some kind of strong cord, something like that, but not thin enough to penetrate the skin so I'm thinking, possibly gardening twine or similar.'

She stepped away from the body, trying to compose herself before saying.

'But that's not what is disturbing, look at the wound on her forehead, it looks like someone has tried to carve a distinct mark. You can come up with your conclusions, but for me, it looks like the shape of a number two. Also, look at her left arm *'Look'* she said.

'The whole of her hand has been removed, the whole lot, just cut off below the wrist. I'm unable to tell you at the moment if she was alive or dead, but let's hope she *was* dead. All I can confirm is that she died here, and it doesn't look like this was a sexual assault, all her clothing is still intact. I'll know more later today, what about this afternoon, say around three o'clock, is that okay with you two?'

There was a moment of silence between them, and then almost in unison.

'That's fine,' both officers replied like that was the standard comment under these circumstances.

Both DI Fox and DCI Vickers leaned in to take a closer look at the corpse, Adam making sure he didn't slip, bile coming up into his throat as he saw the bloodied end of the woman's arm. It resembled the look of a pig's trotter he thought.

'What the hell,' said Vickers. 'Why would somebody do that to a human being? Cut their face and then remove the hand, whether she was dead or alive, it doesn't make sense.'

Regaining his composure, and standing back up, Vickers pauses for a second, trying to take in what they've just seen.

'Quick question,' said the DCI, 'any identification on her, purse, handbag, mobile, anything at all to give us an idea of who she is?'

'Sorry, not a thing, the only intriguing thing is the petals around the body, they're as dead as she is. I'm no gardener as you know, but if I'm not mistaken, these are rose petals.'

'Cheers Doc,' said Tom Vickers. 'We'll get out your way whilst you bag and tag and remove the body.'

Before they turned to leave, Adam switched on his mobile phone, taking a shot of the victim's face.

'You'll have images very soon,' said Rachel, slightly annoyed by his action.

'I know, but I need to share this image with the team, get it printed and put it on the evidence board back at the station.'

'That's okay, but you'll still have the images soonest.'

'Thanks a lot,' Adam replied.

As the two of them made their way back along the path, dawn was beginning to break throwing darting images across the path. Neither of them said anything, Adam was trying to get rid of the acrid taste in his mouth, and both trying to take in what they'd just seen. Eventually, he broke the silence turning to Tom Vickers.

'What about the two ramblers I saw when I arrived, have we already taken their statements?'

'You noticed them, did you? Yes, already been done. They'll be available for you to go over when you get back.

I'm heading off to my weekly meeting with the Chief Super, but I'll catch you or chat later no doubt.'

As he slowly walked away, pulling the collar up on his raincoat, Vickers turned back.

'We've got to move on this one Adam, when the Chief Super hears about this, she'll want it wrapped up, so the pressure will be on all of us to get a quick result.'

Adam just nodded and made his way to the car, noticing that the PC was still there, soaking wet, but still covering his duties as instructed.

Sitting in his Audi, he took a mouthful of water and spit it on the damp soil, trying to get rid of the taste of bile in his mouth.

'It's getting the right result that's important. Not a quick one,' he said to himself.

Five

THE CENTRAL POLICE Head Quarters for Derbyshire are based just outside the city centre, a sprawling, three-storey, modern building having only been officially opened several years ago by the local Member of Parliament for the area.

Surrounded by green fields and trees, with a well-manicured lawn at the front, it looks more like a corporate office than a police station.

Before the move several years ago, the original headquarters were based right in the City Centre. An old Victorian five-storey building, which took on the look of an old period house, somewhere the gentry would have lived years before. It was damp, smelt of piss, which was mainly due to the cats trying to keep the infestation of mice to a minimum and was permanently cold.

Economic cutbacks from the previous Conservative Home Secretary had left the force with substantial gaps in finances, so when the rumours started to immerge about new cash being made available from central government, and that a brand-new purpose-built office was to be created, the HR department was inundated with inquiries for jobs, ranging from outside cleaning contractors to internal administrative staff.

Pulling off the dual carriageway, and up the long tree-lined tarmac drive, DI Fox pulled into the first available space and put his parking permit on the dashboard. Noting the manicured striped grass, he made his way across the car park and through the glass doors, located under the sign, CENTRAL DERBYSHIRE POLICE HEAD QUARTERS with the motto, 'Strength United Is Greater.'

Although he was new to the post, the uniformed officer at reception had made it his mission to get to know all the faces of senior officers and pressed the button to allow him through the security doors, CCTV picking up his every move. He didn't take the lift but made his way up the stairs, two steps at a time, with no hint of being out of breath as he reached the top and unlocked his full-length glass office door.

He entered, leaving it open as usual, putting his keys in his pocket, taking off his coat and hanging it up, noticing wet patches under his arms.

When time allowed, which was always a challenge for every DI, he tried to go to the gym at least three times a week. Half an hour on the treadmill, then time on the rowing machine and finally finishing off with the weights, sweating like mad at the end, but feeling so much better for it.

He'd seen too many senior officers let themselves go, due mainly to long unsocial hours, and too many pints at the local village pub. Adam was determined that wasn't going to happen to him, he wasn't a fitness fanatic, far from it, but having a wife as a GP, constantly reminding him about his BMI, certainly focused the mind… and his body.

Adam's office was on the first floor, his official stainless-steel name plaque on the outside glass wall, ADAM FOX – DETECTIVE INSPECTOR. It was next door to the incident room and overlooked the front car park, at least he could keep an eye on his metallic black A4Audi he thought. Although new in post, he'd already made it a place of work, his desk fully operational with a very modern desk lamp, laptop, screen, phone, and a pen and pencil holder.

He glanced at the family photograph, mounted in a slim piano black finished frame, it had been taken a few years ago, on holiday in Cornwall. The three of them looked like one big happy family, he picked it up, took out his handkerchief and wiped the finger marks off the glass, purposely trying to hold back tears.

Looking around, the only thing missing was a bed, he thought facetiously.

His desk faced the office door, which he always kept open, the first floor had numerous open offices, which, according to a recent personnel survey, assisted in cross-functional working. However, when you reached a certain level, you got your own office, and Adam was at that level.

On two sides blue panelling rose from the floor to ceiling. The left side office was where the Anti-Fraud team was located, and to the right was the hub of the floor. The incident room.

This was where the wider investigation team congregated, agreeing on allocations of duties, together with progress reviews.

Adam had always been a real team player, didn't stand on ceremony, expected loyalty and got results, but didn't mind getting his hands dirty. He often wondered if that's where his nickname came from, The Man, someone who, despite his seniority, was still one of the lads.

He'd been on the police fast track scheme, having graduated from Nottingham University with a 2.1 in Criminology, and taking up his first post as a young PC in South Yorkshire.

He was determined from day one at the police training academy that there were no special privileges for this man, he wanted to be treated like all the other officers, despite his early expected potential within the senior ranks of the force.

Most officers at his level didn't pay much attention to personal appearances some paid no attention at all until a close colleague would gently remind them of their position and that a change of clothing, and maybe a shower might be in order.

Adam was different, he always wore tailored fitting suits, at the last count, Kate said he'd got seven.

At 37, he was one of the youngest DI in the job, six foot four inches tall, thirty-four-inch waist, with black hair, just going slightly grey at the sides. He looked more like a senior company executive or a solicitor, than a police officer.

However, expectations from his superiors were that he *'could go all the way to the top,'* but for now, as he sat down in his leather swivel chair, he had a job to do.

Priority number one had to be a thorough investigation, establish what had happened to this woman, get a quick result for the DCI and the Chief Superintendent, *'yes,'* close the case, *'absolutely,'* but do it the right way, the way he'd been trained.

On his desk were the witness statements of the two Ramblers. Mr and Mrs Bob Hubbard are not local people in the area. They'd driven up from just outside Luton and were staying in a small local bed and breakfast for several days.

Now both retired, they were keen walkers and enjoyed the stunning scenery in the Derbyshire and Nottinghamshire countryside.

He opened the light, brown-coloured Central Derbyshire Police crested folder and began to read what had been recorded. They'd separated the couple, putting them in different interview offices, nothing suspicious about that. It was standard operational procedure, ensuring that the investigating team got all the facts as accurately as possible, both statements were almost identical.

Keen to see the sun come up over the Derbyshire hills, they'd come across the body whilst walking through Blythe Woods, at approximately 06:05 a.m. that morning. Getting a signal from his mobile, Mr Hubbard immediately dialled 999, who contacted both the local police and the ambulance service.

He quickly read through the witness statement, then again in more detail, highlighting with a pink marker the points of interest for further investigation.

Adam checked his watch, it was 9:43 a.m. He'd heard nothing from Tom Vickers in his meeting with the Chief Superintendent. He stood up, pushed his chair back, and opened the window to let in some fresh air. This looked one hundred percent like a murder case, he thought to himself. He didn't want to pre-empt what the final autopsy report was going to say, but it was evident that the victim's body was mutilated. Tom Vickers was right, if the papers got hold of this, they'd have a field day, he could see the headlines now.

MUTILATED BODY FOUND
IN DERBYSHIRE WOODS

Once again, he looked at the family photo frame on his desk, thinking of his wife and their beautiful daughter.

He knew he'd got the experience and knowledge to run a full investigation. Ensuring every avenue was covered, every detail recorded, and every lead followed up.

Easing his chair back, he looked out over the front of the building, breathing in the smell of freshly cut grass. Little did he know what lay ahead for him and the team.

Six

ALREADY AN IMAGE OF the victim had been sent from his mobile phone to his mailbox. He was about to press the print button when his door opened, and in walked a slightly overweight man holding two cups of coffee in his hand.

'Morning Boss,' said Detective Sergeant Frank Bailey. 'I've just heard the news, is it true what's going around the station, have they found a body in Blyth Woods?'

'Come on in Frank and close the door. Take a seat, we need to talk.'

Sitting down, he placed the coffee on two wooden coasters on the desk.

'Is everything all right, you look shattered?'

'I'll come straight to the point Frank. Can you explain why no one contacted me about a body being found earlier this morning, and more to the point, why? What the hell is going on here, who contacted the DCI before getting in touch with me?'

Trying to remain professional, Adam was finding it difficult to control how annoyed and frustrated he was, failing badly.

'Listen, I'm sorry. I tried to contact you, but it was your day off, so I had no choice but to contact the DCI. You know in circumstances like this, we have to move quickly.'

Frank was being defensive, which annoyed Adam even more.

'So, let me get this straight, you tried to contact me. But I didn't pick up the call, is that what you're saying?'

'Yeah,' said Frank, 'that's correct.'

'What time did you make that supposed call, my mobile's been on all the time, so when did you ring me?'

Frank stalled for a moment, moving uneasily in the chair, realising that he couldn't continue to lie through his back teeth.

Trying to buy some time to think, he reached over and took a drink of coffee, burning the roof of his mouth in the process.

'Okay, I'll come clean. I'm sorry. I didn't call you, it *was* your day off, and I just thought it was better to contact the DCI Vickers directly. I didn't do it deliberately.'

'Bullshit, that's exactly what you did. You went behind my back and tried to cut me out of the initial investigation so that when I arrived, work had already started. To be honest, the DCI shouldn't have been there in the first place, this was a DI's responsibility, our responsibility, you and me.'

A knock at the door interrupted the conversation, as a young, well-dressed woman in a dark trouser suit placed two photographs of the victim on Adam's desk.

'These have just come off the printer, I thought you'd want them, sir.'

'Thanks,' replied Adam. 'Could you please close the door behind you?'

Adam picked up the images of the woman and handed one to the DS.

'This Frank is what we should be focusing on,' taping the photo with his finger, 'finding out about this woman. Who is she? Where does she come from and what was she doing in Blyth Woods? Not playing office politics with each other and *not* trying to undermine me or any other colleague we work with. We all have a job to do so let's get on with it. If that's okay with you,' he said sarcastically.

'The postmortem is around three o'clock this afternoon with Dr Rachel… Whatever her name is, I want you and me to be there, and *no* DCI, is that understood?'

Frank stood up, eased the chair back, and walked towards the door, turning round.

'Absolutely sir, and I'm sorry again for the misunderstanding. Oh, and by the way, it's Dr Rachel Munroe,' as he closed the door behind him.

Seven

IT WAS A SUNNY DAY, and the outside of Birmingham prison looked more like a modern brewery than a jail. With two grey imposing towers, and steps leading up to a front entrance.

Originally dating back to the Victorian era, it was built in 1849 and situated in Winson Green, close to the centre of the City. It's a category B prison and has been home to Daniel and one thousand four hundred and sixty-odd other inmates for the remainder of his sentence since being transferred from Wakefield.

Mary Ashby had initially tried to arrange for a local taxi firm in Bradwell to pick her up. Then travel to Birmingham to meet Daniel and finally bring him back home, a round journey of approximately one hundred and ten miles.

But village people are fickle, and not one local company was willing to make the journey, after all, they had a reputation to keep. The last thing they wanted was to be associated in any way with a murderer.

Eventually, after ringing around, she'd found a company in Yellow Pages, located outside the Derbyshire area, nearer Birmingham, who didn't know about Danial's background, and due to the distance, was more than willing to do the pickup.

'We don't want any more trouble,' she said under her breath.

Mary had asked her husband Philip if he would take her, but as far as he was concerned, he'd had enough. Daniel wasn't his son anymore and hadn't been since his original sentence all those years before.

'It's the shame of it all, people crossing the road to avoid me, talking in the supermarket, and as for the people at church… We should have moved when I wanted to,' he constantly would say.

But Mary had never given up on their son, *her only son,* she wasn't interested in what people said.

The happy-clappy followers at the local church, stuff them, she knew he was innocent, and one of these days, whenever that was, the truth would come out.

Mary Ashby was a very determined woman.

Daniel had eagerly been waiting for his release from the first day of his sentence, counting the days he'd already served until the halfway point, and then he started counting down all the days left to go.

It was 7.47 a.m. when the heavy cell doors were unlocked, he made his way down the corridors to the reception area for his first day of freedom.

Two prison officers checked the belongings he had with him and then started on the paperwork, which as far as Danny was concerned, was a complete waste of time, but it had to be done. Then he was shown to a holding cell, which size-wise, wasn't too dissimilar to where he'd lived for the last fourteen years. The only real difference was that it had a large safety glass window, letting in welcomed light.

It didn't take as long as he'd thought, the guards had already told him he was the only inmate leaving that morning, so the process would be quick.

Making his way out of prison for what he hoped was the last time, escorted by one prison officer, Daniel couldn't help but feel a pang of sadness for some of the great people he was leaving behind. Some who had helped him when he'd transferred to Birmingham Prison. Others who had appreciated what he'd done for them whilst inside, and some, just for being there.

Listening when we felt lonely, and cracking a joke to cheer them up, they were like an extended family.

The exit and entry doors worked as a two-way electronic system, the external door opened, allowing a view from the inside door. Once that door had closed, the inside opened allowing visitors to gain access. The prison officer pressed the internal and external buttons leading to the outside. Daniel Ashby stepped out to a blue and white sky, fresh air, leafy trees and finally… freedom.

Hi, Mum had arrived about ten minutes earlier, but due to double yellow lines, the taxi had parked just down the road, still allowing a clear view of the front of the prison.

There he was, standing at the top of the grey steps as his mum got out and quickly walked over putting her arms around her son, smelling the odour of prison life on his clothes.

Walking back towards the waiting car, their hands connected for the first time in years.

Traffic was light through Birmingham City Centre, he opened the side window, the wind blowing through his hair, taking in the high-level views over Spaghetti Junction.

The journey took them just over an hour to reach home, the taxi finally pulling up outside Daniel's mum and dad's, a semi-detached house on the outskirts of Bradwell village.

The taxi driver, who went by the name of Mohammed checked the meter and got out of the car. Opening the boot, he took out the only piece of luggage Daniel had left the prison with. Just his personal belongings and some paperwork in an HMP folder.

'That'll be fifty-five pounds Missis, and do you want a receipt?'

Mary opened her handbag and taking out her purse, handed Mohammed the money.

'There you go, sixty pounds, thank you, and keep the change.'

'Cheers Misses,' he replied, adjusting his sunglasses just as another pickup came over the 2-way radio.

'I'll give you some money for that Mum. I got some discharge cash given me, around eighty-three pounds.'

She took hold of his hand.

'Don't be silly, keep your money, just don't tell your dad what the journey cost, you know what he's like about money.'

Walking down the well-trodden path to the front door, Danny noticed how the garden hadn't changed over the last fourteen years.

The lawn was still immaculately cut, striped from one end to the other, some of the shrubs had grown, but the shape of the lawn was exactly the way it had looked before.

The only thing he noticed was rose bushes dangling onto the path, a smell of summer in the air. Pink and red petals sticking to his shoes, as Philip, his dad, opened the front door, before turning around and walking back into the house.

Eight

'WHOSE CAR ARE WE GOING IN?' asked Detective Sergeant Bailey, trying to move on and avoid any further conversations like those they'd had in Adam's office.

'Probably better if we travel separately, I want to try and be home when Vivian comes from work, so I guess that's more convenient for both of us.'

'That's fine boss, do you know the way, or are you following me?'

'I've been before, it's the new place isn't it?'

'Yeah the new Derby Community Hospital, just follow the signs for the Mortuary, and I'll see you there. Hopefully, they'll be parking outside.'

They both walk across the car park, splitting off in separate directions without saying another word to each other.

Adam got in his car just as his mobile phone pinged. It was a text from Viv. **Do you know what time you'll be home? I'm leaving the surgery in about an hour and planning dinner, takeaway I think, if that's okay with you. Viv xxx.**

Adam sent a quick reply, **Hope you're okay. I'll be back home ASAP. Chinese is in order I think, love you, me. xxxx**

He started the Audi A4, put it into drive and set off down the A38 towards Derby City Centre, listening to The Beatles on Spotify.

Adam arriving at the hospital first, parked in one of the five reserved spaces right outside. As he switched off the engine, Frank pulled up at the side of him in his two-year-old Ford Mondeo.

Like the police headquarters, the pathologist department had only opened just over four years ago.

Full of up-to-the-minute equipment it was the main centre for all pathology investigations and had been headed up by Dr Rachel Munroe as Head of Forensic Pathology for the last three years.

Both detectives entered the building, warrant cards in their hands, announcing their arrival at reception, and being told to follow the signs for the mortuary.

It was 2.55 p.m. as Frank pressed the finger-marked entry button located on the wall, both patiently waiting in silence. Footsteps could be heard approaching the entry door, as a tall young man, no more than mid-twenties and in need of a shave, showed them to the autopsy room. It was a place that most middle and senior police officers were familiar with, the smell hitting both their nostrils on entry, was indescribable.

Staff constantly cleaned the white walls and dark blue linoleum floors, wiping every surface with harsh disinfectants. But as far as the two detectives were concerned, it just added to the unique but repulsive odour, the smell of human tissue and blood remains with police officers for days.

The woman's cold body lay on one of four stainless-steel dissecting tables, slightly raised at the top end to allow body fluids to be collected at the bottom. Bright lights reflected off the floor, illuminating every outlined detail of the corpse.

Morticians moved silently around in the background as Dr Rachel Munroe casually stood over the body and began to explain in detail what she'd found out from her initial findings. She lifted the white sheet to reveal the pale face and top of the body, a long Y-shaped incision had been made down the front, enabling the internal organs to be removed and examined.

She had also made a single incision across the back of the head so that the top of the woman's skull could also be studied.

Adam was the first to speak.

'Have we got a cause of death?'

Fully gowned but removing her face mask.

'I think we have gentlemen.' As she stepped away from the stainless-steel table, Rachel began to go through the autopsy findings.

'So, the victim was asphyxiated, which I think we already knew, but just to make sure I've also dissected and inspected the deceased's tongue, which *has* now confirmed that I'm correct.'

She made her way to a side table, collecting a stainless-steel bowl, inside was the dissected tongue.

'More worryingly, we need to understand more about the amputated hand.

What I've identified so far is this, it was cut off after death, *thankfully*. Possibly with a small hacksaw or similar implement, and most likely where the body was found.'

Frank stepped back and glared at Adam,

'What do you mean, her hand had been removed.'

Rachel looked directly at Adam.

'You haven't told him yet, have you… Yes, the left hand has been fully removed.'

Adam looked at Frank, trying to avoid another argument, particularly in front of Rachel.

'We didn't have the opportunity to discuss it and now isn't the time, let's wait till we get back to the station shall we?'

Frustrated, DS Bailey continued.

'Anything else you can tell us?'

'Yes, and this is interesting, we've cleaned all the wounds on her face, there are a few scratches, which, being in the woods, you'd expect.

But, if I'm not mistaken, which is unlikely, the cuts on her forehead, they have tried to carve the shape of a number, a number two. It's a bit of a botched job, but I would say that they were deliberately carved with the same knife that finished cutting off the hand.'

'Any signs of a struggle, or any defence wounds on the body?'

'Apart from her face, we didn't find any, no wounds, no sexual assault, just the carving on her forehead and the removal of her hand.'

'So, she might have known her attacker then, is that what you're saying?'

'That is your job Detective Sergeant Bailey, not mine. I just give you the facts as I see them, the rest is up to you and your team.'

'One *more* thing however before you leave, the hand wasn't hacked off, it was cut cleanly, meticulously, patiently, almost with skill.

Whoever it was took their time, they didn't seem in a hurry I would go as far as to say, it was pre-planned.'

For several moments all three stood there in silence, absorbing what had just been described.

'Oh, and one final point, maybe be nothing to consider, she was being treated for Type 2 Diabetes. Metformin tablets were still in her system, they hadn't fully dissolved.'

'Thanks, Doc, if you could email all the final autopsy reports to both of us, that'd be great.'

Thanking Rachel, as they exited the autopsy room, Adam undid the top button of his shirt, and both made their way back to the parked cars.

The silence was broken by a call on Frank's mobile.
'We have a name boss.'

Nine

THE STATION WAS BUZZING with activity as Adam entered reception. He made his way upstairs, avoiding the lift again and was about to go into his office when his mobile rang.

The caller ID is DCI Tom Vickers.

'Good afternoon, sir,' Adam answered, immediately knowing what the call was about.

'What can I do for you?'

He wasn't sure if the question had taken Vickers by surprise or whether he was checking to see if he was back at the office.

'Can you give me an update on the body found in the woods earlier today? Came the brief reply.

'Just checking I'm back in the office then,' he thought.

'Both DS Bailey and I have just returned from the autopsy, and apparently, we do have a name.'

Adam then took him through the post-mortem outcomes confirmed by Dr Rachel Munroe, emphasising what she'd said about the marks on the victim's forehead and the severed hand.

'Bloody hell, is that what she thinks?'

'Looks like it, her attacker took meticulous time and effort to remove the hand, her words, not mine.

But the bigger question here is, why? Why strangle her and then remove the hand? She was already dead, so there was no reason to stay around, taking the risk of being seen.

And what's happened to the hand? I've got a team searching the area now, but it's getting dark, making it impossible to search thoroughly, I'll have more updates later tomorrow.'

Adam expected some form of reply from DCI Vickers, but there was none.

'I'm just about to brief the wider team with what we know so far. I'll get back to you soonest with anything of further significance, but at least we have a start with the name, hopefully.'

'Make sure you do, I want to be kept fully informed on progress made, and let's do this investigation by the book. The last thing we want is any errors being made, and the press getting wind of it. This isn't South Yorkshire division Adam.'

With that, the call ended.

By the tone of the conversation, the meeting with the Chief Super hadn't gone well.

'His problem, not mine,' said Adam under his breath.

He picked up the witness statements from his desk, checked his emails and printed off the autopsy report from Rachel.

The door to the incident room was just in front of him, he checked his watch, 4:20 p.m. It was going to be a long day, and his plans for the evening with Viv could prove disappointing.

Taking a deep breath, and buttoning his collar, he opened the door, manoeuvring through scattered chairs, taking in the smell of coffee, deodorant and sweat. An eerie silence came over the room as he reached the front.

DS Frank Bailey let out a louder-than-required and unnecessary cough.

'Okay everybody, let's have your attention shall we.'

Adam stood there, eyes following his every move.

He'd done briefings like this many times, bringing a team together. He knew he had a job to do, and although he said it himself, he did it well.

The top brass assumed a quick result, the pressure was on, but Adam would run the investigation his way, the right way.

Methodically and professionally, he expected the whole team to do the same.

Scanning the room, he recognised some faces, including one dried-off uniformed officer he'd met much earlier. But some he didn't. His priority and his focus were on one face and one face only. An image that he knew he would have to become increasingly familiar with, that would be imprinted on his brain, which would ultimately become part of his working life.

It was the picture on the whiteboard behind him, that of the murdered victim.

Ten

'HELLO EVERYONE, good to see you all, and thanks for turning up on time. For those who don't know me, my name is Adam Fox, Detective Inspector Adam Fox, and I'll be the Senior Investigation Officer on this case.'

Standing there, full of confidence, Adam was determined to get maximum engagement from the team at the outset. He always found that telling everyone his first name helped, it put the team at ease.

Adrenaline kicked in, and getting straight to the point, he dismissed instantly, the call he'd just taken from Tom Vickers.

'So, this is what we know so far. The victim's name is Patricia Locke, 66 years of age, a retired schoolteacher. Never married and worked part-time in a local charity shop in Derby City Centre. According to the Forensic Pathologist, initial autopsy results suggest death by strangulation. Possibly with a piece of strong cord, maybe gardening twine, or similar.'

He pointed to an image on the murder board.

'No DNA or prints to go on, and this type of twine is commonly used around the gardens of Derbyshire. You can buy it from any shop on the high street. So, it's going to be difficult to establish where it came from. You've all got a copy of the autopsy report, the basic info so far from Dr Rachel Monroe is this. Patricia's attacker used some type of hammer to subdue her, possibly a heavy one, due to the injuries to the skull, then went on to strangle her. She met and possibly knew her attacker at a location in Blythe Woods. We also believe it may have been prearranged, as there are no signs of a struggle. She had been left for dead, the attack taking place sometime over the last twelve to eighteen hours, we can't be exactly precise due to weather conditions.'

The team took notes, and over the next fifty minutes, both Adam and Frank continued to go over the autopsy report, combined with the witness statements, capturing on the evidence board all the key points that the team had raised around the case.

By the end of the initial briefing, lines of command and individual duties, combined with roles and responsibilities had been allocated to everyone and timelines had been agreed.

'Are there any other questions?' asked DS Bailey.

Adam noted one of the younger members of the team looked quite distressed as she reviewed the briefing notes.

'Why would they cut off her left hand… any hand for that matter, and more to the point, take it with them?'

Alex glanced around at the faces in front of him, it was probably a question everyone wanted to ask but didn't.

'Good question, this is a high-priority case. A life has been tragically taken, and it's everyone's duty in this room to bring the culprit or culprits to justice. *Yes,* these are the types of questions we're going to be asked and must get answers to. We've not a lot to go on, and that includes time, so, let's work together, stay focused, and get a result. Also, let me make one last point very clear, what's discussed in this room, stays in this room. The last thing we want is for any of the press to get wind of this. So, if you're in any doubt about confidentiality or keeping your mouth firmly shut, let Detective Sergeant Bailey know right now.'

DS Bailey stood to his feet, glancing around the room, visibly checking they'd all taken that in.

'Does everyone understand what the DI's just said? If anyone does let anything out, I *will* find out and I'll have their balls on a plate, not including any female officers of course.'

Picking up their empty drinks, and moving the chairs against the outside wall, the team began to disperse, making their way out of the incident room.

Some not speaking a word thinking of the task ahead of them, but others chatting amongst themselves, Frank picking up what one of the officers was saying to no one in particular.

'What sort of person do you think we're looking at? Is it someone who could be a relative? Opportunistic? Mentally disturbed? Or could there be a sadistic killer at large… Getting their kicks from attacking, mutilating, and killing women?

It was a question Frank decided to ignore.

He didn't want to answer, because he couldn't.

Eleven

HE CHECKED HIS WATCH, at 7:46 p.m. as he locked his office door, headed downstairs, and made his way to his car. It had been a long day, and all Adam now wanted was to get home, relax with Viv and try to enjoy their takeaway together, if that was still on.

'Good night, sir, have a nice evening,' said the officer behind the desk, taking a drink from a mug.

'Good night, Stuart, you too.'

Adam made his way across the well-lit car park, reflecting briefly on how the day had gone. The discussion he'd had with Frank earlier in the day *was* necessary, although it probably could have gone better for both of them.

The Beatles on Spotify kicked in as he put the car in gear, the remote barrier opening as he drove down the tarmac drive.

Traffic was light at this time of night, with slight raindrops running down the windscreen like miniature rivers.

The journey only took about 25 minutes, along the A38 towards the city and then taking the A52 towards Ashbourne. They lived around three miles from the town centre in a four-bedroom house.

They'd only moved into the small but exclusive estate around six months ago, having temporarily rented a place since moving from Sheffield.

Locking the car, Adam opened the front door, dropped his car keys into a tray next to a family photo, and hung his coat up. Viv stood at the kitchen door, the smell of Chinese garlic chicken drifting down the hallway.

She looked sensational, even in an old grey sweatshirt and tracksuit bottoms.

As a healthcare professional, Viv wasn't your normal GP. Yes, she took her responsibilities very seriously, her patients were critically important to her, but she did have a life outside the surgery. Cooking, country walks, and spending time with family and friends, always desperately trying to avoid conversations about the lack of government funding within the NHS.

She poured two glasses of chilled white wine, unwrapping the takeaway into warm dishes.

'Have you had a good day?' as she kissed Adam on the side of his cheek.

'Actually, it's been a difficult one. I won't go into detail, but I think the next few weeks are going to be quite tricky, early mornings and probably about this time at night, maybe even later. It didn't get off to a good start either, me and Frank had a bit of an argument. So, I'm sorry I'm late home.'

'Hey, listen, it's not a problem. I know what I signed up for and how important work is to you, as it is to me. As long as we can have *some* quality time together, it'll be fine.'

Another kiss on the cheek.

'How was your day at the surgery? And the CQC audit, did it go well?'

'Good outcome, we passed with flying colours, so Peter was delighted. The only point they picked us up on was our security, they've recommended CCTV cameras on the outside and the reception area, and some type of internal warning systems in the surgery rooms, just in case a patient becomes angry or aggressive during a one-to-one consultation. Other than that, all good.'

Both Viv and Adam tried to keep work out of their personal lives, being a DI and a GP wasn't the greatest combination career-wise.

Research showed that most marriages like theirs broke down, but it had worked, did work, and despite what had happened in the past, their relationship, their marriage, it was as sound and as solid now as the day they wed.

Viv looked directly into Adam's face, tears forming in her eyes.

'I know you've had a tiring day, but is there any news at all, any further progress… Anything?'

'No… I'm seeing a colleague in the next few days in Sheffield, just to have an update, but sweetheart, no, no further developments.'

Twelve

I WAS LOOKING OUT OF THE WINDOW, daydreaming, trying to get over the fuzzy effect of a quick smoke I'd had in the dormitory when the class fell silent.

'I want the boy who's been smoking again to stand up. If you don't, everyone in the room will be punished.'

The rather plump teacher stood at the front of the class, looking over her glasses with a stern look on her ruby-red face.

I'd sat at the window in our dormitory looking out to the lake whilst taking a quick drag, as it was called before we went into class.

Facing the front again, I realised that the teacher looked like she was talking to me. Should I stand up and confess, or keep my mouth shut, so everyone suffers? Looking back, I should have remained in my seat.

***

Five weeks earlier my parents had dropped me off at the boarding school, where generations of boys had attended for over twenty-five years. Chaffinch House was located just on the border of the Peak District in Derbyshire. In its day, it was recognised as one of the best boarding institutes in the area, setting high standards of education, with an emphasis on mathematics, languages, and sport.

I'd never seen such a magnificent building, with large grey- and brown-coloured bricks, lead windows, with two imposing columns shadowing the ornate wooden entrance door.

Looking up, I notice a sign carved out of a wooden beam, SUE SPONTE, which much later I understood to translate to 'On one's own responsibility.'

I waited silently in the high-ceilinged hallway right in front of the headmaster's study, my father stood there with his back to me, talking with him.

I knew I must not cry, not cry, not cry... My father wouldn't want me to let the side down, I bit my tongue as he turned, shook my hand, and left all alone.

Turning around to wave goodbye, I saw through the side window my mother and father drive away down the winding tree-lined drive, past the lake on the left-hand side. That was the last time my parents came to visit.

An older boy showed me to my dormitory. There were eight of us all with single metal beds, mine was on the right. There were just two wardrobes for all our clothes, which we soon found out, meant that they got creased, and creased clothes came with consequences.

The room was cold in winter, with only tiny windows letting any natural light into the room. There were no carpets as such, dark floorboards creaked everywhere you walked.

Discipline was the order from the very beginning. Breakfast, lunch, and the evening meal were set in stone. No deviation, and if you were late for class, even by a few minutes, punishments were handed out.

I soon made friends with a couple of the boys in our dormitory, Simon, and Toby. We tried to do everything together, keeping a close eye out for each other, from the older boys, who got kicks out of bullying the younger ones.

It was only a few weeks before Simon introduced us to smoking.

We didn't know how he got hold of the ciggies, we didn't care, but he always had a pack of ten under his pillow.

Most of the older boys smoked, so, we thought it was big to be seen smoking, the smell sometimes lingering in our dormitory.

As time went on, the three of us almost became like brothers. We thought this friendship would last for years, although sadly it didn't.

Toby, as I understood later, had a stammer, and as we found out, suffered increased bullying from his early days at Chaffinch House. Some of the older boys would make fun of him, push him over in the corridors, throw his classwork over the floor, and deliberately hurt him during rugby tackles.

We hadn't been at boarding school very long before the beatings started. They'd use any excuse to pull you out of bed, making you walk down a dimly lit passage to begin the punishments. Voices and crying echoed from other areas as you walked to a tiny room at the bottom.

This was where they got down to business and the beatings took place. If you wept, it only got worse, so in the end, you just suffered in silence until it was over, returning to your dormitory, a broken figure.

Some nights I would lie awake waiting for the sound of the creaking floorboards, as the dormitory head, only a few years older than me, but far stronger, would approach, footsteps getting louder, delivering his catch to one of the housemasters, taking his financial reward and shutting the door behind him.

As one of them approached me, I could smell smoke on his clothes. Initially, there were two of them in the room, so I couldn't defend myself. I wasn't a tough lad, but I could kick him in the balls and run off.

One of them looked me up and down and then exited the room, so I was left with just the one smelly teacher as I prepared myself for what lay ahead.

It wasn't sexual, it was just sadistic punishment. He removed his leather belt, snapping it together before he whipped me across both my legs until they began to bleed. He grabbed my left arm and shoved it right up my back until I heard it crack, finally, punching me in the stomach a couple of times.

When it was finally over, he pulled a pure white handkerchief out of his pocket, and I noticed the signet ring on his little finger as he wiped the sweat from his forehead.

'That's it, you can go now, and don't forget, this is between you and me, no going to the headmaster or it'll be far worse next time.'

***

Looking over the class; her eyes came into contact with mine, and her facial expression, as usual, was difficult to judge.

'I'll ask a second time; I want to know who has been smoking and I want to know right now.'

Banging her fist on the desk in front of her.

'Which one of you is it? I can smell it in the room?'

Silence engulfed all around me. My legs began to tremble, and unable to speak, my mouth still tasted of smoke and my tongue was dry.

I could feel eyes staring at me from all directions, waiting for an answer.

'It's me miss; I was the one smoking.'

'Come out here boy.'

Slowly, I eased my chair back, a scraping noise across the floor. Making my way to the front of the class, my legs felt heavy, knowing at that point what was going to take place.

She'd punished me before, for no apparent reason, just to demonstrate the power she had over us. She opened the drawer to her desk, which revealed several sized canes. Running her fingers along, she selected the longest one, placed it on the desk and closed the drawer loudly.

'This is what happens to pupils who break the rules, who are disobedient, let this be a lesson to you again and to everyone else in this class.'

She looked down and picked up one of the canes. And for the first time, which I'd never noticed before, she had a smile on her face.

Her hand firmly taking hold of my small neck, she pushed me over the side of the desk, winding me in the stomach. Holding back any tears, I could see the faces of my friends Toby and Simon. They tried to look away as I heard the 'woosh' sound of the cane coming down on my backside. It was a day I'd never forget.

***

Waking up suddenly, my heart pounding, my hands shaking, the bed sheets covered in sweat, I once again relive the recollections I'm desperately trying to forget.

What took place all those years ago, was it my fault? Did I bring this on myself, inviting this torment into my life for eternity?

It's a question I've asked for years and never come up with an answer.

Was I the only one, or did other boys experience the suffering, the nightmares, still trying to confront their demons?

Will this ever end?

Thirteen

'DO YOU HAVE TO GO in *so* early, it's only 6:15 a.m.?'

Viv turned to Adam as they lay in bed, despite the time of year, the morning sun trying to illuminate their modern bedroom.

'I want to get in before the rest of the team. Hopefully, information from yesterday will have come through, throwing light on what took place.'

The previous night, Adam hadn't told Viv too much about what had taken place, it was still very early in the investigation. He trusted her, of course, he did, but due to the serious nature of the case, he had to be careful what he shared outside of the team.

Having showered, and dressed as usual, he made his way downstairs, had breakfast, and took Viv a cup of tea, kissing her on the lips, the smell of garlic still on her breath from last night's meal.

'I'll be back later, won't be too late hopefully, but not sure what time it will be. Have a good day at the surgery and see you later.'

Despite heavy traffic around the Derby Ring Road, Adam arrived at headquarters just after 7:00 a.m. Only a handful of people were around at this time. He swiped his security entrance card, grabbed himself a cup of coffee, and made his way to his office.

The autopsy report had come through overnight, he opened the file and read the content, printing off enough copies for circulation.

By around 7:30 a.m., Frank Bailey and the rest of the team had made their way to the incident room.

Adam was already on his feet at the front.

'Morning everyone. Let me begin by saying that any member of the team that finds what I'm about to say distressing in any way, can be relieved of their duties on the case.'

As Frank looked around, you could hear a pin drop, as everyone sat in silence, and no one left the room.

Turning around, Adam pointed to the photo on the evidence board.

'So, this is jointly what we know so far, the victim's name has officially been confirmed as Patricia Locke, age sixty-six. She was discovered in Blythe Woods by Mr and Mrs Bob Hubbard.

Blythe Woods is approximately eight miles from Derby City Centre popular with families, walkers, cyclists, etc. It even has a local pub nearby, The Gardeners Arms. Miss Locke was savagely attacked on the thirteenth of August and as I've already said, it's difficult to establish an actual timeline due to the heavy rain the night before.'

Frank stood to his feet, buttoning up his tight-fitting jacket and took over from Adam.

'As already mentioned, the victim's left hand was removed. But interestingly, there were also cuts carved into her forehead. Not completely sure, but we believe these injuries could resemble a number, a number two. Currently, we don't know if this has any bearing on the case, but we believe it may have.'

A question came from one of the officers.

'Could it have happened as she fell forward, or something like that?'

'Good question. Possibly, but unlikely. According to the Pathologist, the cuts seem to have been made deliberately.'

'What about the hand, any more info?.

Frank looked at Adam, his face seeking approval to share more information.

'I'll take this one,' said Adam.

'Okay, we understand the hand was amputated after the victim's death, thankfully. Cut with a sharp knife, they then used a saw to sever through the bone. Whoever did this, took their time… They weren't in any hurry it seems.'

Total silence fell upon the room, broken by a question from a female officer.

'Could it be some form of ritual killing? You know, removing the hand and marks on the face? It's just a thought.'

'Maybe, but let's keep an open mind on this one, we can't rule anything out currently. We've very little to go on, but what we have got needs to be used to our advantage. Let's take a quick break, have a drink and come back here in twenty minutes.'

Back in his office, Adam closed the door behind him as Frank sat down.

'We need to start logging every detail, we have very little to go on, so every bit of information must be officially recorded. We can't afford to miss anything on this one Frank.

'As it should be,' he replied.

I remember the first murder case I got involved in.

I was a DS, working at Sheffield Central. My old boss, DI Richard Cummings, made sure everything was documented, we kept a detailed record of the investigation, and the logbook was updated every day, both written and electronically. It was more than just a memory aid on the evidence board, it was the place where we recorded every step of the investigation, witness statements, crime scene images, forensic reports, and what the investigating team uncovered.'

'Did you find out who did it?'

'Sure did, it took some doing, but concealed within numerous witness statements was one name. It kept coming up, time after time, but at the start, no one took any notice, we were all too busy. Tracking down those witness statements finally led to an arrest, a 68-year-old family man, he's still inside I understand.'

Frank got to his feet.

'One more thing, before we go back in. I don't want any reference to the rose petals around the body, we need to keep that to ourselves. If or when the press get hold of this, we'll have all the cranks calling in and confessing to the murder, so, for now, let's keep this to ourselves.'

By 6:15 p.m. every team member knew exactly what they'd got to do. Adam returned to his office and tidied up his desk, placing his laptop in its case. Locking the door, he made his way across the car park. Although it was dark, he could see his Audi A4 in the distance.

His mobile rang, it was a Sheffield number.

Fourteen

THE AROMA OF A FRIED BREAKFAST drifted up into Danny's bedroom. To his surprise, his dad redecorated it just before his release, the fresh smell of paint still lingering.

It had been almost six weeks since his discharge from prison, and he was finally beginning to get his life back together.

On entering the kitchen, his mum had once again laid out the table for breakfast. It was becoming a routine, he'd get up, have a shower, come downstairs and the food would be ready.

Mary Ashby's main task was to support her son, look after him, and make sure he'd got everything he needed to get his life back on track.

They both knew it wasn't going to be an easy road ahead, people in small villages have long memories, and don't forget easily what's happened in the past.

But that didn't matter, as far as Daniel was concerned, he'd done the time, despite the injustice of his sentence, this was *his* time, and he was going to make the best of it.

He helped clear the fine bone China pots off the kitchen table, then made his way outside. His dad was in his garden shed. As he entered, the electric lathe was turning what looked like a wooded figure. Rows of assorted tools hung on hooks behind him.

Switching off the machine, the humming noise coming to a halt, Philip Ashby looked up at his son, Daniel noticed a look of disdain on his face.

'What are your plans for today?'

Danny could still sense some form of resentment in his dad's voice. Back as far as he could remember, they'd never been close.

His career in the army had always come first. It was his mum that he had spent most of his early childhood with, his dad spending weeks at a time abroad on military duties.

He always thought he preferred to be away from home, with his regiment, doing his own thing.

'Well, if you're interested, I'm seeing an old friend of mine later, we used to work together in the past, and he wants me to give him a hand with some garden landscaping he's doing, may become permanent, we'll have to see how it goes.'

Philip Ashby let out a sigh.

'You need to get a proper job, one that offers a secure future, career prospects, potential for promotion, not just going from one thing to another.'

'Dad, I had a career, my landscaping business was my own, it was what I wanted to do, and you know what? I was good at it. We don't all want to be highfliers, some of us just want a steadier life, and that was my choice.'

Switching the lathe back on, Philip Ashby picked up a sharp chisel and again began to turn the wooden figure, shavings covering his hands.

The conversation was over.

Mary Ashby was looking through the window as he made his way back to the house, tears forming in her eyes.

'Was your dad okay this morning? You know what he's like, a very proud man.'

'As a usual mum, he always goes on about me getting a proper job, it doesn't matter what I do, what I like doing, I'll never come up to his regimental expectations.'

She wiped her eyes on her apron.

'Listen, Daniel, your dad was never here when you were younger, he didn't see you grow up into the wonderful man you've become. He'll struggle to change now, he had *his* opinion on your sentence, and we had ours.'

Danny put his arms around his mum, detecting for the first time how much weight she seemed to have lost.

'Can I borrow your car? I'm meeting an old friend in Derby for coffee, he might have some work for me.'

'Of course you can, the keys are in my coat pocket, help yourself, there's plenty of petrol in the tank.'

He kissed her on the cheek, 'Thanks, mum.'

The journey only took around twenty minutes. As Danny pulled into Costa Coffee, he noticed the black Ford Ranger parked up. JJ Landscape Services sign on the mud-stained driver's door.

Joe and Danny had known each other since their early primary school days, lost contact, then later, bumped into each other at the local pub. Joe was watching the Saturday football match, when

Danny entered, he noticed him analysing player tactics over a pint of John Smiths.

He went over, slapped him on the back and said, 'Hi mate, long time no see.'

After the conviction, Joe went to see Danny in prison every couple of weeks, sometimes taking his mum with him.

He always knew he was innocent.

They ordered their drinks and found a table at the back of the coffee shop, out of the way of prying ears.

'So, it's good to see you mate. Sorry I haven't been in touch sooner, just been busy with the landscaping business.'

'Hey, listen, that's fine, I've only been out a few weeks. Keeping a bit of a low profile until I see how the land lies, and you did come to see me when I was in prison didn't you?'

'It was the least I could do, we go back years, and I knew you didn't do it, you couldn't have, not Danny Ashby.'

They both took a drink of their coffee.

'The trouble *was* Joe; I didn't have an alibi. Me and Arthur Richardson had argued several days before about some gardening work I'd done for him. He didn't want to pay me for the job I'd done, and I'd said I'd get my own back, which I immediately regretted. A member of the public reported that to the police and that's when the trouble started.'

They both took another gulp of coffee as two hot toasted sandwiches arrived.

'They came to the house and arrested me in front of my mum, I became aggressive and the next thing I knew, they'd got me on the hall floor in handcuffs. They took me to the old police station in the city centre, going through what I'd been arrested for. They showed me images of the body, trying to shock me into a confession, I guess. Producing a pair of gardening gloves in an evidence bag, with my DNA on them, not *just* my DNA, but still it was there. You know what it's like, you lose those types of things all the time, but they wouldn't accept my argument that anyone could have got hold of the gloves.'

Danny took a bite of his sandwich, the cheese oozing from the sides.

'They then began asking questions about my whereabouts on the actual day. Earlier that morning, I'd gone for a walk to calm down and clear my head. Me and my dad had had a massive row, nothing unusual about that. As you know, we've never seen eye to eye. I put it down to the fact he was never there when I was young, and his time in the army, I think it changes some people, it did my dad.'

Apart from background noise, several minutes passed in silence, before Joe replied.

'So, what are you going to do now, what's your plans?'

'I'm going to try and get back to what I did before my sentence, landscape gardening services, I had a good customer base, customers liked what I did, and I was good at it too, so, yes, that's my plan.'

Joe put down his sandwich, wiping his mouth with a paper serviette.

'Well, that's where I come in, I need some help with a big job I've secured, full landscaping, probably about six to seven weeks of work, are you up for it?'

'What do you think… It'll give me an income, get me out of the house, and start to pay my way again. I'll give you my new mobile number.'

Danny got out his phone as they shook hands, finished their coffee, and walked across the car park to their separate vehicles.

'I'll give you a call in the next few days,' Joe opened the door to his 4x4 then closed it again, walking back to Danny's mum's Vauxhall Corsa.

'Interestingly, one more worrying point about your prison sentence is not only the injustice. The killer could still be out there.'

Fifteen

BRIGHT RED LIGHTS like firecrackers illuminated the M1, heavy with traffic going North, as Adam made his way up to Sheffield.

He'd answered his mobile and arranged to meet his colleague at a local hotel in Chesterfield, just outside the town centre, avoiding any rumours by meeting at South Yorkshire HQ.

Detective Inspector Chris Mitchel and Adam knew each other, they'd worked together for several years and then become friends.

He'd been appointed the Senior Investigating Officer assigned to the case involving Adam and Vivian's daughter, Scarlett.

Adam walked through the sliding doors of the hotel, put his mobile on silent, and glanced round to check if Chris had arrived, he'd checked the car park but didn't know what vehicle he was now driving.

Chris stood up, waving to catch his attention. Immediately recognising him, he noticed that someone was with him.

A young woman, probably mid-twenties, dressed in black trousers and a tight-fitting blue top.

'How's The Man? Good to see you again mate, can I introduce DS Sarah Ward, Sarah?, this is D.I Adam Fox.'

They shook hands, sat down, and called a waiter, ordering a pot of coffee for three.

'So, how's it all going down in the East Midlands? Hope you've settled in well. Tom Vickers can be a bit of a stickler I've heard, a proverbial pain in the arse apparently.'

'Early days, but all good thanks. At the moment DCI Vickers is letting me run things the way I want. He seems happy, I'm sure I'll know when he isn't.'

Adam wasn't going to tell either of them about the murder investigation, the fewer people that know, the better.

'Adam, I've asked Sarah to join us, as she's going to be taking over the day-to-day running of your case. It's not going off the radar, just priorities and resources. It isn't my choice, but you know how it works.'

Adam wasn't sure how to respond, in the back of his mind, he knew that at some point a decision would be made on Scarlett's case, it was just a matter of time.

Hundreds of children go missing every year, known as MISPER, some are found, others are not.

But this was different, this was his daughter. She wasn't missing… As far as he was concerned… She'd been abducted.

'Adam, are you okay with this? Sorry about the changes, I'm still going to be involved, but from a distance I guess, Sarah will be your main contact going forward from today.'

Detective Sergeant Ward bent down and pulled a well-thumbed folder from her briefcase, placing it on the table in front of them.

'I have your file here on Scarlett's disappearance, but if it's okay with you, can you talk me through again what you believe took place that day, or as much as you can remember?'

He took a deep breath, finding it difficult to recreate what took place all that time ago.

'Well, I'm going back almost four years. The eighteenth of August. We'd had a lie in, it was a Saturday morning after all. My wife Vivian was a GP at a practice in the centre of Sheffield, and she'd had some early mornings that week, and was tired. After a late breakfast, I went to my local gym, which must have been around 11:00 a.m. Viv stayed at home with Scarlett, she'd be around twenty-two months old at that time. We'd planned to drive to the countryside later in the afternoon.'

'What time did you get back from the gym?'

It's all in the records. I quickly called and picked up a coffee at the local café, then came back home around twenty past one in the afternoon. I parked the car and went into the house via the front door. We always kept the gate to the back of the house locked, that's where the kitchen door was.'

'So, what happened then?'

'Scarlett was playing in the garden. Earlier on, I'd put down an old car rug on the grass, she was on that. I went upstairs to take a shower, I usually showered at the gym after my workout, but I'd forgotten a towel. Vivien was in the dining room, which is at the front of the house. We'd had a dinner party on Friday night, Chris and his wife Fiona came over for dinner, together with two other friends.'

Chris looked at Adam and nodded, sensing how difficult the conversation was, and the memories it was bringing back.

'I came downstairs into the kitchen to make some coffee, and immediately noticed something was wrong. Scarlett wasn't on the car rug. Instantly I ran out of the kitchen to check if she'd managed to crawl along the grass and down the side of the lawn, little ones do that don't they? That's when I noticed the gate into the garden.'

'What about it?,' said DS Ward.

'The gate had been forced open, the lock and bolt were on the path, in two separate pieces, two of the screws were still on the gate, the others were on the ground. I opened the gate onto the road, and everything looked normal.

Nothing was happening, nothing out of the ordinary. Just people walking by, and cars being driven, but no sign of Scarlett. She was gone.'

Several minutes passed in silence, DS Ward making notes in the open folder.

'Did, sorry… does Scarlett have any distinguishing features at all?'

'She has beautiful blond curly hair, blue eyes and a mole on the side of her left cheek. We saw a Paediatric Dermatologist at The Hallamshire Hospital, a friend of Viv's, but they said it was nothing to worry about.'

Chris checked his watch, turning to DS Ward.

'Listen, I think we've covered enough today. We have all the facts in the file, I suggest we leave it for now. Both keep in touch by phone and if you want another face-to-face meeting, you can arrange that between yourselves. Give me a couple of minutes would you Sarah?

I need a quick word with Adam.'

As DS Ward collected all the paperwork, Adam looked directly at Chris Mitchel, then waited to speak until she'd left.

'I'm never going to give up trying to find out what happened you know. Whether she's still alive or not, I will find the truth and I'll *never* let this go, even if I have to do my investigations, it's what I'll do, both for Scarlett and Viv.'

Chris let out a deep sigh. 'Listen, Adam, it's none of my business, and I say this as a true friend, you know that. I think you should take a step back; I hate myself for what I'm about to say, but the truth is… your daughter will probably never be found, that's what the statistics show, you know that as well as I do.'

Adam and Chris had been colleagues and close friends for years, and the wives had a good friendship too, so the comment wasn't what Adam had anticipated.

'You know what Chris, you're a good friend to both me and Viv, but you're right… It's none of your business.'

The instant he said that he regretted it, Chris had stood by him throughout this ordeal. He'd have to apologise, but at a later date perhaps.

Making their way out of the hotel, Adam switched his mobile back on. It pinged, two missed calls, one from Detective Chief Inspector Vickers, 'he can wait.' he thought, the other from Viv.

He got into his car, opened the side window, and watched the two officers drive away.

Sixteen

JOINING THE MOTORWAY at Junction 31, Adam felt mentally exhausted. He ran through in his mind what had happened that day and what he was going to tell Viv.

He understood why they'd had to downgrade the initial investigation, it was almost four years since Scarlett was taken and very little progress had been made, if any at all.

Coming up to the services just before Junction 29 he indicated and parked up. It would be easier to make the call to her whilst not driving, he needed to concentrate on what to say.

Buying a drink, he got his head around the conversation he'd got to have, trying to avoid sounding disillusioned. His mouth became dry. Taking a drink from the coffee cup in the centre console. He made the call.

Viv had always blamed herself for Scarlett's disappearance, if she'd stayed in the kitchen, keeping an eye on her. If she'd gone into the garden with her she'd have let her sleep instead of waking her up. Too many ifs and no answers.

The question that's never been answered is why? Why was Scarlett singled out? Was it opportunistic or preplanned? The fence surrounding the back garden was old, with gaps opening in the wood, so if anyone wanted to, they could look in without raising any suspicions.

Was this personal? Was someone getting back at Adam? He'd brought down several organised drug gangs in Sheffield, putting away one gang leader for almost fifteen years.

The ringleader used to get his men to travel down from Leeds, recruit young individuals to be delivery people, pay them handsomely at first in cash, and then over time, a threat of violence if they tried to refuse.

There'd been numerous hardened criminals that had had their finances confiscated, it wasn't out of the question that this could therefore be some form of retaliation.

Or was it to do with Viv? As a GP in an inner-city practice, she comes across all types of patients, most want some health advice, a listening ear, and a diagnosis. But some, particularly those on hard drugs, being prescribed Methadone… Well, they needed more, much more than in most cases, Dr Vivian Fleming could offer.

That was one of the reasons that they'd decided to relocate to somewhere that offered a better lifestyle, not the main reason, but one of them.

Working as a city centre GP isn't an appealing career, as you're dealing with wide social issues. Domestic violence, drug use and abuse, and in some cases, threats to life, as Viv had experienced in the past.

So, when the move to Central Derbyshire Head Quarters came along for Adam and Viv to have the chance to join a thriving GP practice, with the possible potential of a partnership at some point, they jumped at the chance.

A fresh start for both of them.

Being a police officer, at any rank, allows you to get closer to an investigation than that available to the general public. You understand more about the process, the procedures being taken, the potential downfalls and the possible outcomes.

Being a Detective Inspector offers extra benefits, you can speak with colleagues who are closer to the case, request information that isn't normally available, and in some cases, pull rank to get answers.

He opened his mobile, finding Viv's number immediately, and then dialled.

'You're through to the mobile of Doctor Vivian Fleming. I'm sorry I can't take your call right now, but if you leave your name and number, I'll get back to you as soon as possible. Thanks for the call.'

'Shit,' said Adam under his breath. He started the car and headed for home.

Seventeen

VIV'S SKODA 4X4 WASN'T ON THE DRIVE as Adam pulled in. He locked the car with the fob, noticing for the first time all the hanging baskets and pots, despite the month, still in full bloom at the front of the house. Viv was the gardener, she said it relaxed her and took her mind off work, although he did all the mowing.

Opening the front door with his key, he took off his coat and hung it on the banister. There was no smell of food from the kitchen tonight.

It was only just after 4:00 p.m., but already he had to switch the light on in the kitchen, the lounge and the top landing, the house seemed eerily quiet.

He took off his suit, hanging it up as he always did, putting on a pair of designer jeans, a Christmas present from Viv's mum and dad last year. As he walked out of the bedroom, he glanced over at the family photograph of the three of them, sitting down, Scarlett in the middle, Mum, and Dad on each side.

It was going to be a difficult conversation, but he'd got to have it with Viv, he knew that.

In the early days of Scarlett's disappearance, he often used to ask himself, was he personally and professionally doing enough?

Could he have become more heavily involved in the case from the start? His DCI at the time was putting pressure on him to get results. South Yorkshire Police were constantly under scrutiny, any sniff of impropriety had to be avoided at all costs. So, Adam took the difficult decision to step back and let the investigation team, headed up by DI Chris Mitchell, get on with the job.

The problem was, after almost four years, they still didn't have any idea or any leads about what happened to their beautiful daughter.

Car lights shone through the bedroom blind like railway lines on the bed and carpet. Indicating that Viv was finally home.

As he walked back onto the landing he glanced into the third bedroom, slightly opening the door. Unpainted walls shadowed what would have been Scarlett's room, including some of their daughter's furniture from the house in Sheffield.

Walking into the kitchen, Viv stood at the sink, looking through the window into the back garden. What is she thinking? Adam wondered.

'Hi sweetheart, have you had a good day?'

As she turned around, he noticed just how tired Viv seemed. Her pale face looked drawn and haggard, the energy she always seemed to have had evaporated away.

'It's been all right. As is the norm, too many patients to see and not enough time. The fifteen-minute allocation per person just isn't sufficient, but it's the same everywhere. I guess they're lucky to get an appointment with a GP. At least at our practice, the patients can see a healthcare professional within twenty-four hours. In Sheffield, well it could have been days.'

'It does sound like Dr Johnson runs a good practice, putting the patient at the heart of everything you do, isn't that what the saying is nowadays?'

'He does, he's very committed to all the patients, the practice, and the staff. I think he feels it was a calling for him, to go into medicine. Helping people, always being there as necessary, often going above and beyond what's required.'

'It sounds too good to be true. So long as you're happy there, that's all that counts in my mind.'

'You know what. I am. It's good, the support staff are kind, we have all the latest gadgets, the practice is thriving, and more patients coming on board, which means more funding for expansion.'

Viv walked over to the kettle, filled it with water and switched it on.

'How did you get on in Sheffield?'

Adam swallowed hard, then replied.

'You *know* Chris Mitchell. He told me today that he's moving on and being replaced by Detective Sergeant Sarah Ward. She's going to be handling the case from now on.

We went over all the details again, and I ran through the events on the actual day, Sarah made loads of extra notes too.'

'So, have there been any further developments? Are we, or are they any closer to finding what happened?'

He took Viv into his arms, holding her tightly to his chest.

'Listen, they're doing the very best that they can, the investigation, well that continues to be ongoing, and Sarah won't let this slip. She's promised to keep me up to speed with any new information, she's nice. You'd like her.'

Their bodies separated abruptly.

'I'll take that as a no then.'

As Viv stepped back, tears ran down her face, once again she turned to face the back garden.

Eighteen

ADAM SAT IN TOM VICKERS' OFFICE, glancing down at his watch, it was 7:45 a.m. He noticed the Forensic Pathology report was on the DCI's desk.

Tom stood up, opened the office blind, and poured two cups of black coffee, handing one to Adam.

'Thanks for coming in, I wanted to get an update on the Patricia Locke case. The Chief Super's asking questions, and we both need answers.'

'It's coming together sir. The team is working on different angles, under the day-to-day supervision of Detective Sergeant Frank Bailey. But to be honest, it's very early days, and Patricia Locke seems to have had a very private life. A retired schoolteacher, she worked part-time in a charity shop, had very few friends as we've found out, and apart from attending the local church, she seemed to be a bit of a loner. She has no immediate family, was an only child, privately educated. And from what we now understand, both her parents died whilst on holiday, a coach crash apparently, years ago. She inherited the family home and has lived there ever since. Her only pastime apart from her charity work was walking, which according to some of her friends at church, she did regularly. It wouldn't be difficult for someone to know her movements, most mornings she used to take the same route towards Blythe Woods, walking along the open path before entering by the trees, it would be easy for anyone to track her down. We've checked out all social media, Facebook, Twitter etc. No success there either. As you know, there wasn't any DNA. No fingerprints, or footprints, so little to go on. And the weather didn't help, what evidence there was may have been washed away by the rain.'

DCI Vickers tapped the folder on his desk with his index finger.

'I've read the Forensic Pathologist report in more detail. Do we have any more information on why the hand was removed? And what about this cut on her forehead, what's that all about?'

'Rachel Munroe always believed it was done deliberately like it was carved into Patricia Locke's face. According to Rachel, both the hand removal and the cuts on the face were done after she died. Oh, and no, there was no sexual assault, so this isn't that type of crime.'

Adam took a drink of his coffee.

'One last point, the autopsy indicated no defence wounds, no scratches on her hands or arms and nothing under her fingernails, so we now believe she possibly knew her attacker.'

He put his coffee mug back down on the desk, running through in his mind what other questions Detective Chief Inspector Vickers might throw at him, deciding instantly to go first.

'Couple of other points, I'm going to interview the two people who first discovered the body, Mr and Mrs Hubbard. They live just outside Luton. We have their statements, but I need to meet with them. They potentially are the last people to see her alive. I'm going down in the next couple of days. Secondly, if you remember at the crime scene, rose petals were scattered around the body, we're keeping that quiet, the team aren't aware of that, apart from DS Bailey, we're trying to avoid any crank calls.'

Tom Vickers leaned back in his well-worn swivel chair; it creaked under his weight. Placing both hands behind his head, he interlocked his fingers.

'Well, it sounds as though you're on top of your game, Frank Bailey's a good officer, use him, he'll be invaluable to the investigation. He's good at what he does, has lots of local knowledge and the troops respect him.'

'I plan to sir.'

Adam stood up to leave, making his way to the door.

'One more thing, I know you have your reasons for travelling to Sheffield but try and keep away from the South Yorkshire division. You're with Central Derbyshire HQ now, you work for us, DI Fox.'

Nineteen

'SO HOW DID IT GO?' Did you meet your friend for coffee? What did he have to say? Can he help you find a job?'

Mary Ashby was sitting in their lounge, her feet up on a stool, reading a magazine, a tray of tea and biscuits on a small side table.

For the first time, Daniel noticed that all the walls in the lounge were painted the same colour, Magnolia, just like his bedroom. As he glanced around the room, he also noticed that the only photographs were of his dad, in uniform or with other officers, all other family photos had been removed.

He sat down at the side of his mum, sinking into the cushions on the settee, helping himself to a drink and a chocolate biscuit, a luxury he'd not known for quite some time.

'It went well mum, Joe's picked up a big gardening job at a nursing home, needs some help, and he knows he can trust me, at least I hope he does.'

'Is this the same Joe who used to come and see you in prison? He picked me up a couple of times didn't he?'

'The very same mum, he stood by me when others didn't, including Dad. Where is he by the way? In his shed?'

'No, he's got a GP appointment and then he's going to church, something to do with decorating the outbuildings or something. You know your dad, a very private man.'

They both sat there silent, drinking tea, eating chocolate biscuits, and not knowing what else to say to each other.

'Mum were you and dad okay with me being away for so long? I often used to think about how things were at home. I didn't want to ask you when you came to visit, just in case you got upset. Is everything all right?'

'Look, Danny, I've spent more than half my married life without your father, the army was always his priority. I, we, always came second.'

'Well, I'm home now and I'm going nowhere, so he'd better get used to me being around, don't you think?'

Daniel noticed that his mum deliberately avoided the question.

Ever since he can remember his parents had a difficult relationship. He would come home from school and his mum would wipe tears off her face, trying to avoid eye contact with him. When he was at senior school, his dad was never available when parents' evening came around, his mum always attended alone.

There would be days when they didn't speak to each other, arguments, triggered by anything.

So as far as Daniel was concerned, the more his dad spent away from home, the better for him and his mum.

Mary put down her drink, turning to her son.

'What was it like in prison Danny?'

He knew that at some point someone was going to ask him the question. He thought it might have been Joe when they'd met earlier in the day, but instead, it was his mum.

'You know what, I was one of the lucky ones, I kept my nose clean, avoided trouble, didn't get into drugs or anything like that, and I had a good inmate at Birmingham.

Mick, whom I shared a cell with. He was illiterate, not his fault either, he came from a broken family. Always in trouble when he was young and never went to school. So, I used to read all his mail from his Auntie Maud to him, he never forgot that.'

He paused for several minutes, considering what to include and what to leave out.

'The early days were hard, *I knew* I hadn't done it, but the evidence, well you know, the police said it was clear cut. There was only one time when I was really scared, I was taking my weekly shower and two guys came in, looked at me, and I realised what was going to happen. I was young, quite fit, and alone. They approached me and were about to make their move when Mick came in.

He *was* clothed but had a wet towel in his hand. It didn't take too long for him to bring the two of them down, kicking them in the groin, and telling them to.' 'Piss Off.'

For the remainder of the afternoon, they sat there quietly, Danny going over in his mind what life had been like for him, how he coped with the violence, seeing the drugs being taken, and the despair in some of the prisoners.

There were the no-hopers, the ones who'd spent most of their lives behind bars, prisoners who'd tried to go straight, but for one thing or another, found themselves back in jail.

And the ones like Danny, who'd had an interest, his being landscape gardening, used that to their advantage. The warden had permitted him to hold group sessions on the subject, only a handful attended to begin with, but after a while, he was holding five outside sessions a week.

Not only was it enjoyable, but it also gave him the chance to be outside, and more importantly, protection.

The front door opened, and Philip Ashby wiped his feet on the doormat and walked into the lounge just as the two of them had finished their conversation. Danny noticed paint under his fingernails, and that hc looked anxious as he sat down.

'Is everything alight?' asked Mary. 'How did you get on at the GP's? Was your diabetic checkup okay?'

With a heavy sigh, he turned to his wife.

'The diabetic checkup was fine, they're going to change my medication, moving to a generic version, to save money no doubt.'

'Did you get the decorating done?' asked Danny.

'Only a bit, I've just come from church, and there's a rumour going around that one of our congregation has gone missing. She hasn't been to any services recently, no one has seen her, heard nothing from her, complete radio silence.'

'Who is it?' asked Mary,

'I didn't know her particularly well, but her name is Locke, Patricia Locke,' came the reply.

Twenty

DS FRANK BAILEY SAT PATIENTLY at Adam's desk as daylight illuminated the office. He checked his watch. It read 7:12 a.m., they'd arranged to meet up at 7:00 a.m. sharp, but the traffic on the A52 Derby ring road was solid, according to local radio, there had been a two-car collision.

Adam had spoken to Frank the previous evening following his meeting with DCI Vickers, he needed an update and progress made on the case.

'Morning Frank, sorry for being late, traffic was a nightmare.'

He had two cups of coffee in a cardboard tray, handed one to Frank, and kept one for himself.

'So, what's the news, any further headway on Patricia Locke?'

'We've checked out her house, nothing there to report. She doesn't seem to have had any direct family either. The whole place was quite sparse, she led a very private life, with no family photos around the place. The only interesting thing we did find was a picture hung on the wall in the living room, it looks like it was taken some years ago, I've taken a copy on my mobile. I'll show you later, we're going to be late for the appointment at the church. To be honest it looks like she's a bit of a loner, the only real interest she seems to have had, apart from the charity work, is attending the church in Edgewater. It's a small town about five miles northwest of Derby City Centre.'

'I know where Edgewater is, Viv's GP practice is based there, although I've only been there once, for an open day to get new patients to enrol.'

'When was the last time you went to church?' asked Adam, as they pulled into the car park.

Frank sat there for a moment, trying desperately to remember.

'Crickey must have been, I don't know, twenty years ago, when we got married, yeah, that would be about right.'

The journey over had taken them around twenty-five minutes, Frank knew the back road to the town where the church was located.

They'd travelled together in Adam's Audi, having arranged to meet the Vicar at 10:30 a.m.

Edgewater Community Church was a brick-fronted, single-storey building, with blue and green frosted windows on either side of a double door entrance. A large rectangular illuminated sign above, announces to everyone, JESUS SAVES.

The last time Adam had been to church was his niece's christening about two years earlier. Viv didn't want to go, it would trigger too many sad memories, she said, but Adam talked her around.

The Minister, Steven Andrews walked out of a side room, wiping his hands on a paint-covered rag, tucking his shirt into his trousers, limping slightly. He introduced himself, as both Adam and Frank showed their warrant cards.

He was a well-set man, aged around late forties, early fifties, dressed casually in black trousers, and a smart white polo shirt, a name badge on the left side, about five inches below the collar, announcing his name to his flock of followers.

The church was much larger inside than it looked from the car park. With high ceilings and a wide central aisle down the middle, with what looked to be around fifty to sixty chairs on either side, set at an angle to the front. Unlike many places of worship, the floor at Edgewater Community Church was carpeted in a heavy blue and gold floral pattern, clearly recently fitted, that new smell still lingering.

'May I get you gentlemen a tea or coffee?'

'Thank you, said Adam, we're fine, we don't want to take too much of your time.'

During the journey, both men had agreed that Frank would lead the interview, as local knowledge could be helpful.

'How long had you known Patricia Locke?'

'She's been one of our parishioners some years before I moved here, and that was around twelve to thirteen years ago, I came down from Tyne and Wear.'

'So, a Geordie then,' said Frank.

'Actually no, I was originally from the Derbyshire area, and did my initial training here, assisting other ministers, taking services at local schools, that sort of thing, so it's nice to be back home as such.'

'How well did you know her?'

Steven Andrews stood silent for several seconds before replying.

'Not well at all really. Patricia was a private person, a keen walker. She helped at our charity shop in the city centre several days a week. We try and support homeless people in the city where we can. That's what I'm doing right now, painting a new building we're planning to open. As far as Patricia is concerned, I understand from other people who attend our church that she was a retired schoolteacher, but that was many years ago. To be honest outside of the church community, as I've said, I didn't know her too well. On an average Sunday, we can get around ninety to a hundred people coming to worship, it's a large flock to look after.'

'Did Patricia ever mention anything about feeling threatened, uneasy about anything, worried at all?'

'Well if she was, she certainly didn't talk to me about it. We hold one-to-one sessions every couple of weeks, people can come and open up about all sorts of issues, anything from utility bills to a lack of faith, it's all part of what we do here.'

'May I ask a question; how did you find her name? Who she was?'

'Her neighbour,' Frank replied. 'She noticed she hadn't seen her for several days and contacted the police. The local officers used a neighbour's key to enter the house, looked around, checked all the mail at the front door, and found her passport in the bedroom draw, which confirmed who she was.'

'Well, I'm sorry I can't help you any further. She will be sadly missed but is in a better place now, God Bless her.'

'A twisted ankle? Asked Frank, looking down at Steven Andrew's leg.

'No Detective Sergeant Bailey, arthritis in my knee. It started at university after a sports injury, I've had it for years.'

'Which university was that, just for reference?'

'Newcastle studied Physiotherapy, had a difficult time, which resulted in a nervous breakdown, didn't finish my studies, and went into the ministry. My parents were big churchgoers, so I guess that influenced me, sadly they're no longer here.'

Thanking the minister they made their way out the front door, Frank checked his notes. Turning around, he could see Steven Andrews watching them making their way across the car park, sadness in his eyes.

'Well,' said Frank. What do you think? Could he be a suspect? He knew about her movements, where she lived and the fact that she did a lot of walking. No one would ever suspect a pastor, a man of the cloth to be a murderer.'

'He's not a pastor Frank. He's a minister, and he certainly isn't a man of the cloth, that's for sure. No, I don't think he has anything to do with Patricia's death whatsoever. But let's check him out, get in touch with Lancashire police, see if there's anything we should know about.'

Adam started the car and was about to put it into gear and open Spotify when he remembered the photo in Patricia Locke's house.

'You said you'd found something interesting at Particia's house.'

'Yes, maybe nothing, but maybe be something.'

Frank unlocked his iPhone, unlocked it, and pulled up the image he'd taken earlier.

Cupping his hands to shield from the sunlight, it showed a group of around sixty boys, the front row sitting on the grass, legs crossed, the second row seated on what looked like wooden benches, and the third back row, standing.

On either side were several adults, both male and female. To the right of the picture stood a young, casually dressed woman, there was no mistaking it, the facial features, and the height, it looked like a young Patricia Locke.

The picture was in black and white, brown fading at the edges, but there was no mistaking who it was. And printed across the bottom in bold letters.

THE CLASS OF YEAR THREE.

Twenty-one

VIV PARKED HER SKODA Kodiak 4X4 into one of the four reserved spaces marked, GP PARKING ONLY. She looked at the digital clock on the dashboard, it was 7:32 a.m.

The journey from home to Edgewater Medical Centre normally took between twenty-five to thirty minutes. A lot depended on local traffic entering and leaving Derby City Centre and of course, the dreaded school run.

Before taking up the post, Viv researched several practices and spoke with medical colleagues. Making sure that she secured a post that offered a cross-section of patient care, whilst allowing her to concentrate on her chosen specialty, Diabetes Management.

Her initial interview with the senior partner Dr Peter Johnson, hadn't gone as well as she'd expected. She had arrived late, due to a major incident on the southbound carriageway of the M1. Trying to place a call from her mobile phone had proved useless, as it was permanently engaged each time she tried.

Her second and final interview was far more successful, she took the opportunity to share her experience and knowledge on Diabetic Management, referring to a clinical paper on Endocrinology she'd had published in The Lancet some three years previously. More importantly, and what seemed to secure her position was how raising patient awareness and changes in their lifestyle, could potentially reduce their reliance on prescription drugs.

Opening the remote boot, she took out her computer bag and walked over to the main entrance, noticing for the first time the newly installed CCTV cameras. Apart from Dr Johnson, who was the Senior Partner, several other GPs were working at the medical centre, bringing the total to five. One was Vivian, and three of the remaining GPs were full-time, with one other being a locum who came into the medical centre three days a week, including emergency cover on alternative weekends.

Viv still smiled to herself as she glanced at the new plaque firmly screwed to the wall. DR VIVIAN FLEMMING. MRCGP. MRCP.

The main receptionist, a small woman of around thirty who went by the name of Beth, short for Elisabeth, had already disabled the security system, switched on all the lights, and unlocked the five consulting rooms.

Rows of bright green plastic chairs were arranged for patients waiting to see a healthcare professional, two TV screens announcing their timed appointments.

Beth sat behind a glass-enclosed area where upon arrival, further members of staff would deal with all telephone appointments, queries, and requests from patients, acting as a liaison team with all the doctors and nurses.

Edgewater Medical Centre was one of the largest independent GP Practices within Derbyshire and certainly the largest to service the surrounding countryside. Offering a range of professional services to approximately ten thousand patients, travelling in some cases, ten to twelve miles to see Dr Peter Johnson, who'd established himself as a caring and dedicated GP, carrying on the excellent medical care that his late father used to offer.

Acquiring the practice when his father died suddenly, Peter continued to be the doctor that patients wanted to see, and in the early days that was fine and manageable.

But as the patient list increased, he decided to extend the property to create a much larger building and expand the medical team, which now included Viv.

She'd been there almost seven months now, taking up the position much sooner than Adam, and travelling down from Sheffield every day, trying different shortcuts, but accepting over time that the journey was always going to take around fifty to sixty minutes.

Peter suggested she stay over at a local bed and breakfast, there were lots in the surrounding villages, or even at his cottage, but she declined.

Viv opened the door to her consulting room, sat down at her desk and switched on her computer, a screen saver of Adam, Scarlett and herself sprang to life.

Checking the number of patients, she'd be required to see today, on average three per hour, with fifteen to twenty minutes per patient. 'A busy day,' she said under her breath.

There was a knock at the door, and Beth entered with a cup of steaming tea and biscuits on a plate.

'Morning Vivian, she said. Are you okay, you're in a bit early aren't you?'

'I wanted an early start, must go out at lunchtime, and need to leave on time tonight, date night. Is Peter in yet? I didn't see his car when I arrived?'

'Just come in, had his filtered coffee and asked me to ask you to pop in and see him before the patients arrive.'

Viv took a sip of her tea, biscuit in hand, and made her way to Peter's consulting room, which was at the other end of the reception, a smell of coffee leading a trail to the door.

'Morning Vivian, just a quick word if I may.'

Dr Peter Johnson was dressed as usual, casual trousers, an open-neck shirt and a dark blue Paul Smith branded sweater, he didn't like wearing suits, in his mind, smart casual dress generally put patients more at ease.

At five foot eleven inches tall, he carried his weight well, although he would admit he could do with losing a few pounds, too many takeaways, he'd say.

Living alone it's far too easy to just pick up the phone and call for an Indian or Chinese to be delivered and leaving the Medical Centre frequently late in the evening didn't help either.

He'd never married, and after qualifying as a doctor from the Medical School in Nottingham, he stayed local, initially working at the hospital connected to the medical school and then deciding to join his father's GP Practice.

During a one-off conversation with the practice nurse, she'd let it slip to Vivian that after his father's death, his mother, who he'd lived with and cared for, had died quite suddenly from pancreatic cancer, which had hit him very hard.

'We have a practice meeting tomorrow lunchtime,' he said. 'You're still available to attend? Beth has arranged for the practice to be closed for an hour and organised some sandwiches.'

'Yes, that's fine, I've got to get off on time tonight, but tomorrow's okay. Is everything all right?'

'Yes, no problems. It's just a while since we've had any time together and I wish to discuss a couple of points with you. I'll see you then. Have a good day.'

As Viv returned to her consulting room, she began considering what Peter wanted to discuss. Was he concerned about her patient's diagnosis? Had there been some negative feedback? Or had there been a formal patient complaint?

She didn't know, but she'd soon find out.

Twenty-two

ADAM'S ALARM CLOCK went off just after 6:15 a.m. He'd slept in the spare room to avoid waking Viv, and kept the curtains slightly open, to allow the morning to wake him up.

Showering quickly, he grabbed a cup of coffee and hit the road at 6:40 a.m. He wanted an early start, to hopefully beat the traffic as he and Viv were going out for dinner this evening, and he had to be back home on time, 'no excuses,' she'd told him the night before.

Hanging his jacket in the back and loosening his tie, he put the location for Mr and Mrs Hubbard into his satnav, a village about six miles southeast of the centre of Luton.

It showed the route and expected arrival time of approximately 8:45 a.m. Following an earlier telephone conversation, he'd agreed to meet with them both to go over their statements at home, as they didn't want to travel to Derby.

'You'll know you're heading in the right direction when you see the aeroplanes coming into the airport,' said Mr Hubbard.

Taking the A52 ring road he joined the M1 motorway at Junction 25 and headed south. Traffic was light to begin with, so setting the Audi's cruise control at seventy, he opened Spotify and said to himself. 'Time for some Beatles.'

Entering the village, he passed a sign reading BRACKENRIDGE WELCOMES CAREFUL DRIVERS, and a green face lighting up, to show his speed of thirty miles per hour. The Hubbard's lived in a traditionally built bungalow, dating back to the late seventies, with two curved double-glazed bay windows on either side of a dark blue painted entrance door, a large number seven screwed in the centre.

He parked the Audi right outside the house, without blocking the curved drive to the left of the property.

Mrs Hubbard and their dog had already seen him through the window. The front door opened, and Mr Hubbard held out his hand; it felt rough to the touch, Adam thought.

To make sure he'd arrive on time, Adam hadn't stopped on the motorway. So, he asked if he could use the toilet before they began, also checking in the mirror to fasten his tie and wash his hands.

'Can I offer you some tea or coffee officer?' said Mrs Hubbard, as they both stood facing him, side by side.

'Coffee would be great and please call me Adam. This isn't an official interview, I just wanted to take a little more time to cross-check both of your statements.'

Mrs Hubbard made her way to the kitchen, followed by the dog, who settled down in its basket.

'Please take a seat,' said Mr Hubbard.

Adam sat down on a plain grey leather settee, facing the front windows, opposite was a single yellow leather chair which Mr Hubbard made himself comfortable in. Coffee and biscuits arrived, Mrs Hubbard sat next to Adam, placing the tray on a glass-topped coffee table. Adam noticed how modern the lounge was with plain beige carpet, leather chairs and settee, and white walls throughout. Two vertical black blinds covered the front windows.

It was very minimalistic, although he'd expected a more traditional layout. Surprisingly, despite their ages, Mr and Mrs Hubbard seemed to have a modern outlook on life.

'So… thanks for taking the time to meet with me. As explained on the phone call, I just wanted to go over in more detail the statements you gave to my officers, is that okay?'

'That's fine, we're more than happy to help in any way we can, and it's Bob and Sandra by the way.'

'Nice bungalow, how long have you lived here?'

'We moved here from the North, Sunderland to be exact, I was coming up for retirement, I'd spent nearly thirty years in the steelworks, and we wanted a quieter life, somewhere nearer the grandchildren. My son works abroad a lot, flying from Luton, so to be nearer the family, we decided to sell up and relocate south, this property came on the market, we made an offer and here we are.'

Adam opened the folder he'd brought in with him and began to read through Bob and Sandra's statements.

'So, in your own words, can we just go over the events of the day once again? I understand that this has already been done, but in most cases, certain points come to light after the event, and we just need to make sure we've captured everything.'

Bob Hubbard leaned forward, gathering his thoughts.

'Well, apart from the grandchildren, walking is our main hobby. We have a nature reserve a few miles away, spend a lot of time there, walking around, and looking at the wildlife. And the

Derbyshire countryside has always been a favourite spot, every time we go there, we see something different, the landscape changes from season to season. For several years we've stayed at the Fox and Hounds Hotel in Bakewell, a family-run place, it's just on the edge of the Peak District. However, the owner sold up and it was taken over by a larger company, the service just wasn't the same after that, so we decided to try somewhere different. Anyway, on this particular day, we took an early morning walk to Blythe Woods with our dog. It'd been suggested we try it out by the owners of the bed and breakfast where we were staying. They said it would take us about twenty minutes to walk to the entrance unless we took the car, which Benji doesn't like really.'

He takes a drink of coffee and picks up a biscuit.

'I guess we must have left between six and six fifteen. We said we'd have breakfast when we got back. There are several paths leading from the entrance into the woods, but we took the main one. Apart from ours, there were no vehicles in the car park, and we didn't see a soul the whole time we were out walking.'

He placed his coffee cup on the table and helped himself to another biscuit.

'I'd say we'd been walking for about ten to fifteen minutes when we came across an open area which was surrounded by trees… And there she was. At first, we didn't know what was going on and couldn't make it out. As I got a little closer, I visibly noticed it was a body, a cord around her neck, Benji wanted to take a closer look, so I pulled him away immediately. We realised this would potentially be a crime scene, so we didn't move any closer to the body. I'd estimate we were about ten to twelve feet away; I took out my mobile phone and fortunately, there were three bars on it. I called 999 and was immediately transferred to a police officer who took all our details.'

'How did you know where you were?'

'That was easy, I'd installed What3words on my mobile phone several months ago, you never know when you might need it. It virtually took the police right to where we found the body.'

'Did you notice anything else about the body that you can recall now, anything at all?'

Bob Hubbard sat back in his chair and let out a deep sigh.

'I don't think we did. Both me and Sandra have been trying to remember anything that we might have forgotten when we made our statements at the station. I'm sure you can imagine, it was a huge shock to us both, finding a body like that, it takes some getting over.'

'I can appreciate that; it's not something you experience every day… thankfully. One final question before I go, are you sure there was no one around either when you were walking into the woods or coming back out.'

'There was certainly no one around when we set off, although it was early in the morning I guess. One of your officers escorted us back to our car, and explained what was going to happen next, apart from that, no one.'

Adam collected all the paperwork and stood up from the settee, sticking slightly to the leather as he did so.

'Thanks for taking the time to meet with me, I wish it was under better circumstances, but I'm sure you can appreciate, that we have to cover every angle on an enquiry as serious as this one. Just in case anything else springs to mind, here are my contact details, all the information is on the card.'

The three of them made their way to the front door, Benji making his way out of the kitchen, Sandra finally speaking.

'Can I ask one further question Detective Inspector, are you allowed to tell us the name of the women?'

Adam thought for a moment.

'Patricia Locke, her name was Patricia Locke.'

Back in the car, Adam was surprised to see that he'd had no missed calls on his mobile, he'd expected one from DCI Vickers, but maybe he was letting him do the job he's paid to do.

As he made his way out of Brackenridge Village, he wondered how this might affect the Hubbard's. It's not every day you come across a body after all.

Twenty-three

THE M1 MOTORWAY GOING back wasn't too busy, although traffic was beginning to pick up the further north he went. Checking his watch, it was 12:50 p.m., time for lunch his rumbling stomach announced, as he saw a sign for Watford Gap Services one mile ahead.

The Beatles were playing 'A Hard Day's Night' as he pulled carefully into a parking space. Checking his mobile phone again he decided that he would call DCI Vickers himself, better to take the initiative to chat he thought,

GREGGS was always an excellent choice for a sandwich and a cup of tea, he placed his order, got a receipt, and made himself comfortable on one of the vacant chairs.

He never had an issue in claiming meals, drinks etc. on official expenses, some senior officers frowned upon it, saying that they were paid enough already, but Adam's view was different, the system allowed for claiming, and that's what he did, absolutely no regrets.

Opening the statement folder on the table in front of him, he reviewed the notes he'd made following the interview with Bob and Sandra Hubbard. Disappointed in the way that they couldn't offer any further information about the day in question, but at least it was covered.

Deciding not to go into the office he made a call to Frank, bringing him up to speed with developments from his meeting and arranged for an update first thing in the morning.

Next call, DCI Vickers, who picked up on the second ring.

'Adam, I was just thinking about you, how did you get on with the… sorry, what were their names again?'

'Hubbard, Bob, and Sandra Hubbard sir. Essentially, they couldn't throw any further light on what took place on the day, it's all in their original statements, they were unable to add anything else of significance really.'

'So, a wasted journey then, is that what you're saying?'

Adam put his hand over the receiver, 'For god's sake, this man.'

'No, that's not what I'm saying, the key point was to revisit their statements and ascertain if any further information came to hand after the event. Both Bob and Sandra Hubbard were clear about certain things, when they arrived, no other people were hanging around, no vehicles either. They're our only witnesses to finding the body, we've very little to go on at the moment. I'm not saying the investigation has stalled, however, outside of talking with them, leads are very limited.'

Adam could feel the hairs on the back of his neck stand up, he wasn't going to be put under more pressure from the DCI, he'd stand his ground as he'd always done.

'First thing in the morning the whole team are meeting for a debrief, we may have further details to share then, I'll keep you posted sir.'

'We just need to make sure we're on top of this Adam, the Chief Super is looking for a quick closure, avoiding any unnecessary bad publicity for the division, I'm sure you appreciate that, having experienced the kickback in South Yorkshire.'

The line went dead, leaving Adam wondering what the DCI had said to the Chief Super, 'was he up to the job? Are his personal issues clouding his judgement? Or hopefully, *he can and will run* this investigation, no concerns on that score.'

The rest of the journey home was uneventful, stop, start around East Midlands airport, then take the A52 towards Derby ring road, arriving back home at just after 4:50 p.m. perfect timing.

He'd just finished changing when he heard Viv's car on the drive, the table at the restaurant was booked for 7:30 p.m. so she'd got plenty of time to get ready. Opening the front door, he noticed how tired she looked, dark circles under her eyes, they needed a holiday, he thought, sooner rather than later, but the way things are going, it'll be later no doubt.

Forty minutes later, walking down the stairs, she looked radiant, dressed in a black low-cut dress, falling just below the knee, black shoes and a grey stole, what an amazing transformation from earlier on he thought to himself.

La Petite Maison restaurant was just on the outskirts of Ashbourne, about a ten-minute drive, they arrived around fifteen minutes early, just right for pre-dinner drinks.

Adam was driving so he ordered a slimline tonic, Viv had a large glass of chardonnay, just as the waiter showed them to their table.

Although the restaurant was busy, the tables were quite intimate, with low subtle lighting, great for a romantic French dinner for two.

They both had the same starter, pate with onion relish, Viv then going for the salmon, Adam having a steak, medium to well-done, finishing off with crème Broulee and Tarte Tartan, and coffee for two.

The restaurant began to get increasingly busy as Adam paid the bill, leaving a ten-pound tip at the table. They'd parked their car on one of the side streets, stopping occasionally as Viv saw something of interest in the shop windows.

'We must come for a day out to Ashbourne, it's such a lovely place, quaint shops, nice restaurants for lunch, and not too far for us to travel.'

Adam saw Viv's reflection in the shop window glass, he still remembers the first time he set eyes on her, at a local pub in Sheffield City Centre, The Dog and Parrot.

All the young students met there. He noticed her across the bar, made his way over, offered to buy her a drink and started talking. They both shared their life stories and over the next few months became closer, finally deciding that they wanted to spend the rest of their lives together.

That was almost fifteen years ago, both carving out extraordinarily successful careers for themselves and now living a more rural life in Derbyshire. But, and it's always a big but, Scarlett their beautiful daughter will constantly be at the forefront of their minds.

They both try to hide it from each other, but now and again, something triggers a memory, seeing a little girl holding their parents' hand, the laughter of a small child, family photographs at home, they all trigger memories that will never fade.

As they walked back to the car, on the opposite side of the road, three young lads, probably in their mid-twenties, fell out of the front door of a pub, loud voices echoed off the shop fronts, strong language, filling the air.

Doubtless, too much to drink Adam guessed. But that wasn't what made him take a second glance.

What raised his attention wasn't what they were doing or the foul language, it was what one of them was wearing. A cap… and then he remembered.

He'd forgotten about the figure with the black and white baseball cap.

Twenty-four

FRANK'S MOBILE RANG, vibrating on the bedside table, immediately going to voice message.

'Morning Frank, not sure what time you're planning to come in today, but I need to see you in my office ASAP. We also need to get the rest of the team together, can you give me a call when you get this message, Oh, sorry, it's Adam by the way.'

They'd both had a late night, Frank and his wife, Julie, staying up too late, chatting about what to do with her mother and both drinking too much alcohol.

They hadn't noticed the early signs of Dementia, although, like a lot of people of Julie's mother's age, she did begin to get forgetful.

The investigation team had been gathering what little information there was, but it was now time to share more widely any progress made to date, which was the reason Adam had requested for all of them to meet him and Frank in the incident room at Central Derby HQ.

The evidence board had taken on a fresh look, images of Mr. and Mrs. Hubbard had been added, only as a reminder to Adam of the interview he'd conducted. Next to Patricia Locke's photo was one of Steven Andrews, taken from the website he was the minister for.

On the other side was the larger photograph Frank had taken on his mobile phone; he'd printed it out in black and white.

It showed what looked like staff and pupils at a boarding school back in the day, and what they thought was a much younger image of the victim.

'Thanks to everyone for coming in so early, have you all got tea or coffee?' said Adam.

There were nods all around as he turned to face the evidence board.

'So, yesterday I interviewed Mr and Mrs Hubbard, just as a reminder, they were the couple who first discovered Patricia Locke's body. Unfortunately, they can't add any more information other than what's in their original statements, so there is limited progress there. However, both Frank and I have also interviewed Steven Andrews.' He tapped the image with his finger, nodding at Frank to take over.

'We're going to run a check on this guy, but this is what we know so far. He's the minister of the church that Patricia Locke went to, Edgewater Community Church. Patricia Locke was a regular attendee at the church, and as we know, volunteered in their charity shop in the city centre.'

All eyes were on Frank, frantic notes being taken, the smell of strong coffee wafting across the room.

'He moved down from Newcastle, although he originated from Derbyshire. I'm going to contact Tyne and Wear division to get further details on him, although being honest, it may not lead to anything.'

Looking around the room, Adam was trying to judge the mood of the team. From the look on the officers' faces, he knew it was difficult to continue to encourage an investigative team when there was little to go on.

Generally, they were feeling under pressure to get results. To make a name for themselves and stand out from the rest.

A dark-haired, clean-shaven PC towards the back of the room raised his arm and stood up. He opened his notebook, looking directly at Adam, obviously keen to say something and contribute.

PC Gavin Turner had been a police officer for just over four years, and progressed from a special constable, but was originally a self-employed delivery driver.

'I've interviewed the neighbours on either side of Miss Lock's house, Mrs Maureen Spencer, she was the key holder. According to her, Miss Locke *was* a retired teacher at a private school, until about ten years ago, but she's not sure where. She *did* inherit the property from her parents, now deceased, and had lived there ever since. Both neighbours also confirmed that she was a keen walker, and went most days, always taking the same route. It wouldn't be difficult for someone to trace her steps or follow her towards the woods, without raising any suspicion.'

'I've also interviewed the staff at the charity shop,' said a female officer. 'Miss Locke volunteers there three days a week, mostly in the afternoon.'

Making sure she got the facts right; the officer opened her pocketbook.

'One interesting point, a staff member did say that she believes Miss Locke and the minister argued several weeks ago, well maybe not an argument, but voices were certainly raised apparently.'

'Did they say what this argument was about?' asked Frank.

'No sir, they didn't know, but outwardly Miss Locke seemed quite upset by it.'

Frank updated the evidence board with a black felt-tipped pen, then, wrote in bold red letters, the name, Steven Andrews, POI.

Person Of Interest.

Returning to the office, Frank sat down as Adam unlocked his desk drawer and pulled out the police logbook, updating every little detail that had come out of the briefing. They both checked the notes so far, there was very little detail to talk about. No witnesses as such, no motive, no further information following door-to-door enquiries, just a name and a mutilated corpse.

'Are you going to update the DCI tomorrow? In the meantime, what do you want to do about Steven Andrews?' asked Frank.

'Leave Tom Vickers to me. I've written his name down, Steven Andrews. Don't forget to check him out Frank, he may be completely innocent, on the other hand, he could be involved. What was the disagreement about at the charity shop, why was Patricia Locke upset?

If he is hiding something, anything, we need to know.'

'And one more thing, which I purposely didn't raise in the incident room. Do you remember me telling you about a person quite close to the murder scene? I think it was a man. Anyhow, they were taking notes or photographs, dressed in a long dark coat, and black and white baseball cap. I don't think it was a local reporter, as the body was quickly removed by the Pathology team. So, what were they doing there, and more to the point, why were they taking photos?'

Twenty-five

DR PETER JOHNSON sat around the medical centre conference table, laying out papers in preparation for his meeting with Vivian. He checked the clock on the wall, seven fifty-five, he'd cancelled the lunchtime sandwiches, as they'd agreed to meet earlier than originally planned, between eight and eight fifteen, surgery generally started at nine.

Parking her car in the usual space, Viv made her way across the car park, past reception with a quick 'Good morning' and walked straight to the conference room, knocking on the door, not waiting for an answer.

'Morning Vivian, thanks for coming in earlier, hopefully, this won't take too long to go through.'

She pulled a chair from under the table and took a seat, noticing the papers neatly arranged in front of him.

'It's fine Peter… is everything all right? I was a little surprised when you asked me to meet up with you, one to one, as such.'

'Yes, sorry about that, I hope you weren't worried, it's just I needed to have a chat with you about a couple of issues that are connected with you, and not the rest of the team.'

He opened a black leather folder, branded in the top right-hand corner with a pharmaceutical company's logo, his name printed in gold in the centre. DR PETER A. JOHNSON.

He paused for several minutes, checking his notes.

'The police came to see me yesterday, a uniformed officer. He was asking questions about one of our patients, your patient, Miss Patricia Locke. She has been found dead, and he wanted to see if we could offer any information on her background, family, friends etc.'

For a moment Viv sat there motionless, as she could recall, she'd reviewed Miss Locke's condition face to face only several weeks ago. Her new medication seemed to be working, and she had also made a concerted effort to lose a few pounds in weight, so all was good.

'I take it that your husband Adam will know what's going off? I understand from the office he's actually in charge of the case?'

'He hasn't said anything to me about it, but he did mention that he was working on something that might interrupt our way of life you know, early morning starts and getting home late, but he hasn't mentioned what or who it involved.'

'Well regretfully it was Patricia Locke, I did say that you would be available if required, although I don't think we can throw any further light on her background apart from a clinical perspective, but they may need to speak with you.'

There was a knock at the door and one of the other receptionists brought in two coffees, placing them on coasters and leaving without saying a word.

Taking a drink to quench the dryness in her mouth, she looked directly at Peter.

'You mentioned that there were a couple of points, surely nothing is as serious as this?'

'No, the second point is to do directly with the practice.' Peter checked his notes once again.

'Over the last few months, I've been looking at how to diversify some of my commercial holdings in the practice, and coming straight to the point, I'd like you to consider becoming a full partner in the medical centre.'

Viv wasn't sure how to answer, she'd run through on the journey in what Peter could want to talk with her about, but didn't expect this at all, coming as a complete surprise.

'Well, thank you Peter for the offer which obviously I'm interested in discussing further. I'd need to talk it over with Adam of course. It would also depend on the finances. One quick question though, why me, why not one of the other doctors?'

Peter leaned forward, lowering his voice slightly.

'To be honest Vivian, you're the best choice. You've made a huge difference to the clinical work done here since you joined, and if you don't consider accepting then I'll look further afield, which I don't want to do if I'm honest.'

'So, no pressure from my side then,' she said with a smile.

'Look, talk it over with Adam, come back to me when you can and we'll progress further, I've already done the sums, so you don't need to worry about that, we can go through them when you want.'

Standing up, they both shook hands, as though the deal had been done there and then.

'Oh, one more point Vivian, please don't discuss this with any other team member, until we know the outcome.'

Smiling, she turned and replied, 'My lips are sealed,' closing the door behind her.

Twenty-six

STRONG DISCIPLINE WAS CONSTANTLY maintained at Chaffinch House boarding school both from the teachers and the older students. The three of us, Simon, Toby, and I decided to avoid trouble and try and stay together wherever possible, watching each other's back. The older boys went around like packs of wolves, mostly left alone to their own devices, and selectively mistreating the younger boys.

Toby was picked on and bullied, we don't know why, although he was easy meat, quite skinny for his age, stuttered when trying to talk, and couldn't look after himself. He was also extremely clever, exceeded in most subjects, and was on course for exceptional year-end grades. He often would get up early, find somewhere quiet and just study.

The weekends were when we could plan to spend time together. Saturday morning was taken up in class, leaving the afternoon and all day Sunday to do what we wanted, including smoking, although Toby never took a drag, ever.

We decided in the afternoon that if it was a warm day on Sunday, we'd go swimming in the lake, we knew we shouldn't, but no one would see us at the far end, near the trees.

The sun rose early, so after breakfast we got our trunks and towels and made our way across the car park, down the drive to the far end of the lake, laying our towels out on the warm grass.

Checking that we were okay, I took off my wristwatch, we all got undressed and entered the lake, the water was clear, reflecting our faces as we made our way in.

It was quite shallow and became murky as our feet disturbed the silt until we hit a ridge, then it dropped about three feet to the bottom, the water was clear and still safe for us to stand up.

Simon and I were strong swimmers, visiting the indoor pool regularly, Toby was not so good, he kept himself near the edge, not venturing out any further.

As I try to recall, we hadn't been there very long when we noticed two of the older boys coming down the path, straight in our direction.

Toby looked nervous as all three of us swam to the side, he went first as it was easier for him to get out from the lake, soaking wet, we walked back to where our towels were.

'Nice watch,' said one of the older boys, picking it up and putting it on his wrist, adjusting the strap to fit.

'Leave that alone, it's mine, that was my grandads, it's not yours, hand it back.'

'Sorry boy finders' keepers. I found it in the grass, so it's mine and what are you doing here anyway, the lake is out of bounds?'

The punch in my stomach took me by surprise, doubling over in pain, trying to get my breath, the other boy holding Simon's hands behind his back.

Toby looked on in horror, unaware of what was going to happen next, but finding the courage to speak.

'Get off them, leave them alone, pick on someone your size you cowards.'

Getting my breath back, both Simon and I looked at each other.

'Toby, it's okay.'

Turning to the boy with his new acquisition.

'You can keep the watch just leave us all alone, we'll go back to the dormitory and keep out of your way in future.'

The other boy turned to the one who'd hit me and smiled.

'You two, just piss off, we need a quick chat with clever dick here.'

'We all go, or we all stay, we're not leaving Toby here alone.'

'He's not alone, he has us, we'll keep him company.'

'Not a chance, he's coming back with us.'

I fell to my knees, as another thump, much harder than the first, hit me again in the stomach.

Struggling to stand up, Simon turned to me.

'Come on, let's go, it's only going to get worse if we stay.'

Gathering our belongings, we made our way down the path and across the grass, occasionally looking back, they were prodding Toby in the chest with their fingers, pulling his hair. He called out to us.

'I'll be okay, d – d - don't worry about me, I'll see you later.'

As we approached the front of the house, I wanted to go back, to help Toby. To stop the bullying. Simon grabbed hold of my arm.

'Don't do that, it'll make it worse for all of us, including Toby.'

Back in the dormitory, we both sat on my bed wondering what the boys were doing, and when Toby would return.

Other than heavy breathing from the other boys in the dormitory, and a smell difficult to describe, everywhere was still quiet when I woke the following morning.

Simon was still asleep in his bed, but Toby wasn't, *'he must be studying'* I thought to myself.

As with every other morning, breakfast was a military operation, you made your way to the school canteen, got in line, and selected what you wanted finding somewhere to sit, we always tried to find three vacant seats if we could.

Simon sat at my side, looking pale, as though he hadn't slept last night.

'Have you seen Toby this morning?'

'No, I haven't, but I guess he's studying as usual.'

'What about yesterday, what was that all about? Taking your watch and letting us go but keeping Toby behind.'

'I don't know, I'm not bothered too much about the watch, but I'm worried about Toby, I hope he got back all right.'

'Do you know the boys that came to the lake? Simon asked.

'Only the one who took my watch, I've seen him around quite a lot, but not the other boy.'

'Do you think we should report it to the headmaster?'

'What's the point, it won't get us anywhere, and anyway, he just turns a blind eye to what's going off here.'

Simon looked up at the large ornate clock on the wall above the entrance door, I could see a look of concern on his face.

'We should make a move,' he said, 'it'll be morning service in fifteen minutes or so, and I've got to get my tie and jumper.'

As usual, the noise in the main hall was filled with voices, mostly from the older boys, standing and paying attention as the teaching staff entered the hall, silence moving across the room.

The headmaster entered last, making his way to the front of the podium, the crest of the school carved in wood, his black gown moving with every step.

He turned around, looking at the staff lined up behind him, before asking everyone to 'take a seat.'

He had a solemn look on his face, as he shuffled several papers in front of him.

'Good morning gentlemen. Today is an extremely sad time at Chaffinch House boarding school, sadly and tragically we've lost one of our own. I am deeply sorry to have to report that one of our most promising pupils, Toby Curtis, we believe drowned last evening whilst swimming in the lake. We understand that he may have become trapped in the reeds and unable to swim to the surface. I appreciate that this will come as a deep shock to the whole school and in particular to his close friends, you know who you are. The police have obviously been informed, and they will be here for most of the day, they may need to speak with some of you, although it does look like this was an unfortunate accident. Toby's parents are scheduled to arrive later today too. All studies will be cancelled for the remainder of the day, as a mark of respect for Toby, and will resume as normal tomorrow morning. If you have any further questions, speak to your form teacher, thank you gentlemen and good morning.'

As the headmaster and staff left the room, I still recall Simon turning to me, not knowing what to say, tears forming in his eyes. We'd lost one of our closest friends, we always said we'd look after each other, but we'd failed.

As I turned to face Simon, I knew it wasn't an accident, those two boys were involved, whatever they'd done, Toby's life had ended.

As we made our way out of the hall, I glanced around, checking to see if the boys were still there. To the right of me, I noticed one of the culprits, the main one smiling to himself.

The boy who took my watch, who was pulling Toby's hair and pocking him in the stomach. I knew his name, he knew that, and I never forget a name.

Twenty-seven

THE ROADS AROUND DERBYSHIRE were clear as Danny and Joe made their way to the nursing home on the outskirts of the Derbyshire Dales. Joe had collected Danny from his parent's house just after seven twenty. Danny's mum had got up and cooked him breakfast, bacon, sausages and two fried eggs. A strong mug of piping hot tea, and two slices of brown toast on the side.

'You've got to start the day Daniel on a full stomach,' she said.

Joe had tendered for the landscaping job several months earlier, and to be honest, he was surprised when the general manager of the home had contacted him to confirm that the quote he'd forwarded was acceptable. It was going to be a huge undertaking, the whole front gardens were going to be redesigned, based on the drawings that Joe had initially submitted. A brand-new rockery was to be built, with separate seating areas, all surrounded by trees, shrubs, and hedges.

A water fountain was to be erected in the middle, which according to some of the nursing staff, relaxed the patients and aided recovery.

Joe had already taken on labourers to do the heavy work, but he and Danny would oversee the operation, making sure that everything was going to plan, delivered on time and most importantly, within budget.

Danny's experience would be invaluable, which was one of the reasons he'd offered him the job.

Joe had insisted that the men made an early start and as they pulled up in front of the building, several small JCB diggers were already at work, removing soil and levelling off the ground, a smell of diesel fumes lingering in the air.

Danny looked up into the sky, the sun had already broken through, and it was going to be a great day. They both got out of the Ford Ranger and made their way to where all the action was taking place, Danny noticing just how much earth they'd already moved.

As they stood together taking in the work involved, taking a drag of a cigarette, Joe turned to Danny.

'Can I ask you a personal question?' Danny nodded.

'Do you still think about the conviction? Why it went against you? Being accused of murder in the first place? Your time in prison?'

'That's a lot of questions Joe, some of which I'm still trying to come to terms with myself. I was in the wrong place at the wrong time, didn't have an alibi, and as you know, they found my DNA on the gardening gloves. Looking back on it now, I think I was set up by the police, they wanted a result, and as far as they were concerned, I was in the frame, no question'

As Joe finished his cigarette, stubbing it out on the floor, Danny continued.

'All I want to do is clear my name, I'm not interested in anything else, making people accountable, wanting compensation, anything like that, no. I just want to make sure people know I was innocent, thankfully my mum already knows that.'

'If it was me,' Joe replied, 'I'd want answers. Why they didn't widen the investigation, look for other suspects, motives, that sort of thing? Fourteen years of your life were taken Danny, you'll never get that back. I wouldn't rest, I'd want to know what went wrong. The bigger question is, why? Why arrest you in the first place? Was the investigation thorough enough? Did the people involved cut corners?'

'I understand where you're coming from Joe, and in the past, I've asked myself those same questions, but, and it's a big but, you must move on, life's too short to get bogged down in things of the past. And I've also got to think of mum, she stood by my side the whole time, never giving up, always there when needed, pity I can't say the same about my dad.'

Just as they were about to check on the workers, casually making their way into the garden, a rather short, chubby man was walking towards them, Joe noticed him out of the corner of his eye.

He put his foot on the cigarette, rubbing it into the ground, turning to face Danny, talking in a quiet voice.

'Here we go,' he said, 'this is Mr Robinson, the general manager of the nursing home. I bet he's come to ask if everything is going according to plan. I wanted this contract, it'll support the company's finances, but I think this guy is going to be a pain in the proverbial.'

'Good morning gentlemen,' said Mr Robinson. 'Good to see that everyone is making an early start, and the weather looks like it's going to be kind to us too.'

Danny casually glanced at his digital watch, it was only twenty past eight, but already Mr Robinson was dressed in a three-piece pin-striped suit, shirt and tie, with a multi-coloured handkerchief in the top pocket of his jacket. A plastic name badge pinned below MR DAVID ROBINSON – GENERAL MANAGER.

For several minutes, the three stood looking over the garden, towards the lake in the background, unsure how to move the conversation on.

'How long have you been the general manager Mr Robinson?' asked Danny, trying to be polite.

'This building has been a nursing home for about fifteen to sixteen years; I took it over about five years ago. We have three in the company this one, is named The Lakes, obviously because of the view of the lake One in Staffordshire, Sycamore House, and another one in Derbyshire, Woodthorpe Grange. Although my name badge says general manager, I'm the Managing Director of the organisation and the major shareholder. But I try and avoid our clients and patients knowing that it makes life so much easier.'

'What was this before it was a nursing home?' continued Danny.

David Robinson considered the question for several minutes, then replied, 'I think it was a school. Boarding school if I'm not mistaken.'

Twenty-eight

THEY ARRIVED HOME earlier than normal, Adam pulling on the drive about five minutes before Viv.

He'd arranged a one-to-one update with DCI Vickers, which on reflection, had gone better than he thought. Tom Vickers gave the impression he was pleased with progress to date, and whilst there was little to go on, the investigation was uncovering some key elements to the murder.

Just as important, from the Chief superintendent's point of view, the press had kept a distance, so no pressure from that angle at least.

Viv's last patient, Miss Cartwright, hadn't turned up for her appointment. She checked her patient list for the following day, saved an X-ray to her PC and left the medical centre about thirty minutes earlier than planned. Peter was holding the fort, and he'd already agreed to lock up the building, setting the alarm system for the night.

'What shall we have to eat?' said Viv, 'we could order a takeaway or maybe cook something ourselves… Probably a healthier option don't you think?'

'Home-cooked food sounds great, there's a Chardonnay already chilled in the fridge, I'll lay the table if you want to start.'

'If we're drinking white wine, I'll grill some fish for us and a large green salad, that sound good?'

He moved to the other side of the open-plan kitchen and opened the cutlery drawer, taking out two knives, forks, and several serving spoons. As he closed it, he glanced down and noticed the Beatrix Potter cutlery set Viv's parents had bought for Scarlett on her first birthday, it still looked brand new.

They had both decided to keep it with all the other things, it was another reminder of what was missing in their family, their little girl, she'd never be forgotten.

Clearing the table and setting the dishwasher, they made themselves comfortable in the lounge, wine glasses in hand. Adam drew the curtain, blocking out the light on the outside door entrance. He put a CD on the Bang and Olufsen stereo system Viv had purchased as a new housewarming present, the glass doors opening as he approached.

'I'll happily listen to anything, 'said Viv, 'but please let's have a change from The Beatles.'

'Andrea Bocelli it is then,' you can't beat a bit of culture, he's coming to the Royal Albert Hall, we should go and see him if you want.'

'That would be nice,' said Viv, 'the break would do us good, but let's not plan anything for the moment, we're both busy at work.'

She sat at the side of Adam on the leather settee, positioning her head into his shoulder, flipping off her shoes, and pulling her knees up to her chest.

'Peter called me into a meeting earlier, I think I told you about it the other day?'

'Yeah, you did mention it. Did it go okay, is he happy with the way things are going, clinically I mean?'

An unforced smile came across her face.

'He must be, he's asked me to consider going in as a partner, taking a share in the medical practice, what do you think?'

Adam sat there for several seconds.

'Sounds like a great idea to me, but it's up to you, do you think you're up to it?'

'Cheeky sod, of course, I'm up to it. That's not the issue, it's if we can afford the investment, we've already got the mortgage to consider.'

'Look, the mortgage is easily taken care of with our joint incomes, we're one of the luckier ones, good jobs and equally good salaries.'

'How much do you think he'd be looking for?

'I've looked into it, only briefly, and I think Peter would be seeking an investment of around a hundred to a hundred and twenty thousand pounds, but he's already started doing the sums, so we'll know later in the week.'

Sitting up from the settee, Adam turned to Viv.

'Listen, if this is what you want, and it sounds like a fantastic opportunity, then I'm all for it. We'll find the money somehow, and being a partner, it's what you've always wanted.'

As Viv sat there next to Adam, she thought to herself.

'This is what I've always wanted. Being a partner, however, is a big step. Am I up for it? Can I make a difference in the forward-thinking, dynamic medical practice that Peter has created?'

But more importantly than all of that, far more important, she had to avoid wiping away the fond memories of her beautiful daughter, a daughter that they can never forget, no matter what the circumstances.

Twenty-nine

THE SEVEN-FORTY TRAIN into Newcastle Interchange arrived two minutes late, moving away from the crowded platform, she checked her watch. The Senior Personal Officer decided to walk the twenty-minute journey, the sun had broken through and after all, she'd got to continue doing her ten thousand steps, staying on track in preparation for the Great Northern Run.

Calling in at Starbucks, and purchasing a medium skinny latte, Emily Carnell looked down at her smartwatch again, checking she wasn't going to be late.

Detective Sergeant Bailey from Central Derbyshire Constabulary had contacted her the previous day and arranged a further call at nine fifteen.

Her office was on the ground floor, just down the corridor from the two arched main entrances to Newcastle University. It occupies a campus site close to the City Centre of Newcastle upon Tyne, with the medical school adjacent to the West.

Hanging up her pink Burberry coat, Emily sat down at her desk, opened her desktop, and typed in her password, double-clicking the file she'd already read over the day before.

After their initial conversation, Emily had insisted that DS Bailey email her to confirm that the enquiry was legitimate, from an HR point of view, data protection and personal security of all students past and present was mission critical.

Frank had asked Adam if he could use his office for the call to the university, and permission was granted.

Dialling the direct number Emily had given him, Frank waited for pick up, it was answered almost immediately.

'Good morning, HR department, Emily Carnell speaking.'

'Morning Emily, Detective Sergeant Frank Bailey, thanks for offering to speak with me again, really appreciated.'

'That's fine Detective Sergeant, delighted to help where we can.'

'Thank you, and please call me Frank. As mentioned yesterday, I'm seeking further information about one of your past students, Steven Andrews.'

Emily had already printed off all the information that they held on Steven. Including the fact that he only completed twenty months of his Physiotherapy degree course at the medical school.

'So, what can you tell me about Mr Andrews?'

'Well, looking at his file, he only completed just over half of the three-year course for Physiotherapy. He must have left the university, as we don't have any more details after that.'

'Is that it? Nothing else? Just left the university without any reason?'

The query prompted a question from Emily.

'Can I ask *you* something?... Why do you want to know about Steven Andrews?'

Frank had to be careful how he replied, he didn't want to jeopardize the investigation by giving too much away, after all, he could be completely innocent.

'He may be able to assist us with an ongoing investigation down in Derbyshire, he isn't a suspect, we just need to fill in some gaps... Why do you ask?'

'Because looking at his file, and I'm not sure I should tell you this, there is a red flag warning. It states that Steven Andrews was interviewed by one of the HR team for inappropriate behaviour towards a female member of staff.'

Frank instantly sat up in Adam's chair, immediately interested in what Emily had to say.

'When was this?'

'Around two months before he left the university, it doesn't mention the name of the female, it could have been an administrator or a lecturer, just shows NFA, no further action.'

'Is it possible for you to forward a copy of the file on Steven Andrews, I could get a warrant if necessary?'

There was a pause on the other end of the line.

'There's no need for that, I'll email it to you right away, give me your details.'

Frank gave Emily the contact details for Central Derbyshire Constabulary, confirming his email address.

'If you send the file over to me, I'll update my boss and if we do need any further details, am I okay to come back to you?'

'Yes, that's fine.'

Emily Carnell was about to put the phone back in its cradle.

'One more point Frank, he didn't always have the surname of Andrews, he changed his name just before he left the university. Previously, before the red flag, he was known as Steven Gilbert.'

Thirty

ADAM LOOKED OUT OF HIS office window and yawned so wide, it hurt his jaw. He and Viv had talked about the partnership and Scarlett until the early hours. With a sudden knock on his door, he turned around, just as Frank entered.

'He's arrived, I've put him in interview room two,' said Frank.

'Okay, thanks, I'll be down soonest, let him stew for a few minutes.'

He unlocked his desk drawer and pulled out the logbook. Everything, no matter how small or unimportant needed to be recorded, no excuses, it'd paid dividends on a previous investigation and would do so again.

As they both walked in, a uniformed officer walked out, gently closing the door behind him.

A rectangular table stood in the middle of the room, plastic glasses, and water in the centre. Two chairs on one side and one on the other, and a tape recorder located on a side unit at the back of the wall, unlike what you see on the TV, there was no two-way mirror.

Steven Andrews stood up from his chair, a slight look of puzzlement across his face. He was dressed in a dark grey suit, a silver cross on the left lapel, he looked more like he was going to a church meeting than a police interview.

Frank walked over to the recording equipment, unwrapped a tape, inserted it and switched it on, it made a distinct buzzing sound.

'Good morning, Mr Andrews, thanks for taking the time to come in to see us, please take a seat.'

Both detectives pulled out chairs and sat opposite, Adam placing the official logbook on the table in front of him, Frank opening a brown-coloured folder.

'Can I ask what this is all about officer?' turning to face Adam.

'Firstly, thanks again for coming in today, just for your information, under PACE guidelines, this interview is being recorded.'

'We're following up on the investigation into the death of Patricia Locke, which we spoke to you about several days ago.'

'Yes, I do remember, and as I explained at the time, I didn't know her much, apart from her attending the church that is.'

'We understand that,' said Frank, 'however, new details have come to light about a possible disagreement you had with Miss Locke at the charity shop several weeks ago, would you like to explain that to us?'

'I don't recall arguing with Patricia, as I've already mentioned, I didn't know her too well.'

'So, you don't know anything about it, is that what you're saying?'

Minutes passed as Steven Andrews sat there, linking, and unlinking his fingers in his hands.

'Can I have a glass of water please?'

He took a drink, placing it down on the table, his hands shaking slightly.

'Look, we didn't argue, she asked me a question about my past, and I happened to say that it was none of her business. Maybe a little too harshly, but it wasn't, it had nothing to do with her.'

'What about your past?' interrupted Frank.

Pausing for a second.

'I changed my surname by deed poll, it used to be Gilbert, but during my time at university, I changed it, that was all it was.'

'So why change your name to Andrews?'

'Have you ever been to university Detective Sergeant, young people can be very cruel, girls in particular,' he took another drink of water.

'A surname like Gilbert and studying in Newcastle at the time, it draws attention.

Students began to spread vicious rumours about me, was I related, was it my dad… I was struggling with my studies, so, I changed my name to Andrews, it's as simple as that. Patricia Locke found out and wanted to know more. I explained that it was all in the past and to let it drop, so, yes, we had words, in the shop, but nothing else.'

'Do you want to take a break?' asked Adam.

'No thank you, let's just get this over with, I've got meetings arranged for this afternoon.'

Frank leaned forward in his chair, looking down at the folder on the table.

'Tell us about the inappropriate behaviour recorded on your file whilst at the university'

As he looked down, both Adam and Frank could see they'd hit a nerve, when he looked back up, his face was deathly white.

'How did you find out about that? You have no right to bring that into the conversation, it was a long time ago, a time I'd rather forget.'

'Steven, can I call you Steven?' replied Adam. 'We have every right, we need to know what happened, surely you can understand that?'

'I bet you've been talking with Emily Carnell; it wasn't my fault. One of the female lecturers started showing more interest in me than I wanted. She would me to stay behind to discuss my work, would tell me how nice I looked when I'd had my hair cut, things like that.'

'Then one night she followed me out of the campus and asked me if we could go for a drink, I did not want anything to do with her. The next thing I knew, I was called to a meeting with HR, a complaint had been made against me. Apparently, I'd inappropriately touched her, and she'd reported me for it. It was all a pack of lies, but by then the damage was done. About six months later I had a breakdown, left the university, and changed my surname.'

'Thanks, Steven for explaining that, this *is* an ongoing investigation, so we may have to speak with you again.' said Adam. 'In the meantime, that's all for now.'

They all stood to their feet, Frank switching off the recorder, Adam opening the interview door, low low-pitched background voices entering the room.

'One more thing,' said Frank. 'What was wrong with the surname Gilbert? Why the rumours? What were the students accusing you of?'

Andrew Stevens turned and stared them both in the face.

'Check it out Detective Inspector Bailey, John Wilson Gilbert, you'll find out what was wrong.'

Thirty-one

'IF YOU DON'T MIND ME SAYING, you look dog-tired,' said Frank as he closed the door to Adam's office.

'We stayed up late last night, something to do with Vivian's work. That led to a conversation about Scarlett, and what more we could do. I could do in finding out the truth. I know what you're going to say, Frank, thousands of children go missing every year, but that's not the answer. *I've* got to find out what really happened that day, I'm a detective for god's sake, I'm paid to find answers.'

They'd both collected a coffee out of the machine on the ground floor, Adam grabbing a sandwich, for once taking the lift, avoiding spilling the drink on the stairs.

Sitting down they compared notes on the interview with Steven Andrews, Adam bringing the logbook electronically up to date.

'Look, Adam, I know we got off to a bad start earlier on, but if there's anything I can do to help with the investigation into Scarlett's disappearance, you've only got to ask. I thought Chris Mitchell was on the case?'

'He is… was, but resources are running thin, and he's got more important things to focus on, so it's been passed to a DS Sarah Ward. I met them a few days ago, she seems competent enough. But you know what it's like, as time passes, I guess it'll become less important. Anyway, that's where we are presently. No further progress, no sightings, nothing to go on, and a mother desperate for answers. Which regretfully, I cannot give.

Until it happens to you, no one can understand the impact it has on your life, particularly Vivians. It's like losing a part of your body, you know it's there, but you can't see or feel it. I don't think either of us will ever escape that feeling, not until we find out the truth.'

Frank deliberately took his time before asking the next question.

'So, what do you think of the vicar, sorry, minister?'

Adam rocked back in his office chair, which squeaked slightly.

'Honestly speaking, I don't know. It sounds genuine, maybe too genuine. Is challenging someone over a name change a reasonable motive or was there something else going on between him and Patricia Locke? I think we need to keep an open mind on this one.

Keep Steven Andrews on our radar, in the meantime, check out his story about John Wilson Gilbert, and see what you can uncover. I don't think there's any mystery behind this, all he did was change his name due to peer pressure, but it'll answer another outstanding question. We'll meet up again later, is that okay?'

Frank returned to his desk, opened his Lenovo PC, and started typing.

***

Adam looked up at the digital clock on his office wall as Frank knocked and walked in, it was twenty-past two in the afternoon. He'd finished his sandwich, and a can of Diet Pepsi, wiping away the crumbs on his desk as Frank sat down.

'Do you have any contacts at Newcastle Police HQ? By the looks of it, I think they're based at Wallsend, North Tyneside,' Frank said.

'No, the furthest I got up North was Sheffield, did you speak to anyone?'

'Yeah, they came back to me officially. If we wanted any information on John Wilson Gilbert, a request has got to come from our Chief Super to his counterpart.'

'So, a dead end on that one then.'

'Not necessarily, you'd be surprised what you can find by searching on the internet, I've printed off what I've managed to uncover.'

Frank passed several sheets of A4 paper across Adam's desk, retaining the same for himself.

John Wilson Gilbert (born 1951) was a British serial killer based just outside Newcastle upon Tyne, he attacked numerous women in parks and woodland during the 1980s.

The crimes were often referred to in the local and national papers as "The Northern Murders", with the press often referring to Gilbert, once he was identified, as The Butcher of Tyneside.

Whilst at school he was once excluded after coming into class covered in blood, he'd killed one of the rabbits with his bare hands.

In 1979 a woman was attacked and left for dead in a parkland near to where Gilbert lived with his parents. She survived, but over the following eighteen months, three other victims, all female, were murdered, mostly at night and all in isolated areas.

The Newcastle Police immediately initiated an urgent investigation, named "Operation Network", to apprehend the perpetrators, they initially thought there was more than one person involved.

The women described their attacker as a tall, slim man with a tattoo on his right hand.

At this time, DNA technology wasn't available, but some suspects could be eliminated by blood grouping: one attacker believed to be the tall, slim man, was an "'A' secretor with a certain PGM factor in his blood". Unlike DNA, many people share the same blood grouping, so this evidence could eliminate suspects but not identify the offender or offenders.

On the evening of the 10th of December 1982, a 19-year-old woman, named Julie Lockwood was on her way to meet her parents at their farm located in the countryside. Gilbert had been driving around and saw her get off the bus for the short walk to the family home. He drove past where Julie Lockwood was walking, stopping the car several yards in front of her. As she approached, he exited the car and asked her for directions, he then hit her on the head and forced her into the back of the vehicle. Once the attack was over, Gilbert left her for dead, but she survived and gave a fairly accurate description of her attacker, including the tattoo on his right hand, it was an army crest.

The attempted murder of Julie Lockwood changed the investigation, they finally had a lead, the army symbol on the right hand.

The inquiry was taken over by Detective Superintendent Booth (a highly experienced and respected Newcastle murder investigator) he immediately linked this attempted murder with the previous ones.

Gilbert, a former army officer and latterly, a school caretaker, was identified by Detective Superintendent Rodney Booth as a suspect. He was already known to police as he had been previously charged with the stalking of females. A type of rope was found in his parents' house. This linked him to the second murder victim, who had been tied up before being strangled. His experience with using these ropes in the army linked him to the method of strangulation using "Double Braided" rope. Several other people were also interviewed as Detective Superintendent Booth believed that Gilbert did have an accomplice, someone he may have known from the past, but due to a lack of concrete evidence, no one was identified, so no further action was taken.

Gilbert was arrested on the 13th of April 1984 while following a woman in a secluded park. Items linking him to previous crimes were discovered, including a selection of ropes in a rucksack. Detective Superintendent Booth believed that there was sufficient evidence to charge him with two attempted, and three recorded murders. He was questioned about the crimes, and the next day he was charged on all counts. Newcastle Police believed that Gilbert had not committed the offences alone, but he was not forthcoming about any accomplice.

Gilbert went on trial in August 1985 and was convicted of three murders and two attempted murders. He was given a minimum tariff of 30 years by the judge, later extended to a whole life tariff by the Home Secretary at the time.

Following his conviction, Gilbert revealed to a prison Chaplin what the police knew already: that he had not operated alone, but he never released any further details.

During his time in prison, interviews were conducted under caution, and further cases were put to him from police archives to try and jog his memory, and if he remembered any of these cases. He made it noticeably clear that he knew he had information on these crimes but would never give accurate details.

John Patrick Gilbert died in HMP Barlinnie in Scotland in 2008, taking with him all his secrets and, who if anyone, was the other accomplice.

They both sat there in silence, taking in what Frank had discovered from searching the internet.

'Do you think we should contact the Chief Super and ask for assistance with Newcastle Police, just to get a clearer picture of John Wilson Gilbert?' Adam paused for a second, checking his notes in the logbook and running his hand through his jet-black hair.

'I don't think that'll be necessary, Steven Andrews wasn't related to this guy, otherwise, it would have shown up when we conducted the initial checks. All it will do is take up valuable time and resources and take us down a track we do not need to investigate. And after all, it was over forty years ago, its history.'

Frank made his way to the door, holding the handle, he turned back. 'Tell you this much, if that's what university students are like,

I'm glad I wasn't clever enough.' Adam picked up a red ballpoint pen and drew a line through the name of John Wilson Gilbert.

Checking his mobile phone for any messages, he put in his password and opened the diary app. Entering a reminder, **call DS Sarah Ward, reference Scarlett's progress.**

Thirty-two

DR PETER JOHNSON REVERSED his metallic red Jaguar F Pace into the reserved parking space, checking the rear-view camera on his dashboard.

He'd only had the car a few weeks, it still had that brand-new smell inside. Getting up early that morning, he'd left the cottage he lived in just after six thirty, listening to the BBC news on Radio 4, he also liked Classic FM, but couldn't stand all the adverts.

Approaching the front door of the medical practice, he looked around to check that the security company had installed the correct CCTV equipment as the sales executive had recommended during their initial survey. Staff and patient safety were of paramount importance, it offered security to the staff, and confidence with the patients.

As he reached the front door, he put in the security code and walked into the reception area, he still got a thrill from knowing that patients continued to come to *his* medical centre after all these years.

Switching on the lights he opened the metal box behind reception and took out all the relevant keys, going around unlocking the doors, smiling to himself, it was almost like being a prison officer.

Arrangements had been made for him and Vivian to meet at ten a.m. to further progress the possible partnership they'd discussed previously; his accountant had already prepared a financial breakdown to share when they met.

He got himself a tumbler of water from the dispenser and made his way to the room that everyone used as a meeting area, laying out all the paperwork in front of him.

Viv was in her consulting room by eight fifteen, checking her patient's appointment before the ten o'clock meeting. She and Adam had both agreed the night before what amount of money they could raise immediately to enable the partnership to go ahead if it remained on the table.

'Morning Vivian, would you like a drink before we start?'

'Thanks, no I'm fine, I had a strong coffee before I left home.'

'So, have you had the chance to discuss my proposal with Adam? Hopefully, it's good news?'

'Yes, we discussed it last evening, in fact, until the early hours of the morning, and subject to the financial contribution, I'd like to take you up on your generous offer.'

'That's great news, I've already had my accountant draw up some official papers on what he believes to be a reasonable figure, which hopefully ties in with your thoughts.'

Sliding a white envelope across the polished wooden conference table, Viv picked it up and took out the forms.

Everything was detailed on Edgewater Medical Centre headed paper, two A4 pieces stapled together. Although she tried to give the impression of taking time to read through the document, she quickly went to page two.

About two-thirds of the way down was a figure that gave her some surprise but relief, one hundred and thirty-seven thousand pounds, for a thirty-three percent share.

The figure was more than they'd calculated initially, but Viv thought it was manageable.

'So, Vivian, what do you think? Do we have a deal? I know you'll have to speak with Adam again, but essentially what are your thoughts?'

'Honestly… it's a higher figure than we've discussed, but I don't think it'll be an issue, I'll speak with Adam tonight and come back to you in the morning.'

Peter stood from his chair, taking out another envelope from his black leather folder.

Dr Peter Johnson – Private & Confidential.

'Once you've signed the documents, if you put them in *this* envelope, I'll countersign and arrange to pass it onto our solicitors for witnessing.'

Opening his wallet from the inside of his jacket.

'And if you've got any further questions, here's the business card for my solicitor, give him a call if you need any further details.'

'Welcome on board Vivian, it'll be good to have you as a partner, someone to bounce new ideas off, fresh clinical services, new patient initiatives, etc.'

'Thank you, Peter, I won't let you down.'

Vivian opened the meeting room door and walked out into reception and back to her consulting room, avoiding direct eye contact with anyone, a big smile on her face.

Dr Peter Johnson sat back down at the conference table; a sense of relief came over him. He picked up his wallet and noticed the photograph in the transparent plastic flap. It was of him and his mother, taken in their cottage garden, she was sitting on a wicker chair, her son seated on her knee, both looking directly into a camera, the direct sunlight making their eyes squint.

A moment of sadness came over him as he looked once again at the image.

'If only I could have done more for you,' he said under his breath, 'you would still have been here now, but I didn't, *I let you down* and I will never forgive myself for that.'

Thirty-three

AFTER ALMOST THREE AND A half weeks of hard graft, the work at The Lakes Nursing Home was finally taking shape. The land had been levelled, all the small JCB diggers had gone, and both Joe and Danny were delighted with the progress, as was Mr Robinson.

It was a glorious sunny afternoon, and as Joe looked up to the sky, he decided for once, that it was time to take an early break from work.

'Hey Danny,' he shouted, 'do you fancy a quick pint at the local pub, we passed one on the way in this morning?'

'If you like, but can I just check these drawings with you, I've made some changes, and we need to start work on the footing for the water fountain?'

Danny laid out a copy of the plan on the bonnet of the Ford Ranger, due to the sun beaming down, it felt quite warm to the touch. They both decided that the alterations he had suggested made sense and Joe agreed to get in touch with the builder to do all the footings and pipework.

The car park to the Wheatsheaf pub was quite busy for the time of day, Joe had to park the pickup so close to the car on the passenger side, that Danny had to get out first. As they walked through the front door, the combination of food and beer was a welcome smell in their nostrils.

A young lad in black trousers and a dark blue t-shirt approached them, menus in his hand, his name badge read, Zack Clarke.

'Table for two?' he asked.

'Yes mate, somewhere quiet if you can,' Joe replied.

He led them to a table near the window, overlooking the car park, and asked if they wanted anything to drink.

'I'll have a pint of Fosters, and a lager shandy for this chap,' said Danny, he knew Joe had a real aversion to drink driving, although he did like a full-bodied red wine.

'Cheers Danny, good to be working together, we make a great team don't you think?'

'I guess so, it still seems a bit strange, working again after my time… well, you know where.'

'Listen, that's all in the past, you've got the whole of your life in front of you, and we've got a good thing going here. If we pull this work off and over-deliver what mister managing director is looking for, we stand a good chance of getting more business. You never know, he might want some work done at the other places he owns. I've been considering expanding the landscape operation for some time now… Why don't we pool our experience and resources and go at it together?

There's plenty of work out there if we target the rural areas of Derbyshire and Nottinghamshire. Councils are outsourcing the park maintenance for example, so instead of being competitors, let's work together to our advantage. I've got all the necessary equipment, and you had, sorry, have got a unique flair for landscape gardening, so, it's a no-brainer in my book.'

Danny's stomach was beginning to rumble, he wasn't sure if it was the medium to well-done steak he'd ordered, or the excitement of the fact that Joe, his old classmate from junior school, was looking out for him.

He looked out the window, then turned back. 'You know what Joe, I think that's a terrific idea, I had my own business before all the troubles, being my boss again, working with you, as you've just said, we make a great team, so yes, if this is an offer, I'd be delighted.'

With a wide grin on both their faces, they raised their glasses and took a well-deserved gulp.

Thirty-four

IT WAS ALMOST FOUR O'CLOCK when Joe dropped Danny off at home. As he made his way down the path, he could hear raised voices coming from what he thought was the lounge.

His mum was sitting in her usual chair, tears in her eyes, his dad looking down on her in what looked to Danny like a threatening manner, a half-empty glass of something resembling alcoholic on the little side table.

'You can hear you two from outside, what's going on?'

'It's okay Danny, we were just having a conversation about your father's military guns, I think it's time he got rid of them, too many bad memories for my liking.'

Danny noticed red marks on his mum's wrists and looked at his dad directly in the face.

'What have you been doing to mum?' he asked.

'This has nothing to do with you, it's private,' his breath smelled of whiskey.

'Wrong. It's got everything to do with me, so big man, tell me what you're up to?'

Philip Ashby picked up the whiskey tumbler off the table and stormed out the back door, slamming it as he left.

'What's going on mum, has he been hitting you?

Danny's mum wiped the tears from her face.

'Has he been hitting you? Look at your arms, when did this start?'

'It only takes one little thing for him to lose his temper, all I said was, I thought it was time to get rid of his army guns, that's all it was.'

Danny sat down next to his mum; minutes passed as she rested her head on his shoulder. *'You never forget a mother's love,'* he thought to himself.

'How long has this been carrying on?'

'Just after you went to prison, only occasionally at first, but then it became more regular.

He's never normally been a violent man, I don't think diabetes helps, he seems to get mood swings and then becomes aggressive.'

'So, this has been happening for the last fourteen years, which is what you're telling me?'

Mary lifted her head off his shoulder.

'Listen, Danny, you're home now, I can look after you, you can watch out for me, it's not a problem, honestly.'

She stood up, pulled down her cardigan, and made her way up the stairs, leaving Danny alone in the lounge.

He could hear the lathe running as he walked out the back door and down the path to the garden shed.

Opening the door, he flicks the mains switch, waiting for the mains light and machine to stop working.

His dad stood there; his fists clenched like he was ready to throw the first punch.

Danny closed the shed door, the only sunlight coming through the small glass window.

'I'm only going to tell you this once… If you ever touch my mum again, in any way, you'll regret it, do you understand?'

'Oh yeah, you're home, the *big* man now, threatening me. Is that what you did to that other man? Did you threaten him too? Lose your temper, and kill him? Is that what happened?'

Danny didn't answer, he just banged the door behind him and walked back up the path.

Thirty-five

AFTER SEARCHING THE INTERNET and social media on my desktop on and off for three consecutive evenings, I'd finally found the name I was looking for.

There were thirteen references with the same name as I recalled the day of the headmaster's announcement.

The search took me longer than I thought, and although I could still remember what he looked like from my boarding school days, faces changed over time. But names stay the same.

After digging further into the details I'd uncovered, the actual image I pulled up *was* of him, no doubt in my mind. According to his details on the social media platform, he'd moved away from the Derbyshire region, and was now living and working in Nottinghamshire, so he hadn't moved away much at all.

It always surprised me how much personal information people include on certain search engines.

Looking back, he'd want to project himself as the most valued employee any company would want to offer a job to. Getting that all-important position that he believed he was entitled to have, and as far as he would be concerned, openly believed he deserved.

I'd found out his full name, date of birth, which may not have been accurate, where he roughly lived and finally. And most importantly, where he worked.

Sitting there at my desk, recalling my time at Chaffinch House, I still remember the look on the face of my friend Simon, his eyes full of tears, like mine.

As the months and years at school went by, we gradually drifted apart, maybe it was Toby who'd kept the three of us together all the time.

Later, on several occasions, I'd tried to contact Simon, but I'd heard that after he'd left the school, he'd moved abroad with his parents, and consequently, I had never heard from him since.

Double-clicking on the image on my laptop brought the photograph to life. I could see several people gathered on a brightly lit stage, the back of people's heads in the foreground, it must have been some formal gathering, they were all dressed in suits, with shirts and ties.

As I looked more closely at the screen, moving the cursor from left to right, a pang of excitement kicked in, as I finally knew I'd found the person I was looking for.

His hair was cut quite short, greying at the sides. He'd grown taller and put on some weight, but that's not what convinced me I'd got the right person. As I zoomed into the picture, one thing stood out more than anything else, on his right arm, just above his hand, was the watch. It now had a stainless-steel strap, but there was no mistaking what it was, the same watch my grandfather had given me years before.

Thirty-six

DETECTIVE SERGEANT SARAH WARD was drying her hands in the ladies' toilet when her mobile rang, the name on the screen. Adam Fox.

It was her day off, but she'd decided to call in the office at Sheffield Central Police HQ to pick up some material she'd been working on before her appearance at court in a few days.

'Adam, good morning, this is Sarah. How's things with you?'

'Hi Sarah,' replied Adam, 'I'm fine, trust you're well. Listen, I know this is very short notice, but is there any chance you and I could meet up later today? I'd like to chat about progress on Scarlett's disappearance, if any'

Adam and Viv had talked about arranging to meet with DS Ward the previous evening whilst sharing a bottle of Sauvignon Blanc at dinner.

Viv wanted to go along to meet with her and find out more about what further steps had been taken to find their daughter.

Frustratingly, Adam didn't think it was a good idea, after all, he was an investigating police officer, so as such, he should be able to manage the situation.

Viv on the other hand had a different view, 'two heads are better than one,' she told Adam, if DS Ward could meet with Scarlett's mother, it might, just might, change the dynamics of the situation they find themselves in.

Reluctantly, Adam agreed but decided not to tell Sarah about Viv coming along just in case she felt under more pressure.

The journey up to Sheffield from Derbyshire was uneventful. The M1 motorway was, as usual, congested around the junction with the M18. After they'd been travelling for about ten minutes, Adam opened the conversation about the medical centre partnership, they hadn't had the opportunity to discuss it when Viv came from work the previous evening.

'So, how did it go yesterday with Peter and the partnership proposal, is it still on the cards?'

'Well, yes, we'll need to chat about the final figure, just you and I, but essentially, it's what I've been aspiring to, and I think we can raise the money he's looking for.'

'Was it around what we discussed.'

'Slightly higher, one hundred and thirty-seven thousand pounds to be precise, giving me a twenty-five percent share in the practice.'

'Okay, so we'll have to find a bit extra, any ideas?'

Viv sat silently for several minutes, considering how to position her next sentence.

'I'm going to ask my parents. They've always said they would help me financially like they did when I went to uni and medical school. I never had a student loan. Dad paid all my fees.'

Adam turned to her, keeping his eyes on the road ahead.

'We could probably fund it ourselves you know, without involving your mum and dad.'

Since Adam had two brothers and a sister, funds money-wise from his parents were never flowing, he'd always had to pay his way in life, even at police college.

His dad worked in a factory and his mum was a school catering assistant. And with four children to feed and clothe. Spare cash wasn't available.

'It's fine Adam, I'll speak with Dad and explain what we want the money for, they'll both be thrilled that a partnership is being offered from Peter, so I know it won't be an issue.'

Adam didn't want to argue, it did make sense to take Vivian's parents' money, but it didn't sit too well with him, not one bit.

To take his mind off the conversation, Adam opened Spotify, looking to play The Beatles, but decided not to bother, as Viv had closed her eyes.

Pulling his Audi into a parking space at the garden centre they had agreed to meet which was located just southwest of the city centre, Adam checked his watch, they were about twenty minutes early.

Viv opened her eyes and suggested Adam go and get a table, whilst she just looked around the plants and bulbs. The ceramic pots at the front of their house needed replanting.

DS Sarah Ward arrived right on time, looking around to see if she could locate Adam, noticing him sitting towards the back of the restaurant, a second person occupying the table.

They both rose to their feet as Sarah made her way through the tables and chairs, trying to avoid dog leads and shopping bags.

On introducing Vivian, Adam asked what everyone wanted to drink, and went to place the order, checking the table number as required.

The conversation was already underway as he returned, Sarah was showing Viv the folder she'd brought with her, explaining in detail, he thought, how the investigation was progressing, if it was.

'Thanks for meeting us, Sarah, and at such short notice, we both appreciate it.'

'That's fine, I'm off today and Chris Mitchell is in Leeds. He seems to spend a lot of time there. I'm at a bit of a loose end anyway. Court appearance in the next few days, so I was going back to my flat and read up on my notes.'

'So, you two have made introductions. Vivian, this is DS Sarah Ward. Sarah, my wife Dr Vivian Flemming, but I call her Viv.'

Viv opened her Filofax and took out a business card, 'Here you go Sarah, my contact details, just in case you can't get through to Adam, even though I struggle sometimes.'

Sarah took the card, looked over it and put it in the folder she had in front of her.

As their coffee arrived Sarah was explaining the progress made on the case, Viv looking on intensely, taking in every word spoken, despite the annoying background voices.

'I'm going to be honest with you, there hasn't been much progress made since you and I last met Adam, however, one piece of information has come to light.'

Viv put down her coffee mug and eased forward on her chair, Adam looking directly at Sarah.

'You mentioned on the actual day of Scarlett's disappearance that when you went through the broken gate onto the road, there was nothing that you could see that looked suspicious, everything seemed normal, that's correct isn't it?'

'Yes, as I recall, people were walking about, cars travelling up and down the road, so just a normal day I guess.'

'Well interestingly, checking the investigation notes further, a possible crucial point has come to light. On the day of Scarlett's disappearance, two officers conducted both door-to-door enquiries, as well as the local shops opposite your house. The house enquiries came to nothing, however, the greengrocer's store run by Mr Charlie

Walters, was due to close later in the day, due to a week's holiday. So, I've been back to talk to Mr Walters. Recalling the day was obviously a bit sketchy, but he's confirmed something that was originally missed.'

Picking up her coffee mug, Sarah took another drink, before checking her notes again.

'On the actual day that your daughter went missing, Mr Walters remembers a car, driven he thought by youngsters. He didn't get the registration number, or make, just a white car, driving slowly up and down the road several times. Most of his customers buy from outside the shop as they're passing. So he's always there selling his vegetables and taking the money. He said to me that he thought it was odd, as on that very sunny, sweltering day, people were walking around, so there were plenty of parking spaces on the road, why therefore would someone be driving up and down?'

Was this the news that Adam and Viv had been waiting for, finally a breakthrough, bringing closure to their family nightmare?

Adam thought for a moment, getting his head around what DS Ward had just revealed, then asked.

'So, no make of car, or registration number, just a white vehicle, I know there isn't any CCTV either, but did he see how many people were in the vehicle?'

'As he can recall, although it was a long time ago, he was certain there were two people, one at the side of the driver… but that's not the critical point.'

'So, what new information is there then?' asked Viv.

'Well oddly, although it was a warm day, apparently both passengers were wearing what he thinks were black and white striped baseball caps, probably to conceal their identity I would suggest.'

Thirty-seven

Grabbing the car keys from my jacket pocket, I unlock the drawer to the right of my desk and take out what is now a well-worn envelope. Originally, it was pure white, but over time it's become damaged and torn.

Before locking it again, I look at the trophies I've gathered over the years. Moving them around like a living thing, a reminder of my unforgettable past.

Opening the flap, taking out a photograph, laying it down on the top of the desk, flattening it with my hand, CHAFFINCH HOUSE – YEAR THREE.

I begin to refresh my memory of all the individuals in the picture, trying to remember some of the names of the teaching staff and pupils on each of the three rows, noting that two already had thick red crosses through them. On the third row just off centre was my next victim, I smiled to myself, a sense of pure satisfaction kicking in.

***

Cresta Communications had a very impressive office block right in the centre of the financial area in Nottingham, with easy access by bus, train, and the recently upgraded tramway system.

Not wanting to draw attention to myself I locked my car, checking for any CCTV that might be around, there wasn't any, and took a walk.

It was only seven fifty-four when I returned to the car park, which still only had several vehicles in it. I knew it was going to be easy to identify who I was looking for, I never forget a face, even after all this time.

Whilst he might not be working in the office on this particular day, it was certainly worth a punt, and if I had to come back repeatedly, it wasn't a problem, I just had to plan my time accordingly.

The journey across two counties, Derbyshire to Nottinghamshire was easily done by the A52, aptly named Brian Clough Way, due to the famous Nottingham Forest and Derby County football manager.

Checking my mobile for any messages, the time showed eight twenty, and as I looked through the windscreen, three further cars pulled up, parking in well-defined spaces.

Then, there he was, large as life, exiting the passenger side and walking round to the driver's door, window down, a friendly wave to someone who looked much younger than him.

Casually dressed with a lanyard around his neck, he entered the building for what I thought would be a full day's work, planning that he'd probably finish around five o'clock in the afternoon, I'd be there for four, just to make sure I didn't miss him.

Nottingham itself is steeped in history, from famous authors like D.H. Lawrence, and poets like Byron, right through to Robin Hood of Sherwood Forest, who robbed the rich and gave it to the poor, so lots of things to occupy my mind. But on this day, I decided to spend my spare time at Nottingham Castle, and the surrounding gardens. It had recently been renovated and opened up to the public after almost four years.

***

The road along the Riverside adjacent to the river Trent was far busier than I had imagined, it was almost four fifteen when I finally pulled into Cresta Communications, some cars had already left by the look of vacant spaces. I could feel my blood pressure rising as I wondered if, after all this effort, I'd missed him. But relief came over me when the same car from this morning pulled up just as he exited the revolving front door of the office.

There was no casual wave this time, after looking around, just a quick peck on the driver's cheek.

The bright green Peugeot 3005 takes a direction towards the southeast of the city, joining the long traffic queue leaving the city centre. Starting my car, I followed them at a safe distance, unaware of where we were going, but ensuring I didn't lose them.

Traffic was heavy and on a couple of occasions, I thought I'd lost them, however, the colour enabled me to maintain visual contact without them being aware of being followed.

We'd probably been travelling for around twenty minutes on the main road out of the city when the Peugeot indicated, braked, and took a sharp turn to the right, leading down a one-way street, old, terraced houses to both sides. By the look of them, they probably dated back to the early nineteen hundreds, some clearly in desperate need of repair.

As their car approached a T junction at the bottom, they again indicated and turned left, and to my amazement, a couple of hundred yards down the road, the Peugeot slowed to a crawl right outside a modern block of flats.

The building was four stories high and in a row of three, the first, second and top levels all had balconies, overlooking a park opposite. Right in the centre was what looked like a security entrance, which could potentially be an access problem.

Not wanting to draw attention to myself, I stopped my car about fifteen yards behind them. Minutes later, the Peugeot set off again, turning immediately left at the bottom of the road.

I followed closely behind, but not too close to be seen, it led to a car park at the back of the flats. I drove by, turned around and parked at the side of the road, right opposite the back entrance.

'Should I follow them,' I said under my breath. 'Or wait here to see what happens next?'

Instead, I decided to walk around to the front of the flats, unassumingly, sitting on a park bench, taking a closer look. Several minutes passed, and to my surprise, the bifold door opened on the second floor, and two individuals walked out, wine glasses in their hands, sitting on black metal chairs.

The driver of the car, the younger one, looked to be around the mid to late twenties, slim with short-cropped blond hair and dressed in tight-fitting denim jeans and an off-the-shoulder top. I knew he was several years older. A cradle snatcher.

They looked over towards the park, chatting about something, their days at work, planned holiday together, anything. They must have seen me sitting there and yet, they had no idea who I was or what I was doing there.

If this young woman did live here with the person I'd hunted down, it was going to make my plans so much harder to execute. She was the innocent party… but then again, you can't make an omelette without breaking some eggs.

Returning to my car, and driving around the block, I once again approach the flats from the one-way system, parking some way up, on the opposite side of the road, but allowing me to have a full view of the flat and the two people, and *if* they were a couple, where they lived.

As I sat there, the daytime sun begging to set, finally planning how I was now going to get my retribution on the man I'd hunted down.

It became obvious circumstances had changed, as he apparently, didn't live alone.

I checked the time on my phone once again and was just about to call it a day and return to Derbyshire when the front door of the flats opened. Out walked the young female, a leather computer bag over her left shoulder, and a designer handbag in her right hand. As she walked towards the back car park, she turned around, looking up at the balcony, where moments before they'd been drinking wine. She waved to the man and shouted.

'I'm off home to pack, I'll see you in a week's time Ross, the usual time for pick up, love you.'

'Love you too, enjoy the holiday, and don't burn your bum.'

I waited several moments and then started the engine, waiting for the Peugeot to exit the back, concluding that the driver had had a lucky escape and that my plan could finally be put in place.

I had a whole seven days on my side, smiling to myself, '*plenty of time,*' I said under my breath.

Knowing that he was going to be on his own made what I'd planned so much easier, and after hours of internet searching, I'd finally identified the right person. Ross Sulivan, I've never forgotten that name.

Thirty-eight

'DO YOU MIND IF WE TALK about this later in the evening?' Adam said. 'I need to drop you off at work and then go to the office, there's a couple of things I need to chat to Frank about.'

They'd both left the garden centre at around twelve-forty, thanking Sarah for the update and the work she'd done on the case. As far as Viv was concerned, she thought it was a breakthrough.

At least someone had seen something, which was better than not knowing anything at all.

Almost four years had passed since her beautiful daughter, Scarlett, had disappeared and she had never given up hope of finding her… alive. There wasn't a moment went by when she hadn't wondered what had happened on that ill-fated day, if only she hadn't gone to the front of the house to tidy the dining room, or Adam hadn't gone and had a shower, all would have been different.

But that wasn't the case, they *had* turned their backs, just for a few minutes, in that time, someone or somebody had come into their garden, and taken their only child, right under their nose.

Joining the motorway, going South, Adam set the cruise control at sixty-eight and began to go over in his mind what DS Ward had told them. He didn't want to disregard the update that had been discussed but, equally, it wasn't the news he'd hoped for.

Thousands of children go missing every year, statistics show that whilst a substantial number are found safe and well, others are never seen again. But as a father, husband, and senior police officer, he would never give up hope.

He couldn't, for the sake of his daughter and his marriage. He had to remain positive that one day, whenever that day was, he would ultimately find out what happened to Scarlett and bring her home safely to the loving arms of her mummy and daddy.

***

To Viv's annoyance, someone had parked their 3 Series BMW in her reserved parking space. It didn't matter too much, Adam was going to pick her up from the medical centre after work, but it did frustrate her.

Walking into reception, the place was heaving with patients, every seat was taken, and several people were standing. She walked over to the glass-covered counter, where a very tired-looking receptionist explained that the locum GP had called in sick, so Peter and the other doctor were trying to manage the best they could.

'Okay,' said Kate, 'I'll take each patient in turn, and we'll soon get the numbers down, don't worry, it'll be fine.'

'Just before you go, there is also a sales representative here to see you, he says he's got an appointment, but there's nothing in your diary.'

'That explains the BMW,' Viv said under her breath.

A pharmaceutical representative's job was a lucrative career. Good salary, performance bonuses, and a fully expensed company car. A lot of General Practitioners didn't offer to see salespeople, but Viv was different. You could hear and learn a lot about new drugs being planned for launch into the market, alternative medications, and switching prescribing habits, which ultimately, could save the practice money, and, they had a job to do, so treat them with respect, which was her view.

'Ask them to hang around, I will see them when I can,' she replied.

***

Adam grabbed a coffee from the machine and made his way up the stairs to his office, passing Frank, who sat at his desk, looking intensely at his computer screen.

Avoiding standing over him, he stood to one side, trying not to invade his personal space.

'Hi Frank, everything all right?'

'Oh, hi boss, yeah, all okay here, just clearing some emails and bringing the case file up to date.'

'Great, can we have a chat in about fifteen minutes, just a 'heads up' on the investigation, that's all?'

'Sure thing,' Frank replied.

Sitting down at his desk, Adam rubbed his eyes, trying to focus on the computer screen he'd just opened.

He'd had a test about twelve months ago, and all was fine, but lately, he'd noticed that he sometimes struggled to read some of the emails, maybe it was stress related, he'd speak with Viv tonight.

Picking up the telephone he dialled the direct number for DCI Vickers. Frank would have told him if there were any critical changes in the investigation, nevertheless, it's better to take the initiative and speak with Tom first, rather than waiting for his call, putting him on the back foot.

A quick knock on the door and Frank entered, the case file for Patricia Locke in his hand.

'Are there any further updates to put in the logbook?' asked Adam.

Frank opened the rather slim file, placing it directly on the DI's desk.

'Nothing of any importance, all enquiries by the team have resulted in zilch, it's almost like Patricia Locke didn't exist at all. No immediate family, limited friends, apart from the next-door neighbour, just a retired schoolteacher, regular church goer and charity worker.'

'Well, somebody knew her, had a grudge, arranged to meet her in the woods and took their revenge, we're missing something Frank, but I don't know what. When the officers visited her home, apart from the school photograph, did they find anything else of interest?'

Frank studied the file once more.

'No, just the photo, and her passport, found in the draw next to her bed.'

Adam pushed his chair back, stood up and walked over to the window which overlooked the car park.

'What about her mobile phone, that's what we're missing here, her phone. Who doesn't have a mobile phone nowadays, and if you're a regular walker, surely you'd take it with you, just in case.'

Adam sat back down, writing this info into the logbook together with the date.

'Frank, get in touch with all the national mobile network companies, there'll be an organisation out there that has her phone contract and details. We just need to know when it was last used, and the location.'

'We may need a court order boss?'

'Tell them this is a murder investigation, we don't need a court order, we just need tracking information.'

Thirty-nine

THUNDERSTORMS HAD BROKEN my sleep, but now it was a lovely sunny Saturday morning when I woke up. Despite having a bad night of continuing dreams and nightmares, I decided to clear my head of all the punishing thoughts and take a drive to Chatsworth House in Derbyshire, the gardens are wonderful and inspiring at this time of year.

Sitting at my desk the previous evening I had taken out some A4 plain paper and planned what I was going to do. Making a list of all the essential items required, ensuring I didn't forget a thing, and enjoying several glasses of red wine at the same time.

The fact that the young woman didn't live at the address of Ross Sullivan made the situation far easier than originally assumed. My plan was relatively straightforward. I'd already located what floor he lived on and the location of his flat amongst all the others. Just gain access to the property from the rear car park, make my way up the stairs and bingo, fulfil the execution.

Now, it was just a matter of selecting a day, work permitting. Choose a night when he'd be at home, decide on the time, probably later in the evening, his girlfriend, fiancé or whoever she was, wasn't going to be visiting, she was on holiday. I can finally take my revenge, revenge for me, Simon and most importantly, Toby.

I arrived home early afternoon, after having lunch at Chatsworth farm shop, poached eggs on fish cakes, and a bottle of sparkling water. A glass of white wine would have gone down well, but not when I'm driving, I can celebrate later, hopefully.

The journey across the A52 didn't take me as long as I thought, traffic was relatively light, which was unusual as this A road was a direct link between the two cities, so I arrived at the property slightly earlier than planned.

Stopping at an ESSO petrol station, I purchased a bunch of red roses and a newspaper from outside the shop, paying cash to the counter staff.

'Someone is going to be lucky tonight,' she said, speaking through the microphone, 'red roses, and it isn't even Valentine's Day.'

'If anything, I'm the lucky one,' I replied.

Earlier in the day I'd packed everything up together in a brand-new black bag I'd purchased several weeks earlier, no markings on it, so not easy to identify.

Making sure I had everything at my disposal, I did a final check of the contents, plastic loops, strong gardening twine, hammer, scissors, and a selection of very sharp knives, all had latex covers on the tips.

There wasn't going to be any DNA left behind, nothing must be left to chance.

Initially, I'd planned to park my car at the rear, but as I was about to turn into a vacant parking space, I changed my mind, driving to the bottom of the road, turning right and parking on the side street a little distance from the flat.

Avoiding drawing attention to myself, I picked up the newspaper and read the headlines, it would shield my face. As I waited until the sun started to go down, I opened my side window slightly to let some fresh air in.

I had to ensure that he was in the flat, and as it was now getting dark, I thought the location would be illuminated confirming his accessibility, if he wasn't, I'd have to come back another night and another, until he was.

Luck was on my side, the lights were on, and I could see him walking around the room overlooking the park. He was either talking to himself, on a speaker phone, or singing along to some music, quite entertaining.

I walked back around to my car, collected the black bag from the boot and picked up the roses from the front seat, several petals dropped into the footwell, I'd clean those out back home.

It was beginning to get dark as I made my way to the back entrance to the flat, and my out-and-out surprise was, that just as I arrived, someone was leaving through the rear door, kindly holding it open for me.

I decided to make the first move, 'Good evening,' I said, 'thanks for holding the door, I don't want to damage the roses.'

'You have a lovely evening,' they replied and casually walked away into the darkness, thankfully they hadn't noticed the black leather gloves on my hands.

Adrenaline kicked in as I climbed the four flights of steps, two at a time, arriving at the front door of Ross Sulivan, not even out of breath. Taking my time to look around, there were no CCTV cameras, why would there be, it's only a block of modern flats after all, and thankfully, no spy hole in the modern hardwood-grained front entrance. Just a number screwed to the wall, a number three, how ironic.

My heart was thumping like I'd held my breath too long, as I stood there about to meet the man who'd systematically tortured and killed one of my closest friends.

A friend whom both Simon and I had decided was the glue that had held our relationship together at boarding school… Toby.

I knocked on the door with the signet ring I placed on my finger earlier, gold on wood.

Hearing footsteps approaching.

Forty

'HOW IS EVERYTHING AT HOME?' Is your mother-in-law making any improvements?' Adam sat at his desk enjoying his second cup of coffee, Frank sitting opposite.

He'd arrived early at Central Derbyshire HQ, deciding to spend time catching up on paperwork, updating the logbook and electronic file and replying to outstanding emails. 'How much more time would we have without emails?' he thought to himself.

He'd noticed over the last few days how drained and out of sorts Frank had looked, pale-faced and unshaven, he wasn't even dressed like a Detective Sergeant, although to be fair, compared to his immediate boss, he never really did.

Was it the investigation? Okay, there'd been very little progress made, no one's fault, it was like many standalone cases, with little to go on. No real witnesses, no motive, no DNA, and a victim who on the surface of it had no enemies.

But Patricia Locke was brutally assaulted, body parts removed and murdered, which made Adam think to himself, why? Why her, why now, and what secrets did the old school photograph hold?

Thankfully, DCI Vickers wasn't putting any pressure on Adam, Frank, or the wider team. He'd have had firsthand experience of difficult murder investigations in the past, and he'd know how making little progress was frustrating for all concerned.

Frank looked Adam directly in the face. 'Julie thinks, sorry, knows, her mum has the first signs of dementia, and to be honest, so does her GP. Just trivial things, she forgets my name occasionally, walked past our house last week and couldn't remember where we lived, and the language, she's never sworn in her life, now she's eefing and blinding like the rest of us. And last week, she smacked Julie right across the face, just because she hadn't put any sugar in her tea.'

Adam could see the hurt in Frank's eyes. From what he'd heard on the grapevine, their marriage hadn't always been a bed of roses, much like a lot of police officers' relationships. But Julie was always his number one priority, if she was happy, that was fine with Frank.

'Do you want to take some time off? I can clear it with Tom Vickers, not holidays, just compassionate leave, might do you and Julie some good, get your head around what to do for the best.'

Frank sat there, considering the offer the DI had given him.

'We've already started looking at care homes, the diagnosis isn't good, the results from tests done by the medical team at Derbyshire Community Hospital are pretty conclusive.'

Adam looked away through his office window, thinking about the case when Frank broke his thoughts, bringing him straight back to the conversation, what he said made him sit up straight and listen intensely.

'I've been checking over old investigations, murders like Patricia Locke's are few and far between around this part of the world, so I did some digging and what I've uncovered might be of interest to this case too. Going back about fifteen years, I recall a man was brutally murdered in the area, almost the same location as this recent case, I was just a PC at the time, and I'd forgotten all about it, until an old drinking buddy of mine reminded me.'

'Can you dig out the old investigation files? I'd like to take a closer look at them. See if there's any similarities to the Locke case.'

'I've already put in a request, we should have them by tomorrow morning, but in advance of them arriving, I do remember a couple of things, the senior investigation officer was *one* DI Tom Vickers. And the suspect who was charged was a chap named Daniel Ashby.

Daniel Ashby has recently been released from Birmingham Prison and has returned to live with his parents, they live locally, in Derbyshire.'

Forty-one

TURNING INTO THE estate, Adam parked his Audi A4 on the drive, next to Viv's Skoda. Switching off Spotify and listening to the clicking sounds as the engine started to cool down, he couldn't get Daniel Ashby out of his mind.

As he made his way through the front door, he noticed the wet patches on the tarmac, Viv must have watered the pots and hanging baskets when she got home, the smell of flowers drifting towards his nose.

Dropping his car keys in the Murano bowl on the hall unit, Viv stood at the top of the stairs, she had a look of inquisitiveness about her.

Making her way down, flip flops clicking on her heels, she opened her arms and held Adam tighter than usual, they'd always had a strong relationship, both honestly, emotionally and sexually. There had never been any impropriety between them and there never would be.

'I know you don't always like takeaways, but I've ordered one to arrive about eight-ish, so get showered and I'll pour us a drink.'

The bedroom was cool as he entered, hanging up his suit, he ran the shower, hopefully washing off the stress of the working day, still thinking about Daniel Ashby.

Eight o'clock on the dot, the security light illuminated the porch, as a knock came at the door, Adam could smell the Chinese food as Viv paid the young man who delivered it, making her way to the kitchen, two dinner trays laid out on the marble counter.

'I've ordered for two, but as usual, I think there's too much, so I hope you're hungry.'

They both piled their plates high with crispy duck, lemon chicken, sweet and sour pork, and egg fried rice and made their way into the lounge; white wine in large glasses was already on the coffee table.

'Shall we listen to some music? Adam said. Or watch something on Netflix? We've still got several episodes of Emily in Paris to watch?'

'Nothing too heavy, Emily in Paris sounds perfect to me.'

As the credits went up and the last episode ended, Adam decided to open up about Scarlett and the information they'd received from their meeting with Sarah Ward.

It was no good sweeping it under the carpet, he'd got to try and be as honest as he could with Viv, without her losing all hope of seeing their daughter again.

'I'm glad we took some time to meet with Sarah, aren't you? It was interesting what she said about the car driving by and the passengers wearing baseball caps, I'm not sure where it leaves us, but at the very least it's something to follow up on.'

If he was being honest with himself, Adam wasn't convinced that this information changed anything at all. Almost four years had passed since Scarlett's disappearance, and despite Chris Mitchell's investigation, there hadn't been one solitary breakthrough, at least until now.

'How do you think we should play it? Meet up again with Sarah. Wait a while or you try and do some more digging? That's what you're good at you know.'

'That's true, but you know, we've got very little to go on, and I don't want to be seen to be treading on Sarah's toes. She may have uncovered a link between the car and Scarlett's disappearance, but, and it's a big but, it doesn't give us any firm information. And the longer this goes on, the less concrete leads we do get can be relied upon.'

He realised that this wasn't the way Viv wanted the conversation to go, he understood how overwhelming it must be for her only daughter to go missing.

He missed her every single day too, but his job brought him in contact with crimes like this all the time, sometimes even worse. Viv on the other hand had her challenges as a GP but was shielded from the realities of MISPERS.

'I know you're doing your utmost to find Scarlett, and I also know you'll never stop looking,' tears began to run down her face. 'I just want her back Adam, to hug her, hear her voice, and hold her close.'

He put his arm around Viv's shoulders, as she sobbed uncontrollably, feeling the hurt inside himself.

'I'm off to bed, early start tomorrow, MMR vaccination day, so I need to be in early and Peter's off for a few days.'

As Viv stood to her feet, Adam got hold of her hand, 'I'll never give up looking for her you know, one way or the other I *will* find out what has happened to our daughter, I promise you.'

He decided not to go to bed straight away, Viv needed her sleep, and he wasn't that tired, so finishing off the last glass of wine, he went into the kitchen, took out his laptop and began searching for details on Daniel Ashby.

Forty-two

AS FRANK HAD ARRANGED, the file on the Daniel Ashby case was on Adam's desk when he entered his office. Opening the window blinds and putting down his first cup of coffee of the day, he sat and opened the folder in front of him.

It was all there, the victim's name Arthur Richardson, the initial investigation headed up by Detective Inspector Thomas Vickers, witness statements, police interviews, the whole nine yards.

Over the next fifty minutes or so Adam turned over page after page of information. He also came across various local paper clippings, cut out and pasted on cardboard from two main publications, The Derbyshire Times, and The Nottingham Evening Post.

Landscape Gardener Charged with Murder was the headline on the front page of the Derbyshire Times. The mother of a local man who says her son is innocent was featured on the bottom front page of the Nottingham Evening Post, accompanied by a photograph of Mary Ashby being interviewed by a local reporter.

As Adam read the interview with Daniel Ashby's mother in detail, he began to wonder if there *had* been a miscarriage of justice. Was Daniel Ashby innocent of murder, or has he started his murderous campaign once again?

A knock on the office door made him look up from the folder he'd been absorbed in, it was Frank, he looked refreshed and a big improvement from the previous day.

'I've got you a fresh cup of coffee boss, and a Dark Chocolate KitKat, apparently chocolate is good for brain function, I have a Mars Bar every day and look at me.'

'Cheers Frank, I could do with a break from this, excuse the pun. You look a lot better today, did you and Julie chat about taking some time off, I can swing it with the DCI.'

'I did and I think we're going to be okay; we talked about her mum last night and we've decided that she needs twenty-four-hour support, we'd already started looking at care homes, and we've found a local one, not far for us to travel and the CQC is the regulation authority rate it five stars if that's how they measure places like that.'

'I had a word with Viv last night about your mother-in-law's dementia, she described exactly the symptoms that you're experiencing, and apparently, it only gets worse as time goes on. I'm sorry Frank if that sounds harsh, it's not meant to be.'

'Thank you, we know what's ahead of us, that's why we made the decision we have; it's the best thing for all of us.'

Frank noticed the open file on the desk, and the two paper clippings laid out in front of them.

'I see you checked the file out then, what's your opinion, is Daniel Ashby our killer, or did we put away the wrong man?'

Normally, I wouldn't be concerned about putting a killer away… Just as long as the investigation has been as thorough as necessary, and the CPS accepts the evidence offered, then fine, it's then down to the jury. After all, some do get away with murder, mainly due to the mishandling of the case, and then the CPS throw it out, although we know they've done it. But there's something about this case that feels wrong somehow, no motive, no real witness, just somebody hearing an argument between Richardson and Ashby. And the gardening gloves, yes, they did have DNA on them, but they could have been picked up at any time by anybody and then used and thrown away at the crime scene. You've done the right thing to bring it to my attention; I think we should bring Daniel Ashby in for questioning.'

'I'll get on to it straight away, shall I schedule for tomorrow morning, first thing if I can, he still lives locally, so it shouldn't be a problem.'

Just as Frank was leaving, his hand on the door handle, he turned back to Adam. 'Watch your back, Adam, Tom Vickers was the SIO on the Richardson case, he still has a lot of influential friends here in Derbyshire, just saying.'

Forty-three

ROSS SULLIVAN TURNED DOWN the volume on the Bang & Olufsen CD player, he had been singing along to Rod Steward's Greatest Hits when he thought he heard a knock at the door to his flat.

'If this is the next-door neighbour, wanting some IT advice, they can stuff off,' he thought. 'I'm not their exclusive PC expert.'

Walking down the tiled floor passageway, he closed the door slightly to the bathroom, he'd just been to the loo, and the extractor fan wasn't working too well.

The sound of the security chain being taken off the door and opening, made me stand back slightly. For the first time in a long time, I was face-to-face with my next victim.

'Is this where Ross Sullivan lives?' I asked. Already knowing what the reply would be *and* who he was.

He looked slightly confused by the question, clearly not expecting anyone to be calling at this time of the day.

'Who wants to know? I think you've got the wrong address mate,' he asked with an air of annoyance in his voice.

As I pushed the heavy door open, it connected with his forehead and he lost his balance, crashing backwards onto the pure white tiled floor, bone-crunching as blood began oozing from a small cut on his head.

He began to panic, to try and cry from the attack as the first hammer blow came down, causing severe damage, a ridge the size of a fifty pence coin on the right-hand side of his head, followed by two further blows.

I didn't initially want to kill him outright, but if he did die. Well, so be it.

I put down my black bag and the roses and dragged him down the passage. As we made our way to the lounge, marks from the back of his shoes, left black lines on the tiled floor.

He was beginning to make unrecognisable noises through his mouth as we moved past the bathroom door, his eyes filled with sheer terror.

'Change of plan,' I said under my breath. I was going to close the lounge curtains to make sure that no one saw what was happening to my victim, but the bathroom… Considering that as an alternative, *that* was sheer genius, easier to wipe up the blood from a tiled floor.

I turned on the light, the extractor fan making an irritating grinding noise as I put the stainless-steel plug hole in and began to fill the bath with cold water.

He was staring into my eyes, unable to speak, horrified, as I got out the sharp knife, taking off the silicone cover. Blood began to run into the corner of his left eye as I gouged the number three on his forehead the best way I could. Before I used the long black plastic loops to tie his hands behind his back, and his feet together, I noticed the watch on his right hand, removing it left a white mark on his wrist. Finally, it was returned to its rightful owner.

He was still groaning as I lifted him on his knees, and leaned him over the edge of the bath, tying the garden twine tightly around his neck, down past his waist and in between his groin, pulling it so hard that his head jerked forward, as I fastened it to the black plastic loops.

Looking at him from behind, I wanted to believe that he knew what was going to happen to him, to take place. And what terror was going through his mind, looking down at the floor, noticing that he'd pissed himself, which brought a sense of pleasure to my plan.

As the water increased in depth, he began to try and lift his head, tightening the twine even more, spluttering, trying desperately to breathe as the water filled his mouth and nostrils, choking with every move.

Taking out the sharp kitchen scissors I cut back chunks of his scalp and hair, putting a section into a plastic bag I'd packed earlier, bits of flesh fastened to it, letting the rest float on the surface, forming strange shapes as it moved around the bubbles left from his last breath.

Switching off the light, I sat on the edge of the bath, letting my body come down from a high, surveying my handiwork whilst I waited, just to make sure that he was dead, before closing the front door to the flat, scattering a handful of rose petals on the floor behind me.

Forty-four

DANIEL ASHBY SAT on a rather uncomfortable chair in reception at Derbyshire HQ. They were deliberately designed that way. His mother, Mary Ashby sat at his side, a maroon handbag on her knee, the desk sergeant had got them both a cup of tea, initially, Mary had refused a drink, then on second thoughts, had changed her mind.

Frank had called their landline in the afternoon of the previous day, the home number still on file, requesting that Daniel attend a meeting at HQ the following morning.

His mum took the call and immediately contacted Danny on his mobile. He was on-site at the care home, didn't hear the phone and she left a message.

'Danny, this is your mum, can you please call me as soon as you get this message, the police want to talk with you. They won't tell me what it's about, but they've asked that you arrange to go to Central Derbyshire headquarters tomorrow morning, call me when you can, love you.'

The landscape job at the nursing home was taking shape, and it looked like they'd finish a few weeks earlier than originally planned. Joe had told Danny he was taking a few days off, apparently to finish off some more quotes, and do the VAT return, which was fine, he was the boss after all. Normally, the whole team would call it a day around four thirty in the afternoon, but it was nearer five fifteen as Danny got into his mum's car and checked his mobile for any messages.

The journey home seemed to take longer than normal. He turned off the radio and opened the car window, letting some fresh air hit his face, so he could think more clearly about what the police wanted to talk with him about. Had someone come forward with fresh evidence? Would they open the case again after all these years? Finally bringing an end to his long-standing ordeal, proving his innocence.

***

Adam closed down his PC, locked his office door and made his way down the stairs to the reception area. Observing Ashby's body language from above, he looked relaxed he thought to himself.

Frank joined him about halfway down, briefly explaining his call to Mary Ashby the day before.

'By the tone of her voice yesterday on the phone, I think they're under the impression it's good news. Mrs Ashby was happy to pass on the message to Daniel that we wanted to see him she couldn't have been more helpful.'

Adam held up his identification lanyard, introducing himself and Frank to Daniel. 'Mr Ashby, Mrs Ashby, thank you for taking the time to come in today. My name is Detective Inspector Adam Fox, and this is my colleague Sergeant Frank Bailey. We'd like to ask you some questions if that's possible?'

Daniel and Mary followed the two police officers to interview room four, Adam in front, Frank holding up the rear. All the interview rooms were a mirror image of each other, this time, there were four chairs, two on each side of a grey plastic-covered table.

'Can I get you both something to drink, tea, coffee, water?' asked Adam.

'We've already had a drink,' replied Danny. 'Can I ask what this is all about? I've had to take a morning off work to come here.'

'We'd like to ask you some questions if that's okay with you?'

'Is this concerning my prison sentence, I was innocent, you *do know* that don't you?'

Adam smiled, trying to lessen the tension. But glancing at Mary Ashby's face, he'd failed miserably.

'Am I okay to call you by your first name, and if so, do you prefer Daniel or Danny?'

'Everyone knows my son as Danny, detective inspector,' intervened his mother, 'what's this all about, hasn't he suffered enough from the police?'

'I understand your concern, however, this has nothing to do with the sentencing of your son. This is a separate investigation, and when I explain the circumstances, I believe you'll understand why we've asked Danny to come and speak with us.'

'Several weeks ago, a woman's body was found in Blythe Woods, she'd been brutally attacked and died at the scene. On checking our records, it is almost the same location where Danny was sentenced for the murder of Arthur Robinson. So, you can see why we needed to speak with you if nothing more than to eliminate you from our enquiries.'

Danny's demure evaporated almost immediately, from being relaxed to being on his guard, he'd experienced interview techniques like this before and it didn't end well.

'You people… you never give up, do you? You put my son in prison for a crime he didn't commit, and then as soon as he comes back home, you start persecuting him all over again, shame on you detective inspector.'

'Mum, calm down, let me handle this. Is this an official interview, and if it is, do I need a solicitor?' asked Danny, already sounding both irritated and nervous as he spoke.

'We're not recording the interview,' said Frank, 'at this time Danny you're not under caution or arrest, this is a voluntary interview. You're just assisting us with our enquiries and free to leave at any time.'

'How long is it since you were released from prison?'

Daniel hadn't been in a police station or interviewed by them for over fourteen years, his stomach started to churn, as he tried to calm himself down… losing his temper was the last thing he needed to do.

'I've been out nearly four months now, living back home with my mum and dad… I've done my time in prison for a crime I didn't do, all I want now is to get my life back on track, build up my gardening business once again and look after my mum.'

Avoiding looking at his Apple watch, Adam studied the clock on the opposite wall. They'd been interviewing Danny for almost an hour and putting it down to either a copper's intuition or just a gut feeling,

Adam was convinced that Daniel Ashby had nothing to do with the murder of Patricia Locke. Although it hadn't been a complete waste of police time.

Thanking both of them for their time as he opened the door, Frank showed them out, and Danny turned to both officers.

'I thought you were going to tell me some fresh evidence had come to light, that you'd uncovered discrepancies in the initial investigation… I didn't do it you know,' repeating himself, 'I didn't do it.'

'Do you fancy a sandwich in the staff canteen? I'm starving, as I skipped breakfast this morning.' Viv regularly nagged Adam about skipping meals. 'It's not good for you, you need to have regular food inside you, you'll be getting ulcers if you're not careful.'

Picking up a tray each, they waited in line to be served. Adam ordered tuna with mayo, whilst Frank had a cheese and tomato cob, two bottles of Harrogate sparkling water were also placed on their trays.

The lunchtime rush for food was ending as Adam found a quiet table in the corner, away from prying ears. As they both took bites, Frank looked up from his plate, 'So what do you think, did we send down the wrong man?'

Considering carefully how to answer, Adam thought for a moment and then replied.

'I think we did, and if that's the case then I have some real areas of concern.'

He opened his hand and held one finger at a time. 'One, did we conduct a thorough investigation at the time? Two, did we sentence the wrong man for the murder of Arthur Richardson? Three, was the DI under pressure to get a quick result? And if that is the case then we have a major problem on our hands.'

'Did Tom Vickers cut corners to get a quick result?' asked Frank.

'That may be the answer. He certainly hasn't spoken to me about the similarities between the investigation we're working on and the Daniel Ashby case. But that might just be an oversight on his part, so let's not jump to conclusions. But that's not what I'm worried about.'

'So, what is it?' replied Frank. 'Will the Ashby's take legal action against the force?

Adam considered his response carefully.

'No, Frank, that's not my worry. *My worry is,* I think we have a Serial Killer on the loose.'

Forty-five

MELANIE WATKINS REVERSED her Peugeot 3005 into a reserved parking bay, checking the rear-view camera and audible sound, she'd hit the concrete pillar driving forwards before, so this was the safer option. Collecting her laptop bag off the back seat, she made her way to the main road and opened the unlocked front door to Watkins, Fletcher and Simpson, WFS Estate and Letting Agents.

The office had two very large modern, grey-painted windows, and a central door, all looking out onto the main road of an upmarket suburb just outside Nottingham City Centre.

WFS marketed themselves at the higher end of the estate and letting industry, offering a very personal service to their client base, who often were seeking to buy a house, flat or barn conversion with a price tag ranging from six hundred thousand up to one and a half million pounds.

She dropped her car keys on the desk which was purposely sited right in the centre of the office, overlooking four other desks, so she saw all the potential clients entering the office and allowing her to keep an eye on the staff.

'This business is highly competitive,' she often told the team. 'If we all want to be successful, we have to give a hundred and ten percent.' She knew that was impossible, but it appeared to keep the staff on their toes.

Business was buoyant at the moment. The market for larger properties was in heavy demand, partially due to a well-established and recognised hospital and medical school, and two great universities, Nottingham, and Nottingham Trent.

Making herself a cup of strong coffee and a glass of filtered water, she sat at her desk and opened her laptop. Having just returned from a week's vacation in Portugal, seven days of no emails was just what she wanted.

By ten forty-five, Melanie Watkins had cleared around sixty percent of her messages, some just deleted, with the important ones being actioned.

Picking up her mobile phone, she called Ross Sullivan, whom she hadn't spoken to whilst away and wanted to agree on a pick-up time for the morning.

After the fourth ring, the phone clicked in, ***'Hi, you're through to the mobile of Ross Sullivan, I'm not available at the moment, so please leave a message and I'll get back to you as soon as I can, thanks for your call.'***

'Hi Ross, this is Melanie. Hope you've had a good week, and you've missed me loads. Just giving you a quick call to see what time for pick up in the morning and if you're up for going out for dinner tomorrow evening. Give me a call when you get this message, love you, sweetheart.'

Just before the lunchtime break, Melanie made a second call to Ross, leaving a similar message to the first one. By three-thirty in the afternoon, she decided after a third call and no answer, to contact his office to check that everything was okay.

She hadn't got Ross's office number on her mobile, so checking online, she found the main telephone number for Cresta Communications and made the call.

'Good afternoon Cresta Communication, Joanne speaking, how may I help you?'

'Yes, hello, my name is Melanie Wilson, could you put me through to Ross Sullivan's office please?'

'One moment, I'll see if he's available.'

'I'm sorry caller, Mr Sullivan isn't answering his phone, may I take a message?'

'Where the hell is he?' Melanie thought. 'Is it possible to put me through to his manager please, it's quite urgent?'

Minutes seemed to pass slowly until a voice came back on the line.

'Hi, this is John Hawkins, Ross's colleague, who am I speaking too?'

'Hello John, my name is Melanie Wilson, I'm Ross's partner and I wondered if you'd heard from him at all today?.'

'Thanks for calling Melanie... actually, no we haven't. I've checked his work plan, and he's supposed to be in the office both yesterday and today, we've heard nothing from him, and he hasn't phoned in sick. He might have decided to work out of the office. I do know he had a big PowerPoint presentation to work on, so maybe he decided to stay at home with no interruptions. Although normally he'd let me know, so a bit odd to be honest.'

Momentarily, Melanie was too worried to answer back, had he been taken ill, all alone in the flat, or was he in hospital, no one knowing who he was?

'Thanks, John for letting me know, I'm going to go round to his flat and check that he's all right. I'll remind him to give you a call in the morning if he's planning not to come in.'

With that, she ended the call, opened the drawer on her desk picking up her car keys.

Due to heavy traffic crossing the city, it was almost five thirty before Melanie arrived at the flat. Parking her car at the back, she made her way to the entry door and used the security code that Ross had typed into her mobile phone to let herself in.

As she opened the door, calling out Ross's name, she noticed black marks on the floor, and dead rose petals moving backwards and forwards in the wind. Initially, she thought nothing more about it and made her way into the lounge.

One of the side lights near the B&O stereo was still on, she could feel the heat coming from the bulb as she switched it off.

Looking around before she checked out the bedroom, all looked tidy. And his bed hadn't been slept in.

'Ross, are you in? This isn't funny. I'm getting worried, and work isn't too happy with you either… where are you?'

The unnerving silence began to concern her as she retraced her steps back down the corridor, noticing the bathroom door on her left was closed, which was unusual.

Ross had promised to get someone in to fix the extractor fan, suggesting that they leave it open to let some fresh air in.

She knocked on the door, switching on the light before entering the bathroom.

Seeing Ross on his knees, she thought he was throwing up in the bath, then she saw the blood marks on his scalp. Initially too shocked to react, she stumbled back into the corridor, and then an ear-piercing cry echoed around the flat.

Placing her hand on the wall to steady herself, she took a deep breath, trying to hold back from throwing up, pulling out her mobile phone, Melanie Watkins dialled 999.

Forty-six

FOLLOWING AN UNSCHEDULED phone call Tom Vickers exhaled. He put his glasses on his desk and popped two Nurofen tablets out of the silver foil strip.

Pushing his well-worn black leather swivel chair back, he glanced out of his office window which looked over the front car park at Central Derbyshire HQ.

Cynthia Vickers, his wife of almost fifty years had been nagging him again about early retirement, spending more time together on holidays, relaxing with her sister and brother-in-law, whom she was very close to.

'Not on your life,' he said under his breath, 'I'd rather stick pins in my eyes than spend time with those wasters.'

He'd got almost eighteen months to go until his sixtieth birthday, then he was eligible for a full pension. Tom loved his wife very much and would do almost anything to please her, but regular holidays with her sister, no can do.

Sitting back down, he opened the brown folder in front of him. Adam had requested to meet him about the current investigation and a possible connection with a previous crime.

Tom's whole working life had been in the police force just like his father before him. In the early days, he'd just been one of the lads, working the beat, over time, rising from an unambitious PC to the rank of Detective Chief Inspector.

In that time, he'd seen many a copper turn a blind eye to criminality, a driving offence, theft, low-key burglary, for a backhander, it happened, but murder, categorically no way, not on his watch.

He'd pulled the file from the archives, no questions asked and tried to familiarise himself with the case; it was a long time ago, over fifteen years, and a lot of water had passed under the bridge since then.

Daniel Ashby: age twenty-two. Parents: Mary and Philip Ashby. Occupation: Landscape Gardener.

Victim: Arthur Richardson. Retired finance manager. Verdict: Guilty of second-degree murder. Sentence: Minimum fourteen years in HMP.

A knock at his office door made him look up to see DI Adam Fox standing there, his hand on the door handle.

He put the file to one side. 'Hi Adam, come on in, can I get you a drink?'

He put on his glasses, opened his drawer, and withdrew a bottle of Scotch and two glasses.

'Not for me sir, a bit early, but I'll take a coffee if the machine is on?'

Tom got himself a drink, the bottle clinking on the glass as he poured, Adam helped himself to a coffee at the machine on the unit at the far side of the office.

Both men sat there for several moments, not saying a word, just holding their drinks, Adam breaking the silence.

'Thanks, sir, for agreeing to see, me at such short notice, I wanted to A, bring you up to speed with the Patricia Locke investigation, and B, we think there may be a possible connection with a similar murder some years previous.'

'Well, I certainly want to know the latest on the case, that's for sure, but a connection, I don't think so Adam. If it's the one I believe you're referring to, and I think it is, it was a long time ago.'

'I understand that sir, however, there are some similarities between that old case and the one we're currently investigating.'

Tom took several moments to compose himself before replying.

'Daniel Ashby *was* found guilty. The evidence was solid, and a thorough investigation took place. I was the SIO on the case, but you know that already. It's all there in the file, he had a personal grudge against Arthur Robinson, something to do with some work he did. And Mr. Robinson refused to pay.

And the gardening gloves, his DNA was on the gloves, they were found near the body, straightforward evidence Adam.'

'Yes, I know all that, but both Frank and I have interviewed Daniel Ashby again, and if I'm being honest about this, I believe we put away the wrong man.'

Tom Vickers sat there; he could feel his blood pressure rising as his heart began to beat faster.

'Does Frank Bailey think we put the wrong man away? He was involved in the case from the outset, has *he* got the same idea as you DI Fox?'

'So, we're moving to official name status now,' thought Adam. The tone from his boss had changed instantly, instead of wanting to discuss the case, he'd gone on the defensive.

He also noticed perspiration forming on his forehead, as he took off his glasses, placing them in front of him, interlocking his fingers, calmly pausing.

'Listen Adam... it was a long time ago, we were all under pressure to get a result, the local press was on our back and the Chief Super wanted the case closed. Daniel Ashby *did* have a motive, didn't have an alibi, and we had a witness who heard him threaten Mr Robinson, it all stacked up at the time, and there was no one else in the frame. Yes, Daniel Ashby denied ever being involved, but no one could vouch for his whereabouts, not even his parents, all he said was that he went for a walk to calm down, near the woods. So, let me ask you this question. Would you have done anything any differently? We got the right man, Adam, don't make this an issue, the last thing we need is another investigation. I thought you'd have had enough of that at Yorkshire, leave it alone, and that's the end of it, understand?'

Tom Vickers poured himself another drink, whilst Adam helped himself to his second cup of coffee, trying to control his frustration. Sitting back down he realized it was pointless carrying on the discussion, it would only lead to an out-and-out argument, and his judgement told him that neither of them was in the mood for that. He also knew that he wouldn't be doing himself or Frank any favours by questioning the decisions made on a case years before.

Opening the logbook, he ran through the lines of enquiry the team were following, reviewing the progress made, or the lack of it, on the Patricia Locke case.

He emphasized that whilst the team were pulling out all the stops, following up on every possible lead, and there weren't many, frustratingly, they had to conclude that at the moment there was very little progress being made.

As Tom Vickers's blood pressure began to return to normal, he asked a question.

'Changing the subject completely, is there any further news or progress on Scarlett?' I cannot image what you and Vivian must be going through right now.'

As Adam also calmed down, he replied.

'Well, no actual progress, but we did meet with Detective Sergeant Sarah Ward recently, and she *has* found some new information that might have a bearing on her disappearance.'

'I thought Chris Mitchell was handling the case, or has he backed away now, bigger fish to fry knowing Chris?'

'Chris remains involved, but more from a distance, you know what it's like, eventually, you get moved to investigate other cases, that's what's happened here I understand.'

'Well look, Adam, if there's anything I can personally do to help, my door is always open, you know that.'

Tom Vickers looked at his watch, just as his desktop lit up, the screen reflecting in his glasses.

'I've got to go, sorry, the Chief Super has asked me to meet with some reporter from the local rag, something to do with community policing, what a load of crap.'

As Adam stood up to leave, Tom's phone rang, picking it up on the fourth ring.

'Yes, I know, I'll be down in a minute, show them to the meeting room and I'll be there as soon as I can. The reporter's arrived, so, are we done here for today?'

'I guess we are,' replied Adam as they both walked to the office door.

'Don't forget what I said, let it drop, there's no sense in racking up the past.'

As Adam made his way down the corridor and back to his office, he muttered under his breath.

'You might want to let it drop Tom, but I won't.'

Forty-seven

MARY ASHBY COVERED HER HEAD with her coat hood, rain beginning to fall as they walked across the police headquarters car park to her Vauxhall Corsa.

Neither of them looked back, walking in silence, waiting for each other to say something. Although Danny's mum could drive, whenever they went out together Danny always took over the duty, he wasn't a particularly good passenger either.

Making their way back home from the interview, his mum turned down the radio and placed her hand on Danny's knee.

'Are you okay?' she asked him.

Before replying, Daniel ran through in his mind what had been discussed with the two officers, his opinion was, that they didn't think he'd committed the crime all those years ago, but equally, they couldn't come up with an alternative suspect, so the case remained closed, at least for now.

'I'm fine mum, not sure if this will ever end for me, but I know the truth, *we* know the truth and that's all that matters in my book. You know what, I got the impression rightly or wrongly, that Detective Inspector Fox has some misgivings about the case, don't ask me how, it's just a feeling I get. Maybe I'm mistaken, maybe they'll call me back in for a second time, but I know the truth and that'll never change.'

It started to rain more heavily, the windscreen wipers moving the rain to one side. Danny checked the time on the dashboard, it was 2:37 p.m. and they'd had no lunch.

A couple of hundred yards ahead was the pub that he and Joe had stopped at several days ago, he switched on the indicator and began to move to the centre of the road.

'I think a nice lunch is in order mum, anything you fancy, my treat?'

'That would have been lovely, but I need to get back home to finish preparing a meal for your dad, he has to eat at regular times due to his medication, maybe next time, if that's okay?'

Danny noticed the sad look on his mum's face, he couldn't pinpoint what it was, but he was determined to find out more.

He'd previously noticed the bruising on her arms and warned his dad to leave her alone. '*Nobody mistreats my mum,*' he said to himself.

Turning the corner into the road where they lived, he noticed a black Ford Ranger parked just outside the front wall.

'We have visitors by the looks of it,' said his mum.

'It's Joe, the chap I've been working with, he's the landscape gardener, and he texts me to say he might pop round.'

Making their way into the lounge, Philip Ashby and Joe sat together, two glasses of what looked like whisky on the coffee table in front of them.

'Hi mate,' said Joe, standing up to shake hands.

'I said in my text that I might call round, your dad's been good enough to entertain me, showing me his gun collection, talking about the olden days in the army, he's led an interesting life hasn't he?'

Danny picked up the glass and put it to his nose, *it was whisky.*

'I thought you didn't drink and drive Joe, or are you planning to get a taxi back home?'

'Calm down Daniel,' said Philip Ashby annoyingly, 'it's only one drink, he'll be fine.'

'It's okay Danny, I haven't taken a sip, your dad had poured the drink before I could say anything.'

Philip Ashby picked up his drink and downed it in one, put the glass down heavily on the coffee table, and then picked up the second glass.

'You kids, you don't know how to live, back in my day if someone offered you a drink, it was courteous to accept, anyway… more for me.'

Mary Ashby looked at her husband, choosing her words carefully before saying.

'Don't you want to know how he got on at the police station?'

Philip Ashby didn't reply, he just turned away, picked up the two guns, walked towards the kitchen and out through the back door, slamming it shut.

Joe turned to Danny, an embarrassed look on his face.

'Joe, before you ask, I'll tell you some other time, but not right now if you don't mind.'

Danny's mum asked Joe to stay for dinner, which he kindly accepted, she'd already started preparing a chicken casserole before they'd left for the police station, so there was plenty to go around.

It was almost ten o'clock before Joe left the Ashby house, arranging to pick up Danny early the following morning to do some final checks on The Lakes Nursing Home.

Forty-eight

FRANK BAILEY POPPED HIS HEAD around the door of Adam's office, a slight smirk on his face.

'Coffee and KitKat boss, you look like you need one?'

Taking a deep breath and trying to compose himself, Adam replied.

'What I need is a Detective Chief Inspector with some balls, not a superior officer who thinks it's fine to brush a possible miscarriage of justice under the carpet. There's something not right here Frank, having interviewed Daniel Ashby, can you honestly say hand on heart that you think he's capable of second-degree murder? What did he have to gain… Nothing whatsoever. No motive, no financial benefit, all that took place was an argument over a gardening fee, which Arthur Richardson refused to pay. So, Daniel confronted him, and it led to a disagreement. And look at Mary Ashby, she doesn't seem like a person who'd turn a blind eye to murder, even if her son had done it, I think she'd have talked him into giving himself up. But no, instead, whilst he's been in jail all that time, she's stood by him, fighting his corner, and no, Frank, I don't need any coffee. I'll be off the ceiling if I'm not careful, but I'll take the KitKat, thanks.'

Reaching into his jacket pocket, Frank pulled out a four-finger chocolate bar, bits of fluff sticking to the outer wrapper, breaking it into two sections, he passed one to Adam as he sat down on the chair opposite.

'So, it didn't go as well as expected then I guess?' Frank still sporting a smile on his face. Honestly, you know what Tom Vickers is like, always has to be right, doing the right thing and all that.'

'Are you having a laugh? He sat there and frankly told me not to rock the boat, let it drop. So being honest with you, I don't think he's doing the right thing, not one bit.'

He took a bite of his KitKat.

'He told me that you were involved in the case, is that correct?'

Frank sat there for several seconds, getting his head around the question and what to say, choosing his words carefully.

'Well yes, I *was* involved in the case, but only on the peripheral, door-to-door questioning, searching the woods for evidence.

Following up on lines of enquiry, all the general stuff, you know how it works Adam. But remember I was only a PC back then, and I'd only been in the force for about eighteen to twenty months, not wet behind the ears, but still learning on the job. The two main investigators were Tom Vickers and Chris Mitchell. Chris at that time was a Detective Sergeant, just before he was transferred to Sheffield, but you know that anyway. You've worked with Chris Mitchell of late, he's as straight as a dye, a very experienced copper, he wouldn't compromise on an investigation, *would he*?'

'I'm sure you're right Frank about Chris, but between me and you, something in the back of my mind is telling me that the decision to charge Daniel Ashby was a mistake, and a big one at that.'

'Anyway, what's the latest on the Patricia Locke case, have we managed to trace her mobile phone?'

'The mobile phone company have now confirmed that she made just one call on the day she was murdered, we traced the number, it was made to our Minister friend, Steven Andrews, after that… nothing.'

'Can you follow up with Steven Andrews and see what the call was all about, I still think he's hiding something, but at the moment I don't know what?'

Frank took a drink of his coffee, shoving a KitKat finger into his mouth.

'Will do boss unless the phone is switched on, it's impossible to find its location, and since it hasn't been used since the day of the murder, they cannot tell us where it is, so it's a waiting game I'm afraid.'

'It was never found at the scene of the crime was it, so can we surmise that wherever or whoever may have the phone, could, just could have something to do with the death of Patricia Locke… we need to find that phone.'

As Frank picked up his coffee mug and made his way to the door, Adam called him back.

'The conversation we've just had is between me and you. If Tom Vickers did make an error of judgement, then that's something he'll have to live with. But from what I see so far, I think we put away the wrong man. And if that is the case, then the murderer is still out there.'

Frank closed the door behind him as he left.

Forty-nine

JULIE BAILEY HAD ALREADY started making dinner as Frank came through the front door of their nineteen eighties semi-detached house. The smell of fish wafted through the hallway as he closed the white double-glazed front door.

He stood there for several seconds considering what Adam had said about the Daniel Ashby case. Hanging his coat on the stainless-steel hook next to his wife's, he made his way towards the kitchen, it had been one of those days, and he could eat a horse.

Julie had heard him come in and had already poured him a large glass of white wine, Frank wasn't choosy, any wine would do, just as long as it was alcoholic.

As usual, the kitchen like the rest of the house, was immaculate. Julie was extremely proud of the house they'd both created over the years. She always hoped it would become a family home, but despite years of trying and IVF treatment, both by the NHS and latterly privately, bringing a baby home was not to be.

Frank took off his jacket and pulled two kitchen stools from under the breakfast bar, dropping it on the back. He opened the cutlery drawer and put two knives and forks next to brightly coloured placemats.

As Julie opened the oven door, hot air filling the room, she turned to her husband.

'My mum hasn't been too good today. I was going to call you, but didn't want to trouble you, you know, with the case and everything. Her carer called me earlier and said that she wanted to know why she was in her house, what she was doing there, she even picked up the phone and started to call the police. I've been over, and she's a lot more comfortable now, but I think we do need to decide on the nursing home, we can't go on like this for too much longer, she needs help, we all need help.'

'Listen, sweetheart, you can call me at any time at work, either on the office landline or my mobile, as Adam repeatedly tells me, and he knows more than most… family first. I know it's not easy for you, and if you think the time is right, let's make that decision. I love your mum; you know that she was great over the IVF funding.

However, she does need support and care, and I don't think we can give her that anymore.'

He picked up his glass of wine and took a long gulp, buying himself a little time to consider what to say next.

'Let's make another appointment with the home we've been to and get things moving. It will cost us, and we'll probably have to sell your mum's house to fund the expense, but if that's what's needed, then that's what we'll do.'

Frank had always had a good relationship with his mother-in-law, ever since her husband died of a sudden heart attack almost ten years ago, he'd taken it upon himself to help where he could. Every alternate Saturday if work allowed, they'd both go over, Julie would take her mum to the local Tesco store whilst Frank did the gardening, decorating and bits of DIY, that sort of thing.

He'd never had a strong connection or affection with his parents, his dad worked shifts at a Co-op warehouse, and his mum ran a hairdressing salon, she was good with her customers, but a terrible businesswoman. He recalls the massive arguments they both had about money, or more to the point, the lack of it. His dad would piss it up the wall every Friday and Saturday night, then blame his wife for spending too much.

As time went on, they both began to drift apart and eventually went their separate ways, his mother died several years later and his dad, whilst still alive he believes, doesn't have anything to do with him.

After dinner they cleared the pots, placing them in the dishwasher and setting the timer for a four-hour delay.

Frank always moaned about the cost of energy, and how they should be saving money. Before adjourning to the lounge, Julie opened the fridge door, cool air hitting her face, she removed a second bottle of white wine and switched off the kitchen light on her way out.

Frank made himself comfortable in his favourite chair, a beige leather electric recliner they'd bought in the sale, it didn't quite match the settee and other chairs in the room, but it was comfortable in the furniture store and lived up to its expectations now.

Julie took a sip of her wine, putting the glass on the side table next to the chair she'd sat on.

'What sort of day have you had, is there any more progress on the case?'

Frank had always had an understanding with Julie. Once the front door was closed, conversation on the job stopped, too many marriages in the force had ended in divorce, and he wasn't ever going to take that risk.

She noticed how tired he looked, pale and withdrawn, he'd also lost some weight, only a few pounds, but it showed in his face.

'Is everything all right at work? I know you don't talk about it, but you seem miles away tonight.'

Taking a large swig of wine, he sat forward, placing both hands over the cool glass.

'To be honest, it's been a shit day. We're making little progress on the Patricia Locke case, and to cap it all, Adam's had a big row with Tom Vickers. A case going back over fifteen years, and he now believes after all that time, Tom might have put away the wrong man. But listen, let's not talk about that, let's leave work at the front door, we need to focus on sorting out your mum, making her as comfortable as we can, for as long as we can. That nursing home, The Lakes, I think it's perfect for her. Expensive, yes but it's close by, has great patient reviews, and excellent assessments by the Care Quality Commission.'

'How do we break the news to my mum, putting her in a nursing home, she'll see it as the last resort, losing her independence, it'll be a big step for her, for all of us I guess.'

Frank topped his wine glass up and refilled Julie's. 'Listen, sweetheart, we knew this day would come, we'll sit down with her, both of us and explain what we would like to do and why.'

Julie felt sick in the pit of her stomach as tears began to form in her eyes, grabbing a tissue and wiping her face, she stood up, walked over to the wall unit, and picked up a framed photo of her mum and dad taken on holiday in Whitby around twelve years ago.

'It won't be the same you know… But I think she'll be much happier at a nursing home. She'll be surrounded by people with similar conditions, and hopefully, staff that will look after her. We'll still be able to visit, won't we, take her out for the day, and apparently, she can have certain pieces of her furniture in the room, so she'll still have some familiar items that will help.'

'I'm off in a couple of days,' said Frank, 'why don't you make an appointment tomorrow and we'll go over and discuss all the final plans, dates, costs etc.'

Frank picked up the brochure they'd collected from The Lakes Nursing Home on their last visit, a well-presented, glossy booklet covering all the amenities that it could offer. He studied it for several moments, then placed it on the coffee table.

Fifty

THE MORNING SUN HAD MADE the inside of Frank's car stuffy as he unlocked the doors with the remote key fob, holding it open for Julie as she sat down in the passenger seat, putting the nursing home brochure in the footwell and clipping on her seat belt.

His father-in-law had always opened the door for Julie's mum, and it's something that Frank had picked up and carried on with.

The Lakes Nursing Home could see them the following morning, Frank had called Adam to ask for a few hours off, which he knew he'd agree to.

The journey only took around thirty minutes, joining the outer ring road of Derby city centre, then taking the A52 towards Crich.

The Lakes was located approximately three miles outside the town centre, in open country, flanked with trees on either side of the road as they approached the nursing home.

Making their way down the gravelled drive, the place looked more like a five-star hotel, with a well-maintained lawn at the front, and a large lake surrounded by a path in the foreground, several large vehicles were parked to one side, with several people working on the garden and planting a range of shrubs.

Parking the car in a space marked visitors, Frank and Julie stood for several moments, taking in the surroundings before walking to the front entrance. A well-dressed woman in a dark blue uniform stood at the front of a large oak-opened door, holding out her hand.

'Mr and Mrs Bailey, how nice to meet with you. My name is Karen Lattimer, and I'm the Matron at The Lakes Nursing Home, welcome.'

The three of them made their way to a small but well-appointed office, where tea and coffee were offered, Frank accepted a cup of tea, but Julie declined.

'I understand that you've already met our Managing Director Mr Robinson on your first visit to us and you're now looking for residential care for your mother, is that correct?'

Julie looked once again at the brochure in her hand and replied, 'Yes, it's for my mum, unfortunately, she's been diagnosed with

Dementia. And although we've both tried to look after her, we think the time has come for her to have supported care, as you offer here.'

After discussing all the matters in connection with Julie's mum, including the financial costs, Karen Lattimer suggested that the three of them take a final look around the home, which included the room that Julie's mum would be in. Walking down the expensive carpeted corridor, Frank noticed that all the rooms were named after well-known locations and sometimes famous people, Sherwood, Chatsworth, Lawrence, etc.

Julie's mum's room was Byron, which Frank understood must have been named after the poet Byron.

By the end of the tour, they were satisfied that The Lakes Nursing Home was the ideal home for Julie's mum. Hopefully, she'd be well looked after, and with it being relatively close, it would allow Julie and Frank to visit regularly.

Karen Lattimer escorted them back to the reception area at the front of the house, opening the large oak door and apologising for the work being done on the gardens.

'The workers should be finished by the end of next week, just the finishing touches. It's taken them longer than expected, although the bad weather hasn't helped either.'

As they walked down the steps Frank checked his phone, turning to Julie.

'Whilst we're here shall we take a stroll round the lake, I've not got to get back straight away, so we might as well enjoy the free time and the scenery.'

The path around the water was further than they thought, deciding just over halfway, they'd turn back and make their way to the car. As they walked hand in hand, Julie noticed a large wooden garden seat partially hidden by overgrown bushes. Gently moving the shrubs to one side, taking care not to sting herself on the nettles, she noticed a blackened brass plaque on the back of the seat, taking out a handkerchief, she wiped it clean, it read:

IN MEMORY OF ONE OF OUR OWN - TOBY CURTIS –
ALWAYS REMEMBERED - NEVER FORGOTTEN.

Just before reversing the car out of the parking space, Frank's mobile rang, and then it pinged, Adam's name appeared, and he answered it immediately.

'Hi Boss, we're just leaving now, I'm going to drop Julie off at home and then I'll come straight to the station, I should be with you in about thirty to forty minutes.'

There was a delay on the line as though the call had been disconnected.

Frank switched the call from the speaker and put the phone to his ear.

'Are you there Adam,? I can't hear you.'

'Frank, I've just texted you an address in Nottingham, get yourself over here without delay, blue light it if you have to.'

He turned to Julie, a confused look on his face.

'Sorry sweetheart, I've got to get over to Nottingham urgently, can I drop you off at your mum's? It's closer to the A52.'

'That's no problem Julie replied. I need to speak with her anyway… Nottingham, that's not on your patch is it?'

'No, it's not,' replied Frank.

Fifty-one

LIFTING THE BUNCH OF KEYS off the hook in the garden shed I select the right one and unlock the drawer once again taking out the school photograph at Chaffinch House, smoothing it down with gloved hands, you can't be too careful.

Killing Ross Sullivan had been the easiest one so far, you know the old saying, '*If you fail to plan, you plan to fail.*' And yet, when I'd identified my latest victim, I thought it wouldn't be as simple as it was, a seamless execution, though I say it myself.

Picking up the red felt tip pen I place a cross through the image of my latest victim, smiling to myself as I recall the expression on his face, that look of fear. Knowing that something horrifying is going to take place but not knowing what or how it will happen.

I wished I'd have taken a picture now, but that was far too risky.

Opening the small plastic zip bag I'd packed, I took out the blooded hair and attached flesh and put it in the drawer along with all the other trophies that I'd gathered quite a collection, but still more to come.

Peeling off the black leather gloves and putting them in the black bag with all the other items, I move some of the gardening tools to one side, making sure that they are well hidden and out of sight.

Looking back at the school photograph, there were now three red crosses striking through the images of the people I'd hunted down.

Arthur Richardson was my first victim, viciously killed. It seems such a long time ago as I look down and notice the gold signet ring in the black metal box, turning the key, locking it, as I've tried to lock out the horrors of my time at boarding school for all these years.

Fifty-two

FRANK COULDN'T REMEMBER the last time he'd used the small blue emergency flashing light on his car. But dropping off Julie at her mum's, he opened the glove box and attached it to the roof, making his way along the A52 towards the address Adam had texted him. Adrenaline kicks in as he uses the car horn to get other vehicles to move out of the way.

Exactly twenty-seven minutes later, as he turned a corner a cluster of police vehicles met him, crime scene tape wafting in the wind. He parked several meters down the street, making his way to where all the action seemed to be taking place, a modern block of flats outside Nottingham city centre.

Several uniformed officers stood around the POLICE – DO NOT CROSS blue and white plastic tape, Frank was unable to identify any of them until he noticed Adam and his black Audi A4. He was in discussions with someone who looked familiar, but he was too far away to recognise them.

Locking his car, he walked up the road, showing his warrant card to a sombre-looking officer registering all the names attending the scene, raising the tape as Frank ducked underneath.

Looking to his right, several people had already begun to gather on the opposite side of the road, most of them standing, but several sitting on what looked like park benches, waiting for something to happen.

Making his way to where Detective Inspector Adam Fox was standing, looking as usual, totally professional in his three-piece suit, well-groomed jet-black hair, heavy in conversation with a colleague that Frank now recognised.

'Frank, I'd like to introduce Detective Chief Superintendent Craig Slater from EMSCO, Craig this is my right-hand man, Detective Sergeant Frank Bailey.'

DCI Slater repositioned himself, so he was right in front of Frank and shook his hand firmly.

'Good to meet you Frank, Adam speaks highly of you, I appreciate you coming over so quickly.'

EMSCO stood for East Midlands Serious Crime Organisation. It's one of the largest collaborative policing units in the country, carrying out and delivering specialist capabilities and services on behalf of the five East Midlands police forces.

As the three of them made their way to the front door of the impressive modern building, Adam couldn't shake off the feeling of dread as they made their way up the stairs to the second floor.

The frenzied activity met them at the front door of Three Ashcroft Court, Nottingham.

Before entering the flat a young police constable handed them white Tyvek overalls, a white face mask and blue overshoes.

Adam took a deep breath and stepped inside, Craig and Frank several steps behind, as they made their way along a hallway to what looked like the lounge.

As the three of them entered he immediately spotted Rachel Munroe, the Forensic Pathologist from Derby, a forbidding look on her face, she was talking to another colleague who was taking notes on a clipboard.

She spotted Adam, excused herself and walked over to meet the three of them.

Frank was the first to speak.

'Hello Rachel, why are you here, this isn't your patch?'

'Hi guys, no it isn't, but the Senior Forensic Pathologist for Nottingham is on maternity leave, and I'm the next in line.'

The four of them made their way back down the hallway, Adam noticing for the first time several dead rose petals on the floor, a spine-chilling thought went through his mind.

Rachel began to slow her pace allowing both DS Bailey and DCI Slater to get ahead of her, she asked Adam to hold back.

'It's the same killer, Adam,' she said quietly. He's been tied up, head shoved into a bath full of water, scalped in certain areas on his head, for trophies I presume, and like the others, a number carved into his forehead.'

As Adam entered the bathroom, he bent down to examine the trussed-up figure.

Sure enough, his hands were securely tied together, a cord running down the front of his chest, through his crutch and tied to the back of his hands. It was evident that if he tried to move, his head would go further into the water, there was no way out.

The back of the man's head had several deep wounds, and the blood was still moist due to being in the water. The skin on the victim's face was wrinkled, making him look much older than he probably was. And right in the centre of his forehead, just as Rachel had described, was carved a number, a number three.

Fifty-three

THE BATH WATER MADE a gurgling sound as the stainless-steel plug was released, swirls of diluted blood circling down the drain.

Not wanting to be seen to be pulling rank, DCS Craig Slater stepped forward to take a closer look at the victim, mentally taking in what he saw in front of him. Adam immediately noticed his body language, he didn't seem to be phased by what he saw, absorbing the crime scene like it was an everyday routine to him, which he guessed it probably was.

Frank suggested that he move out of the bathroom, there wasn't a lot of space in there, and with four adults, it was getting too cosy for his liking.

Craig Slater turned to Adam. 'Before you arrived, Dr Munroe was suggesting to me that she believes there are similarities between this murder, and one currently being investigated by you and the team back at Central Derby. A female named Patricia Locke. Not the same in terms of the way both victims have been murdered, but likenesses in the way the bodies have been marked, and the cuts to the forehead of both victims. No guessing here Adam, but what's your take on this?'

Adam had only met Craig Slater once before, it was around eighteen months ago, he'd attended a briefing meeting at Sheffield Central Head Quarters in connection with a drug bust that Adam had worked on.

The people involved had gone down for a long stretch, and Craig wanted to understand more about the 'Best Practice tactics' used in the case.

Adam stood in the bathroom looking at the victim and the horrendous wounds to the back of his head, recalling what he saw when he attended the crime scene involving Patricia Locke.

Deciding not to answer Craig's question immediately, he turned to Rachel standing next to him.

'What do we initially know about the victim?'

'You mean apart from him being dead? Well, we know his name and where he worked, but apart from that, not a lot. According to a neighbour, his name is Ross Sullivan, the neighbour's lived here for almost three years and he was here when they moved in apparently. The alarm was raised by his girlfriend or fiancée, not sure which, her name is Melanie Watkins, a local estate agent, highly successful by all accounts. She's downstairs with one of the pc's if you want to speak with her, but go easy Adam, she's clearly in shock.'

Adam called out in an unusual formal manner to Frank. 'DS Bailey, can *you* go downstairs and interview Melanie Watkins? Get as much information as you can on Ross Sullivan What's their actual relationship? Where did he work? Family and friends, remain professional but don't go easy, we need answers. Then try and find out how they'd get access to the property, check for any CCTV at the front entrance, the road outside etc. Speak with the neighbours, they may have seen or heard something, I'll see you back at the station later.'

From the tone in Adam's voice, there was no suggestion of going in easy.

Craig Slater lifted his arm, pulling back his shirt cuff to check his watch, he was still waiting for an answer.

As Adam stepped back from the corpse, he noticed some of the rose petals had travelled onto the bathroom floor.

Remembering the question, Adam asked Rachel to excuse him and suggested that he and the DCI talk downstairs. This wasn't his patch; he needed to understand the ground rules. The last thing he wanted at the moment was an official complaint going back to Tom Vickers, after all this *was* outside his area.

As they made their way to the front of the flats, several uniformed officers were keeping onlookers and probably the local press at bay.

The crowd in the park opposite was now about four deep in parts, some standing on a bench trying desperately to see what was taking place.

They stood there for several minutes and then Craig Slater turned to Adam.

'I've already spoken with Tom Vickers first thing this morning Adam, explained to him that if these cases are linked, and from what Dr. Munroe has indicated, then initially it looks like they could be. If that is the case, I want well-thought-out, systemized cross-functional working between Derbyshire and Nottinghamshire police. No politics, no stabbing in the back, just focused collaboration, that's what EMSCO is all about. He's agreed to offer *your* full support on this, so let's talk tomorrow when you've had the opportunity to pull more details together. In the meantime, if you do need any further information, just pick up the phone.'

Before Adam had the time to reply, DCS Slater held out his hand, looked towards the crowds in the park opposite, and manoeuvred his way around the uniformed officers, walking down the road to a waiting car.

Rachel Munroe had got rid of the Tyvek suit and face mask and was now standing at the front entrance to the flats, dressed in civilian clothes, putting a comb through her hair.

Maintaining his discipline of professionalism at all times, Adam fastened the button on his jacket and walked back to the entrance, stopping for a moment to look up at the balcony where Ross Sullivan had lived.

'So, this is the second one, first Patricia Locke and now Ross Sullivan?'

The comment from Rachel took Adam by surprise, he was about to reply when his phone pinged.

He typed in his code, and the message read.

'Hi Adam, I've returned to the station as Melanie Watkins didn't hang around, so I've arranged to interview her first thing tomorrow morning, see you when you get back, Frank.'

Adam looked directly at Rachel. 'When will you have the autopsy reports back? We need to move on this one Rachel, and no, this probably isn't the second one, but I'll come back to you on that.'

Before Rachel could respond, Adam had begun to make his way to his car, the onlookers in the park opposite had begun to dissipate. Starting the engine, he decided that this wasn't the time for Spotify, putting the car into reverse and checking his rear-view mirror.

'What the F..., he said out loud. The image he saw first took him by surprise, as blood ran cold through his body, he jumped out of the car, but the figure in the crowd had disappeared.

He looked right then left, scanning the faces in front of him, then walked towards the park benches, but he or she was nowhere to be seen.

It was a figure dressed in a long dark coat, wearing a black and white baseball cap.

Fifty-four

VIVIAN'S DAY AT WORK hadn't started well. She'd arrived twenty minutes late due to leaving home without her laptop, normally she'd leave it in the hallway, but last night she was checking a recipe and left it in the kitchen, so had to turn back.

Then there was a hold-up on the main road out of the village, and to cap it all, when she tried to log in to her computer, there seemed to be some type of malfunction, 'or playing up,' at least that's how the practice manager had described it.

Her first patient of the day hadn't turned up for their appointment, so as she sat at her desk, she hoped things would get better as the day progressed.

Dr Peter Johnson had introduced a new policy at the GP Practice. If a patient didn't keep their appointment, and they hadn't got a valid reason for not turning up, or contacting reception to cancel, this was recorded on a database and discussed at the monthly practice meeting. What action might be taken was never actually agreed.

Viv decided not to complete the task, as her second patient, a young mother with a fourteen-month-old baby with suspected whooping cough took longer than the allocated time.

There was a knock at the door and one of the receptionists walked in with a mug of coffee and three digestive biscuits on a tray.

'I thought you might need a drink; the practice manager's told me that your PC's gone down, is there anything I can do to help?'

Viv looked up from her desk, she'd been checking the number of recent cases of infantile whooping cough on her laptop, which according to the updated records, had increased by a dramatic twenty-seven percent.

'Thanks very much, that's just what the doctor ordered if you'll excuse the pun. I'm fine thank you, my laptop's got all my patient appointments for the rest of the day, including a meeting with the new sales representative from Forden Pharmaceuticals at twelve-thirty, give me a buzz when they arrive would you?'

The coffee and biscuits went down a treat, both she and Adam had made it a rule to try and not eat any biscuits or cakes during the week. Viv had put on a few pounds and Adam, due to workload hadn't been going to the gym, according to him, his suit trousers began to feel tight, but as she finished the last digestive, she thought, 'three biscuits won't make much difference to the waistline.'

After seeing six more patients, when Viv looked at the time on her PC, it was ten past twelve, with one more patient to see before twelve-thirty.

Right on time her office phone rang. The receptionist confirmed that her appointment had arrived.

There was a knock on the consultation door, and Viv replied to come in. Jason Fletcher introduced himself as the new territory business manager for Forden Pharmaceuticals.

Viv thought he looked around mid to late twenties, as he sat comfortably in front of her desk. Opening his briefcase, he got out his company's branded folder and handed her a business card.

Viv took a few minutes to read it, **Jason Fletcher – a.b.p.i – Territory Business Manager – Forden Pharmaceuticals.**

Viv noticed immediately that he wasn't dressed as most other salespeople usually were. Instead, he wore beige chinos, an open-neck shirt and a dark blue jacket. He went on to explain that this was a new company initiative, to see if it put targeted customers at ease, Viv wondered what targeted customers meant, but had to agree, it did seem to work.

Almost forty minutes later Jason Fletcher presented a brand-new prescription drug for the management of certain conditions with patients that have been diagnosed with Diabetes.

He would like the practice to select an agreed number of patients, evaluate the trial and if successful, consider switching targeted patients to this new drug. Viv explained that she would have to discuss this with other clinical colleagues, agreed to bring this up at the next practice management meeting, and suggested that Jason make a further appointment in around six weeks.

That would allow time for the wider team to take a closer look at the clinical data and decide the next steps.

'Thanks for your time Dr Flemming, it was nice to meet you, and I trust we'll see each other again in the next few weeks. In the meantime, if you do require any further information or details about the trial please give me a call or send me an email, my contact details are on my business card.' And with that, he stood to his feet, exchanged a handshake, and left Viv's consultation room.

It was the middle of the afternoon when Peter popped his head around Viv's door, 'Hi Vivian, sorry to trouble you, is it convenient for us to meet up before close of play? I need about fifteen minutes of your time, to go over the partnership agreement, is that okay with you?'

'Yeah Peter, that's fine, shall we say around six o'clock, is everything all right with the paperwork? Your solicitor has checked it and they seem happy with the content and the final amount to be paid.'

'Yes, everything's fine, it's just a couple of points to go over and we're good to go,' as he closed the door, 'see you around six-ish.'

Unfortunately, two further patients cancelled their afternoon appointments, which gave Viv a little time to look at the clinical papers Jason Fletcher had detailed for further review.

The sun was beaming through the opaque window, making the meeting room feel warm as she walked in, Peter was already there, several papers laid out on the conference table in front of him.

'Everything is in order Vivian; all I need is a couple of signatures and the partnership is complete.'

Viv and Adam had already read all the documents a couple of nights ago, it looked acceptable.

Peter moved his finger across two pieces of the documents, 'If you could just sign there and there, and that's it… Welcome partner.'

She picked up the pen and signed as required, placing it back down on the conference table.

'Can I ask you a personal question Peter, why me, why offer me a partnership?'

He considered her question for several minutes, then replied.

'As I mentioned before, since you joined us, Vivian, the practice has taken on a new look, staff morale seems to have increased, patient numbers are up and we're even getting CVs from other GPs for consideration to join us. But the main reason is that I want someone to carry on the good work of the practice. Someone dedicated to patient care, keen to look at new ideas and treatments, and to work on growing our patient numbers. You probably don't know, but I inherited Edgewater Medical Centre from my father almost sixteen years ago.

He died very suddenly from a massive heart attack, leaving my mum and I to pick up the pieces. It was hard at first, Mum took his death badly, actually, she never really recovered, but I had to try and carry on for the sake of my patients and my dad, that's why I need a partnership, to carry on the good work for everyone.'

Sitting back in her consultation room, Viv did know about the sudden death of Peter's father, but none of the staff had ever openly discussed it, nor would she expect them to. It was a very personal matter and something that had nothing to do with anyone else but Peter and his mother.

She tried to open her desktop computer and was delighted to see that it had been fixed, just as she was checking her appointments for the following day her mobile pinged, checking the message she saw it was from DS Ward. As she read the message her hands began to tremble, and her legs felt like jelly.

The message in capitals read. **CALL ME WHEN YOU CAN, WE'VE RECEIVED MORE NEWS ABOUT SCARLETT'S DISAPPEARANCE.**

Fifty-five

ADAM'S CAR WAS ALREADY on the drive when Viv pulled up at the side, switching off the engine and pausing for several moments, noticing that all the hanging baskets and flower tubs were wilting desperate for water.

Deciding not to call Adam from her mobile but hoped he'd be at home when she arrived.

The traffic was unusually heavy when she'd left the medical centre, taking her almost thirty minutes to get home, minutes in the car that seemed to last hours.

Walking through the front door, and placing her laptop case on the floor, she heard voices coming from the lounge, and as she entered she realised that Adam was on speakerphone to Frank.

'The point is Frank, if my observations are correct, we've now got three unsolved deaths, all of them planned, and not a single motive to go on. We've now got to include Arthur Richardson as potentially being the first victim, although it was years ago, and someone was found guilty, I truthfully don't believe that Daniel Ashby had anything to do with his murder. He was just in the wrong place at the wrong time, something I'm going to speak to Tom Vickers about tomorrow. You were there at the interview, hand on heart, do you honestly believe for one moment that he could have viciously butchered the body like that? You've read the report, the injuries to the skull, the burnt fingers… it just doesn't fit Frank. Look at his mum, Mary Ashby, she doesn't seem the sort of person to me who would sit back and say nothing.'

'I hear what you're saying Adam, but he'll be as mad as hell you know, after all these years, questioning the outcome of his investigation,' replied Frank.

'Yes, I know, and I'm not looking forward to it, but if there has been a miscarriage of justice, for whatever reason, then we must call it out, surely you understand that don't you?'

'Of course, I do boss. I'm just warning you of the possible consequences, Tom's got friends in high places, he plays the political game, and I don't want him to make life difficult for you… Or for me as far as that goes.'

'I'm going to keep your name out of this, you were a uniformed officer at the time, it wasn't your responsibility to bring Daniel Ashby to justice, you were only doing what you were told to do.'

There was a pause in the communication before Frank replied.

'Okay Adam, so I'll see you in the morning, first thing, I'll get the team together for the briefing and we can review any further progress. Just one more thing before I go… *Do* you think we have a Serial Killer on the loose or just a madman… Or woman?'

'Let's talk about it tomorrow, have a good evening.'

Switching off his mobile, Adam had only just noticed that Viv had walked into the lounge, he walked over and gave her a huge hug.

'I'm sorry sweetheart, it's the final call of the evening, promise.'

'Have you heard from Sarah Ward at all today? She left me a text message earlier this afternoon.'

'No, but my phone has been on and off most of the day, you've probably picked up from my conversation, that there's been another killing, this time in Nottingham.'

Viv opened her mobile phone, typing in the code. 'Take a look at this,'

Adam scanned the text message, then read it once more.

Viv couldn't control her emotions anymore.

'What do you think it means, a breakthrough, do you think it's to do with Scarlett's disappearance, have they found something, have they found our beautiful daughter? Anything Adam… anything.'

'This is D.S Sarah Ward, I'm sorry I'm unable to take your call, but if you leave your name and number, I'll get back to you as soon as I can, thanks for your call.'

'Sarah, this is Adam Fox, we've just picked up your text message to Vivian. Can you please call me back on this number as soon as you can? I'd appreciate it, thanks Sarah.'

'Have you eaten? Asked Viv, 'I don't know if I fancy anything, but I'll get you something if you like. Maybe a pizza, there's one in the freezer.'

'I'll get it, why don't you sit down, try and relax and I'll get you a glass of wine, how does that sound?'

There was already a half bottle of Chardonnay opened in the door of the fridge, he got out a glass and poured Viv a drink, taking it back into the lounge.

'Here you go, get that down your neck, I'll put the pizza in the oven, get myself a beer and I'll be right back.'

He flipped the top off the beer bottle, and as it spanned around on the work surface Adam considered in his mind the content of the text message.

Was there a breakthrough? And if yes, what did that mean?

He returned to the lounge, beer bottle in hand, Viv was just sitting there, staring into the wine glass.

'Viv, I don't know what Sarah has found out, and I'm sorry if I missed her call to me, but at least she's got back to us, all we've got to do is wait to hear from her and see what she's got to say.'

Viv didn't answer immediately, then replied. 'I know, but the waiting is killing me, all this time Adam, not knowing what has happened to our daughter, and then when there is a possible breakthrough, Sarah's words not mine, neither of us was there to pick up the call, what does that tell you?'

'It tells me that we both love our daughter very, very much and that we will never give up hope of finding her alive. However, life does go on, and I'm not saying that missing Sarah's call doesn't matter, of course, it does, she'll come back to me just as soon as she possibly can, both she and Chris Mitchell are on our side you know, never forget that.'

The timer on the oven seemed to make a louder-than-normal buzzing sound, announcing that the pizza was ready, Adam made his way to the kitchen, the smell making him feel rather hungry.

His mobile phone rang. It was Sarah Ward's name on the screen. He pressed the green button and answered the call.

Fifty-six

BOTH VIVIAN AND ADAM HAD'NT slept well at all. They'd stayed up talking until the early hours, only agreeing to go to bed when Viv suggested they would be tired in the morning if they didn't get some sleep.

The alarm clock announced it was time to get up, the bedside clock read, 6:30 a.m. Adam showered first, followed by Viv which took longer as she had to dry her long blond hair.

Normal conversation over breakfast would have been about their day ahead, but today, it was all about the text message from Sarah Ward the day before.

Adam had promised to call Sarah just as soon as he got into the office, giving her time to arrive at South Yorkshire Central Station, or he'd call her on her mobile on the way to work. He explained that if he couldn't get hold of her, then he'd give Chris Mitchell a call, he'd know what was going on it was hoped.

By twenty past seven Adam was at his desk, he'd collected his second cup of coffee from the machine downstairs, stirring it, but it still looked like vegetable soup. Switching on his computer, he checked his email, noticing one from Tom Vickers, it read.

Adam, I would like to meet with you in my office at 08:30 this morning, I've sent you a meeting request, please accept and I'll see you then, Tom.

He checked his watch, *'Time to call Sarah,'* he said out loud.

Sarah's mobile phone connected and on the fourth ring she picked it up, 'Adam, good morning, this is Sarah Ward, I've been trying to get hold of you since yesterday.'

'Yes I know Sarah, I'm sorry, I was tied up on a case and had my mobile switched off, however, Vivian has explained the text you sent to her, something about a breakthrough, or possible breakthrough, is that right?'

'Well yes, I've got some new information on Scarlett's disappearance. But I don't want to discuss it over the phone, is it possible for the three of us to meet up, preferably down your way this time if that's convenient?'

Adam wasn't sure what the comment meant but agreed in principle.

'Sarah, that's fine, Vivian and I will work around your commitments, we could do it later this afternoon if that's okay, or maybe meet for an early dinner at a local pub, what's best for you?'

'I'm tied up for most of the day, but an early dinner sounds great, it'll be good to get out of the flat for a change, shall we say five thirty, how does that sound?'

Adam scribbled the time on a Derbyshire Police jotter pad on his desk. 'I'll contact Vivian, I'm sure that's going to be fine, I'll find a pub not too far from the M1 and book a table for three, I'll text you the address and the actual time if it's different to what we've agreed. Is there anything you can tell me beforehand; I'm sure Vivian will ask?'

'Let's wait until we see each other later.' With that, the line went dead.

Fifty-seven

ADAM DECIDED NOT TO TEXT VIV, but to call her at the medical centre. He checked his watch, it was only ten past eight, so she wouldn't have any patient appointments until later.

'Good morning Edgewater Medical Centre, you're speaking with Joanne, how may I help you?'

He was quite surprised that he hadn't been put on hold in a queue, normally, that's what usually happens when you ring for a GP appointment.

Viv asked Joanne to transfer the call. 'Adam is everything all right, have you talked to Sarah yet?'

'Yes, I have, and we've arranged to meet up later today, I've suggested five thirty at a local pub if that's okay with you. I'll book the table and go back to Sarah with the details.'

For a moment Adam thought he'd been cut off as Viv didn't answer. 'Are you there, did you hear what I said?'

'Sorry darling, I was just thinking what Sarah is going to say, will it be good news, and what does a breakthrough mean, are we going to be any nearer to finding our daughter?'

Adam knew that the disappearance of Scarlett almost four years ago had ripped the heart out of Viv, it was hard for any *father* to lose a child, but for the mother, it was almost impossible to describe how they must feel. She didn't openly display her emotions, but he knew that underneath that hard exterior, she continued to blame herself.

Her chosen career as a medical doctor had exposed her to life's encounters that some people can only begin to imagine, dementia, drug reliance, and childhood cancer. But whatever had happened to Scarlett for Viv remained difficult to grasp.

'Let's hear what Sarah has to say when we see her later, I'll text her the details and pick you up at work around five o'clock, will it be okay to leave your car overnight there and I'll drop you off tomorrow morning?'

'That'll be fine, I'll let Peter know about leaving my car in the car park, the security cameras will keep an eye on it overnight, and there's a barrier anyway, see you later, love you.'

As Adam began to text Sarah with the meeting details, his office phone rang, picking it up, thinking it was Frank, he answered.

'I'll be with you Frank in two minutes, are the team ready?'

'Adam, this is Tom Vickers, we have a meeting organized for eight thirty, it's now twenty to nine and I'm waiting in my office, can you come down now please?'

As he made his way down the corridor to the DCI's office, he tried to run through in his mind what the meeting could be about, was Frank right, did Tom Vickers have friends in high places? '*Shit,*' he said under his breath, I should be meeting Frank and the team in the incident room right now.

Tom Vicker's door was slightly ajar, he was sitting at his desk when he saw Adam at the door.

'Come in Adam, thanks for coming, I'm sorry to drag you away, but there's a couple of things I need to chat with you about.'

Adam moved the office chair back from the desk and made himself comfortable, then replied.

'I'm sorry I'm a bit late, there's been a possible development with Scarlett's disappearance, and I had to call Vivian to check something out. Also, if you don't mind, can we make this quick, I've got a briefing meeting with Frank and the team following events from yesterday?'

Tom picked up his pen and started rolling it through his fingers, a senior psychologist once explained to Adam that this was a typical sign of someone nervous, unsure of a situation, concerned about creating conflict or telling downright lies.

'Don't worry about the briefing, I've already spoken to Frank and he's going to brief the team and you later on, and I hope whatever the news is on Scarlett, that it's what you and Vivian have been waiting for. No, what I wanted to chat about was DCI Craig Slater and EMSCO, you met him I understand yesterday in Nottingham.

He'd already called me to explain the situation and asked for your assistance, which I granted straight away. Did *you* know that Ross Sullivan had been linked to an organized drugs gang in Nottingham? EMSCO had been keeping him under surveillance for nearly two years now, that's why Craig Slater's got involved.'

When he arrived at the crime scene, Adam had wondered how someone like Ross Sullivan could afford the exclusive luxury apartment, expensive furniture, the Bang and Olufsen stereo, and also why someone from EMSCO would get involved in a suspected murder case but discounted the fact that it could be based on the probable link to other crimes.

'Obviously, you'll continue to report directly to me, but you've now got a dotted line to DCS Slater, I expect you to give him your full support, and to keep me in the loop on everything, is that clear?'

Finally putting his pen down on the desk, Tom looked Adam straight in the face. 'I understand having spoken to Craig Slater this morning, that there seems to be a connection between the murder in Nottingham and that of Patricia Locke, is that correct?'

'I believe there are sufficient similarities between the two killings to make that a direct possibility. Dr Rachel Munroe, you know Rachel of old don't you? She's attended both crime scenes and in her opinion, the parallels between the two cannot be ignored. It's the markings on the victims' foreheads, Patricia Locke had what looked like a number two carved into her, and Ross Sullivan yesterday, he had a distinct number three carved into his face.'

Tom looked down at his desk, opening a folder in front of him, picking up his pen once more, he ran down the pages until he found what he was looking for.

'I've pulled the file on Arthur Richardson, there's not a huge amount of information in there, but, interestingly, did you know that *he had* carved on his forehead, marks that evidence photographs show what could resemble a number, a number one.'

As Adam stood and made his way to the office door, Tom Vickers called him back. 'Adam, just a minute, you may as well take this, you're probably going to need it.'

He handed over the file to Arthur Richardson.

Fifty-eight

FRANK BAILEY MADE HIS WAY from the staff canteen with two cups of strong white coffee and two KitKats, just as Adam arrived back in his office.

'Here you go boss, I thought you'd want a drink and some chocolate, how did it go, did he give you a hard time?'

Adam sat at his desk, going through in his mind the meeting he'd just had with Tom Vickers, it wasn't what he'd expected, and started wondering if there was a hidden agenda here. Or was he overthinking it?

Frank put the coffee and the KitKats on the desk and pulled up one of the two chairs situated in front of the desk.

'Actually Frank, it went better than I expected, I thought I was in for a bit of a bollocking, but he was quite calm. He wanted to update me on the killing yesterday of Ross Sullivan, and more importantly, how, I'm sorry, we are going to work with DCS Slater at EMSCO. Have you ever been involved with this high-level unit before?'

'Never, but I did recognise the DCS though, but I've no idea where I've seen him before, maybe in one of the internal police journals that get handed around, *but* he does seem a highflyer.'

'Well, get used to it, because I've explained to Tom Vickers that if I'm going to be involved with EMSCO, then you are too. It took a bit of persuasion, but in the end, he was fine with it, he's going to update Craig Slater later himself.'

Frank picked up his coffee cup taking a big gulp.

'Sorry I didn't make the briefing, but I understand you handled it anyway, any further updates from anyone?'

Frank opened the folder he'd bought in with him, 'Well, if we're talking about Patricia Locke, there's no further progress at all, all current leads, and there haven't been many, have delivered nothing. We've just come to a dead end. In connection to yesterday and the murder of Ross Sullivan, being honest, I didn't go into great detail at the briefing. It wasn't on our patch, not sure what Tom Vickers and Craig Slater had agreed between themselves, I wasn't going to step on anyone's toes believe me.'

'You did right Frank, I need to take some direction from DCI Slater and what is our potential next move, until then, we need to concentrate on finding everything else we can about Patricia Locke, don't know what it is, but we're missing something here. One interesting point, DCI Vickers is coming around to accepting that there could be a link between the murder of Arthur Richardson, all those years ago, Patricia Locke and yesterday's butchering of Ross Sullivan. He's just handed over the file to me, he didn't go into detail about Daniel Ashby, but I think our assumptions are correct, he *was* innocent.'

As soon as Frank had left the office, he picked up the two empty cups of coffee, and gently closing the door behind him, Adam opened the brown folder Tom Vickers had handed him.

The smell of old paper wafted up towards his nose as he scanned the document on Arthur Richardson.

The head and shoulders photograph of him didn't do him any favours, he looked older than the sixty-three years recorded. He was employed at Derbyshire County Council as a finance officer, until taking early retirement at the age of sixty. Apparently, he'd always lived in the same village and had never been married. Tom was right, there were marks on Arthur Richardson's forehead, and it did resemble the look of a number one figure, but that wasn't the only thing that startled him, as he continued to read the report, his eyes came across one sentence, a sentence that confirmed in his mind that all these killings were connected.

Petals… rose petals were found scattered around the body of Arthur Richardson.

Fifty-nine

THE OFFICE FELT HUMID as he opened the window and took a couple of deep breaths. Going back to his desk Adam opened the drawer, took out and updated the logbook, checking all the critical points that Frank, the full investigation team, and himself had found out and electronically recorded.

He was struggling to concentrate, too much coffee, probably. He must remember to tell Frank that he now only drinks black coffee, he's going to lose a few pounds, but keep bringing the KitKats.

His mind began to wonder what Sarah Ward was going to tell him and Viv when they met later in the day, and more to the point, how was Viv going to react. He'd text Sarah the location of the pub. The Shepherds Rest, located just off the M1, Junction 28, and Viv to finally confirm the pickup time from the medical centre.

Looking back down at the folder on his desk, arguably by now, a picture would be emerging on the murder of Patricia Locke, but with little progress made, and no new leads, it was time to acknowledge that the three murders – Arthur Richardson, Patricia Locke and Ross Sullivan yesterday, could all conceivably be linked?

Removing a rusty paperclip from the front page, he took the image of Arthur Richardson to the photocopier on the far side of his office, lifting the lid and pressing the button for COPY.

It was twenty past four when he next looked at his watch, he'd agreed to collect Viv at five thirty, hopefully, the traffic shouldn't be too heavy, but he wanted to give himself enough time, he couldn't afford to be late, not for this meeting anyway.

Closing his office window, Adam made his way down the corridor, purposely passing the incident room.

Although the door was slightly open, there remained a distinct smell of body odour, probably triggered by the heat coming through the open blind windows.

At the front of the room was the whiteboard, several names had been written in black felt tip pen, one included Daniel Ashby, which had been underlined, together with lines linking the names.

Adam picked up one of the small magnetic disks and placed Arthur Richardson's image next to Patricia Locke's, taking the black felt tip pen and purposely drawing a black line connecting the two images. He stood there for several seconds, contemplating when Ross Sullivan's name and photograph would be added.

Sixty

VIV WAS STANDING OUTSIDE the medical centre as Adam pulled into the car park. Driving forward, reversing into a space, and then pulling up right in front of the main entrance, noticing for the first time the security cameras scattered around the building.

Before Viv got into the car, he turned off Spotify and The Beatles track playing, YESTERDAY, it was the wrong thing to be listening to, he thought to himself.

As he'd joined the A38 to drive to the GP practice, he'd considered calling Craig Slater. From what he understood about the DCS, he encouraged his team to take the initiative and be proactive. Even though Adam wasn't officially one of the full-time squad for the investigation into the murder of Ross Sullivan, legitimately, he was one of the boys, at least for now.

Considering whether to make the call, he turned on Spotify selecting The Beatles soundtracks.

LET IT BE came up, and glancing at the clock on the dashboard, which read 4:55 p.m. he decided that tomorrow morning would be better. After all, it was the DCS who would set the ground rules for his involvement.

Viv opened the back door to the Audi and placed her laptop in between the seats, making sure it was out of sight, they'd discussed several nights ago about the number of recorded thefts from vehicles where laptops had been left in plain sight.

She leaned over and gave him a peck on the left cheek, as she strapped herself into the front seat.

'So, what sort of day have you had?' she asked, 'hope it's been productive. Peter called me to see him earlier on, to go over the final details of the partnership, it's all fine by the way.'

'Well, that's good news, when do we have to transfer the money?' asked Adam.

'I've given the solicitor all the information, and they'll make the transfer as required, probably in the next couple of days.'

Adam still had some reservations about taking a loan from Viv's parents, but she *was* their only child, so it did make some sense he guessed.

'Interestingly, he was telling me earlier today about how he came to be running Edgewater Medical Centre, it was his fathers. He started the practice years earlier, but unfortunately, passed away very suddenly from a massive heart attack, leaving Peter and his mum. They only had one son, so Peter inherited the business as such, and took overall control, making changes, by expanding the footprint of the building and over time, expanding the patient number and subsequently, the medical team.'

For several moments neither Adam nor Viv said anything, just the sound of Steve Wright on radio two in the background, Adam deciding not to talk about *his* day at work.

The digital clock in the car read 17:17 so they were a little early for the meeting with Sarah. It would give them time to find a suitable table somewhere away from the main restaurant where they could talk confidentially.

As they were shown to their table, DS Sarah Ward arrived and made her way through the restaurant to join them.

She was dressed in a dark trouser suit, pale blue blouse and matching blue shoes, giving the appearance that she'd dressed for the occasion rather than just coming from work.

'Hello, you two, it's so nice to see you both again. Thanks for agreeing to meet here, it's convenient for me as one of my best friends lives nearby, just outside Mansfield actually, so I'm going to call in and see her later.'

'It's good to see you too,' said Adam 'How is everything going at Sheffield, is Chris keeping well?'

'I think Chris is fine. To be honest, I don't see him much at the moment, he's tied up on a big drugs case. Coming down into your part of the world, Derbyshire. They're using the M1 motorway as a run down from Leeds to London, it's becoming known as the number one drug route. They leave early in the morning, travel down, drop off the goods and then back home by early afternoon, no questions asked. I have a fortnightly review meeting with him on all the cases I'm working on, including Scarlett's, other than that, he leaves me to my own devices.'

Adam picked up one of the menus on the table, 'Well, you must be doing something right then Sarah, that's Chris's style, let's you get on with it, that's the way you learn.'

After making their choice of food, and taking note of the table number, Adam walked over to the bar and ordered, waiting whilst the drinks were prepared, two white wines and a pint of lime and soda for Adam, still keeping an eye on his waistline.

He turned back and noticed that Viv and Sarah were already in deep conversation, the expression on their faces giving nothing away.

As he sat back down, he picked up the thread of the conversation.

'And so, when I got back to my desk, there was a message on the office phone. It was from the chap who ran the fruit and veg shop on the road opposite the gate to your back garden… Sorry, Adam, I was just explaining to Viv about the call from the man who ran the shop.'

Before Adam had time to reply, Viv asked.

'What did he have to say?'

'Well, it's interesting. If you recall, he was going on holiday the following day, so he was hurrying about trying to get everything done before the shop closed. He'd remembered the car and the two people in the front with what he described as baseball caps or similar.'

'I remember that Sarah, we've discussed that previously,' Adam interjected, then realising that may have sounded too harsh.

'Yes, I know, and that's in the case notes. But following the phone message, I've been over to interview Mr Walters, and he now remembers an incident that he'd forgotten all about.'

Just as Sarah was about to go into more detail, the food arrived, a large tray and stand placed at the side of their table.

'One chicken fajita, one hamburger, no fries, and one steak and salad,' said the server. 'Does anyone want any sauces or anything else? If not, enjoy your meal.'

'Thanks,' they all said in unison, picking up their cutlery.

'What Mr Walters now recalls is that he saw two men, he described them as casually dressed, walking up and down the opposite side of the road, intermittently trying to look into your back garden through the broken fence panels. He then recalls a loud noise; he thought it was a car backfiring but now realises that it could have been the gate being forced.'

'Would he recognise the men if he saw them again? Asked Viv.

'Well, you're talking almost four years ago, so whatever they looked like then, you can bet your bottom dollar, they won't look like that now.'

'Is that it, nothing else? said Viv, regretting the comment immediately.

'No, there's something else, something that throws more light on Scarlett's disappearance. The shop owner also recalls a woman carrying a small child in her arms, towards a waiting car. Nothing strange about that normally, except that the man who held the back door open, was, he believes, one of the men who was walking up and down the road earlier.'

'So, you now believe Scarlett was taken from the back garden by a woman, possibly opportunistic? Said Adam, attempting to understand what Sarah was trying to get at.

'And what's Chris Mitchel's take on this, has he any thoughts on what might have taken place?'

Sarah considered her response for several moments then replied.

'I mentioned it to Chris last week and he had the same opinion as me. We now believe that Scarlett's disappearance wasn't opportunistic as you've described, nor a spare-of-the-moment decision.

No, looking at the evidence that we have so far, which to be frank is limited, Scarlett was taken against her will, but for whatever reason, we have no idea.'

'We believe it was organised, previously arranged in the way she was taken, deviously planned. We now believe your daughter was taken to order.'

Sixty-one

IT WAS WELL INTO THE NIGHT before Viv and Adam managed to get some sleep, the time they'd spent with Sarah had raised more questions than it had answered.

The journey back home was only filled with silence, neither of them wanting to talk, unable to get their heads around what they'd heard, but Adam was now beginning to wonder if they'd see their daughter ever again, alive or dead.

They decided to collect Viv's Skoda from the medical practice to avoid Adam having to make the journey the following morning.

Peter had also arranged for a company to come in and conduct some advanced PC training, following an upgrade to their computer systems, which started at eight-fifteen sharp, Peter Johnson was a particularly good boss, but a real stickler for timing.

Viv looked tired Adam thought, as they sat in the kitchen, having their usual breakfast, homemade muesli, fat-free yogurt and black coffee, he'd made a mental note not to tell Viv about the KitKats.

Typically for Derbyshire, the weather consisted of sunny periods, thunderstorms and heavy rain, which resulted in the traffic being heavier than normal.

Adam made his way to Derbyshire Police HQ, and for once he welcomed the delay, it gave him time to go over in his mind what he was going to do next.

Organized gangsters were often known to seek retribution on the people that grassed them up, if they couldn't get to them, they'd target their immediate family, there were a lot more families with new identities than the general population knew about.

But why would someone want to take his daughter, they weren't wealthy, not unless someone knew more about Viv's parents.

Her father held a senior position at Sheffield University, as the Professor of Economics until he retired about three years ago, now doing the odd lecture for a ridiculously high daily fee.

Her mum was a senior partner in a law firm in Coalville, Leicestershire. Until recently, she practised a couple of days a week, so, yes, in most people's eyes, they would be seen as financially secure.

Viv was their only daughter, ever since they both met, some of his friends, including Chris Mitchel and his wife, had always teased him about her being a good catch in more ways than one.

Parking his car as near to the main entrance as possible, he pulled up the collar on his dark blue suit, entered the building, showed his security pass to the officer on duty, and made his way up the stairs from reception.

Turning immediately left towards the staff canteen, avoiding the drinks machine, and ordering a black coffee from one of the catering staff, who greeted him with a smile, saying 'Good morning to you sir.'

His sidekick, Frank had requested to take another day's holiday, so that he and Julie could move her mum into The Lakes, which Adam had authorized.

He wanted to get the whole team together but agreed with Frank that he needed to take a sounding from DCS Slater before involving anyone else, making a note on a yellow POST IT NOTE, to call him, sticking it on the edge of his computer screen.

If Scarlett's disappearance was for financial gain, which when he thought about it, sounded preposterous, they'd have heard something months or even years ago… Then it must be connected to either Viv or himself.

He remembered when she was a GP at the Sheffield Central Medical Practice, only because she hadn't been there very long, there was one occasion when she had to have a mother and son removed from where they lived, due to domestic abuse.

The police were called, and the man was arrested, threatening in temper, to get his own back, as Adam recalls, then being released on bail several days later.

So, there's a motive, he thought to himself. Losing his son and having his collar felt by the police, *was that* a reason, possibly, but unlikely?

Was it something that *he'd* been associated with whilst at South Yorkshire Division? He'd been involved in several high-profile cases. Organised crime, prostitution, drug smuggling, to name just three.

The main one was when they uncovered thousands of pounds worth of cocaine coming in from Amsterdam into Hull, transported along the M18 to Sheffield or Leeds and then sold on.

After nearly two and a half years of investigation, including some of his team going undercover, the gang had finally been brought down, the key people involved were all doing time, scattered in high-security prisons across the country, not scheduled to be released for years, and from what Sarah Ward was saying, it sounded like Chris Mitchell was continuing the fight.

But the ringleader, the person or person's calling all the shots, making all the money, the brains behind the organization, well, they were never brought to justice. Early release bargaining with some of the offenders was offered but never taken up, either through loyalty or the sheer fear of retaliation. Adam and some other senior officers always knew and understood that there was no such thing as absolute safety or protection against thugs in a high-security prison.

It was over four years now since Scarlett had gone missing from the garden at the back of the house, one minute everything was fine, and the next she was gone.

He avoided going over the same thing repeatedly, it didn't make any difference, he was only punishing himself.

If only he'd not gone upstairs to have a shower, if Viv had tidied the dining room later that afternoon if he'd mended all the broken fence panels, which his father-in-law had offered to do, if only, if only, if only.

The ping on his mobile phone brought him back from his deep thought pattern, he typed in his code and read the message, it was from DCS Slater.

Hi Adam, I've just spoken with DCI Vickers and we've both agreed that we need to run a parallel investigation on this murder case. Can you please arrange to meet me at EMSCO headquarters tomorrow at 9:10 a.m.? I would also like DS Frank Bailey to attend. Thanks, Craig Slater.

Adam immediately called Frank's mobile, and as expected, it went to voice mail, he left a message about the meeting, suggesting that they meet at Central Derbyshire HQ and travel in together, he'd never been there before, so safety in numbers.

It was dark when he finally left the office, placing a call to Viv's mobile as he walked across the car park, she picked up on the third ring.

'Hi sweetheart, how are you, you OK?'

'What time will you be home?'

'Just leaving now, so should be with you in about thirty minutes, traffic permitting. Is everything all right?'

Viv sounded strangely on edge like she didn't know what to say down the phone to Adam.

'Are you okay? You don't sound your normal self.'

The line went silent for several seconds, and then Viv replied.

'I was fine until I came upstairs and popped my head into what was going to be Scarlett's bedroom, it's brought it all back to me, the day she went missing. I should have kept an eye on her, not left her, not for a second. And now look, from what Sarah said last night, it's unlikely we'll ever see our daughter again… and please don't tell me we will. That will just make things worse.'

For the first time in years, Adam didn't know what to say. Viv was normally the positive one, the one who always approached issues with an open mind, normally using a clinical paradigm as a solution.

'I'm going to be home soon, let's talk more about it then, *try* not to get upset. I'll be there soon, love you loads,' and with that, the call ended.

He parked at the side of Viv's Skoda, placing his hand on the bonnet, it was stone cold, she'd arrived home early.

Walking into the hall, and closing the front door, he expected her to be upstairs, calling her name, but instead, she was curled up on the settee in the lounge, her eyes red and wet with tears, mascara leaving dark lines down her face.

He knew that at some point since Scarlett's disappearance, they'd have to have a difficult conversation about what may happen in the future, and where do they go from here.

Hundreds of parents lose their children, every year, many through enormously tragic circumstances, some of which both Viv and Adam had first-hand experience of, but that didn't make it any easier.

Taking off his jacket, he undid the top button of his shirt, easing the knot of his tie down, deliberately sitting at the side of her, as close as he could, letting her rest her head on his shoulder.

Viv's body began to shake, and for the first time, he realised just how vulnerable she had become, a vulnerability which was hard to control.

Sixty-two

THE LAKES NURSING HOME looked stately in the sunlight, the front glass window reflecting the rays, like dragon's eyes looking down on them.

Frank and Julie drove down the tarmacked drive, slowing over the bumps, parking their car in the gravelled visitors' space.

His mother-in-law wasn't a good backseat passenger. She wasn't a good traveller at all, and the last thing Frank wanted was her throwing up on the rear seats.

Earlier in the day, Frank and Julie had arrived at her mum's bungalow, it hadn't been the difficult conversation with Julie's mum as they'd expected. Sitting down in her lounge, Julie noticed a slight whiff of urine masked by a smell of disinfectant in the air.

They'd explained earlier in the week that life was clearly becoming increasingly difficult for her at home, and maybe the time had come for her to look at moving into a brand-new home, a home where people, including her daughter and son-in-law, could look after her.

To give them some space, Frank went into the kitchen and made some tea, they'd brought some milk with them, as the last time they were there, it had gone off in the fridge. When he came back, Julie's mum was chatting and smiling away, seemingly happy to be making the move to the nursing home.

It had rained the night before, giving the stonework to the front of the house, a glow, almost resembling the look of granite.

As the three of them got out of the car, Frank noticed two other vehicles, a private ambulance and a Black Ford Ranger nearby, two people inside, he observed that they were having what looked like an in-depth conversation. As he looked more closely, he recognised the passenger as Daniel Ashby sitting in the front seat, next to a man of similar age.

As they made their way to the front of the house, a female stood at the door, stepping down to greet them.

She looked around mid-forties, dressed in a dark blue uniform, dark tights, and black slip-on shoes. Frank immediately recognised her from their previous meeting and noticed again the name badge, Karen Latimer, Senior Matron.

She knew who Julie's mum was and held out her hand, smiling warmly and welcoming her to The Lakes Nursing Home.

'I'm going to go with Mum to her room,' Julie said, turning to Frank. 'Would you mind going to the main office and sorting out the final bits of paperwork, there's just the standing order payment to check and sign, I think everything else is covered.'

'That's fine, shall I come to your mum's room or see you outside?'

With tears in her eyes, Julie replied, 'I'll see you at the front of the house, I just need a few minutes with Mum on our own if that's okay?'

As the three of them made their way down the brightly lit corridor, Frank noticed Julie put her arm around her mum, squeezing her shoulder.

He made his way to the front of the house, checking his mobile phone, noticing that the Black Ford Ranger was still in the car park. JJ GARDENING AND LANDSCAPE SERVICES advertised on the muddy door panel.

Daniel Ashby and the other man stood side by side, talking and pointing at something towards the lake in the distance.

Frank wasn't sure how long Julie would be, so after several minutes, he walked over to the two of them and said, 'Hello.'

Although they had their backs to him, it was Joe who first heard the rustle of gravel as Frank came closer, turning round, as Danny noticed who it was.

'Hi, Detective Sergeant Bailey,' he said, 'have to come to ask me some more questions, or just following me around to see what I'm up to?'

Frank didn't rise to the bait replying.

'Mr Ashby, it's nice to see you again, and no, I'm not following you and don't have any further questions. I'm here with my wife on a personal matter. But I'm glad I bumped into you. My boss, Detective Inspector Fox has asked me to thank you again for giving up your time and coming to see us. I hope it wasn't too inconvenient, and we appreciate the information you gave us about the current case we're working on. At the moment, we don't believe we'll have to speak with you again, if that does change, then clearly we'll be back in touch… What brings you to The Lakes Nursing Home… I'm just inquisitive, there's nothing intentional in my question?'

'That's okay Sergeant. I understand you have a job to do, but I want to move on, get my life back in order and forget what happened in the past. Sorry, I should have introduced you, this is Joe Jackson, a colleague of mine, we've been doing some landscaping work here, and we're just checking the completed job before Joe sends them the final invoice. It's been quite a long project, redesigning the front garden, installing a fountain and making sure the whole outlook at the front of the house is as the Managing Director wanted. Although I say it myself, I think we've done a great job.'

Joe pulled out a business card, 'Here's our contact details, if you ever want any gardening service Detective Sergeant, give us a call.'

Frank held the card in his hand and was just about to reply when Julie called him to see if he was ready to leave.

Heading back to the car, he turned around to face both men, 'Thanks for the contact details, I'll keep you in mind, good to see you again Daniel, Joe, nice to meet you too.'

Walking back to the 4x4 Joe wanted to ask Danny what DS Bailey was talking about, he'd told him that he'd been interviewed by the police, and said that he'd tell him some other time, maybe he still didn't want to talk about it.

Deciding not to ask any questions, avoiding looking directly at Danny, he looked through the dusty windscreen towards the front of the house.

'Did you know, before this was a care home, nursing home, or whatever it is, it was a boarding school? I'm going back years now, but I spent some of my time here when I was younger. When my mum and dad died, I went to live with my godparents, Uncle Charles, and Auntie Cynthia. They weren't my relatives, but Charles was my dad's best friend and accepted the responsibility of taking care of me, they were great and welcomed me into their family like I was one of their own.'

'Both had demanding jobs and spent time away from home, so together with their other boy, we went to this boarding school, Chaffing House. I was much older and only attended for two terms, leaving at sixteen, and getting a job at a local garden centre, that's how I got into the landscaping business. Whilst at the school some of the boys used to describe what went on with the members of staff, horrible things, punishments, abuse, and mistreatment. It's a time in my life I prefer to forget now.'

Danny knew that Joe's parents had been killed in a tragic car accident some years previous. All three were travelling on the M1 northbound back from London when the tyre on an articulated lorry burst. It crossed the centre reservation and ploughing into their car, killing his parents at the scene. Joe was seated in the back of the vehicle and wasn't injured, apart from a few scratches.

Being an only child, he went on to inherit the family home, death in service from his parents' employers and savings and investments, allowing him to set up his business.

As Joe looked up at the front of The Lakes Nursing Home, he turned to Danny, 'I wonder what secrets continue to lie behind that old wooden door?

Sixty-three

ADAM CHECKED HIS SMART watch as they walked out of Central Derbyshire HQ, and across the car park to his Audi.

It was twenty-past eight in the morning, Frank had arrived much earlier in the day, he'd got a pile of paperwork to catch up on having been off the day before with Julie and her mum.

On the way back from The Lakes, they chatted about how they would manage things in the coming weeks, regarding visiting duties and more importantly, the funding for her mum's care.

The bungalow was already on the market with a local agent, who gave the impression that it could sell reasonably quickly, particularly if it was priced competitively, which both Julie and Frank agreed to.

It did want some work done to it, rewiring, and new heating, but according to the agent, it was an ideal property to invest in, renovate, and then potentially sell on.

In the meantime, her mum did have some funds available to bridge the gap whilst the sale hopefully went through, so money at this stage wasn't an issue.

Local radio was playing as they joined the southbound M1 at junction 28. Storm clouds drifted over as they followed the directions that Craig Slater had emailed with the location of EMSCO.

'Is this the best we've got to listen to?' chimed up Frank. 'I thought you were a Beatles fan; can't we have some quality music in the car?'

Adam opened Spotify and selected the Beatles' assorted tracks, YELLOW SUBMARINE started playing, followed by YESTERDAY.

'Hey that reminds me, I saw Daniel Ashby at the nursing home when we dropped off Julie's mum. He's been doing landscaping work there with a friend, a Joe Johnson, no sorry, Joe Jackson. Hope you don't mind, I explained that we won't need to talk with him again, but if we do, he seemed fairly unperturbed by it.'

'Yeah, that's fine, I think we both now know that he'd nothing to do with the murder of Arthur Richardson. The pressure would be on to get a result, resources would be limited, even in those days, and Daniel Ashby fit the frame as far as Tom Vickers was concerned. Even though he conceded that mistakes were made, the investigation *was* rushed, so he handed the file over to us. Taking the pressure off him just in case Mr Ashby takes it any further. It's now our responsibility to check the similarities between that murder and the ones we are now working on. If I'm right, and I hope to God I'm not, whoever murdered Patricia Locke, and potentially, Ross Sullivan, also murdered Arthur Richardson all those years ago. The question we've now got to ask ourselves is.'

'Why do it? Who did it, and will there be any more?'

Sixty-four

THE DIRECTIONS CRAIG Slater had emailed Adam instructed them to leave the M1 south at Junction 25. Then take the third junction on the left towards the village of Sandiacre and the Holiday Inn.

Turn right at the second junction just before the hotel and follow the signs for East Midlands Storage.

They pulled up outside what looked like a run-down office block just as the heavens opened, torrential rain beating down on the roof of the Audi.

Wiping mist from the side window, Frank could see several old wooden pallets which stood outside the building, the wind lifting remnants of plastic sheeting, and also noticed three cars, an old silver Vauxhall Omega, a Ford Mondeo and a Transit van, parked right outside. The van supports a red and white logo on the side panel, EMS – East Midlands Storage.

Adam kept the engine running, ensuring the front windows didn't steam up too much. 'Are you sure this is the place?' asked Frank, 'I thought the old HQ in Derby was bad enough, but this looks derelict.'

'This is what DCS Slater sent me yesterday, I don't think he'd give us the wrong location, do you?'

Frank took a second look, then replied.

'Probably not, there's only one way to find out, and that's to take a look.'

Adam checked his watch once again, 9:03 a.m. 'Let's give it a couple more minutes, hopefully the rain will settle, then we'll make a move, I don't want us to be late.'

As quickly as the rain came, it stopped.

As they made their way to the front of the building, finding themselves at the entrance, allowed access by a blue double-glazed door, the bottom panel had been damaged and was boarded up. To the right of the door was what looked like a flimsy intercom system fastened to the wall, with a green button, PRESS FOR INFO.

Frank took the initiative, pressing the button, probably longer than necessary Adam thought.

After several rings, a voice announced. 'EMS how can we help you?'

'Good morning, my name is Adam Fox, I'm here with a colleague, Frank Bailey, we have a meeting with Craig Slater at ten past nine, trust we're at the right location.'

The line went dead, which left Adam wondering if they'd been cut off, then suddenly, there was a loud click, and the blue door opened to allow both of them to enter.

The reception area was smaller than they expected, with a frosted glass sliding panel to the left, two black plastic chairs to the right-hand side, and a smell that Adam couldn't put his finger on.

Expecting the glass panel to open, they were both surprised when a door at the bottom of reception opened, and in front of them stood Craig Slater.

'Gentlemen, good morning, you managed to find us then I see?'

He was casually dressed, dark grey trousers, a white shirt, no tie, but cufflinks, and back loafer shoes.

Both Adam and Frank had agreed to go suited and booted, there was a dress-down policy at police headquarters, but that might not have extended to EMSCO.

He held the door open with his foot, 'Shall we go upstairs, and I'll show you round the place?'

As the three of them made their way up a flight of stairs, the aroma of fresh coffee reached their nostrils. Voices became louder as they reached the top, it wasn't what either Adam or Frank expected.

The floor was completely open plan, with pale blue walls, and a white suspended ceiling, illuminated with bright downlights.

Craig walked over to the coffee machine and poured three drinks into pure white mugs, 'How do you take your coffee?'

'Black no sugar,' replied Adam.

'White two sugars,' replied Frank.

'If you follow me I'll take you to my desk, it's in the corner over there,' pointing to a large desk in the far corner.

As they made their way across the floor, Adam noticed the one-way windows, which reduced the natural light, he also counted around twelve circular workstations, with three desks at each location, casually dressed officers occupied the desks, apart from three vacant ones, all looking at computer screens or heavily involved in paperwork.

Craig pulled a chair from behind his desk and placed it at the end, Adam and Frank sat directly to one side and placed the hot coffee mugs on coasters.

'So, you managed to find us then?' I guess it's not what you expected. EMSCO don't have an officially recognised Head Quarters. We use *"ghost"* premises as office facilities, which go under fake company names, such as EMS, to remain as covert as possible, we even have a company van for additional impact.

This location covers the northern part of the East Midlands, Nottinghamshire and Derbyshire specifically, we also have alternative locations, similar to this one, to facilitate access to all parts of adjoining forces, generally using unmarked police vehicles, such as the ones outside.'

'Can I ask a quick question,' said Frank, 'What type of cases do you get involved in here, and what's the connection with our investigations?

Craig looked around the room, observing the officers at the workstations. 'That's a good question Frank, and I'll come to that later if I may, in the meantime, I'd like you to go over the current investigation, warts and all.'

Adam glanced up at one of the digital clocks around the room; it read 11:55 a.m. They'd just finished updating DCS Slater on their current investigation.

Both had already decided on the journey down the motorway to cover every detail, if they *were* going to work together, then total transparency was vital.

He showed specific interest in the marking on each victim's forehead, and what did the numbers tell them. More importantly, why was there a gap between the murder of Arthur Richardson? If there was a connection there, what did the rose petals signify? What had they got to do with the victims, if anything at all?

Adam kept the sighting of the baseball cap wearer to himself. Frank knew only about the first one but wasn't aware of the figure outside Ross Sullivan's flat.

After their second cup of coffee and a comfort break, they returned to Frank's original question about what EMSCO did.

'As a general rule, me, and the officers here, get involved in all forms of serious crime, which could be anything from people trafficking, money laundering, gang warfare, to multiple murder investigations, hence our involvement here. We identify, disrupt, and prosecute those individuals or groups causing the most damage to communities in the East Midlands. Actively work with other agencies cross-functionally to plan and prepare for major incidents and equip those agencies with information and knowledge to maximise protection against crime and the criminals involved.'

Several seconds passed as Adam and Frank absorbed what they'd just been told.

'That's a massive operation, DCS Slater,' said Adam, 'so why specifically do you want *us* to get involved?

'Firstly, the murder victims, were they random killings. Or is there some connection between the three of them? It certainly looks that way by the markings. Arthur Richardson, I now understand was the first victim, a number one carved into his forehead, then Patricia Locke, the second victim and finally, Ross Sullivan. All the bodies were mutilated in some form or another, trophies were taken, gathering body parts as mementoes.'

Adam was about to speak, but DCS Slater carried on.

'So, are we looking at a vicious and sadistic killer, someone who's known to the victims, plans in detail their slaying, or just random killings for the sake of it? Is it someone who wants to get noticed, their name on the television, press coverage? We don't know at this stage, that's where you guys come in. You need to continue your investigations into the first two murders and liaise with me directly in connection to the murder of Ross Sullivan.'

'Where do you think Ross Sullivan fits in all of this?' asked Adam.

'Ross Sullivan was on our radar, he'd been under surveillance for months now, and we understand he had direct links with organised drug gangs both in The East Midlands and beyond. Cannabis, cocaine, and heroin specifically, but they were also getting their hands on synthetics, such as methamphetamine and fentanyl, serious stuff.'

'Why didn't you move in on Sullivan?' asked Frank.

'Well, we wanted him to point us to the main ringleaders, and give him enough rope to hang himself, but we then realised he was just a middleman, one of many who just did as they were told, terrified of the consequences if they grassed anyone up. We also identified another person we'd got tabs on.

Again, surveillance for months, and then suddenly, he disappeared. Weeks later his body was found in Sherwood Forest, his tongue had been cut out. He'd been nailed to a tree, his wrists and ankles cut open, and by the time anyone found him, he'd bled to death.'

'My god,' said Frank, 'what sort of individuals are these people?'

'These people Frank are animals; they'll stop at nothing to get what they want and to keep it. It's a business to them, and like any other business, if it gets disrupted or competitors come in, serious actions must be taken. They demand and expect complete loyalty from their people, step out of line and you'll suffer the consequences, in more ways than one.

Sixty-five

TOM VICKERS HUNG UP the phone and eased his chair back, revealing stretched buttons on the bottom of his shirt. His wife had been nagging him for weeks to lose a bit of weight, to no avail. At one time, police officers had one of the higher death rates of any profession, too many late nights, unsocial hours, microwaved food and whiskey in the drawer, a recipe for early death.

As Adam sat in front of the DCI's desk, he reminded himself what Viv had commented about his waistline, 'Must tell Frank, no more KitKats,' he thought to himself.

'That was the senior editors of the two local papers, The Derbyshire Times and The Nottingham Evening Post, I've pulled in a favour and asked them not to cover any stories relating to the current cases. As and when we get a result, they'll be the first to know. But for the moment it's radio silence from both of them. So, how did it go yesterday? You found the place I take it?. I've never been to that location, but I understand it's a sod to find.'

'Yeah, it went fine sir, interesting building from the outside. But once you're in, it's a great operation. DCS Slater took us through what they get involved in, and why he'd asked us to meet him. Ross Sullivan *was* a serious drug dealer or at least supplying drugs. He'd been under surveillance for months, they were hoping that he'd lead EMSCO to the people at the top, but that didn't happen. Maybe he became frightened, scared of what might happen to him if he was arrested, and from what we heard yesterday, you wouldn't want to mess with them.'

'You got involved in drug gangs in Sheffield didn't you?, sent a number of them down if I recall. Do you think there's a connection?

'Not sure if I'm honest with you, these people spread their pursuits far and wide, the ones we took down operated out of Leeds, but we didn't get the ringleader, and from what I heard yesterday, I can see why no would talk.'

'Did he say anything about Arthur Richardson?'

Adam nodded his head from side to side.

'Not specifically, and we didn't raise it either. Whatever evidence there was against Daniel Ashby, with respect sir, was wrong. He didn't murder Arthur Richardson, but I think we should avoid discussing this any further, don't you? Like us, Craig Slater believes that the murders *are* all linked, the marks on the victim's foreheads. And don't forget the rose petals, you'll remember, they were around Patricia Locke's body where she was found, and also in the hallway of Ross Sullivan's flat. We've now agreed to keep each other updated on developments, reading between the lines, I don't think Craig Slater will get too involved, it's just with three outstanding murder cases and one possibly linked to drug gangs, that's meat and veg to EMSCO.'

***

Just as Adam was about to enter the incident room his phone rang.

It was Vivian.

'Hi, it's me, are you free to talk for just a minute?'

'Yes,' Adam replied.

'Might be a bit late home tonight, a pig of a day, but I'll tell you about that later. Shall we go out for a meal? It's ages since we had a night out, thought it would make a change, give us a break from cooking and get us out the house for the evening.'

'Great idea, I'll text you when I'm about to leave, but I'll have to go now, see you later.'

As soon as he'd pressed the red icon on his mobile, he regretted the abruptness of his reply.

He opened the door to the incident room, seeing the two images of the victims on the whiteboard at the far end of the room. Frank had arranged for several tables to be put together, and the assembled team sat around as he sat in a vacant chair next to DS Bailey.

He checked his watch; it was just after 3:00 p.m. as he looked up from the logbook and photograph of Ross Sullivan that he'd collected from his office just before his call from Viv.

'Thanks for joining us everyone. This is now the fourth briefing we've held in connection with the suspected murder of Patricia Locke, as you'll see from the whiteboard, there is an additional image. This is a photograph of Arthur Richardson; he died in what we now understand to be remarkably similar circumstances to Ms Locke, although his death was around fifteen years ago.'

Frank handed out photocopies of Arthur Richardson.

'We now believe Arthur Richardson was the first victim, DS Bailey and I have interviewed the original suspect, who has recently been released from prison, and we now know that he was in fact, innocent.'

Handing our additional copy images of Ross Sullivan, Adam continued.

'We also have some further significant developments, here is a photograph of Ross Sullivan, he was murdered in Nottingham several days ago. Similar MO, to the previous victims, savagely attacked with markings on his forehead and body parts taken as trophies.'

He waited a few minutes for the team to take a closer look at the facial image. 'Following this recent killing, this is now being upscaled into a full-blown investigation, nicknamed Operation Flycatcher. I will remain thc SEO, and continue to report directly to DCI Vickers, and until further notice, a dotted line to a DCS Slater, based in Nottingham. DS Bailey will be your main contact and all relevant details about these cases must continue to be channelled through to him.'

It was 16:37 when Adam looked up at the digital clock on the wall, he wanted to finish the meeting on time, to get home before Viv arrived from work. Date night.

Frank had issued out the responsibilities to the team with one of the offices writing on the top of the whiteboard in black felt tip pen, OPERATION FLYCATCHER.

He stood to his feet, addressing the whole team, 'So, you've all got your assignments, are there any further questions from anyone?'

One of the young officers put down his notebook, raising his hand to indicate he had one.

DS Bailey, have we considered if there were any connections between these three people? For example, did they all belong to the same social media contacts? Were they related in any way? Have any of them had a criminal record, or reported any concerns to the police?

Adam looked up and recognised the young officer, he'd spoken to him at the crime scene, the one whose parents wanted him to go into teaching, 'He's got the makings of a good officer' he thought to himself.

Frank answered, 'That's a good question young man, at the moment we're unaware of any connection between the three victims. Arthur Richardson was sixty-three, widowed and until recently, worked as a financial officer at Derbyshire County Council.

According to the records, his body was found near some open ground not too far from his local pub. Patricia Locke, was sixty-eight, a retired schoolteacher who worked in a local charity shop in Derby City Centre. Big churchgoer, we've already interviewed the Minister who knew her, body found in Blyth woods. Finally, Ross Sullivan, aged forty-eight, is an I.T. manager at a communication company based in Nottingham. His body was found in his flat by his female partner. So, at the moment, there's no clear connection between the three victims apart from what we already know. Oh, and one last point, each corpse had rose petals scattered near or around the body, what that tells us, we're unclear of at the moment.'

Adam looked directly at the young officer who asked the question.

What's your name son?' asked Adam.

'Cartwright sir, P.C Cartwright.'

'Okay, thanks, P.C Cartwright. One further point that you all should be aware of. Ross Sullivan was potentially involved in some form of drug smuggling or supplying drugs. He may have been working for an organised drug gang, which could be related to his death, that's why the Nottingham team are getting involved. And one more point, please keep the rose petals confidential, we don't want anyone outside this room knowing about that, keep it to yourself please.'

Before everyone left the room, for some moments there was total silence, officers looking down at the notes taken, checking their allocated duties, and everyone absorbing the details of Operation Flycatcher.

Sixty-six

'IF YOU DON'T MIND BOSS I'm going to get off. I promised to pick Julie up from the nursing home in, the early days but things have gone well with her mother.'

After the team had left the incident room, Adam picked up the logbook and the two made their way back to his office, normally Frank would pull up a chair, but not today.

'Yeah Frank, that's fine, I'm just going to catch up on some paperwork. I plan to be out of here by five o'clock avoiding any time with Tom Vickers.'

As Frank grabbed the door handle, Adam called him back, 'Oh, and one more thing, don't bring me anymore KitKats until further notice, Viv's put me on a health kick.'

The journey didn't take as long as he thought, arriving home before Viv, and parking the Audi on the left-hand side of the drive. Viv always parked her Skoda 4x4 on the right as she worried about opening the driver's door and damaging Adam's sacred metallic black AUDI A4.

Getting out of the shower, he checked his weight on the scales, he'd lost three more pounds, 'maybe I can go back to the chocolate bars' he thought.

He was dressed in beige casual trousers, a black POLO shirt and a Ralph Loren sweater, and had already booked a taxi to pick them up at 7:00 p.m. taking Viv to one of her favourite restaurants.

Hearing the car pull on the drive, he opened the fridge door and took out an unopened bottle of white wine, twisting the plastic screw cap and pouring two large drinks into cut glass glasses, a wedding present of six, no idea who's brought them.

Opening the front door, Viv leaned her laptop case against the wall and made her way down the hall to the kitchen, seeing Adam all dressed up made her smile.

'Hi, that's great, you're home earlier than I thought, I wasn't sure what time you'd arrive, I've booked a taxi for seven o'clock, so you'd better get your skates on young lady.'

He kissed her on the cheek, and passing her the glass of wine, noticed how tired she looked, he cautiously asked, ‘You still want to go out don’t you,? I’ve booked our favourite restaurant.’

‘Of course I do, give me twenty minutes sir,’ saluting him as she made her way out the kitchen.

Vivian Flemming would look good dressed in a black plastic bag, but tonight as she walked down the stairs, she looked absolutely stunning. As Adam looked up towards her, she stopped momentarily, letting him admire the red and black floral dress, showing off her slender curved figure.

‘Dr Vivian Flemming… You look fantastic, I’m the luckiest guy in the world being married to you, do you know that.’

‘You’re not too bad yourself, Detective Inspector Adam Fox… and I’m the lucky one.’

The taxi arrived just as they’d finished the second glass of wine, switching the hall light on, Adam locked the front door and helped Viv into the back of the car, linking fingers as it drove away.

He’d reserved a table for two in a secluded corner of the restaurant, the waiter lighting a candle as they sat down. Viv loved Italian food, she would maintain that not only did it taste good, but in moderation, it was healthy, avoiding too much garlic bread of course.

Adam ordered drinks before the meal, a gin and tonic for Viv and another glass of white wine for himself.

‘So, what sort of a day have you had? You mentioned it was a bit of a pig.’

The tiredness had evaporated from Viv’s face now, she looked more relaxed as she picked up her gin and tonic, taking a large gulp.

‘It’s been one of those days, two patients didn’t turn up for their appointment, which annoyed me, as one of them I’m having to monitor their blood sugar levels, as they can’t do it at home themselves. And then to cap it all, Peter and I had a real disagreement about possible new drug evaluations at the medical centre. He accused me of making decisions over his head, which I didn’t and wouldn’t do.’

‘How did you leave it, was it resolved before you left work?’

‘I suppose so, it wasn’t his fault the patients didn’t turn up, *that* did put me in a bit of a mood, but I’d never go behind his back on anything clinically, and I told him so.’

'Wow, Dr Flemming, you've certainly got your bee in your bonnet about this, haven't you.'

'Well yes, I suppose I have. There's a formal agreement about clinical trials, they're discussed at the monthly practice meetings between the medical team, and a decision is taken to either go ahead or not. In the last meeting, Peter cancelled, as he was away for a couple of days, hence it was never discussed.'

'So, how did he find out about the evaluation.'

'The company, Forder Pharmaceuticals came to see me. It's a potentially new drug for diabetes. Unbeknown to me, they also wrote to Peter confirming that a trial discussion had taken place and been arranged accordingly, which isn't the truth. However, if the company rep has reported that a trial discussion took place between the two of us, well then I can see where the confusion has come from.'

Viv took a further gulf of her drink, 'she was on a roll now,' Adam thought to himself.

'How did you leave it with Peter, did you kiss and make up?'

'Don't be ridiculous Adam, that's a stupid thing to say.'

'Hey, I'm sorry, I was only trying to lighten the mood.'

'No… I'm sorry, I shouldn't have snapped at you like that. Once I'd explained to Peter about the background to the misunderstanding, he was fine and apologised for his behaviour he'd had an off day too.'

It was almost a quarter to ten when the waiter, a short thin man came over and announced that their taxi had arrived, placing the restaurant bill on the table.

The same driver picked them up earlier in the evening, informing them that this was his last drop off, as he pulled up in front of their house.

They decided that another drink was probably too much, they'd already downed two bottles of wine and two large gin and tonics, so bed was probably a good idea.

As they lay side by side, Viv turned to Adam, 'I'm sorry darling, I've been rabbiting on about *my* day, what sort of day have you had?'

Adam considered the conversation they'd had with DCS Slater and the drug gangs, deciding that tonight wasn't the moment to discuss it any further.

Placing a bottle of spring water at the side of his bed, he switched off his side light, the moon escaping out of the clouds, illuminating the bedroom, turning over, Viv moved towards him, her breasts resting on his chest as their lips and tongues locked together.

Sixty-seven

THE MOBILE PHONE PINGED, waking Adam from a deep sleep, opening a bottle of water at the side of his bed and taking a gulp, he checked the time and the message, it read, 06:24 across the top.

Can we meet in your office around 08:15? There are a couple of things I need to discuss with you, thanks CS.

Viv was having a shower, so he went downstairs and made some fresh coffee for a change, instant never tasted the same.

Breakfast was over by 7:35 a.m. as they both made their way out of the house, Adam setting the alarm just before closing the front door.

As Viv picked up her laptop and walked round to her car, she checked the hanging baskets and pots with her finger, 'We need to water these when we get home, otherwise, they'll be dead.'

'I'm not sure what time I'll be back,' replied Adam, 'but if I'm home first I'll do it, save you the job.'

She blew him a kiss as she opened the door to her car, started the engine, checked the rearview mirror and rear camera, reversing out the drive. Putting down the passenger window, she called out 'Hope you have a good day, see you later, Oh, and did I thank you for last night, thanks again, it was great, you're the man, in more ways than one.'

'Behave,' he replied as her car glided down the road, indicating right at the bottom, and she was gone.

DCS Slater was already seated in Adam's office as he opened the glass door, glancing up at the clock on the wall, it read 07:58. Craig Slater put down a notebook and pen, and stood up.

'You're not late Adam, I was hoping to catch Tom Vickers, but he's either not arrived yet or out for the day.'

'I'm not sure of his whereabouts, but I can check with his secretary when she arrives, can I get you some coffee?'

'That would be great, I don't suppose they do Latte's here do they, if not, white, no sugar will be fine.'

'White, no sugar it is then.'

Placing the drinks on his desk, Adam checked to see that his mobile was still on, just in case Tom Vickers phoned him, he could relay the message about DCS Slater wanting to see him.

'You said in your text, that there were a couple of things you wanted to chat with me about, is it following our meeting yesterday?'

'Yes, it is, but I didn't want DS Bailey to hear what I'm about to say. I've been looking at your records from your time in Sheffield, it looks like you were heavily involved in drug gang warfare, is that correct?'

'Yes, I suppose so, amongst other things. We did bring down a network of drug dealers, operating we suspected out of Leeds, and travelling down and up from London for distribution, why?'

'If our intelligence is correct, and we believe it is, then the drug gang you and the team took down in Sheffield, could be associated with the gangs we're currently investigating. And if that is the case, Adam, then you'll be aware that they won't let anything get in their way, stopping at nothing to protect their merchandise. The body in Sherwood Forest is an example of the lengths they'll go to protect their business and their anonymity… I'm just giving you a 'Heads Up' because if it is connected with the gangs from your time up north, then you, at the very least need to know what you're dealing with, we all do.'

Scenarios began to circulate in Adam's mind.

'It was quite a long time ago sir, and I was only onc of several investigating officers in the team. Chris Mitchell headed it up, have you spoken to him about your concerns, I understand he's still heavily involved in some investigation?'

'As you should be aware, South Yorkshire Police sits within The Yorkshire and Humber Regional Organised Crime Unit, similar to EMSCO. They'll have had a similar conversation with DCI Mitchell.'

Craig Slater checked his watch.

'Before I go, have we interviewed Melanie Watkins, Ross Sullivan's partner, the one who found the body?'

'Tomorrow sir, she's seemingly been on holiday when DS Bailey called to speak with her about her statement. According to staff, she's only just coming back from holiday, odd time to go again.'

Adam picked up his office phone, dialling an internal number. 'DCI Vickers office, Wendy speaking.' 'Hi, Wendy, DI Fox… yes good morning. Could you tell me if DCI Vickers is in today? There's someone in my office who wants to speak with him...

Yeah, okay, what time is he scheduled to be back... Later this afternoon.' He looks up at Craig Slater, who under his breath mouths. 'I'll leave it to another time.' 'Okay, that's fine... No, not to worry, they'll catch up with him some other time. Can I pass on a message to the DCI? Asked Adam.

'No, it's fine, it was just a catch-up, you know, it's always better to keep the senior guys in the loop.'

'Operation Flycatcher, that's what we've called it, a joint operation between Derbyshire and Nottinghamshire.'

'Great name Adam.'

'Oh, it wasn't my idea, it was thought up by one of the officers working on the case. A PC Cartwright, I think he's got a great future in the force.'

Craig Slater checked his watch once again. 'Anyway, keep me updated on the interview with Melanie Watkins, she might be able to throw some light on Ross Sullivan's background. We've already spoken to Cresta Communications, an exemplary employee, with nothing on his work record, and no disciplinaries. Apparently, everyone seemed to like him.

Through the open panes of glass, Adam watched DCS Slater make his way along the corridor, walking with confidence and authority, casually looking both left and right before taking the stairs leading to the ground floor.

Grabbing a takeaway coffee from the canteen, Adam decided to get some fresh air to clear his head. Walking outside, he made his way towards several wooden tables and chairs, where, weather permitting, officers and civilians could take a break or sit and have their lunch in peace. Luckily the sky was blue, so hopefully no rain today.

Placing the recyclable coffee cup on the table, he began to run his finger across the lip, trying to take in what DCS Slater had told him. What if the drug gangs did seek revenge, what if they had him or Viv down as targets? The people he'd put away whilst in Sheffield, knew his name, they could easily find out where he lived, and if that was the case, had they already made their move.

If they couldn't get at Adam or Viv, they'd do the next best thing. Take the one thing that meant more to both of them than life itself, their daughter. Scarlett.

Sixty-eight

MELANIE WATKINS ARRIVED at her office unlocked the front door and entered the security code. As well as a team meeting to discuss house sales and lettings, she also had two important viewings. Which if she pulled them off, could generate an additional revenue of around twenty thousand pounds.

Both properties were at the higher end of the market, one within easy commuting distance to Nottingham University, the other, a three-storey period house located in The Park, which with a fair wind could fetch around one and a half million pounds.

WFS was solely owned by Melanie Watkins. She'd acquired the Fletcher estate agency when it was on the market around eighteen months ago. Simpson was her maiden name before she married and then divorced Mark Watkins, a day she never regretted.

She put the kettle on and took two WFS-branded mugs from the cupboard, one for herself and one for the appointment with Detective Sergeant Bailey.

He'd called her the day after she got back from a long weekend in Milan, arranging to take a statement following the death of Ross Sullivan.

Sitting down at her desk, she opened her laptop, checking the final timings for the client visits, they were back-to-back, so she couldn't be late.

The main road where Watkins, Fletcher and Simpson estate agents were located was lined on both sides with an array of coffee shops, restaurants, and health food outlets, not a charity shop in sight.

Frank Bailey arrived right on time, introducing himself and showing his warrant card, although Melanie Watkins had already met him once before at the flat in Nottingham.

She'd booked out the small conference room so they could have some privacy, taking their coffees in there just as a member of the sales team arrived.

'So, Detective Sergeant Bailey, how can I help you?'

The abrupt approach threw Frank off his guard for a moment, quickly recovering, he explained the purpose of his visit.

Melanie Watkins stood dressed in a dark grey one-piece outfit, with several square silver buttons running down the front, and a gold pendant suspended around her neck.

Frank estimated that she was around her late twenties to early thirties, clearly from her dress sense, highly successful. In Frank's opinion, she didn't have time for pleasantries, just get on with it, which seemed to be her attitude.

'We need to take a statement from you, Miss Watkins, following the death of Ross Sullivan, and just for the record, this may take slightly longer than you planned, it would have been far better if you'd have told us you were going away straight after his death.'

She looked very irritated at Frank's comments, 'Not the sort of person who likes being told off,' Frank thought.

'It was a last-minute decision, *I* needed to get away, finding Ross in the bathroom, have you any idea what that was like, we'd only seen each other a couple of weeks previously, just before I went on a week's holiday.'

'Must have come as a shock, once again I'm very sorry for your loss.'

Forty minutes later, Frank put down his pen on the conference table, finished his coffee and passed the statement for Melanie Watkins to read.

There were no errors, as usual, Frank had recorded every detail accurately, and she signed the statement at the bottom handing it back, showing no emotion.

Just as they were about to leave the room, Melanie stood still for several seconds, then asked, 'Do you know why there were rose petals in the hallway at the flat, Ross suffered from Asthma, so he used to avoid things like that?'

'At the moment we are keeping an open mind on that. If they weren't already in the flat at the time, then we could assume they are associated with the crime.'

As he walked out the door, he glanced through the front window, briefly checking out the price of bungalows, this was going to be the next task, finally selling his mother-in-law's property.

Back at police headquarters, he went straight to Adam's office, seeing him seated at his desk, he knocked and opened the glass door.

'Hi boss, do you have ten minutes to go through Melanie Watkins statement? She's some work that one.'

'Certainly Frank, I could do with a break, do you want some coffee?'

'No, I'm fine thanks, it'll be lunchtime soon, anyway, no more chocolate for you until further notice.'

Sitting around the small breakout table, Frank let Adam read the signed statement, occasionally clarifying some key points.

'So, they intermittently took recreational drugs in the flat then, clearly, for personal use only.'

'Yes, although she doesn't give me the impression of a regular user, no bloodshot eyes, just when she was in his flat. However, one thing of interest. Ross Sullivan's parents.'

Frank pointed to the statement with his pen.

'They live in north London, he used to travel down to see them regularly, she once asked him about it and he just told her that they were getting elderly, and he needed to keep an eye on them. I also placed a call with his workplace, Cresta Communications. He was a middle manager not on a huge salary, so how did he manage to buy a flat like the one he had in Nottingham is anyone's business? Looks like the drug connection is a goer.'

'Thanks for this, I'll read it again and let you have it back. I'll also scan and send an email copy to DCS Slater.

He came to see me earlier today, just a quick update about the case. He wanted to speak with Tom Vickers, but he hasn't been in today.'

'Any idea why, maybe it's to do with Arthur Richardson?'

'I doubt it, but I think it's better we leave that alone, don't you?'

Sixty-nine

JOE JACKSON'S FORD RANGER pulled outside Danny's mum and dad's house. Throwing a copy of The Derbyshire Times into the back, he turned down the volume of radio one, as the presenter announced it was 'seven forty-five.'

Locking the 4x4, he walked down the path to the front door, noticing that the roses on either side required pruning, 'A job for Danny' he thought to himself.

Knocking on the door it took several moments for it to be opened, Mary Ashby standing right in front of him, wiping her hands down her floral apron. 'Morning Joe, come on in, Danny won't be too long, he's just taking a shower, sit down at the kitchen table and I'll get you a cup of tea, is tea all right or would you prefer coffee?'

'Tea's fine Mrs Ashby, thanks'

'Call me Mary, Mrs Ashby makes me sound so old, which of course I am. Have you had breakfast?'

'No, I set the alarm on my mobile phone, but the battery was flat, so I've over slightly.' As he replied, the smell of grilled bacon made his mouth water.

'Daniel normally has two bacon sandwiches with brown sauce, would you like one?'

Without hesitation, Joe replied, 'Yes please, and I'll have brown sauce too.'

She was pouring him a mug of strong tea, just as Danny walked down the stairs, he was dressed in his working clothes, shaved and his hair was still slightly damp.

Although they'd been working together for weeks for the first time, Joe noticed how his appearance had changed from when he was first released from prison.

He looked refreshed and energised and as he walked over and sat at the kitchen table, he finally seemed to have a purpose in life.

Mary Ashby placed two plates of bacon sandwiches in front of them, and a bottle of brown sauce, picking up the teapot and pouring Danny a drink.

'Here you go boys, that'll set you up for the day, have you got a busy one?'

'Yeah,' replied Joe, swallowing his food quicker than expected, 'We've got a meeting with the owner of the nursing home we did some work for, he wants us to quote for various gardening work at one of his other homes, so, fingers crossed, we'll get that business too.'

Joe was still eating when Danny got up from the table, 'Give me five minutes Joe and I'll be with you, I just need to get my coat from upstairs.'

'Don't worry about that, it's a lovely day, no rain forecast and there's one in the Ranger if you need it.' Finishing his tea, he stood up. 'Thanks, Mary for the breakfast, we'd better shoot off, but I'll overlay again if that's all right with you, the sandwiches were great.'

'Here's the postcode, can you put it in the sat nav, and we'll get off, you know what a stickler Mr Robinson is for timekeeping. Joe put the 4x4 into gear and set off down the lane, turning the radio down so you could hardly hear it.

'I didn't see your dad this morning, is he okay?'

'He always goes for a walk first thing in the morning, Blythe Woods, done it as long as he's been home, which hasn't been very much.'

'What rank was he in the army?'

'He finished up being a sergeant, based up in the north. I think the place was called Otterburn, but not sure if I'm honest. I didn't pay much attention, as I've mentioned before, we didn't get on, still don't if I'm honest with you.'

Joe looked down at the sat nav, fourteen miles to go, checking the time of arrival, they would be there on time.

'When I was at your house last time, your dad showed me the guns he had from his army days, does he keep them in the house, and has he got a license?'

Danny considered the question for several minutes before replying. 'Don't know about a license, I guess he does, but he keeps the guns under lock and key in the garden shed unless he's cleaning them, it's always locked away in his draw with all his other memorabilia, why?'

'Oh, no particular reason, it's just I'm looking at buying a hunting gun, for the weekends, you know, I think I've got to have a firearms certificate, just wondered if your dad's got one?'

'If he has, he's never spoken about it, but then again, we don't speak, so I wouldn't know.'

Rain clouds began to form as Joe put on the Ford Ranger's indicator, and approached a turning on the left, the sat nav announced, 'You have reached your destination.'

Mr Robinson stood outside Woodthorpe Grange Nursing Home, glancing at his watch to check they'd arrived at the agreed time.

He talked them through what he had in mind, as Danny made several notes in his workbook. Joe occasionally recommended an alternative idea to the one he had in mind, which surprising to both of them, he considered and accepted.

The job value wasn't to the level of The Lakes Nursing Home, but if they got the quote right, it would give them further income to buy some additional equipment, which for a young growing business, was important.

Before leaving, Joe suggested that they take a look around the garden to familiarise themselves with the job before forwarding the final quote, 'It's always better to walk the ground, get a feel for the earth underfoot' was his opinion.

He pulled up his collar as the dark clouds turned to rain, 'I've got a coat in the back of the Ranger Danny, if you want it, we don't want you coming down with a cold.'

They both walked back to the vehicle, Joe using his key fob to open the automatic boot, as Danny leaned over, picking up the black coat, something caught his eye.

Looking closer, he noticed two stainless-steel knives on the scruffy rubber matting, one around six inches in length with a wooden handle and the other, shorter, around four inches.

'You shouldn't have seen those,' Joe whispered in his ear. They're my gutting knives, I usually put them in a safe place, be careful, they're sharp, and they're used when I go fishing.'

'I didn't know you fished; they look dangerous.'

Joe picked the longer one up, running his finger down the length of the blade.

'Yeah,' he replied, 'you're right, in the wrong hands they would be.'

Seventy

ADAM ENJOYED DRIVING Viv's Skoda. It held the road well in wet weather, and you were high up, so visibility was enhanced. They'd decided to take her car as Viv said it was far more comfortable on longer journeys than his Audi A4, and she was probably right.

'What time do you think we'll arrive, I said I'd text my mum to give her an ETA?'

It was Adam's weekend off and Viv had agreed to visit her mum and dad at their country cottage in the Cotswolds, it was only a small place, but ideal for a holiday break or weekends away.

It was almost two months since Viv had seen her parents, she Facetimes her mum every week, but with the pressure of work and the unsocial hours that Adam sometimes has to keep, it always proved difficult to arrange for the four of them to get together.

When Scarlett was around, it was different, her mum and dad would offer to stay over and babysit, allowing them to get out for the evening.

But when Scarlett disappeared, Viv's mum and dad avoided talking about coming over for the weekend.

A missing child is a nightmare every parent dreads, a time that both Adam and Viv tried to put behind them, and yet they always wanted her to continue being at the forefront of their minds.

***

Frank Bailey sat alone, quietly, in the incident room, laid out in front of him were three A4 black and white images of Arthur Richardson, Patricia Locke and Ross Sullivan.

He recalled what the young PC had said at one of the briefing meetings. 'Have we considered if there were any connections between these three people? Did they all belong to any social media groups? Related in any way? Did they have a criminal record? Or had they reported any concerns to the police?'

Thorough background checks on all three victims had come up with nothing. They weren't active on social media; they weren't related in any way both Richardson and Locke were on the surface of it… Loners. None had criminal records, but Ross Sullivan was on Nottinghamshire's radar. And finally, there was no record of them reporting any concerns about their safety to the police.

'What are we missing?' he said out loud. Knowing full well no one would hear him. The only connection linking all three murders was the carvings on the forehead, the taking of body trophies, and those rose petals. Presently, no witnesses to question. What is going to be our next move?

Flesh sliced from their faces, numbers one, two, and three, what did that mean, Frank wrote down the numbers in bold black letters.

Is there someone out there hunting down innocent people, gathering information about their personal lives? They must know something about the victims, their movements, schedules, where they live, and what they do, or do.

As he looked down at the black numbers on yellow A4 paper, two frightening thoughts went through his mind.

The body nailed to the tree in Sherwood Forest, investigating the murder of Ross Sullivan, could the drug gangs seek out and take revenge on any officers determined to uncover evidence and bring them down?

And secondly, and more worryingly.

Would there be a fourth victim?

***

It was just after 6:15 p.m. when they arrived at Willow Cottage, almost the same time that Viv had confirmed to her mum.

Soon after setting off, she'd reclined the car seat and slept for most of the journey, waking as the security light at the front of the cottage floodlit the inside of her car.

Adam suggested Viv go inside whilst he unloaded the Skoda handing her two bottles of wine they'd purchased from a Majestic store on the way down, one red and the other white.

Roger and Maureen Flemming were both in their late sixties, he was old school, wearing an open-neck shirt and cardigan, and supporting a blue and white cravat.

If you casually passed Maureen in the street, you'd put her at around mid-fifties, smartly dressed in a petrol blue trouser suit, with matching shoes, Adam always hoped Viv would inherit her mother's genes.

They both stood at the entrance to the cottage, Roger holding out open arms, giving Viv a big hug, Maureen waited for Adam to unload the luggage.

'Hello, you two,' she said, it's lovely to see you both, hope you had a good journey. Bring the cases in Adam and put them down in the hall, Roger can take them into your bedroom later.'

'Hello darling' said Roger, stepping back to admire his daughter, 'Let me look at you, you look great.'

'Thanks, Dad, I'm fine. We're both fine thanks for asking, looking forward to a weekend away in the countryside.'

'Well, you've come to the right place, the weather hopefully is going to be good over the next few days. So hopefully, we can have a long walk tomorrow and stop at the local pub for lunch if you wish.'

'Sounds wonderful,' said Viv, accepting the invitation for both of them.

Knocking at the bedroom door woke Adam from a deep and restful sleep, as Maureen quietly placed two cups of freshly made coffee on the bedside table, 'Breakfast will be in about half an hour if that's okay?'

'Thanks, Maureen, I'll wake Vivian up and we'll get showered.'

'No hurry, it's scrambled eggs, so easy to do, when you're ready.'

Whether it was the smell of the coffee or the opening of the bedroom door, Viv opened her eyes, blinked several times, and focused her vision on Adam's face.

'Hello you, sleep well?'

'Yes thanks,' avoiding the usual reply 'Like a baby.'

'Your mums brought some coffee for us breakfast will be in about thirty minutes… I'm going to take a quick shower.'

The table was set in the dining room, Willow cottage kitchen wasn't large enough to include a breakfast bar or anywhere else to eat for that matter.

After a sumptuous breakfast of scrambled eggs and smoked salmon, more fresh coffee, they all got togged up and made their way out of the front of Willow cottage, Roger setting the alarm and locking the door behind him.

Willow cottage wasn't particularly isolated, there were several other properties scattered along the road, but it did enjoy a wider than normal pavement, allowing the four of them to stroll side by side for the majority of the walk, only occasionally having to step to one side for the odd vehicle to pass.

Roger had booked a table at the Hare and Hound pub for twelve-thirty, explaining on the walk that it served 'The best food in the whole of the Cotswolds.'

'It would do,' Adam thought to himself.

Adan took the order for drinks whilst Roger, Maureen and Viv made their way to the table, paying in cash.

'So, what are you planning to do for your birthday?' Roger asked looking directly at Viv.

Turning her head towards Adam, she replied, 'We haven't really discussed it at the moment, but I'd probably like a small gathering at home, just family and a few friends, nothing too extravagant.'

'Will your parents come over Adam? Asked Maureen, she knew what the answer would be, but it still didn't stop her asking.'

'I think that's unlikely; they don't like travelling too far these days, but we have planned to go up and see them in the next few weeks.'

Viv's mother and father had only met Adam's parents once, at the wedding, and it was evident that it wasn't going to be a long-lasting relationship.

It didn't bother either Adam or Viv whether they got on or not, just so long as they avoided spoiling the wedding celebrations, which they did.

'You'll be able to come and stay with us for my birthday mum and dad, won't you?'

'Wouldn't miss it for the world,' replied Roger.

It was almost four o'clock when Viv hugged her dad and kissed her mum. Adam packing the car up for the journey home.

'Thank you for a lovely weekend, we've really enjoyed it, it's made a nice break for both of us.'

'You're always welcome here,' replied Maureen, 'Text me when you get home, just so I know you've arrived safely, and we'll talk later in the week.'

Remotely closing the boot, Adam walked over, shaking hands with Roger and giving Maureen a quick peck on the side of her cheek, instantly recognising she was wearing the same perfume as Viv.

The journey back was uneventful, apart from the fact that Adam for once, didn't put on Spotify.

'Is everything okay, you seem distant somehow?'

'I'm fine, it's just I knew your dad would want to talk about the loan for the partnership. I don't mind, not one jot. But we could have managed to get the money together somehow without going to Roger and Maureen.'

'Probably so, but it would have stretched us financially, and with everything else going on, I didn't want to put any more stress on either of us, surely you can see that?'

He paused before replying. 'Of course I can… I'm sorry, it's just that I like to think I can look after everything, including our finances.'

'You're doing a great job… Remember, you're the man.'

Switching on Spotify, he considered what he'd just said. 'I can look after anything, but not my daughter.'

Seventy-one

PETER JOHNSON'S JAGUAR stood alone in his designated spot when Viv arrived at Edgewater Medical Centre, she checked her watch to check she wasn't late. Thankfully, no, Peter had arrived early.

She felt refreshed and energised following the weekend with her parents, and thankfully, although Roger and Maureen do try his patience, Adam seemed to enjoy the break.

Although she'd got a full day of patient appointments if they all turned up, she wanted to speak with Peter in connection to the clinical trial. The pharmaceutical sales representative was scheduled to meet with her later today, after her last patient.

His door was open as Viv made her way to her consulting room, so she decided to pop her head around the door.

'Morning Peter, everything okay?'

His face seemed illuminated by the PC screen he was looking at, turning his head, he replied.

'Good morning Vivian, yes I'm fine thanks, how's you, good weekend?'

'Yes thanks, we went to stay with my parents in the Cotswolds, made a nice break.'

Checking notes, he'd just jotted down, he replied.

'I've just been researching FORDEN Pharmaceuticals, you've got a meeting with them later today I understand?'

'Yes, that's right, we spoke about it, if you recall. They want to conduct a phase three clinical trial on a brand-new diabetic drug they're planning to bring to market. They selected this practice due to the higher number of patients we have with diabetes, and to be honest, my clinical interest in the disease.'

'Well, from what I've briefly delved into, they seem to be at the forefront in pharmaceutical research and development. Privately owned, a family organisation, and based just outside Manchester. So, yes, I think it's something we should get behind and support. It's your decision at the end of the day, but from what I read, let's do it. And the other attraction, they're based outside London and the Southeast, attracting investments for the north of the country.'

It was coming up to six o'clock by the time the meeting with FORDEN Pharmaceuticals had ended. Jason Fletcher their account manager had been accompanied by the company's clinical research director, Dr Dirk Classen. He'd explained in great detail, graphs and all, the results of the drug trials to date and was delighted that Edgewater Medical Centre had decided to consider a number of their patients.

Kate explained that they would now run a database of diabetic patients, obtain their voluntary consent, and give them sufficient information about the new drug allowing them to make an informed decision.

'If all goes to plan, I can have all the details back in the next ten days or so, does that work for you?'

'Absolutely Dr. Flemming,' replied Dr. Classen, a look of delight on his face.

***

'What are we missing?' Frank was seated across from Adam's desk early Monday morning. 'There has to be something, we've got three murder victims, and the only connections are cuts on their foreheads and bloody rose petals.'

Adam sensed the frustration in Frank's voice, it wouldn't be long before Tom Vickers started putting pressure on them to come up with some results. It was probably the involvement of Craig Slater that was buying them some breathing space, but that wouldn't last too much longer.

Adam studied Frank in front of him for several moments.

'Do you remember me mentioning at the crime scene of Patricia Locke? Someone observing what was going on, taking notes, and dressed in a dark coat and black and white baseball cap? Well, back in my car after coming out of Ross Sullivans' flat, I noticed through my rear mirror, a figure in the crowd, interestingly, they were dressed the same… By the time I'd got out, they'd disappeared, the question is this. How do they know where to go?'

'I hope you're not suggesting *I'm* passing on information to a third-party gov. I know we didn't get off to the best of starts at the beginning of this case, but I'd never compromise an investigation.'

Adam's intention wasn't to accuse Frank. He knew he was a good honest copper and a solid right-hand man, but he couldn't hide from the fact that someone was leaking information.

And if that is the case, then they may not only know the killer but more chilling, could know who the next victim might be.

Seventy-two

WAKING FROM TORMENTED nightmares, I reach over to get a tumbler of water, spilling it on the bedsheets, as my hand is shaking so much.

For most people, enjoying a good night's sleep enables them to wake refreshed and ready to take on the day ahead. But the visions are so real, that I'm continuously taken back to our time at Chaffinch House.

Both Simon and I tried desperately to overcome the pain and loss of our friend Toby, and as the weeks and months passed, our thoughts turned from sorrow to survival.

The ill-treatment and beatings continued to take place, smelling the stench of smoked breath and thumping into my stomach, becoming the norm for me.

We never talked about what was happening to us, although sadly, I often noticed Simon returning to our dormitory, bruising above one of his eyes.

Maybe he suffered worse than I did. Experiencing beatings that he didn't wish to discuss, we couldn't talk to anyone, and we'd been warned to keep quiet. So, for both of us, remaining silent was our only option.

Unlike many others, Chaffinch House wasn't a particularly religious boarding school.

Yes, there was always a daily service first thing, the headmaster leading it from the front. However, Sundays were very different, no classes and no studying.

Most weeks a local vicar would come to the school, take a service, speak to some of the youngsters who were possibly homesick and needed someone to talk to, and generally spend the day supporting the boys as required.

Normally after the early Sunday morning service, Simon and I made our way out of the breakfast hall, not always knowing how the day would go.

'What are we going to do today?' I asked Simon.

He looked at me for several seconds, unsure what to say.

'My mum and dad are back in the country for a few days, so they're driving over this morning, taking me out for the day, hopefully, a nice lunch too.'

I avoided showing my disappointment, although I think Simon knew how hard it was at times for me. My parents hardly came to visit, always using the excuse, 'Really busy son, my dad would say, we'll come over to see you very soon, but we love you, you know that don't you?'

I wave goodbye to Simon as he gets into the back of his father's car, shouting a little too loud, 'Have a great day and I'll see you when you get back.'

He gave me a thumbs-up, as the light green Range Rover made its way down the drive.

Taking a deep breath, thinking about what I'm going to do for the day, I glance over towards the water, trying to forget the fateful day that Toby died, but still recalling what one of the older boys did to him.

With Simon away for the day, I was going to be at a loose end, and not wanting to return to our dormitory, I decided to take a walk around the lake.

We'd both avoided it since Toby's demise. But being on my own, maybe it was time to put the memories of that chilling day behind me.

I'd been walking for about ten minutes when the sun broke through the pure white clouds, and starting to sweat under the heat, I took off my shirt and tied it around the waist of the shorts.

Several weeks after Toby's death, the headmaster announced that his family had donated money to the school, requesting the purchase of some form of memorial to celebrate his life.

It had been decided that a wooden bench would be positioned overlooking the water, in memory of Toby Curtis.

As I made my way around the side of the lake, a familiar walk the three of us used to take, I noticed the oak seat dedicated by his family to our friend Toby.

Sitting down I put my hand over my eyes, trying to shield them from the bright sunlight of the day.

As my eyes adjusted I could make out a figure walking along the path, a face I didn't initially recognise, until they came closer.

Sitting down at the side of me, they asked.

'Are you all right? You look troubled and upset in some way.'

Hesitatingly I replied.

'I'm okay thanks, just thinking about my friend. He drowned in these waters some time ago, just remembering how we miss him and all the good times we had together. We'd always talked about becoming long-term friends, no matter where we ended up after we left boarding school, we'd always remain close… But it wasn't to be.'

He turns and lifts his hand, wiping away the tears falling from my eyes.

'I'm sorry about your friend, it's so very sad when you lose someone close to you, but you'll have all those fond memories to look back on in the years ahead.'

As the sun continued to beat down on my bare skin, I opted to continue to walk around the far side of the lake, under the shade of the low-hanging trees, making my way back to the dormitory.

Getting up from the seat, they turn to me.

'If it helps, I'd like to show you something that might bring some comfort to you, it's just inside here, behind the seat.'

Apart from Simon, I guess this had been the first time I'd spoken to anyone about my feelings towards Toby's death, it was just something I didn't discuss.

And whilst they were a stranger, having someone to talk to made me feel content, but possibly more vulnerable.

So, as suggested, I stood up and walked towards the bushes.

They followed closely behind, I could feel their breath on my neck as firstly their hand went towards my waist, starting to make its way down my shorts. Trying to move out of the way, they wrapped their arm tightly around my throat.

Taken completely by surprise, I immediately struggled to get my breath, and my eyes began to water, making it difficult for me to move.

Struggling to breathe, and realising that I had to escape, my brain went into survival mode.

I raise my left leg, stamping down on their foot, so hard I could hear a crack, it might have been a twig, but I hoped it was a bone.

As they shouted out and pulled away in agony, they bit the top of my back, between my shoulder blades. The blood dripping down, pain travelling down my body.

Instantly releasing their grip on me and gaining back my strength I ran towards the bench, quickly looking both right and left, then directly turning left and hurriedly, made my way back down the path towards the front of the house.

I was probably about twenty yards from the bench when I slowed down to try and control my breathing, thinking through what had just happened, looking back, and checking that no one was following me.

Thankfully, the coast was clear.

It wasn't until later that I recognised their face, an image I was determined never to forget.

Seventy-three

PHILIP ASHBY POPPED TWO extra strong mints into his mouth as he parked his car outside the Edgewater Community Church. Two hours earlier, he'd stopped off at the pub near Blythe Woods and downed two pints of lager and a whisky chaser. He knew he'd be over the limit if pulled over by the police.

He didn't give a toss, all he wanted to do was to talk with the minister, Steven Andrews before all the celebrations started.

He placed a notepad and pen on the passenger seat, noticing Steven through the windscreen. He was talking with someone who had what looked like a camera around their neck.

In the last few months, he'd struggled with his conscience, remembering what he'd done all those years ago, drinking heavily seemed to numb the horrific memories.

He'd known that at some point, the time would arrive for him to come clean, to act, and bring an end to this haunting nightmare.

The time had finally arrived.

Steven Andrews had built up a sweat, he'd got up early and was currently busy spacing out the additional seating that was required. The local journalist from the Derbyshire Times walked up and introduced himself.

He wanted a brief interview and some photographs for the paper, but due to recruitment issues, all journalists now had to take their photographs. He was already prepared, the camera hanging down from his neck.

Large numbers of the congregation had started to arrive, for what was going to be a really enjoyable day for everyone.

Funding for a project as important as this one had started almost three years ago, initially, just a passing comment from one of the parishioners, but here they were, many months later, officially opening a drop-in centre for anyone and everyone.

Making his way to the middle of the church, Philip turned to the man with the camera, 'Would you excuse us for one moment? I need to speak with the minister.'

Steven turned towards the journalist. 'I'll come and find you as soon as I can, go and get yourself a cup of tea or coffee.'

'Thanks, Steven, I know you're busy but is it possible to speak with you at some point today? I must talk with you.'

'Well, it's going to be a hectic day for all of us, but of course Philip, could we make it later this afternoon? Once all the celebrations have started to die down, maybe my office, let's say four o'clock.'

That wasn't the answer that Philip Ashby expected, he looked around at the mass of people gathering in the church, shrugged his shoulders and casually walked away.

Returning to his car, he noticed there were hardly any spaces left, and as he got closer, he observed that a long-based minibus had parked right next to his vehicle.

He looked through the windscreen again, observing that Steven was already in conversation with the journalist, who was holding a drink in his hand.

'No time, just no time,' he said to himself.

Maneuvering around the minibus, obscured from view, he headed out and drove back to the secluded car park near the pub he'd drunk at hours before.

Parking up, he opened the boot of his car and took out a large dark blue bag, closing the boot and sitting back down in his vehicle, putting the bag on the side near the notepad.

He then began to write.

By the time you read this message, I'll have taken the action I should have done years ago.

I don't know why I have decided to write this letter here of all places, but Blythe Woods is somewhere that has brought some relief to me during my early morning walks.

I'm going out of my mind with guilt and remorse, if I'm being honest with myself, my life's been a mess for years. I miss my time in the army so very much, the discipline, having a sense of purpose, and protecting my country and its people.

I have a few regrets, but my biggest one is some of the people I came into contact with, one person in particular.
If it hadn't been for them, I probably wouldn't be here right now, putting pen to paper for the final time.
I should never have married, my army life made it so that I was never at home, and when I did come back, I was like a stranger in my own house. Daniel being born was a complete shock, he was never planned, and I always struggled to accept him as my son.
So, I have finally decided for once in my life to take control and do the right thing. I hate myself for all that I've done in the past and cannot go on any longer with this guilt, it's tearing me apart.
I should have been a man, gone to the police at the time, admitted to what I'd done, and accepted my punishment.
Detective Superintendent Rodney Booth always knew that John Wilson Gilbert had an accomplice, but they never found me out.

Forgive me.

Philip Ashby

Seventy-four

IT WAS APPROXIMATELY FORTY-EIGHT hours before the body of Philip Lionel Ashby was discovered, deliberately parking his car in an isolated spot near Blythe Woods.

He'd been reported missing the day before by Mary Ashby and her son, Daniel. They'd telephoned Derbyshire police and reported him missing, having explained that he hadn't returned home from going to church for the opening of a brand-new drop-in centre the day before.

Officers from Derbyshire Constabulary started a search, focusing on Blythe Woods, working from information that this was an area that he used to visit regularly.

DI Adam Fox had been briefed on the situation and together with DS Frank Bailey, visited the area before returning to police headquarters to update DCI Tom Vickers.

Walking down the corridor to his office, Adam noted that he was on the phone, knocked on his door and waited to be asked to enter.

Tom Vickers replaced the receiver and called out for Adam to come in, a stern look on his face.

'Is everything all right sir? Asked Adam.

'Take a seat. That was the Chief Constable on the phone, so, we have another death to deal with DI Fox?' replied Tom Vickers, looking up from his desk, his glasses perched on the end of his nose.

By the tone of his question, Adam realised that he wasn't too happy receiving the news about Philip Ashby, knowing that he probably didn't want to hear the name, Ashby, banded around the station anymore.

'We've discovered a body we understand to be that of Philip Ashby, Daniel Ashby's father. He was reported missing early yesterday morning by his wife and son, his body was found in a car, parked near Blythe Woods. DS Bailey and I have visited the crime scene, and the Forensic Pathologist, Doctor Rachel Munroe is conducting the post-mortem this afternoon, we should have the results by tomorrow morning, but in our combined opinion, Philip Ashby took his own life, leaving a suicide note in the vehicle.'

Tom Vickers took off his glasses, placing them on his desk.

'You'll have a full report on your desk by tomorrow afternoon, once the body has been identified,' but we're ninety-nine percent it is Philip Ashby, sir.'

'Do you think this death is in any way connected with the three other cases you're currently working on if we include Arthur Richardson that is?'

That comment came as a complete surprise, the fact that Tom Vickers was finally linking the murder of Arthur Richardson with the two recent ones. After all, he was the SIO on the initial investigation, which was conceivably flawed. And ultimately ended up sending an innocent man to jail.

'No sir, our initial investigations are leading us to a connection with several serious crimes that happened in Tyne and Wear, in the mid-sixties. In the suicide note, Philip Ashby admits he was the accomplice to one John Wilson Gilbert. You'll probably remember the case sir, Gilbert became known as The Butcher of Tyneside, attacking several young women walking alone, it took place during the late nineteen eighties. Detective Superintendent Rodney Booth led the investigation, and he always worked on the assumption that Gilbert had an accomplice. He was finally brought to justice and found guilty of several sexual assaults, spanning several years, and the murder of three women. Whilst in prison, he was interviewed by officers about an accomplice, but he never let on who was involved. He died in two thousand and eight, taking the name with him. I've already requested Frank Bailey to liaise with Northumberland Police, although Rodney Booth passed away a few years ago.'

Mary and Daniel Ashby attended the mortuary the following morning, DS Bailey and Dr Rachel Munroe in attendance, having been informed that Philip Ashby was ready to be formally identified.

Immediately heading back to Mary Ashby's Corsa, Daniel put his arm around his mum's shoulders. She smiled at him as he turned and spoke. 'Let's go home, shall we? Don't worry mum,' we're free of him now, and I promise, I'll look after you from now on.'

He opened the passenger door for her, and they drove away.

Seventy-five

THE FULL REPORT ON THE DEATH of Philip Ashby was attached to an email as Adam arrived in the office early the following morning.

Pressing the print button on his PC, he took hold of all the sheets of paper, sat back down at his desk, and read.

He picked up a yellow highlighter and outlined all the relevant points, which he recorded in the logbook and electronically.

Mary and Daniel Ashby had attended the morgue and identified the body as Philip Lionel Ashby, DS Bailey was in attendance but remained outside the mortuary.

He'd been found by two police officers in his car just outside Blythe Woods at approximately 09:25 a.m. the morning after he'd been reported missing.

The car was initially locked, and after one of the officers gained access by breaking a side window, a gun was found on the passenger seat together with a suicide note. The gun and the written note had formally been confirmed by his wife as her husbands.

Detective Inspector Adam Fox and Detective Sergeant Frank Bailey attended the scene, Dr Rachel Munroe, a Forensic Pathologist initially examined the body and then authorised the transfer to the morgue for further examination.

Post-mortem results confirmed that the injuries sustained correspond with a self-inflicted single gunshot wound to the stomach, ripping through vital organs, causing a loss of consciousness, combined with severe bleeding.

This action resulted in death approximately three to three and a half hours after the initial injury.

Stapling the documents together, Adam walked over to where Tom Vickers's secretary worked and placed them in his in-tray, returning and noticing Frank sitting in his office, two coffee cups in front of him.

'Has the report come through about Philip Ashby?'

'Yeah, I've already read it and printed out some copies, including one for Tom Vickers, he wasn't too pleased when I saw him last, pressure from above I think. Here's a copy for you, as we all suspected, he took his own life regretfully.'

It took Frank several moments to scan the document Adam had passed him, occasionally running his tongue across his top lip.

'How did you get on with Northumberland police, did you get a response?'

'Eventually yes,' replied Frank. 'But honestly, they didn't seem too interested in what's taken place, seems as far as they're concerned, it's finally closed off the case. Just a shame that DCI Booth didn't live to hear the news.'

'Let's go for another cup of coffee shall we gov?, I'm dying for a bacon sandwich,' said Frank.

Adam was about to close the door when the office phone rang, 'DI Fox,' he announced.

'Okay, we'll be right down, thanks.'

'We'll have to forget the coffee, Steven Andrews, the church minister is in reception, he wants to speak with both of us.'

The three sat in one of the side rooms off the reception area, Frank changing the door sign to ENGAGED.

Steven Andrews looked pale, unshaven, and like he hadn't slept much.

Pulling out a chair for him to sit down, Adam asked, 'Can I get you some tea or coffee, Mr Andrews?'

Pausing, he replied, 'No, thanks… He came to see me you know… Philip Ashby came to the church. He wanted to speak to me about something that seemed to be bothering him. I was busy, it was the opening of our drop-in centre, I explained that I was tied up, but I'd see him later, but he never came back.'

'How did you hear about Mr. Ashby?' asked Adam.

'One of our parishioners called me late last night to say that they'd heard that he'd gone missing, news travels fast in a small community like ours.'

Frank was taking notes as Adam carried on with the questions. 'How did he seem when you spoke with him?'

'He seems preoccupied, almost distant he wanted to speak with someone, and that should have been me. I've let him down, should have found the time to talk with him, the journalist could have waited.'

'Journalist, what was that all about?'

'The drop-in centre, The Derbyshire Times were covering the opening, and offered to run an article for us, it's a good cause and free advertising for the church. Is it true he committed suicide?'

Frank looked up and answered, 'It's very early days, we are not at liberty to confirm anything at the moment, his death remains under investigation.'

Steven Andrews just sat there momentarily, unsure what else to say.

Deciding to bring the conversation to an end, Frank, diplomatically put down his pen, looked at his watch and spoke.

'Thanks for coming in Mr Andrews, we'll be back in touch if we need more details.'

Standing, the three of them made their way to reception, Steven Andrews didn't say another word, just walked out of the front door and across the car park.

The two of them took the stairs back to Adam's office, making their way down the corridor, Frank turned to Adam.

'Steven Andrews, he seems to have taken it badly… Losing two of your parishioners, Patricia Locke and now Philip Ashby must be hard to take in.'

'It's unfortunate, to say the least, but I guess in that type of job, you get used to it.'

'Probably yes, but I'll tell you this, Steven Andrews is hiding something, don't know what, but there's something not quite right, coppers nose and all that.'

Seventy-six

WAKING UP TO THE MORNING sun creeping across the bedroom, I realised the nightmares that have haunted me for all these years, seem to be finally coming to an end.

It had been almost two weeks now since the horrific memories of boarding school continually broke my sleep. Leaving me in a state of despair, hopelessness, and misery, could this finally be over?

Maybe, just maybe, I was ultimately being set free, allowing me to live my life as others do. The absolute pleasure I get from hunting the victims down and taking revenge gives me a fulfilment that is difficult to describe.

My attack on Ross Sullivan. I often think about if he recognised me as he looked into my eyes, the day he took my watch and the life of my friend Toby, and how my other friend Simon was, he might have been one of the luckier ones, avoiding what happened to me, it was something we never spoke about then or ever since.

Checking my mobile phone at the side of the bed, it read 7:09 a.m. opening the blinds fully, and looking out of the bedroom window, for once the weather forecast had got it right. It looked like it was going to be a lovely sunny day.

I'd taken a day off work and planned to spend time in the garden, preparing everything for the autumn. Giving the lawn a final cut, planting daffodil and tulip bulbs and cutting back the roses, so a quick breakfast was in order.

Walking through the lounge towards the kitchen, I noticed how quiet the house seemed to be, only broken by the sound of the chime of the carriage clock announcing 7:30 a.m.

It seems such a long time since I lived here with my parents. A house full of fun and excitement, laughter, and enjoyment. That was until I ended up at Chaffinch House.

As it panned out, the quick breakfast didn't happen, as when I opened the fridge door, there were no eggs or bacon.

So, I drove down to the local supermarket, filled up a shopping basket and home by 8:15 a.m.

Parking on the drive outside the house, I noticed the newspaper sticking out of the letterbox at the bottom of the front door, the paper boy must have delivered The Derbyshire Times whilst I was out.

Unlocking the door and putting the shopping in the fridge l took hold of the paper and sat at the kitchen table.

I lick my index finger and unfold the paper, quickly scanning through the pages. Nothing of real interest on the front or inside page, but as I scan through to page three, reading down, there I see it, right in the middle on the left-hand side.

It was a photograph of several people standing right in front of a large cross outside the local church, nothing unusual about that. But as I looked more closely, reading the article and moving my eyes from right to left, directly in the centre, standing out from the others, I spotted it.

Something that makes me want to throw up, my hands begin to shake, as the image before me brings terrifying recollections back into focus memories and scars that I thought I'd left behind forever.

Seventy-seven

WALKING DOWN TO THE GARDEN SHED, my hands continue to tremble.

Sitting down, I open the drawer, taking out and unlocking the black metal box which holds all the trophies I've gathered since I first started preparing the acts of vengeance.

Seeing that photograph brought it all back to me, walking around the lake, sitting on the wooden bench, what I understood was an innocent conversation with someone I thought I could trust, and then what took place.

If I hadn't got away, if I hadn't defended myself, what they were going to do to me haunts me still to this day.

Folding out the school photograph taken at Chaffinch House, I check that the image in the newspaper is the same as the person in the back row. They'd changed, of course they had, but there was no mistaking it, it was them, alive and well.

Alive for the moment anyway.

When I finally fell asleep that night, fear and anxiety returned, despite what I thought, the nightmares were back. Struggling to walk through thick damp fog, grappling to see where I was going, Simon and Toby were at my side, menacing faces in front of me, holding out their hands, trying to grab me. I jolt awake, covered in perspiration, knowing again what I had to do.

Hunting them down this time was going to be easier, they'd almost advertised their location, and all I had to do was turn up at the right time and be prepared with the correct set of tools in my bag.

Fortunately for me, the journalist covering the article in the paper had outlined the times for church meetings. After reading it a second time, I circled in pen. The day I was going to meet my attacker again.

Like all the others, it had to be planned meticulously, take a route with limited cameras, check for CCTV near the church, arrive earlier than the people attending for worship, I'd got to avoid any witnesses, give myself time to get away.

I'd been lucky so far; the police hadn't got much to go on. I'd been careful. No bystanders, no DNA, no connections to the people already killed, and nothing to link me to the crimes… perfection.

I decided to pack the boot the night before, avoiding anyone seeing me load up the black bag I'd used on all the slayings.

Two days previous, I'd made a detour before returning home, taking the route to where they were I thought they lived. It checked out, there were no speed cameras as far as I could tell, but I never exceeded the speed limit anyway.

Driving slowly past the car park, I counted eleven cars, the people attending a service inside the church.

I parked my car about fifty yards down the road, and walked back, casually checking for any CCTV, giving me additional insight into the surroundings.

There it was, on the glass-covered wooden notice board outside, the image of my victim, dressed in a dark suit, a silver cross on his lapel, and right underneath, the opening times for all the church services. The day and time of my plot were confirmed.

Wednesday was initially uneventful. Work demands as normal, but I decided to finish earlier than usual, returning home and having two strong cups of coffee, settling my nerves before setting off.

I checked once again that I'd got all the equipment I needed. I'd recently obtained a gruesome mask to cover my face whilst also putting in one additional item that I might require.

The journey over was unexciting, although the wind did begin to intensify as I drove over the Derbyshire hills. Thankfully, traffic was light, and as usual, I stuck to the speed limit, arriving in plenty of time.

I'd previously checked the car park for CCTV coverage, but there wasn't any, so instead of parking down the road and walking back, I parked just outside the front entrance to the church, next to a SAAB 900.

A sticker on the rear screen stating, JESUS SAVES.

Probably my victims.

One last look around, the place seemed deserted, and I began to wonder if I'd misjudged the situation, made a mistake and that they wouldn't be here.

Taking the black bag out of the boot, and putting on the mask and gloves, finger by finger, I made my way to the front of the church. Noticing that both double doors were open, revealing another door with a small window pane, which was closed. Glancing inside I checked that the coast was clear, and wasn't going to be interrupted, it was.

As I opened the door, the wind blew it out of my grasp, banging it into the side wall, the sounds echoing through the building.

The soft patterned carpet camouflaged my steps as I entered what was much larger inside than it looked from the outside.

Steven Andrews turned off the shower and exited the cubicle, leaving wet footprints on the black tiles floor as he wrapped a large towel around his waist.

The shower and toilet facilities had been constructed within the church several years ago, the funding supported by a late parishioner's will.

Drying himself and casually dressed, he slowly walked across the passageway to his office, noticing how cold it seemed.

He knew the two front doors to the church were left open, but he could have sworn that he'd closed the middle door.

Looking out of his office window, the shrubs were moving in the wind, all in unison, moving in the same direction.

Had he put the door on the latch or had the wind blown it open, either way, he quickly decided to go and take a quick look.

As he started to walk towards the front doors, he glanced down to see several hymn sheets on the floor, which had blown off the small wooden table to the side. He picked them up, light from the large front window, casting shadows across the carpet, and put them back in place, closing the middle door, and returning to his office.

Switching on his laptop, he waits for the black screen to come to life. Unsure initially, then instantly noticing a reflection in the PC of someone standing in the doorway, dressed in dark clothing and wearing a terrifying face mask.

Glaring closer at the screen, he notices that they're holding what looks like a large knife in their hand.

The figure stood completely still, blocking the front exit to safety, the large knife moving backwards and forward, dangling from their hand, glinting in the sunlight.

As fear begins to move up Steven Andrews body, he stands and quickly decides to make a run for it towards the back entrance to the church. But the masked intruder is too fast, closing the distance between them and pushing him to the floor.

He'd never been so frightened in all his life, as he tried to catch his breath from the fall, new carpet fibres filling his nostrils. The intruder kneels on his back, securing his hands in place with a plastic tie.

'Whatever you want, money, the laptop, my wallet, just take it,' cries Steven. 'You can have it all, just don't hurt me, please, I beg of you.'

He gets no answer, as the stab of a knife cuts right into the middle of his shoulder blades.

The pain immediately travels through his body, as he hears what sounds like a bag being scraped along the carpeted floor.

Zipping open the black bag I take out a sharp four-inch knife and a pair of electric wire pliers, laying them down on the floor, like a surgeon preparing for a major operation.

Steven Andrews can feel warm blood flowing down his back and onto his chest as a second stab and then a third, all-penetrating around the same area. He continues to struggle to get his breath, as he inhales, more blood seems to ooze out from the wounds.

With intensified strength, the dark-dressed figure grabs hold of his body and turns him over, pinning his arms and hands to the floor. And for the first time, as his vision began to fade, Steven Andrews looked into the eyes of his killer.

Seventy-eight

SITTING AT THE BREAKFAST BAR, Adam was working on his laptop, making final notes for the unscheduled meeting with DCS Slater.

Viv walked into the kitchen; she was already dressed for work in the new uniforms that Peter Johnson had introduced. Pale blue trousers with a matching loose-fitting 'V' neck top, and the medical centre logo on the breast pocket.

'Coffee smells good, do you want another cup?' she asks.

'Yes please,' and passes her his mug, their hands connecting.

'You're up early, working from home today?'

'Maybe later on, I've got to go over to a meeting at EMSCO, DCS Slater sent me a text late last night. He wants to see me first thing, so I thought to make some notes about the case and catch up on some work beforehand, you never know how long these things last, then come back home later.'

'Why do you think DCS Slater wants to see you, surely it would be Tom Vickers?'

'*It will* be to do with the case. The latest victim was a potential drug dealer, he may have been part of a wider gang, Craig Slater is the SIO. There could be a connection between that case and the one we are working on. I continue to report directly to Tom Vickers, yes, this is just cross-functional working with this other team based in Nottingham.'

Drinking their coffee in silence Viv turns to Adam. 'Have you heard anything from Sarah Ward recently, it seems to have gone very quiet?'

He knew that before long, the subject of Scarlett's disappearance would come up in conversation, as there were no further updates, he'd tried to avoid bringing the subject up.

He'd already contacted DS Ward several days ago, all she could tell him was that the investigation was ongoing, but with no further information and no new leads.

She was struggling to know how to proceed. She did agree to have a chat with DCI Chris Mitchell and see if he had any suggestions, feedback was, that he hadn't.

Adam looked up from his PC, took a further drink of coffee, and quickly thought through how to reply.

'I spoke with Sarah a couple of days ago, I meant to say something but completely forgot. The case will continue to be live, however, at the moment there seems no actual progress. As we know, the witness at the grocery store. He's given an accurate account of what he now remembers, but all trails have gone cold.'

'So, what are you saying, no more leads, no progress… No hope.

He saw the sadness in Viv's eyes. How could he explain that the longer Scarlett was missing, the less likelihood there was of finding her, at least alive?

Delivering bad news to loved ones was always difficult, but part and parcel of the job, turning up at someone's front door, and seeing the hopelessness carved on their faces, it never gets any easier.

But when it's your own, as close to home as it gets, that's when it's impossible to see your way forward.

Adam promised Viv that he'd never give up looking for Scarlett, but as the months and years went by, even he had to bring himself to concede that their daughter could join thousands of other children and ultimately remain a MISPER.

He puts down the screen on his laptop and holds her hand.

'Listen, sweetheart, there is always hope, everyone involved is doing the absolute best that they can to find out what has happened to Scarlett.

We have the best team on the case. I know they're doing everything they can to find out the truth, and I will never give up, not ever, until I know what took place that day. Wherever Scarlett is, I'll find her, and that's a promise.'

The M1 South was already busy with a constant stream of vehicles, mostly cars and vans. But also, the occasional lorry holding up the near side and middle lanes.

Roadworks had reduced the maximum speed limit to 50 miles per hour, frustratingly, apart from the traffic, there seemed to be no work taking place and no sign of human life.

Arriving in plenty of time at EMSCO headquarters, Adam switched off the engine, sitting there, staring out of the front windscreen. Running through in his mind what could he have done differently? Should he have taken the lead in the investigation?'

No, Chris Mitchell was the SIO, and he'd had wide experience of investigating missing children in the past, also, he volunteered, both as a work colleague and more to the point, a personal friend of both Vivian and Adam.

'You too close to the case Adam,' he'd stated. 'It's going to be difficult for all of us, but I'm going to be the SIO, leading the team, running the investigation, getting results. I'll keep you updated obviously, but leave it to me, is that clear.'

And yet here they were, just over four years later, Chris had moved on, and still no answers.

Getting out of the AUDI A4, he locked the doors with the key fob and walked to the front door of EMSCO HQ, noticing the wooden pallets were still outside.

Announcing his arrival, a smartly dressed young woman opened the far side door and asked him to follow her up the stairs, it was only the second time Adam had been there, but they'd already remembered his name.

DCS Craig Slater sat at his desk, talking to someone who'd got their back to Adam, as he weaved his way through the workstations and across the office it wasn't until he got closer that he recognised the overweight shape of Tom Vickers.

Introductions over and coffee ordered, Craig Slater immediately got down to business.

'Thanks for coming in Adam, both Tom and I have been discussing the progress on the case, in particular, the murder of Ross Sullivan. There have been some further developments, we're now certain that he *was* involved in drug smuggling. Probably a middleman, setting up supply meetings, agreeing quantities, negotiating prices, but relatively low down in the food chain.'

A young male officer placed three cups of coffee in front of them; Craig waited until the officer was out of earshot.

'Even if he was still alive, it's doubtful he'd have led us to the top people. Do his time. Keep his mouth shut, and avoid suffering a similar death to the individual we found in Sherwood Forest.'

Adam had come prepared to talk comprehensively about all the individual cases, and he wasn't too concerned about raising the murder of Arthur Richardson if it came up in conversation, the wrong man had been put away, simple as that.

Over the next two and a half hours, the three officers went over every single detail about the murders of Arthur Richardson, Patricia Locke and latterly, Ross Sullivan.

DCS Slater occasionally looked at the two of them as he took copious notes. Tom Vickers just sat at the side of Adam, generally in complete silence.

It was 12:45 p.m. when unexpected food arrived. M&S packaged sandwiches, bags of assorted crisps, orange juice and fruit, typical office working lunch.

'How are we doing with the press?' Adam asked, 'The locals haven't covered anything at the moment, do you think we're at the stage where we need to get them involved, hold a press briefing for example?'

Craig Slater looked at Tom Vickers, then replied, 'I've spoken with both editors of the locals, and they've agreed to continue media silence for the present time, but press briefings may need to be considered, that's your decision Tom,' who just nodded his head up and down in DCS Slater's direction.

'One other important point we wanted to discuss with you Adam, and the main reason that I've invited DCI Vickers here today,' he glances down at the paperwork in front of him.

'I've been speaking with DCI Chris Mitchell, we used to work together, I understand you know him well?'

'We worked together when I was in Sheffield, he's a personal friend too,' replied Adam.

'Do you think that the disappearance of your daughter could have anything to do with the drug gangs you brought down whilst working in Yorkshire?'

Adam enjoyed enormous satisfaction in preparing answers for meetings in advance, in particular when you were in front of your superiors or the press.

Being able to reply with confidence to tough questions made life so much easier in the long run, you weren't playing catch. But this question, a complete curve ball, hit him like a bolt out of the blue.

'It's a scenario I've considered time after time sir. The drug gang I brought to justice, did they plan and take revenge? Not on me or my wife Vivian, but the one thing that bonds us both together, that would hurt us the most, our daughter Scarlett. We never managed to identify or arrest the ringleaders, no one would talk, probably out of fear for their life or their family's safety. So, yes… if I was looking for a sound reason why someone would kidnap our daughter, and recently I have, then the drug gang retribution makes absolute sense.'

Just as he was about to continue the conversation both mobile phones rang in unison, Tom Vickers picked his up off the desk and answered. 'It's for you Adam, DS Bailey.'

'Hi boss, when convenient, you need to leave the meeting ASAP, we've got another murder victim.'

Seventy-nine

RETURNING TO HIS CAR, Adam checked the postcode Frank had texted him over. DE4 5BZ, Edgewater Congregation Church, Crich, Derbyshire.

He knew the route from Central Derbyshire HQ, the satnav telling him that the fastest route was back up the M1 to junction 28, taking the A38 towards the outskirts of the town centre of Crich.

Like the southbound, the northbound carriageway was limited to 50 miles an hour, the traffic heavier than earlier in the day, Adam weaved his way through lines of traffic, deciding that the car's blue lights were essential, informing vehicles of his presence, allowing him to get to the crime scene urgently.

As he approached the church car park, avoiding the onlookers at the entrance, an officer lifted the blue and white POLICE DO NOT CROSS tape.

He parked his car next to Frank Bailey's Ford Mondeo.

Before entering the church, he glances back towards the faces of the people who'd gathered outside, checking that no one in a black and white baseball cap was standing in the crowd.

It was all clear.

Several officers stood in the car park, ensuring no one entered the church unofficially. A PC was standing inside the double doors, recording Adam's name in the logbook, they both looked at each other, not saying a word.

As he entered the church through a single wooden door, it caused red rose petals to dance across the carpeted floor.

Trying to find Frank Bailey he noticed several people fully dressed in white Tyvek overalls, white overshoes, and face masks, two were standing over a body, blood stains on both their knees, someone else was taking photographs, whilst a further person was recording verbal notes.

One of the figures stood upright, lowering their face mask.

'Good afternoon DI Fox, we must stop meeting like this, and I mean it.'

'Hi Dr Munroe, good to see you too, but I'd prefer better circumstances… Does anyone know where DS Bailey is?'

Rachel looks around then briefly answers, 'I think he is taking a statement from a parishioner who found the body, in one of the side rooms I understand. Before you go, can I talk you through our initial findings?'

She walks over to one of the other Tyvek wearers and takes a folder from his hand, focusing closely on the first page.

'So, as usual, we'll know more once we get them back to the morgue. But our initial examination of the body shows that they suffered three deep cuts into their back, in between the shoulder blades. That's not how he died, however. The body was then turned over and their throat was cut with what we believe to be a long sharp knife, from left to right. So probably right-handed, slicing straight through the neck just below their Adam's apple… that's what killed them.'

Adam took a closer look, realising for the first time that the body lying on the floor in front of him was Steven Andrews.

His white face was covered in blood. Three deep cuts on his forehead, one vertical, one horizontal and one connecting the other two. Trying to resemble the image of a number, a number four.

***

Looking around outside the church and away from the body, they checked that the coast was clear, no one was watching them or in hearing distance as they made the call.

The mobile was picked up on the third ring, 'I told you never to call me on this number unless it's an emergency, so what's the problem?'

'There's been another murder, this time it's a minister at a local church apparently, what do you want me to do?'

'Has DI Fox arrived?'

'Yes, he's just pulled into the car park. I'm very nervous, I think he knows something. I don't think I can keep doing this, it's not what I signed up for, it's getting out of hand, I could lose my job.'

'You'll do as you're told, understand. Otherwise, you could end up like some of the others, remember the corpse in Sherwood Forest, you *don't* want that to happen to you?'

There was a deathly silence before they replied.

'I'm sorry, it's just you know, getting too much for me, if they were to find out it was me forwarding the info, I'd be out on my ear.'

'If you don't calm down you'll have no ears for them to throw you out with… Understand.'

'I'll make the call, and the observer will be there as soon as possible, stop panicking, you'll only draw attention to yourself, and neither of us want that do we?'

The phone went dead.

***

Dr Rachel Munroe agreed to have the autopsy with Adam by eleven am the following morning. He knew he was getting in the way of the Forensic Pathologist, excusing himself and making his way towards the side of the church.

Walking towards the front of the building, he looked up at the brightly coloured glass window above him, the sunlight illuminating every panel.

DS Frank Bailey was sitting at a round table, two blue cups and saucers in front of him. He was interviewing a pale-looking woman dressed in a tweed skirt, with a beige-coloured knitted cardigan, introducing her as Mrs Philippa Wilton, one of the church parishioners, and the one who found the body.

She was drying her eyes on a floral handkerchief as Frank introduced her to Adam, a slight smell of lavender coming from her clothes.

'Mrs Wilton, this is Detective Inspector Fox, he's my boss and will be leading the investigation into the death of Mr Andrews.'

Adam pulled up a chair and sat down across from the two of them, replying.

'Thanks for taking the time to speak with us, I'm very sorry that we've had to interview you in this way, but I understand that you were the person who found the body?'

She wiped her eyes again, blew her nose on the handkerchief, folded it up and stuffed it into the arm of the cardigan, Adam noticing that her hands were trembling.

'I usually come and clean the church twice a week, since my husband passed away, it gets me out of the house and gives me something to do.'

'I understand DS Bailey had already taken a statement from you, but could you briefly talk us through what happened when you arrived?'

Philipa Wilton glanced around the room, ensuring that no one else was listening to what she was about to say.

'I arrived at my usual time, about eleven-thirty this morning. Usually, I make a hot drink for myself and Steven before I start cleaning. I went into the side office to see if he wanted tea or coffee. I thought it was unusual as the inside door was open, normally it's closed to keep the church warmer, but today it was left open. I also noticed rose petals on the floor, which I thought was very odd, as there are no rose trees in the garden of the church, either at the front or the back. I didn't think any more about it, I just carried on walking into his office. As I turned the corner I initially just saw the bottom of his feet on the floor, moving further in I then saw the body, lying there covered in blood. I panicked, didn't know what to do, didn't do first aid, and all that blood around his mouth. I dialled 999 on my mobile and was immediately put through to the ambulance service and the police. The person at the end of the phone gave me instructions on what to do. Check for breathing, all that sort of thing, but he wasn't breathing, he was dead. The police arrived before the ambulance crew, two officers in uniform, and then this gentleman arrived, asked me to wait and he'd come and see me later. That's it, that's all I know, it's such a shock, lying there, just lying there, covered in blood. I don't know what the church will do?'

***

He mingled with the crowd that had gathered outside the front of the church, avoiding being seen, images of DI Adam Fox captured on their mobile phone.

He turned away and quietly returned to his parked car, located down one of the side streets.

Starting the engine, he looked in the rear-view mirror, adjusting his black and white baseball cap as he slowly drove away, avoiding drawing attention to himself.

Eighty

DI FOX WALKED INTO THE BRIEFING room and took up his position in front of the whiteboards, now showing images of four victims, Arthur Richardson, Patricia Locke, Ross Sullivan and now the minister at Edgewater community church, Steven Andrews.

Dr Rachel Munroe had emailed over a photograph of the last victim, having cleaned his face of blood before taking the shot, it still didn't show Steven Andrews in a good light, however.

Detective Sergeant Frank Bailey had already started the briefing as Adam entered the room, he'd got an update meeting on the case with DCI Vickers, and knowing him, it could go on for ages.

'We need to focus on the facts everyone, take a look at the images on the board behind me, four people have been murdered by what we now believe is the same person or persons. We've included Arthur Richardson,' Frank taps the photograph of Richardson with his pen, 'he was the first victim, brutally killed almost fifteen years ago. The latest victim is Steven Andrews, a minister at Edgewater Community Church in Chrich, he was viciously murdered yesterday. Before I hand over to Detective Inspector Fox, let me say one final thing. Whoever is doing this isn't going to stop, they're getting a thrill out of it, enjoying seeing people suffer, giving the police a runaround. They're clever, they plan the executions, gather information about their victims, and hunt them down, taking trophies, and body parts. But hey… that's just my opinion.'

'I wouldn't have put it quite like that,' Adam stated to the whole team, 'but you know what, DS Bailey is probably correct. The person or people responsible for these horrendous crimes won't get away with it, we will find them and bring them to justice. They'll make a mistake, they always do, that's a known fact. I know everyone in this room is working to the highest standards and let me say on behalf of DS Bailey and myself, it's appreciated, I couldn't ask for a better-committed team than the one that sits in front of me.'

Pausing, he could feel the emotion in the room, one of gratitude he'd like to think.

'Let's not forget what we're faced with here. There's no motives, no evidence, and no DNA. They must travel by car, but we have no

ANPR recordings. There were no witnesses. No fingerprints. All four of the people involved didn't know each other. Had completely separate lives, different ages and genders. So, we've still nothing concrete to go on.

The autopsy on Steven Andrews should be through later this afternoon, it might give us some further insight, but I wouldn't count on it.'

He takes a step back, glancing at the images on the whiteboards. 'Finally, when we do make an arrest and bring this person or people to justice, we do it by the book. There are no cutting corners, we must get this right, the investigation *will* continue to be conducted professionally and ethically as it has been from the start. As a division, we can't afford any cockups, the case for the CPS must be completely watertight, is that clear? Okay, thanks everyone, now let's get back to work. Frank, I'll catch you later.'

He takes a final look around the briefing room before leaving, the faces of some officers said it all. They were all asking the same question, is there a serial killer on the loose?

He didn't think there was, but he couldn't rule it out.

Adam knocks on DCI Vickers's office door, he doesn't want to be invited in, so he enters.

Tom Vickers sat in his black leather chair, his stomach eating into the top of the desk, his large hands cupped in front of him.

Looking directly at Adam, he asks him to take a seat, his facial expressions looking even more strained than normal.

'Morning Adam, thanks for your time, I know how busy you are presently.' He pauses to gather his thoughts.

'I've just taken a call from upstairs, the chief super is becoming increasingly concerned that 'little progress is being made on the current cases', her words, not mine. We need a breakthrough, I know everyone is working flat out, but I'm under pressure to get a result.'

'If we'd have conducted the first murder correctly, we might not be in this position now,' he thought to himself.

'I've just come from a briefing meeting sir; talked with the team, and explained how critical it is for a result, but we have to get the right one, no more mistakes this time around.'

Tom Vickers knew exactly what he was referring to but kept quiet, knowing he couldn't defend the decision he made all those years ago.

'I understand the pressure you're under sir; I feel the same. Whoever is doing this, *will* come unstuck, people like this, believing they've got us on the run, thinking that they're always one step ahead, they'll make a mistake, and when they do, we'll be there to make the arrest.'

'I know Adam, and I understand why you're applying caution to the investigation, rightly so under the circumstances. You're right, we can't afford another mistake like Daniel Ashby's. That was my fault, but at the time the evidence was sound, or as sound as it ever can be. But, I made a big mistake, put away the wrong man, a decision I'll always regret, and I'll have to live with that decision.'

Moments passed before Adam picked up the conversation once again.

'There's one more point I need to discuss with you, I think we have someone passing on information about the investigations. When I arrived at the murder of Patricia Locke, I noticed there was someone taking notes and photographs on their mobile phone, dressed in a dark coat, and wearing a black and white baseball cap. Didn't think anything about it, just a nosy observer. But then it happened again at Ross Sullivan's flat, the same person, dark coat, and baseball cap, trying to mingle with the crowd in the park opposite. By the time I'd got out of my car, they'd gone, but there's no mistaking it, someone is leaking location details of the murders, and it's not within the team, Frank assures me of that, and I think I believe him.'

'Why do you think someone's passing on information? The press continues to be silent, so no leaks to them. Therefore, what's the aim, and what are they gaining from it?

'I have no idea, sir, interestingly, I didn't notice anything suspicious at the church when I arrived yesterday. It just doesn't make sense, taking photographs for no apparent reason.'

Tom Vickers leaned back in his leather chair; it creaked loudly under his weight.

'This is just a thought Adam, have you considered that it might have nothing to do with the investigations, maybe something completely separate? Remember what DCS Slater said about your daughter's disappearance, if it's gang-related, it could be personal, with nothing to do with the current murders.

They could be coming after you or Vivian.'

Eighty-one

DS FRANK BAILEY WAS AT HIS desk when Adam shouted him over, switching off his PC, he made his way to the DI's office.

'Coffee boss and a bar of chocolate?' 'Cheers Frank, black and I'll take a KitKat.'

Checking his email messages, the autopsy had come through from Dr. Rachel Munroe, Adam printed two copies off, putting them to one side on his desk, just as Frank arrived back.

'So how do you think the briefing went? Were there any further suggestions or comments after I left the room?'

'The team are getting frustrated, everyone's feeling the pressure, there's just nothing much to go on. We've been working completely in the dark, the only link to all the killings is the numbers carved on the foreheads of the victims and those bloody rose petals, what's that all about?'

Adam takes a drink of his coffee and a bite of the KitKat, 'Listen, Frank, it's like I've just told Tom Vickers, we will get a breakthrough, they'll make a mistake, or someone will come forward with information that will lead to a suspect. We're all feeling the pressure, just reassure the team that they continue to get my full support. I told them as such. I also told the DCI about the baseball cap; you know the person taking photographs at the first two crime scenes. He has a different angle on what's going on and doesn't think it has anything to do with the murders, he believes it could be a personal vendetta. Can I speak confidentially? Frank nods his head in agreeance.

'When I went to EMSCO, DCS Slater threw a real curve ball at me about my daughter's disappearance. As you know, Scarlett went missing when she was about twenty-two months old, taken from our back garden when we lived in Sheffield. DCI Chris Mitchell was initially conducting the investigation, we used to work together and he's also a close friend of the family. That's now been passed onto a DS Sarah Ward. Both Viv and I have met up with Sarah a couple of times, more to put Viv's mind at rest, so at least she believes something is being done. But, at present, there's been little progress, a possible sighting of people sitting in a car outside the back fence of the garden, but nothing concrete. The point is, Craig Slater now believes that Scarlett's abduction… well, that it could be linked to organised drug gangs.'

Adam noticed for the first time, a look of emotion on Frank's face, something he'd never seen before.

'I'm sorry boss, that's an awful position to be in, for both you and Vivian, if there's anything I can do to help, anything at all, you just need to ask.'

'The thing is, we never uncovered the top players in the gang, they're still out there, operating as usual, still supplying hard drugs to anyone who'll pay for them. But, if Craig Slater is right, and it's something I've considered carefully, then this *is* personal, they've taken my daughter, we might never see her again, or even worse, she might be dead.'

Adam took another drink of coffee, spitting it back into the cup, it was stone cold.

'If you don't mind boss, I need to get on, and write up the briefing notes, is there anything else we need to go through?

'Yeah, there's one other thing… Can we trust the team we have on this case?, you know why I'm asking, someone is feeding inside information about the killings. The person wearing the dark coat and cap, they were there, at both Patricia Locke's and Ross Sullivans, taking photos on their mobile phone.'

'Can you ever trust a team one hundred percent, the answer to that is no. I've worked with most of these officers for months, sometimes years, and I don't believe any of them would leak details of an ongoing case, I genuinely don't.'

'Well, whoever it is, they must have a reason, financial paybacks, blackmail, personal threats, whatever or whoever it is, we need to find out Frank.'

He reached over and opened the file on the autopsy report, passing a copy over to Frank. Scanning over the document he noticed two sentences which Rachel Munroe had highlighted in BOLD, he couldn't believe what he was reading.

'Bloody hell, have you read this? The second page, halfway down. Steven Andrews's teeth were pulled out, which explains all the blood on his face. Four front teeth in total, numbers seven, eight, nine and ten According to the Forensic Pathologist, he was probably still alive at the time.'

Eighty-two

DR PETER JOHNSON CHECKED his watch, it read 12:47 p.m. sitting at the top of the conference table, his personalised black leather folder in front of him.

He'd arranged the monthly staff meeting for the whole team at Edgewater Medical Centre.

This was something that he'd carried on from when his father had the practice, the quote he'd always used was. '*One of the deep secrets of life is that all that is really worth doing is what we do for others.'*

Peter Johnson knew that he'd never be the remarkable physician his father had been, taken too early in life, but, if he could be half the man he was, he wouldn't complain.

Vivian was the first to take her seat, looking around the room, and deciding to sit opposite Peter, she knew what the main agenda point was going to be, and wanted to be seen as still part of the team, albeit now, she was the senior partner.

By 12:54 p.m. everyone was seated at the conference table, as Peter opened his folder to go through the first agenda point, leaving the announcement of Vivian Flemming to the position of senior partner to the end.

By 1:20 p.m. the hand clapping and words of *'congratulations'* had subsided; it was now time for lunch before the afternoon shift started.

Viv returned to her consultation room, shortly followed by a knock on her door.

Beth the senior receptionist entered, as usual, she had a mug of tea in her hand, placing it in front of Viv. 'Here you go Dr Flemming, I thought you'd like another cup of tea before you start your afternoon patient list, a hot one this time. If you don't mind me saying, the whole team is delighted about your appointment. We need some fresh thinking and ideas in the practice, and I think we'll get it now you're in this new position.'

Viv took a quick sip of her drink; Beth was right, it *was* hot.

'Thanks, Beth, Peter and I are going to do everything we can to ensure that Edgewater Medical Centre continues to offer the highest standard of patient care where possible. We also want to look after our staff, whether full or part-time. Everyone can play their part, from patient bookings to new medications. Please let everyone know that this medical centre is the place to be, both for staff and patients.'

Beth smiled and closed the door behind her.

It was early evening when Viv arrived home. Adam's car was already on the drive, and she noticed that he'd done as he promised days ago and watered the hanging baskets and planters on the front.

As she placed her laptop case on the floor, the smell of Indian food wafted down the hallway, 'No more work for Vivian tonight,' she said under her breath.

Adam popped his head around the kitchen door, a large glass of white wine in his hand, 'The dining room is set, all you've got to do is go and take your uniform off, and the meal will be ready.'

'I think I'll take a shower if you don't mind, and I'll put some clothes on too, just a thought,' winking at him as she climbed the stairs.

Although it was a takeaway, it was nearly two hours before they'd both finished the meal, Adam had made a fruit salad for dessert one of Viv's favourites being very healthy and full of flavour.

He poured her a third glass of wine; they'd already finished one bottle. Making their way into the lounge, putting some music on, Burt Bacharach Live at The Sydney Opera House.

Taking a larger-than-usual drink from the glass, he asked Viv what sort of day she'd had at work.

'It's gone well actually, we had the usual monthly practice meeting and Peter announced to the team about my partnership, he'd already told me he was going to do it, so it didn't come as a surprise.'

'What was the reaction?

'Well, I've only spoken to the senior receptionist, but according to her, everyone seems delighted with the changes. The next three to six months will be the decisive test, if everything goes according to how Peter expects it to go, then we should end up with more patients, increased income, and the opportunity to expand into other services, such as Physiotherapy, as an example.'

'That sounds great, so no regrets on investing the money then?'

'No, not at all, just so long as you're comfortable with it?'

'Yeah, of course, I am, and it was good of your parents to offer us the money, I realise that now.'

Adam had consciously decided earlier in the day that he'd got to tell Viv about the possible abduction of Scarlett by the criminal gangs, but it was easier said than done.

'Listen, sweetheart, there's something I've got to tell you.' He took hold of her hand, noticing the diamonds in her wedding ring, reflecting in the lounge lights.

'I had a meeting with DCS Slater recently, initially, it was an update on the case, but he also mentioned something that we need to talk about. You know that DS Sarah Ward is investigating the disappearance of Scarlett, well, Craig Slater now believes it could be linked to organised crime.'

He knew that trying to dress the conversation up was a waste of time, Viv was used to delivering unwelcome news to patients, she's always wanted to know the full facts.

'It probably stems back to my time in Sheffield when we infiltrated that drug gang if you remember, most of them got long prison sentences, but we never got the top people, they're still out there.'

He takes a further drink of white wine.

'Craig Slater has also spoken with Chris Mitchell; he also thinks there could be a connection. I've spoken to Sarah Ward this afternoon and explained what we now believe may have happened. She's promised to continue her investigation, and to keep me fully posted on any further developments, no matter how insignificant.'

He looked into Viv's eyes expecting tears, but instead, she had a look of relief, almost like it was a release after all this time.

They didn't speak for almost an hour. There were no words to say, they just sat there, hand in hand, alone in their lounge, with their private thoughts.

Viv was the first to move, 'I'm going to make some coffee, would you like one brought in?'

'Coffee would be great; I'll come and give you a hand.'

As she stood at the NESPRESSO coffee machine, placing two pods into the machine, Adam wrapped his arms around her waist.

'Craig Slater could be completely wrong you know; there's no evidence that Scarlett's disappearance has any connection to organised gangs. It's his assumption, and yes, he could be right, they may have retaliated for me bringing down their operation. Whatever happened on that day, I'll never give up trying to uncover the truth, no matter how long it takes. And if that means I have to continue working to bring down these brutal drug gangs. Then so be it.'

Eighty-three

TAKING OUT THE FADED PHOTOGRAPH of Chaffinch House, I smooth the curved edges out and pull the top off the red marker pen. Scrawling a thick X through the image on the back row, identifying the Reverent Steven Andrews, as he was known at that time.

He only visited the boarding school occasionally, and only on a Sunday to take part in the morning service.

If only on that sunny day, I hadn't taken that walk around the lake, making my way into the bushes with him, it would never have happened, but it did, and he had to pay the price.

Still on occasions when I take a shower, I catch sight in the bathroom mirror, of the scar he left on my shoulder blade as he bit into my flesh, drawing my blood.

So, whilst he was still conscious, removing his front teeth with the pliers, making *him* bleed, and hearing *him* beg for mercy, was payback for me and any other boy he'd probably tried to abuse.

***

When Simon returned later in the evening, I decided to tell him about what had happened to me whilst walking round the lake. He said he regretted leaving me whilst he went out with his parents, which was nonsense, but a kind thing to say, I guess that's a true measure of our friendship, a friendship that was brutally taken away from Toby.

As bedtime approached, I became increasingly anxious about what might have happened if I hadn't defended myself. And also, what could lie ahead this Sunday evening? The ruffing up, pulling me out of bed, and dragging me down the corridor.

Unfortunately, it continued to happen.

I wasn't sure what time it was when they hauled me down the dark corridor, the door creaking as it opened. He stood there looking up and down at me, a smile on his face, the older boys, pushing me towards him as they closed the door.

His large hand with the signet ring pulled back my hair, his breath smelling of smoke, as the first punch hit me in the stomach. I leaned forward, winded, as further thumps hit me right in the middle of my back, making me drop to my knees.

I never knew how long the beating went on, just the ending, when he always took the white handkerchief out of his top jacket pocket, wiping the sweat from his forehead.

He always told me the same thing. 'Tell the headmaster and things will get far worse.'

I didn't, but they still did.

Looking back at the photograph, I run my finger along the top row, counting the number of adults, stopping at one right in the centre.

A tall, well-dressed figure in a white-winged collared shirt, black tie, and long black gown, standing at a slightly elevated level than anyone else, indicating their overall authority.

I knew who they were, they had a responsibility to protect the very boys under their control. They must have known what took place at Chaffinch House but chose to turn a blind eye.

Thankfully, I also knew where they lived, I'd been there before, so unlike my other victims, hunting them down was an easy task.

Checking the bag I always use. It still contained my leather gloves, a range of sharp knives, electrical pliers, plastic ties, and the scary mask, just in case.

And right at the bottom, brown, dead rose petals, I was ready, I just had to decide on a suitable day to carry out my brutal slaying.

Taking my thick red felt tip pen, I mark a circle around the face of the final victim I'm going to execute.

One Wilfred Heathcote. The headmaster at Chaffinch House.

Eighty-four

THE POLICE OFFICER EXITED the staff lift and made his way through reception to the outside car park. He turned his head to the right, nodding briefly to the officer behind reception, who was occupied, speaking to someone on the telephone, jotting down some details.

His car was located to the right of the front of Derbyshire police headquarters, the staff car park.

Holding the key fob, he opened the door to the Mini Cooper and sat in the front seat.

He'd only purchased the low mileage car around eighteen months ago, it was his pride and joy, cleaned every week inside and out.

None of his colleagues had ever asked how he could afford an almost brand-new Mini on a police officer's salary. But if they had, he'd rehearsed a very plausible answer, he didn't drink or smoke and to date, hadn't got a girlfriend.

The monthly cash he received from the people he associated with gave him a lifestyle that he'd never be able to achieve normally, but guilt and fear were starting to creep in.

Did his work colleagues suspect anything? He was beginning to think that the Detective Sergeant was, but he couldn't put a finger on why.

However, he found he was continually looking over his shoulder, just to check. But that wasn't his concern, what kept him awake at night, was constant fear, the fear that he could easily be disposed of.

Why did he get involved? He'd got no financial worries, lived with his parents, and his father was proud that he'd joined the force.

But he'd taken the first payment, and he knew there was no way out, well, there undoubtedly was, but it would be the end of a career that he loved.

Also, he didn't want to end up in Sherwood Forest, tongue cut out, nailed to a tree, like a crucifixion.

Looking out of the windows, he checked that no one was around, the coast was clear. The inside of the Mini was cold, but he could feel the perspiration on his forehead and his heart pounding in his chest.

He took out the burner phone he'd been given and dialled the number, placing it to his ear, and waiting nervously for pickup.

'I trust this is important, ringing me at this time of the day,' came the answer.

'I wanted to speak with you straightaway, I've got an update on the case.' The line was silent as he carried on speaking.

'Did you know that Ross Sullivan was dealing in drugs? His death is being investigated on two fronts. He's been murdered, but they think it might also be linked to drug dealings, I just wanted you to know.'

There was no immediate answer. 'Are you still there, did you hear what I just said?'

'Yeah I heard all that, we already knew he was being checked out, if they'd get any closer, we'd got plans to correct the issue. Thankfully, someone did the work for us. Don't worry your tiny mind about that, just concentrate on what you're paid to do, keeping a close eye on DI Fox. We want to know all his movements, what other cases he is working on, that sort of thing.

We already know about his daughter's disappearance; that's not your concern. But listen to me, if you can't do this anymore, then maybe you're surplus to requirements.'

There was nothing more to be said. The call ended.

***

Adam and Frank were already on their second cup of coffee, having arranged to meet up early. They'd already discussed all the key updates on the case, Frank becoming increasingly frustrated with the lack of progress. This frustration came out in language that Adam could only recall from his time at university.

'Listen, I understand how you and the team are feeling. But some investigations take longer than others. Several years ago, when I was at South Yorkshire, we held a joint regional conference with West Yorkshire Police, it was one of the most prolific serial killings ever. What were the key learnings and how could the force have done things differently? It took the investigating team five years to find and arrest the culprit, and it turned out to be one of the most expensive manhunts in British history.'

Detective Sergeant Bailey took his job seriously. Okay, he was a little rough around the edges and didn't bother too much about appearances or personal hygiene at times, but if you wanted someone on your side, watching your back, he was right for the job.

When the body of Patricia Locke had been found, he hadn't initially informed Adam about the situation, instead, he'd gone directly to DCI Vickers. He now realised that was a mistake, a genuine one. But one that he was now trying to put right.

The working relationship between a Detective Sergeant and their immediate boss was always seen within the ranks of the police as a critical one, approached with honesty and integrity.

Frank had reported to several Detective Inspector's over time, some worse than others. In the past, DI Vickers hadn't always been whiter than white, often cut corners, and didn't do things by the book.

But Detective Inspector Adam Fox was different, a little too intense, at times, but his natural intuition for finding the underlying cause of a case made him exceptionally skilled in his job, undoubtedly, he was one of the best bosses he's ever reported to.

'If you don't mind boss, am I okay to take a few hours off tomorrow morning, Julie wants me to go with her to the nursing home. The matron has made a provisional appointment for 10:30 a.m. Don't know what it's about, I can come into the office beforehand if you want me to.'

'That's fine Frank, you do enough non-paid overtime. How is your mother-in-law, does she like her new surroundings?'

'Difficult to say, it's early days, but Julie thinks she's settled in okay. We've got to sell the bungalow to fund her care, but that's in hand now, two offers already, with one above the market price.'

'You didn't use WFS, estate agents, did you?'

'Who, Melanie Watkins?. Not a chance. I'll never be able to prove it, but I'm convinced she knew Ross Sullivan was linked to drugs, but we'll never know now.'

Eighty-five

THE SILVER ROLLS ROYCE HEARSE quietly drew up in front of Mary Ashby's house. A short man in a dark suit got out just as the car came to a halt.

He somberly walked down the rose-shrouded path to the front door, gently knocking twice, announcing the arrival of Philip Ashby.

Daniel opened the front door and informed the funeral director that they'd be a few more minutes, his mum was just putting on her coat.

Mary, Danny and his best friend Joe walked down the cobbled path towards the second silver funeral car. Mary stopped briefly, showing little emotion as she glanced at the coffin, with just one single red rose on the top.

Danny had suggested that Joe travel with them in the second car, although the relationship with his dad wasn't great at the best of times, following a hearse in a black 4x4, advertising gardening services, was probably a little too disrespectful after all.

It would have been a natural choice to hold the funeral service at Edgewater Community Church. But with the sudden death of the minister, Steven Andrews, Danny had suggested the local church in the village, St Wystan's.

They didn't expect many people to attend but had arranged a wake at the local pub, The Hand and Spear, the one they understood Philip had visited before his death.

The church was cold as they entered. Danny held onto his mum's arm, as they made their way to the front pews.

Philip Ashby wasn't a particularly popular individual in the village, yes, he regularly saw people on his morning walks, but he generally kept his head down, minding his own business.

What neither Mary nor Danny had accounted for was his friends from his church, where he used to spend a lot of his time.

So, surprisingly, there were many more people in the congregation than they had expected.

The coffin lay on a stainless-steel gurney, in front and to the left of where his family sat.

Danny looked around the church, his hands beginning to feel warm, as the central heating started to kick in, noticing the numbers from the last service still in the carved wooden church hymn boards.

The vicar, the reverend Charles *'Charlie'* Cooper, climbed the steps to the lectern to begin the eulogy.

He'd met Mary and Danny on two separate occasions, the first to pass on his sincere condolences, and the second time to discuss the life of Philip, what they would like to be included, and more importantly, what to be omitted.

He puts down his notes in front of him and takes his position, his wiry figure leaning towards the congregation, as one of the funeral directors gently closes the church doors.

'In the name of the Father, Son and Holy Spirit, Amen. We are gathered here today to remember the life of Philip Lionel Ashby, loving husband to Mary and father to Daniel.'

Charlie Cooper glanced down at his well-prepared notes. 'We all remember Philip not for what he did, but for the person he was. A god-fearing man who committed his later life to the church, it's wonderful to see so many of his fellow congregation here with us today.'

Reverend Cooper already knew that Philip had had a career in the army, but it was decided very early on that this would be inappropriate to mention.

Mary and Danny had suggested to the vicar that they didn't say anything at the funeral, but if necessary, open it up to the congregation if anyone would like to say a few words.

For several moments there was silence in the church apart from the occasional cough, and then from one of the pews at the back, stood a tall-looking man, who with the aid of a walking stick, made his way to the front, placing his hand on the coffin, resting his stick against the wall as he stood behind a small wooden lectern.

Taking out a single sheet of paper and placing his glasses on, he began to speak.

'I hadn't known Philip for very long, but we used to spend time together decorating the new drop-in centre that's recently been opened. We did become quite good friends during this period, but I sometimes used to see sadness in his eyes, he never spoke about his past, and I never asked. I trust he's now in a better place and finally at peace.'

The Reverend Charles Cooper announced the final hymn, 'Abide With Me,' as Philip Ashby made his final journey back towards the entrance to the church.

Mary, Danny and Joe began to make their way down the middle of the aisle, the coffin taking the lead, row after row of unfamiliar faces staring at them.

As they reached the end, Danny, looking around, noticed a face that looked familiar but couldn't remember where he'd seen it before.

The figure stood there alone, Mary Ashby also glanced at them, and a slight smile came across her face.

Eighty-six

'WHAT TIME ARE YOU MEETING the estate agent?. We need to be at the nursing home at 11:15 a.m. to meet with the matron.

Frank had agreed to be at Julie's mum's bungalow to meet the agent managing the sale, they'd had an offer made, it was just going over the final details.

Looking at the kitchen clock, he replied, 'I'm going now, I'll be back just gone ten at the latest, it's only a twenty-minute drive to the nursing home, so we've got plenty of time.'

All of Mavis Thorpe's belongings had been removed from the three-bedroom bungalow she'd lived in all her married life. Julie had taken some things that held fond memories, with several pieces of furniture relocated to the nursing home.

The rest of the items had been cleared away by a house clearing company, who didn't charge for their services.

Frank offered to paint a couple of the rooms, to brighten them up before the property went up for sale, the smell of fresh paint still lingered as he opened the front door.

He was checking the property one last time when the doorbell rang.

'Good morning Mr Bailey, my name is Roger Edwards. I'm the agent managing the sale of your property, thanks for arranging to meet up with me.'

Frank invites him in, although with no furniture they both have to stand.

'We've had a confirmed offer for the property, I just need to go over some final paperwork, and then it's all systems go.'

All the documents seemed to be in order, Frank checked just once more before signing on the bottom line.

'There's one final question we forgot to ask before. There's a couple of shrubs in the garden that my wife would like to remove if that would be okay, her dad planted them years ago, and she'd like them in our garden.'

'I don't see that as a problem, let me check and I'll call you back later, was there anything else you wanted to discuss?'

'No, I think that's it, we're off to the nursing home now, but call me when you have an answer.'

With that, they both made their way to the front door, Frank locking it for the final time and handing over the keys.

It was exactly 10:40 a.m. when they pulled up outside The Lakes Nursing Home, despite the time of year, the sun was out glistening across the lake.

'We're a bit early,' said Frank as he locked the car, 'should we go and see your mum for a while?'

'No, I'd rather hear what the matron's got to say before I see Mum, it's such a lovely morning, shall we walk around the lake, it won't take us long?'

'Good idea.'

It wasn't too long before Julie came across the wooden bench that she'd spotted on their last walk, the overgrown weeds and branches had all been cleared away, making it a good place to sit down.

'I wonder what the matron wants to speak with us about?' Hope it's nothing serious?'

'Don't worry, we'll soon find out, I'm sure it's nothing to get concerned about.'

As they both stood to make their way back, Julie again noticed the bronze plaque on the back of the seat, it had been cleaned and now shone like brand new in the sun.

'I wonder who Toby Curtis was, maybe a resident from long ago, or someone who worked here?'

Frank didn't pay too much attention, but replied, 'You could ask the matron when we get back, she might have some idea who they were.'

Just as they were about to walk up the steps to the front door, Frank's mobile rang, 'Dam, I'd better take this, I think it's the estate agent, you go in, I won't be too long.'

He made his way back down the steps, and right on time, the matron appeared in the reception area.

'Thanks for coming in Julie, I just wanted to have a quick word with you about your mother, is your husband with you?'

'He's just outside on his mobile, he won't be long, but, go one.'

'Let's go to my office, it's more private there.'

The two of them walked down the corridor, Mrs. Latimer, opened the door and asked Julie to take a seat.

'Your mum's been with us for several weeks now, and she's settled down well. Although we're slightly concerned about her memory, she does seem to be getting quite forgetful, it's not an issue, but we are required to keep you updated on your mum's condition. It's manageable from our point of view, that's what we do, we care for elderly people, irrespective of their symptoms. But I needed to let you know just in case you notice something when you're with her.

'Where was Frank when you need him?' Julie thought to herself. 'Thanks for letting me know, it's appreciated. We'd noticed for a while about her forgetfulness, we just put it down to old age, but then things started getting worse. Thankfully, she's in the best place now.'

The call ended and Frank quickly made his way up the steps, seeing the receptionist as he entered. 'Good morning… my wife has a meeting with the matron today, has she gone to see her mum do you know?'

'I'll have to check the patient logbook,' replied the receptionist, 'What's your wife's mum's name?'

'Mavis, Mavis Thorpe.'

The patient logbook was on the desk, opening it she ran her finger down the various names documented, coming across Mavis Thorpe.

'I'm not sure, they went to the matron's office, if she isn't there, she'll be in the SHERWOOD room, but I'd try the office first, it's just down the corridor second on the left.'

Just as he was about to knock on the door, it opened, and Julie and the matron stepped forward.

'Thank you so much for your time matron, we really appreciate what you're doing for Mum, is it okay if we go and see her now?'

'Yes, of course, it is, and don't worry, she's in safe hands, anything else you need to know, just ask.'

There was something that Julie wanted to ask, but for the life of her, she couldn't recall what it was.

Making their way towards the SHERWOOD room, Julie explained to Frank about her mum's memory loss, and what the matron had mentioned to her.

'I don't think it's dementia, but it could be the start I guess, I'm glad we made the decision we did, aren't you?'

Frank got hold of her hand, 'Of course I am, we did everything we could whilst she was at home, the bungalow's sold, it's all going to plan, and she's in a much better place here.'

Forty minutes later they said 'Goodbye' to Mum and closed the door to her room.

Walking back down the corridor, Julie noticed the matron was in the reception area and remembered what she wanted to ask.

'I've got one more question actually, nothing related to mum. When walking around the lake, we came across a wooden bench, in memory of Toby Curtis. I'm just nosy, do you know who he was?'

The matron paused for several moments, then replied, 'Well, it was before my time, but if I remember correctly, I understand it was a boarding school before it was taken over and opened as a nursing home. So maybe it was one of the boys attending the school. Sorry, I can't help you further, but you could ask the headmaster, Wilfred Heathcote.'

'How would I get in touch with him?'

'Oh, that's easy… He's one of our residents here at The Lakes.

Frank wasn't paying much attention to the conversation between Julie and the matron until he heard the word boarding school, remembering the old photograph on Patricia Locke's wall.

'Would you happen to know the name of the boarding school by any chance?'

'Well, if I'm not mistaken, it was called er… Chaffinch House. Yes, that's right, Chaffinch House.'

Eighty-seven

FRANK DROPPED JULIE OFF AT HOME, explaining that he must get back to the office urgently.

The information the matron had told them threw fresh light on the cases currently being investigated.

He pulled into Central Derbyshire HQ, avoiding the parking bays and leaving his car out the front, quickly making his way to DI Adam Fox's office.

Adam was on the phone as Frank, not bothering to knock, just opened the door and walked straight in.

'Can you finish the call boss; I've something really important to tell you?'

Adam apologised and put the phone down. 'This had better be good, I was just on the phone to DCS Slater.'

'Listen, I've just come back from The Lakes nursing home, where Julie's mum has moved too. When we were there last time, Julie noticed a wooden bench overlooking the lake, we saw it again today when we took a walk around. There's a name on the bench Toby Curtis. Nothing too unusual about that I hear you say. But then, when Julie asked the matron about who Toby might have been, she mentioned that before it became a nursing home, it used to be a boarding school. Chaffinch House. I think it's the same place as the photograph we saw in Patricia Locke's house; the same image that's on my phone. I want to go back, apparently, there's a resident there who used to be the headmaster of the school. Wilfred Heathcote, I want to interview him and see what he's got to say… Adam, this could be the breakthrough we've been looking for, give me a couple of hours. I'll call you later, once I've found out any further details, but we need to run with this.'

'Okay, Frank but keep me posted. I don't want to raise anyone's hopes until we know more, the last thing we need is a false lead, and DCI Vickers on our backs again.'

It only took DS Bailey around forty minutes to arrive at the nursing home. There was no direct urgency, he didn't use any blue lights, just stuck to the speed limit and arrived according to the digital clock in his car at 2:35 p.m.

Entering the reception area, the same person was on duty as had been earlier in the day, they still looked smart in their maroon uniform.

She looked up from the desk, immediately recognising Frank from a few hours previously.

'Hello, back again, you can't keep away, can you?.

Getting out his warrant card, Frank replied. 'Apologies, this is an official visit, could you give me directions to the room that Wilfred Heathcote is in, I understand he's a resident staying here?'

'He is yes, his room is on the first floor, the Byron room. If you take the stairs, at the top, turn right and it's the third door on the left. If you want any more help, please let me know, I'll let matron know you're here too.'

Frank found the Byron room, and stood outside the door, politely knocking, and opening it slowly.

His eyes had to briefly adjust to the sunlight, noticing a chair facing the outside window.

Before he left the office, he'd printed off a copy of the photograph on Patricia Locke's wall, putting it into a plastic wallet.

Walter Heathcote sat in a high-backed chair, a small table to his right-hand side, holding an opened book, The Pickwick Papers by Charles Dickins.

Looking around the room Frank saw a small leather-covered chair in the corner, moving it closer to Wilfred Heathcote.

There was a knock at the door, which opened quickly, as the matron entered.

'Hello Mr. Bailey, what are you doing here?'

'High matron, I apologise, but picking up from what you mentioned earlier, I want to check to see if Mr Heathcote could shed any light on a photograph I've got. Hopefully, it's when he was the headmaster at Chaffinch House. You can stay if you wish, but it shouldn't be too long.

Checking her watch, she replied.

'No that's fine, I've got some other meetings to go to, but I'll just explain to him why you're here. Can I just ask that you don't put him under any stress, however? He has a fairly serious heart condition. But in terms of his brain power… well he's still as bright as the rest of us.'

'Of course, I won't, I just want to show him a photograph to see if he can put any names to the faces.'

The matron placed her hand on Wilfred's arm. 'Wilfred, this gentleman is from the police, it's nothing for you to get concerned about, he just wants to ask you a few questions about the old boarding school, is that okay with you?'

He rubbed his eyes, and picked up his glasses from the side table, perching them right on the end of his nose.

'A policeman… Not guilty officer.'

'I'll leave you to it DI Bailey,' closing the door to his room.

'Hello, Mr Heathcote, my name is Detective Sergeant Frank Bailey, I'm with the Central Derbyshire police, thanks for your time this afternoon. I understand that you were the headmaster at Chaffinch House some years ago, is that correct?'

With a gravel-sounding voice, Wilfred replied, 'Yes, I was the headmaster for almost twenty years at Chaffinch House, and here I am now, finishing my days in the very room that was originally my office. See that picture on the wall over there, that's me sitting at my desk, that desk is still here, used by the matron in *here* office.'

'I was wondering if you could take a look at a photograph I have?, I believe it was taken here some years ago. It shows what we understand to be members of staff and some of the pupils from the school.'

Frank moved his chair nearer and placed the photograph in Wilfred's hands.

'If you look along the top row, I think the person in the middle could be you, do you think that's correct?'

He moved his arthritic finger along and tapped the figure in the centre. 'Yes, that's me, I always used to stand on a wooden box, just to give me an extra bit of height. The other people to the right and left are some of the older boys and teachers, apart from one. The gentleman third from the right, was the local vicar. He used to come to visit on Sundays.'

'And what about the boys, do you remember a boy named Toby Curtis? I think he may have been a pupil at Chaffinch House.'

Wilfred lifted his head, replying. 'It was a sad day, Toby Curtis got into difficulty whilst swimming in the lake, we'd warned all the boys about the dangers, and his body was found some hours later.'

'Could you show me which image is Toby if that's possible?'

Wilfred studied the picture again for several moments, then replied. 'That was Toby Curtis, the young lad on the second row, right next to his two best friends.

'Thanks, Wilfred, that's great, one last question before I go, can you remember the names of the other boys, Toby's friends?'

'Yes I can,' Wilfred replied.

Frank wrote down the first name, which he'd never heard of before, he then wrote down the second name. A name that he was not only familiar with but had come across before.

He took his mobile from his jacket pocket, 'I need to make a quick phone call to my boss Wilfred.'

'You won't get a signal from up here. Try the car park, out the door, turn left and use the service door, that'll take you directly to the car park.'

Frustratingly, there was no answer on either Adam's landline or his mobile, so Frank instantly sent him a text message.

Hi boss, this is me. I've just interviewed the headmaster, he's given me some really useful information, a name, which you're not going to believe. I'm going back to speak with him again and I'll call you before I leave, cheers for now, Frank.

Returning upstairs, Frank thought, 'Wilfred Heathcote, you're a living legend.'

Eighty-eight

MY CAR BLENDED IN WELL with all the other vehicles as I pulled into a parking bay at The Lakes nursing home. I don't know if I'm becoming obsessed with taking revenge, or whether the planned executions of the victims will finally bring some solace to the years of tortuous nightmares I've endured, I truly hope so.

I hadn't initially set out to brutalise my selected prey, but as time went on it became almost an obsession, something that I couldn't control. It was like I'd been taken over by someone or something else.

But they had to be punished, no matter what, and by taking the retribution that I did, hopefully over time, the nightmares will cease, and I can finally return to normality.

I wasn't too concerned about being seen as I got my trusted black bag out of the vehicle, unzipping it, checking that I'd got everything I needed.

It was visiting time at the nursing home. People were milling around, so it wasn't unusual for someone carrying a bag with them.

It now all depends on what I find as I enter the reception area, walking up the steps, I run through the final plan in my mind, one more time.

Over the years I'd been very fortunate not to be seen by anyone, never made any mistakes, or at least I thought, no witnesses. But I still had to remain vigilant, never letting down my guard.

'Perfect,' I said under my breath. The receptionist wasn't there as I entered, giving me the chance to look over the desk, trying to find out if I could, which room Wilfred Heathcote was in.

Suddenly, the door at the back of the reception area opened, and a young lady in a maroon uniform stepped forward.

'Good afternoon, can I help you?'

Although she may have seen me in the car park before, she didn't recognise me, so I can relax, take a deep breath, and respond as planned.

'I certainly hope so. I'm here to see my uncle Wilfred, Wilfred Heathcote, could you tell me which room he's in please?'

She looks down at the register and replies.

'He's in the Byron room, it's on the first floor, if you take the stairs, at the top, turn right and it's the third door on the left. Do you want me to show you the way?'

'Thanks, but that's fine, I'm sure I'll find it.'

The Byron room was exactly in the place as described, placing my gloved hand on the door handle, I took a final look both ways to check that no one was around, then entered the room.

Frank returned his mobile to his pocket, making his way back to Wilfred's room the same way he left. He'd waited in the car park for several minutes to see if Adam would come back to him, but he didn't.

Gently knocking on Wilfred's door, opening it slightly to check that it was okay for him to enter, he walked back into the Byron room.

A figure stood with his back to him, leaning over Wilfred's chair, a large black bag resting on the side table.

For a second, Frank thought it was one of the healthcare workers, checking, making sure their patient was comfortable.

As the figure quickly turned around, Frank immediately saw their face, looking into their eyes… Their pupils dart from side to side, then he recognised the killer for the first time.

Suddenly he saw the knife glinting in their hand, he had nothing to defend himself with, as blood moved down the blade and dripped onto the carpeted floor.

Time seemed to stand still, then the dark-dressed figure in front of him swiftly moved forward, the knife still in their right hand, entering Frank's body just above the waistband of his trousers.

Initially, he felt no pain, just an odd feeling on his skin, but as he looked down, he saw a bright red stain on his pure white shirt begin to increase in size.

He felt dizzy and cold, just before he fell to the floor. Looking up at the ceiling, the figure picked up their black bag, stepped over him and gently closed the door.

Frank tried to get his mobile from his inside pocket, but it slipped out of his bloodied hand as darkness began to creep over his eyes, just before they closed.

Eighty-nine

THE CALL CAME THROUGH TO Adam's office at 4:23 p.m.

The attack had initially been reported to the local constabulary and passed onto Central Derbyshire police headquarters at Ripley.

Ms Latimer the matron at the nursing home had returned to see how DS Bailey was getting on interviewing Walter Heathcote.

Unable to open the door fully, she'd managed to squeeze her body through the gap and saw the detective sergeant on the floor, blood oozing from a wound in his stomach.

Rushing into the shower room, she grabbed a bath towel and secured it tightly around the wound, trying to stop the bleeding.

Another member of staff immediately called the police and the ambulance service. Two traffic cops arrived within seven minutes, and the ambulance was there in ten.

On hearing about the incident, the whole of the police headquarters was instantly placed on high alert. On learning about the incident, DCI Vickers immediately took charge, instructing DI Fox to get himself over to the hospital urgently.

Two uniformed officers had already picked up Julie Bailey from their home and used blues and twos to get to Derbyshire Community Hospital as quickly as possible.

Although it was late afternoon, as Adam entered, the A&E Department was already beginning to get busy, with several people waiting at the reception area.

He stepped forward, showed his warrant card, and apologised to everyone for jumping the queue.

'Hi, my name is Detective Inspector Adam Fox. I understand the paramedics have brought one of my colleagues into the department. Their name is Frank Bailey, could you tell me where I can find out what's happening or where to go?'

The man behind the reception screen didn't initially take kindly to the queue jumping but inputting some details and checking the admissions list on the computer screen in front of him, he noticed it was a police officer who'd been brought in, initially assessed as a category one patient.

'You see the red-painted wall over there, that's where you need to go.'

'Thanks so much and apologies again.'

As he made his way across the A&E department he began to run through in his mind how this could have happened. Frank was in no danger; it was a routine call. He'd just returned to the nursing home to supposedly interview a headmaster who was a resident there.

So, how could it have gone so wrong, and more to the point, how serious were Frank's injuries?

He caught sight of Julie as he turned the corner into the trauma department, she was talking to a young man dressed in a dark blue tunic and trousers.

He didn't interrupt, just listened. 'So, your husband is currently in theatre Mrs Bailey. He's suffered a serious stab wound to his lower abdomen, and we're trying to control the internal bleeding.'

'How serious is serious?'

'Well, your husband has lost quite a lot of blood, but he's a relatively fit man, it's the bleeding inside his stomach that we've got to control, I'll know more later on, please don't worry, he's in the best place.'

Julie Bailey wasn't sure what to say to Adam, as they both sat down on two black plastic seats, a table separating the chairs.

'Can I get you a drink, coffee or tea?'

'I'd love a cup of coffee Detective Inspector Fox, thanks,' replied Julie.

'Anything to eat, a chocolate bar or something?' thinking about Frank and the KitKats.

'No thank you, coffee will be fine.'

He returned, putting two plastic cups of coffee on the table and sitting next to Julie.

'Have you any idea what's happened, Detective Inspector?'

'At this present time no. But officers are at the scene, taking witness statements, so we'll know more later in the day… And it's Adam by the way.'

She picked up her coffee, wrapping her hands around the cup. 'We'd only been at the nursing home a few hours before, had a meeting with matron about my mum, so I don't know why Frank went back?'

'He wanted to interview a resident at the home. A retired headmaster, he believed he may have had some information on the cases that were currently working on.'

Julie took a drink of her coffee before replying.

'Is this to do with a dead boy, Toby Curtis and what the nursing home used to be, a boarding school?'

'Yes, I think it was, it was previously called Chaffinch House, closed years ago and reopened as a nursing home.'

'That's what the matron told us when we asked her about the name on a wooden bench overlooking the lake. Chaffinch House, that's what she said.'

'You know what Julie, according to what DCI Vickers has told me, that matron could have saved Frank's life. She gave him first aid when she went into the bedroom and saw him lying on the floor.'

As Adam finished his sentence, Julie finally began to break down and cry.

Ninety

IT WAS MORE THAN THREE HOURS before the consultant returned to speak with Julie, who introduced Adam as her husband's boss.

He dragged a chair over from the corner of the department and sat down opposite the two of them, Julie noticing for the first time his name woven into his dark blue tunic top, Dr James Smallwood – A&E Consultant.

'Well, it's taken us a while to control the bleeding, but I'm pleased to tell you that your husband is going to be okay. He's out of the theatre and recovering in the ICU. We'll keep an eye on him for the next six to eight hours and then hopefully transfer him to a ward. I've been told that a police officer will be on duty outside, if that is the case, we'll put him in a single-bedded room.'

'Can I go and see him please, just for a few minutes?'

'I don't see why not, but he's going to be very groggy, so not too long, okay. If you follow me, I'll take you to him.'

As they set off, he turned to Adam, 'Only family at his bedside, you'll have to come back later tomorrow.'

By the time he got back to his car, he'd missed three further mobile calls, and one message, all from DCI Vickers, he sat in his AUDI and listened.

'Adam, this is Tom Vickers, I guess you're still at the hospital, I hope Frank is doing okay. Listen, I've been over to the nursing home, unfortunately, the old man, Mr. Heathcote, I think his name is, well he's dead.

Dr. Munroe is in attendance, she'll liaise with you sometime tomorrow with an update. Preliminary examination of the body indicates that he died from a massive incision to his throat, with a long sharp knife. She believes he died instantly, probably using the same knife that injured DS Bailey. Until further notice, I'm taking charge of this case, not stepping on your toes, but that'll allow you to keep in touch with Frank. We need to know what happened Adam, you said that he'd gone to speak with Mr. Heathcote, so what was it about, what did he find out, and more to the point, why

was Heathcote murdered? The receptionist on duty at the time had already given a statement. The old man's nephew apparently came to visit him. We assume that was a lie, so, whoever that was, was probably the killer and who also stabbed Frank. My guess is, he saw his face before he was attacked. I've arranged for officers to be outside the ward, just in case whoever did this decides to finish the job. Get back to me when you can, but as I've said, your priority is finding out as many details as you can once Frank is fit to talk, we need both a name and if he recognised or could recognise the killer. We need to move fast on this one, I don't want this bastard getting away. I'll leave it in your capable hands.'

Adam saved the message, and as he sat there, he began to consider what would have happened if the matron hadn't returned to check on Walter.

Frank could have remained in the room, fighting for his life, or something far worse, bleeding to death.

He wanted to stay at the hospital but realised that wasn't practical, he'd come over first thing in the morning.

Opening his mobile, he scanned for the direct line to Tom Vickers, pressed the call button and placed the phone on speaker.

Not surprisingly, DCI Vickers answered immediately. 'Adam, how's things there? Please tell me that Frank's going to be okay.'

'He's out of surgery sir and has been transferred to ITU. They're keeping an eye on him for the next few hours, but it looks like he's going to be all right.

His wife is with him at the moment and I'm coming back over here first thing in the morning, I told Julie, that's his wife, that if there's anything she needs, anything at all, to call me. Trust that's okay with you… Frank texted me to explain that Wilfred Heathcote had given him a name. But he didn't tell me who it was, just that I wouldn't believe it.

One thing is for sure, DS Bailey *will* give us a name and *should* be able to recognise whoever stabbed him. If it's Daniel Ashby, then I'm sorry. Sorry for not listening to you in the first place and doubting your approach to the initial investigation all those years ago.'

'This isn't the time for apologies or regrets. The critical thing here is putting a face to that name and then let's get a warrant for their arrest.'

It was late evening when Adam finally arrived back home, Viv's car wasn't on the drive, which initially concerned him, but then he remembered that she was going to call at the supermarket straight from work, the fridge was almost empty and there was only one bottle of wine left.

He sat alone in the lounge, staring into a half-empty glass of white Chardonnay, wanting some background music, but deciding against it. He put the glass on the coffee table and closed his eyes for a moment, at least that's what he thought.

The front door opened just as he woke up, checking his watch, he'd been asleep for almost forty minutes. Walking down the hall, both hands full of shopping, and a laptop case over her shoulder, Viv noticed how tired Adam looked.

Dark circles around his eyes, and his skin looked dehydrated.

She put the shopping down on the breakfast bar, her laptop on the floor and placed both arms around his waist. 'Are you okay, you look like hell?'

'I've been at the hospital most of the day, Frank's been stabbed, he's going to be okay, but he's had to have major surgery to stop internal bleeding, they've transferred him to ITU.'

'My god, what happened?'

'He went to The Lakes Nursing Home to interview a retired headmaster, who may have had information on the current cases we're investigating. The matron found him on the floor, a stab wound to his lower stomach. Walter Heathcote, the man he was talking to is dead, I think Frank tried to stop the killer and got in the way, he's lucky to be alive Viv', I'm going back to the hospital again first thing in the morning. The details Mr. Heathcote gave Frank. Well, he thought the name was familiar to us, and the way he was attacked, it's more than likely he saw his face.'

'Do you want me to come along, I could probably get a few hours off, although Peter hasn't been at work today and is off tomorrow, some medical conference he's attending.'

'No, it's fine, Tom Vickers is holding the fort, he's the SIO investigating what took place at the nursing home, liaising with the Forensic Pathologist. I'll go back tomorrow and if Frank's well enough to talk, then hopefully we'll know who the attacker is, and if I'm right in my assumption, then I've made one massive error of judgment.'

Ninety-one

ADAM LAY AWAKE MOST OF THE night. Going over how he could have been mistaken, and that Daniel Ashby could have been guilty all along. Was the disappearance of Scarlett and the subsequent ongoing investigation clouding his judgment?

He always tried to detach himself from personal issues to his work, but this was different, she was his daughter, and he had a responsibility to find out what happened, it was his duty as a senior police officer and more importantly, as a father and husband.

He'd showered and was out the front door by 6:20 a.m. travelling in silence, the journey didn't take long, as traffic at that time in the morning was light. Finding a parking space right outside the A&E department, he made his way in, maneuvering around stationary ambulances and heading straight to the trauma unit where he'd been the night before.

There was only one person at the nurse's station, a young man who Adam thought didn't look much older than his mid-twenties. Showing his warrant card, the nurse gave him directions to where Frank's room was. 'Go down the corridor, past the coffee machine and it's the third door on your left, you can't miss it, there's a police officer stationed there.'

The officer who was sitting outside Frank's room quickly stood to his feet as Adam approached, 'Good morning sir, Mrs. Bailey is in with the detective sergeant.'

'Thanks, go and get yourself some breakfast, I'm going to be here for some time, so take a break for an hour.'

'Thanks, sir,' as the officer walked down the corridor.

As he looked through the window, Julie Bailey was sitting next to Frank's bed, her eyes were closed, as Adam gently opened the door.

'Oh hello, Detective Inspector Fox... Sorry, Adam, thanks for coming back in.'

Julie Bailey stood up, pulling down her jumper to cover the top of her denim jeans, she'd been at Frank's bedside all night, two cardboard cups and a part-eaten sandwich on top of the table across the bed.

Adam took a look at Frank, then turned back to Julie, asking

'How's he doing, has he had a good night?'

'The doctor has been in a few times, just checking him over, you know, blood pressure, all that sort of thing, they seem fairly relaxed about his condition. Thankfully, there *was* no internal damage, and the wound is healing as expected.'

'That's fantastic news. He'll be up and running in no time.'

She moved closer to the bed, leaned over and gently stroked his forehead with her hand.

'He's opened his eyes a few times he knows who I am, but he hasn't said a word. He's full of drugs, so I guess that can be expected.'

'Has he said anything at all about what happened?'

'No, I'm sorry, not a thing.'

'Not to worry, if you don't mind, I'm going to stay around for the next few hours, if or when he comes round, and the doctor's happy, I'd just like to speak with him, no pressure though.'

Julie picked up the sandwich box and two used coffee cups off the table and put them in a flip-top bin in the corner of the room.

'Have you eaten at all?' asked Adam.

'I had a sandwich at about two o'clock this morning and another coffee.'

'I'll go and get you a drink and something more substantial to eat from the cafeteria, what would you like?'

'Could you see if they do a takeaway porridge, you know, the ones that come in a cardboard container, any flavour and a cup of strong tea please.'

She reaches into her handbag for her purse and pulls out a ten-pound note.

'Here you go, there's ten pounds.'

'Don't be silly, I'll get these, you wait here and keep an eye on Frank, I'll be back soonest.'

He opened the door to find the officer back on duty, a look on his face like he'd been fed and watered.

'Did you find the cafeteria?'

'Yes sir, go back through reception and make your way to the exit doors, don't go through, just turn right and there are two swing doors, go through there and the cafeteria is just down the corridor on your left, you can't miss it.'

'Famous last words,' Adam muttered under his breath as he set off down the corridor.

Fifteen minutes later he returned with maple syrup-flavoured porridge, a hot breakfast sandwich for himself and two cups of strong tea, he put them on a side table with four sachets of sugar.

Julie was holding he husband's hand, 'He's just opened his eyes again, only for a moment, but I think he's coming round. You know, he always wanted to be a police officer. Had a tough upbringing, but wanted to prove to his mum and dad he could make something of himself. He's never regretted it; in fact, our only regret was never being blessed with children. Oh, we tried, but it wasn't to be, and then when my dad died we took on looking after Mum, so adoption wasn't practical. He's a good man, did everything for mum after dad died, gardening, decorating, she thinks the world of him.'

One of the female nurses knocked on the door and entered. 'Sorry to interrupt, I've just got to check his blood pressure and oxygen levels.' The doctor will be in to see you later, but we're over the worst, he's starting to look much better, I think he may start to wake up soon.'

'When he wakes up, would it be okay for me to speak with him, maybe just for ten minutes?'

The nurse turned to Adam, replying.

'I don't see why not but don't tire him out. He's still quite heavily drugged, so he may keep falling asleep until the medication begins to wear off.'

'I won't and thank you,' replied Adam.

It was a further two hours before Frank finally opened his eyes once again, a smile came over him when he saw Julie and then Adam's face.

'Hello boss,' they both stood there unsure which boss he was referring to.

Ninety-two

JULIE ASKED ADAM TO STAY with Frank whilst she went to get a member of staff.

He looked around the room, his eyes trying to adjust to the bright overhead lights.

'Hi Frank, how are you feeling?'

'Like I've been hit by a ten-ton lorry.'

'Juile's gone to get the nurse; she'll be back shortly. Do you know what happened to you, can you remember?'

Frank closed his eyes once again and then opening them, he replied. 'I was interviewing the headmaster of Chaffinch House, Walter, no Wilfred Heathcote. I went downstairs to make a call and when I returned, he was there, in his room, crouched over him.'

He began to cough, and Adam poured him a glass of water.

'Thanks.'

'What happened after that Frank?'

'It's all a bit of a blur, but I remember him coming at me with a knife. I noticed the blood on the blade, I tried to step out of the way, but I was too slow, he stabbed me boss… He stabbed me.'

The door opened and Julie and the female nurse entered, looking at Frank and then Adam.

'Hello Frank, you're awake, are you?. Before you start asking him any questions, I need to check him over, if you don't mind, could you leave the room? I'll call you back in when I'm done.'

The police officer was still outside as Adam closed the door. 'How's he doing sir, I hope he's going to be okay; DS Bailey, he's one of the good guys, and if you don't mind me saying, you can't say that about every senior officer.'

'I'm sure you're right constable, on both fronts.'

Adam glanced through the window, trying to see what the nurse was doing, updating notes in a folder that she had in her hand, she put the pen in her top pocket, turned around, and opened the door.

'You can go back in now, he's come round but as explained, he'll probably drift in and out for the next couple of hours, so not too many questions please.'

As he re-entered the room, Adam had to accept that Frank wasn't going to be fully coherent and maybe unclear of all the facts.

All he wanted was a name, a name to the face, the person holding the knife, who stabbed his detective sergeant, leaving him to die.

'Here Adam, take this chair if you don't mind I'm going to the ladies and then get some fresh air, are you going to be okay staying with Frank until I get back?'

'That's fine Julie, take your time, I'm not going anywhere yet.'

'I promise I won't be too long.'

Julie got her coat, picked up her handbag, kissed Frank on his cheek, and then left the room.

'Can we pick up where we left off? You were telling me about the stabbing.'

'They came straight at me boss, I tried to step to one side, avoiding the knife, but I was too slow. The next thing I knew, I was on the floor, trying to get my mobile to call for help. Blood oozing from my stomach, all over my shirt. The very last thing I remember is them stepping over me, a black bag swaying in their hand and then… Nothing.'

'But you saw their face Frank, you can recognise them, yeah?.

'They had a look of sheer hatred, a wild, vicious look of revenge about them.'

'Was it Daniel Ashby? Was he the person in the room, standing over Wilfred Heathcote, was it him that attacked you?'

He closed his eyes as though he was trying to recall the moment it happened, then opening them, he replied.

'Daniel Ashby… wasn't he the lad we interviewed early on… Yes, I remember him, he came in with his mother didn't he.'

For several moments he drifted back to sleep, and then suddenly he opened his eyes, wide this time, with an actual look of fear.

'You need to make sure your wife is safe, protect her… Vivian, she could be in danger, they're all in danger.'

'I don't know what you mean Frank. Vivian's at work, she's not in any danger, she's fine, trust me.'

Trying to lift his body off the bed, Frank grabbed Adam's arm, 'It's not Daniel Ashby Adam, he isn't the killer.

Ninety-three

ADAM CHARGED OUT OF FRANK'S ROOM, telling the officer outside to remain in place, no matter what.

The accident and emergency department was crowded as he tried to manoeuvre himself to his car outside.

Switching on his mobile phone, he immediately called Viv on *her* mobile, she didn't pick up and he didn't leave a message.

Next, he called DCI Vickers, who answered on the fourth ring. Adam quickly explained what Frank had just disclosed, telling him he was making his way to Edgewater Medical Centre.

'You need to wait for backup DI Fox, don't go in there alone.'

'That's not an option sir, my wife's life could be in danger, so I'm not hanging around.'

Five minutes later he was on the A38, blue lights illuminating the number plates of cars in front, but no siren.

He ran through in his mind what to say to Viv if anything happened to her, he would never forgive himself. He then called her mobile once more.

This time she picked up.

'Hello you, you've just caught me in between patients, is everythi…'

'Listen to me Viv very, very carefully. I want you to go to reception and tell the staff that all patient appointments have been cancelled, just think something up, it doesn't matter what.'

'I can't do that Adam; I told you we were busy today; Peter isn't here, and patients are waiting to be seen by both the locum and me.'

Police officers were trained to remain calm in situations like this, but frustration and fear were beginning to creep into his voice.

'I understand that, but you need to clear the reception area, get the staff to leave the premises and *you* need to get in your car and go home. Please do as I say, Viv, this isn't a joke, I'm deadly serious.'

'What's going on Adam? Why are you talking like this? It's not like you, I don't understand.'

'Just do as I say. Don't ask any more questions, clear the premises and make sure you're safe, you know I wouldn't ask if it wasn't critical, but it is, so do it… right now.'

Viv's mobile went dead, she sat there for a couple of minutes, trying to understand what Adam had just told her.

She trusted him with her life, and for once he was trying to prove that.

Opening the door to her consulting room, Viv unhurriedly made her way across to reception, avoiding trying to alarm anyone.

Two staff members were behind the glass partition, she opened the side door and entered.

'Hello, Dr Flemming, is everything okay?'

'I want both of you to go and explain to our patients that due to unforeseen circumstances, all appointments for the rest of the afternoon have been cancelled. Please don't ask why, just do as requested. Then I want you to leave the premises and go home.'

'But we have a full list of patients,' said one confused receptionist.

'Yes, I know that, but this is an emergency, please, just do as I say. I'll go and check on the locum, to make sure he hasn't any patients with him, and he can leave too.'

Adam's AUDI A4 pulled into the car park, coming to a sudden halt just as Viv was getting into her car. Opening the door, he ran over to her, holding her by the arm, telling her to come with him.

Adam took hold of her car keys and locked her Skoda, returning to his car, both sitting in the front.

'I'm sorry I had to ask you to do that sweetheart, but I had no option, you could have been in real danger. I had to get you out of there, you and all the others.'

Vivian had a confused look on her face.

'What the hell is going on Adam?'

He looked through the window, trying to get his head around how to tell her.

'I don't know how to explain this, so please don't ask me to. But the person who stabbed Frank could be responsible for the other murders we're investigating.

Taking hold of her hand.

It's Peter Viv, Peter Johnson.'

Initially shocked, Viv pulled her hand away.

'Are you out of your mind, Peter isn't a killer. He's one of the gentlest-mannered people I've ever met. You're wrong Adam, it cannot be Peter. Anyway, he's not even here, he's at a medical conference in Oxford, he couldn't have attached Frank.'

'And how do you know that, just because he told you where he was supposedly going, and it's in his diary, that means nothing Viv, nothing at all.'

'But how can you be sure, Frank might have made a big mistake, he's only just come out of surgery, and he is probably confused… He *will be* confused.'

Again, getting hold of Viv's hand, he ran his thumb over her wedding ring. 'Listen, sweetheart, Frank didn't make a mistake, he isn't confused, he saw Peter's face. He was holding the knife, he stabbed him in the stomach, and then this gentlest of men, well, he just casually stepped over Frank, leaving him to die.'

'There's no mistake, *I've* made no mistake.'

'It's Peter Johnson.'

Ninety-four

DETECTIVE CHIEF INSPECTOR VICKERS took the call from DI Fox. He informed him of the identification of Peter Johnson, and Tom Vickers immediately contacted the Chief Superintendent who permitted a major incident plan to be put in place.

Slowly Viv began to take in what Adam was saying to her. She worked with Peter; he was her partner now and a personal friend.

How could he possibly be responsible for injuring Frank Bailey and the brutal slaying of all the other victims, he cared for his patients, and he'd taken the doctor oath, 'To Preserve Life.'

'You need to go home now Viv, I've already called headquarters, and an armed support team are on their way to his house, I'm going to join them there.'

'I want to come with you, I need to speak with him.'

'Absolutely not, this is a police matter now, it'll be handled by the team at Ripley, they know what to do. You need to get in your car, go home and I'll call you later with an update.'

As Viv walked back to her car, Adam considered just how much more personal tragedy his wife could take before she broke.

***

Adam pulled up outside the cottage where Peter Johnson lived. A police vehicle was already there, and two officers were inside, waiting for further instructions.

One of the officers got out of the car when he saw DI Fox's car pull up, no blues and twos, just silence.

'Hello sir, is there anything we should be doing,? Our instructions were to wait outside the property and call in if the occupant looked like he was planning to leave.'

'No, that's fine, just get back in the car and wait for the armed officers to arrive, I'm going into the property to try and talk with the suspect.'

'Do you think that's a good idea? Sir, shouldn't you wait for other offices to arrive, he may be armed?'

'All I'm going to do is try and talk to him, calm him down, make sure he isn't anxious, the last thing we need is for him to panic.'

He lifted the latch on the wooden gate, it creaked in the stillness as he walked down the gravelled path, either side was the sweet smell of end-of-season roses, still lingering in the air.

The front door was shut as Adam got closer, knocking, he waited for someone to answer.

A distorted image appeared through the small, frosted window of the door; someone was approaching. First the sound of a lock, then the movement of a bolt, and finally it opened.

'Hello Adam, I've been expecting you, please come in. Excuse my scruffy clothes, I've been tidying up the garden, burning some old tree branches, so I probably smell of smoke… Can I get you a drink?.

Stepping into the kitchen, Peter pulled a chair out from under a large oak table. 'Take a seat Adam, can I get you tea or coffee? I always have a cup of tea at this time in the afternoon.'

'Tea will be fine Peter, thanks.'

'Tea it is then.'

He placed two china cups and saucers, a milk jug, and a pot of hot tea on the kitchen table, placing a large coaster under the teapot.

'Do you know why I'm here Peter?, it's to do with an attack on one of my officers, Detective Sergeant Bailey.'

Dr Peter Johnson stood there for several moments trying to recall the attack against the police officer.

'Yes, I'm sorry about that, I hope he survived. He got in the way you see, it was going so well, and then, before I had the opportunity to leave my mark on the fifth victim, he came into the room and startled me. I had no choice. I'd got to get away.'

'But why Peter, why all those senseless, brutal killings?

The sound of police vehicles arriving outside broke the silence, as Peter Johnson picked up his teacup, carefully considering his next comment.

'They had to be punished for what they did, surely you must understand that?'

Adam, still sitting at the table knew what he had to do. He officially cautioned Peter Johnson and took him to Central Derbyshire Headquarters for further questioning.

'I'm going to have to arrest you, you know that don't you Peter?'

'Yes of course I do Adam. I only wish you'd have done it months ago. Can I just clear the table before we leave? I'm not sure when I'll be coming back home again.'

Detective Inspector Fox stood up from the chair.

'Peter Johnson, I'm arresting you for the murder of Wilfred Heathcote and the attempted murder of Detective Sergeant Frank Bailey. You do not have to say anything, but it may harm your defence if you do not mention when questioned, something which you later rely on in court. Anything you do say may be given in evidence. Do you understand?'

'Yes, I do,' he replied.

They both made their way to the front door and as Peter opened it, suddenly he stopped, taking a final look behind him, realising that it would most likely be a long time before he saw the house again.

There were several police vehicles outside the property, but the armed officers had been instructed to stand down as there was no immediate danger to life.

One of the officers who'd first arrived on the scene was standing outside the front door, he got hold of Peter's arm and together they walked down the gravelled path to a waiting car.

The other officer opened the back door, placed his hand on Peter's head as he sat down, walked around to the other side, and took the seat next to him.

As the car moved away, Peter glanced through the side window, on seeing Adam standing next to the wooden gate, he held up his hand and smiled.

Ninety-five

AS THEY WALKED DOWN the corridor to interview room two, Tom Vickers asked Adam, 'So how has Vivian taken this news? How's she coping with all this?'

Adam remained silent, considering his reply, then said, 'I think she's struggling to take it all in. Peter Johnson was a work colleague and a good friend. He's even offered her a partnership; we raised the money and it's just been finalised, but now he's no longer going to be there. I don't know what will happen now, we'll have to see.'

A uniformed office stood outside interview room two, the sign on the door showing engaged.

As they were about to walk in Tom Vickers took hold of Adam's arm. 'How do you want to play this, by rights, I should lead the interview, but I think under these circumstances, we'll get more out of him if you take the lead.'

'I'd intended to sir; you can take notes... If that's okay with you?'

Another uniformed officer held the door open, walked out and closed it behind them.

Peter Johnson sat alone, as Adam opened a window to let the smell of smoke out and some fresh air in.

In general, all the interview rooms at police headquarters took on the same layout, a rectangular table in the centre of the room, and two chairs opposite where Peter Johnson sat.

He stood up stood up from the chair, looking directly at Adam.

The way he was dressed seemed to be out of character, usually, he would be kitted out in smart casual trousers, a buttoned-up shirt and a matching jumper, but today was different.

Adam pulled out one of the two chairs opposite whilst DCI Vickers set up the recording equipment, unwrapped a tape, and inserted it into the machine, checking that it was in working order. Then sat down next to Adam, placing a logbook folder in front of him.

Adam glanced up at the digital clock on the far wall, confirming the time at 15:35.

'For the benefit of the tape, Dr Peter Johnson is being questioned in interview room two, in the presence of Detective Chief Inspector Tom Vickers and Detective Inspector Adam Fox, this interview is being recorded onto a secure digital network. Peter, could you please confirm for the tape that that is correct?'

'Yes, that's correct.'

'You have also been given the opportunity for a solicitor to be present, which you've declined, is that also correct?'

'I don't need a solicitor; I don't need defending.

'Do you know why you've been arrested?'

'Of course I do. But before I say anything else, I just want to say how sorry I am for attacking one of your colleagues, when he entered the room, I knew I had to get away. I hadn't finished you see, the markings on Wilfred Heathcote's forehead, it still had to be done, so I panicked.'

DCI Vickers looked up over the rim of his glass and abruptly said, 'He'll live, thanks to the quick thinking of the matron at the nursing home.'

As Peter Johnson took a sip of water that was in front of him and looked down at the dirt from gardening in his fingernails, he began to tell his horrific and brutal story.

'It started not long after my parents sent me to Chaffinch House. I was only there for around twelve months, to give my mother and father a break. He was heavily involved with the medical practice and my mother suffered with her nerves, and taking anti-depressants. I soon made friends with a couple of other boys, Simon and Toby, we used to do everything together, always watching out for each other, but it wasn't long before things began to change. It started one night when an older boy pulled me out of my bed and dragged me down the corridor to a room at the end. I tried to get away and shouted for help, but no one came. Two people were standing there, as the older boy pushed me towards them, one of the men left almost immediately. The other man, his breath smelling of cigarettes, looked at me… Then the beatings began.'

He took a further sip of water.

'It became a regular thing, marching me down the corridor, pushing me into the room and being physically abused. It wasn't just me; maybe I was lucky, I would hear other boys crying out in pain, begging for them to stop. He used to enjoy inflicting punishment on me, for no reason, just because he could. In the end, I always remember, he would wipe the sweat off his forehead with a white handkerchief, his gold signet ring glistening in the moonlight. He told me if I ever reported what took place, then it would only get worse, little did I know how bad it would get. It was Arthur Richardson you know. He was a maths teacher, and my first victim all those years ago. I arranged to meet him near the entrance to the woods near the village, didn't think he'd accept, but he was inquisitive and wanted to know more, I guess. During the attack, all I could think of was what he'd done to me, all that pain and suffering, he had to be punished, so I did. I knew it would take the pathologist several days to identify the body, which gave me time to get rid of all the clothes and return to work as though nothing had ever happened.'

'Do you want to take a break for a few minutes Peter?' asked Adam.
'No, I'm fine. The big mistake I made was the gardening gloves. Daniel Ashby had been doing some tidying up at the medical centre, I just picked the gloves up one day, and I knew he wouldn't miss them. But I should have taken them home and not thrown them away in the bushes.'

His eyes began to water, as he took a handkerchief out of his pocket and blew his nose.

'Daniel Ashby was charged with the murder of Arthur Richardson Peter and you just sat back and said nothing.'

'Yes, I know DCI Vickers, and I will take that to my grave. But that is not the worst part of all this. Over the last few days, I've had details that make what I have done over all these years, unforgivable, truly unforgivable'

Ninety-six

IT WAS 8:30 A.M. THE FOLLOWING morning when DCI Vickers and DI Fox re-entered interview room two, setting up the digital recording and taking the same seat positions as the previous day.

Peter Johnson was now dressed in a light grey tracksuit; showing a couple of days' stubble growth, he looked like he hadn't slept the previous night.

Adam opened the interview once again.

'So, Peter, you told us yesterday that murdering all these people wasn't the worst thing you've done. Frankly speaking, I'm not sure what could be worse.

'DI Fox, the worst part of all of this is that Daniel Ashby, the boy who spent years in jail for a murder he didn't commit… Well, he's my son.'

Both Tom Vickers and Adam couldn't believe what they had just heard. Could Mary Ashby and Peter Johnson have kept this a secret for all these years?

'Yes, Daniel is my son. Mary Ashby and I had an affair… years ago. Her husband, Philip, was constantly away, and when he did come home, he never had any time for her or what he understood to be his son. I didn't know anything about Daniel until Mary came to see me as a patient, just after he'd been released from prison. She was having difficulty sleeping, knowing that her son had spent all that time away and was innocent. I prescribed some short-term medication. She then dropped the bombshell about me being the father to Daniel. I couldn't tell her what I'd done, murdering Arthur Richardson… Can you imagine how I felt after realising that my son, my only son, had gone to prison for something that I'd done? I'm going to have to live with that guilt for the remainder of my life. I'd never intended to murder the other victims, but they'd indirectly ruined my son's life as well as mine, so they needed to be punished for that. I had to continue hunting them down, gathering the trophies, seeking revenge not only for myself but for my son. I knew the torment would never go away until I'd finished what I had started.'

Guilt was something that Adam had also gotten used to. He'd endured it for the last four years, not being able to find his missing daughter, so he began to understand the torment that Peter was suffering.

Tom Vickers had no sympathy and tersely said, 'Tell us about Patricia Locke, why was *she* hunted down and murdered?'

'Patricia Locke was victim number two. Simon had introduced both Toby and me to smoking, we used to sit near the windows of the dormitory and take a few drags now and again. On this particular day, I decided to have a smoke before lessons, which was a mistake and one that I'd once again pay dearly for. The class was assembled as Miss Locke, as she was known then, walked into the room. I never understood why she always picked on me, but she always did, regularly. She knew someone had been smoking, she could smell it, looked me directly in the eye and then announced that unless the culprit confessed, the whole class would be punished. Not wanting all the other boys to suffer, I stood up and walked to the front. I remember she had an assortment of canes located in a drawer on her desk. She chose one, holding it firmly in her hand and commenced the punishment. Pushing me over the desk, she brought the cane down on my backside as I watched the boys in front of me. The thing I remember the most was the smile on her face, she enjoyed every minute, as she made me suffer… That's why I cut her hand off, I gathered the trophies you see and saved them in my black box. Patricia Locke, she was victim number two.'

Adam checked the digital clock on the wall, it read 10:17.

'I think we should take a break Peter; I'll organise some drinks for us, and we'll start again at eleven o'clock. Do you need a toilet break at all?'

'No thank you, I'm fine, but a drink of coffee would be nice.'

The officer outside walked in as they made their way out of the interview room, closing the door behind him.

DCI Vickers spoke first, 'So, what do you think, is he cleverly playing with us, or is he completely insane?'

'My initial thoughts, I don't think it's either. He's very intelligent, you can't become a GP without being brainy, and I should know. No, I believe he knows exactly what he was doing, right from the very first murder. But I've got to say, if he'd known about Daniel Ashby being his son earlier, then he would have probably stopped at Arthur Richardson.'

'He mentioned this black box, have we searched his house yet?'

'Officers are currently combing every area inside the house, including the outbuildings, we'll find it soon enough.'

Both detectives entered the interview room at seven minutes past eleven, agreeing beforehand that Adam should continue with the questioning, after all, he was the arresting officer.

Peter Johnson was sitting there, still trying to get dirt from under his fingernails.

'So, Peter, you told us about Patricia Locke, what is the background to Ross Sullivan, based on the condition and markings on the body, we take it that you murdered him too. Was it drug-related?

He sat there for several moments, giving both DCI Vickers and Adam the impression he was thinking hard about the brutal slaying of his third victim.

'I don't know anything about drugs. Ross Sullivan murdered one of my best friends, Toby Curtis, so he deserved to die the way he did, by drowning. He struggled under the bath water, just like I imagine Toby did when he attacked him in the lake at Chaffinch House. We'd just gone there, Simon, Toby and me, it was a sunny day, the water calm and warm. Ross Sullivan and another boy made their way to the lake and started bullying us, he stole my watch, which was my grandfather's. They started picking on Toby, he told us to go, and he said he'd be fine, we wanted to stay, but he reassured us he'd follow us back, but he never did. The next day, the headmaster told the whole school about Toby, he said he'd drowned, in a tragic accident. I knew then what Ross Sullivan had done; I saw it on his face, he'd drowned one of my best friends.'

'How did you find out where he lived Peter?'

'Actually, hunting him down wasn't easy, I noticed an article in a local magazine. Ross Sullivan had won some awards at work, initially, I wasn't sure it was him. But then I noticed the watch, he was still wearing it after all those years. That's what gave him away. I found out where he worked, some communication company in Nottingham drove over and just sat in the car park and followed him home. Well, not him, but what I thought was his girlfriend.

I went back several times to check the surrounding location, then one early evening, entered the flat through the rear door, he lived at flat number three, he was also my third victim.'

DCI Vickers checked the notes he'd made, 'You mentioned earlier about a black box, we're searching your house currently, is that something we'll come across?'

'Yes, my black box. You'll find it in the gardening shed, together with the black bag I used to take with me. I'm not sure where the key is, they took some off me when I arrived, but they might be on a hook in the shed. You can break the lock I guess; you'll find all the trophies I've gathered inside, the signet ring from Arthur Richardson, right up to my last but one victim, it's all there.'

'Tell us about the next victim Peter, why were they hunted down and brutally murdered?'

Ninety-seven

IT WAS A SUNDAY, EARLY AFTERNOON, and I'd decided to walk around the lake, it being a sunny day.

My best friend Simon had gone out with his parents, so I was at a bit of a loose end. There's a wooden bench looking over the lake, in memory of Toby. As I sat there thinking about what he must have gone through, all that water filling his lungs, I saw a figure approaching. They sat down at the side of me, asked me why I looked so sad, and then said they wanted to show me something in the bushes, just behind the seat. I should have ignored what they suggested, but I didn't. He let me go first, then before I knew what was happening, he'd got his arm around my throat, moving their hand down my bare chest to the top of my shorts. I was struggling to breathe, then suddenly, a sharp pain ran down my back as they bit into the side of my shoulder blade, I could feel the blood beginning to trickle down. I had to escape, get away from them, but their grip became tighter. I managed to lift my left leg and stamped as hard as I could onto their foot, they shouted out in pain, dropping their arm from around my neck. I ran back through the bushes and made my way back to the dormitory, frequently looking over my shoulder to make sure I wasn't being followed.'

For several minutes they all sat there in silence, Adam beginning to understand the pain and suffering that Peter must have endured for all those years at Chaffinch House. It was well documented about past abuse at boarding schools, people returning years later, trying desperately to bring closure, but this was too close to home.

And then hearing about his son, Daniel Ashby, that would have been too much for anyone to live with.

'Did you recognise your attacker, was it one of the teaching staff at Chaffinch House?'

'For years I've tried to forget what took place on that particular day, and all the other times. Put them to the back of my mind, and just concentrate on my career as a GP, and my patients. But the nightmares still returned, taking me back, as though I was still there. It was only when I was looking at the school photograph that I recognised their face on the back row, a face I thought I could trust. I didn't intend to hunt them down, but then I saw an article in the Derbyshire Times, the opening of a brand-new drop-in centre, and there they were, standing right in the centre of the picture. It brought it all back to me, what might have happened if I hadn't got away. Finding them was easy, the article handed all the details to me on a plate, all I had to do was plan the execution, and the best part, packing the extra thing in the bag with all the other items I needed. So, I drove over to the church, the car park was empty, and the front doors were open, just the middle door closed. Steven Andrews was sitting at his desk, combing his hair, it looked damp. Initially, I didn't think he had any idea I was there until he saw my reflection on the screen of his computer, and then it was too late. Oh, he tried to get away, but unlike me, he was unsuccessful. The first stabbing was in his back, followed by several more, I turned him over to face me, that look of terror in his eyes. I took my electrical pliers and pulled out four of his teeth, he could never bite anyone again. Finally, using the same knife, I marked his forehead with a number four, and left him to die.'

There was a knock at the door, a uniformed officer entered, asking if one of the detectives could step outside.

Adam looked at the digital clock, they'd been questioning Peter Johnson for almost two hours, and it was approaching lunchtime.

'We're going to take a thirty-minute break now, we'll reconvene at one-forty. Peter, one of the officers, will stay in the interview room and arrange sandwiches for you and a drink.'

'Thank you, DI Fox,' came the reply.

Both detectives stood in the corridor, Tom Vickers suggesting they go to the staff canteen for a sandwich.

'Sir, we've found the black box and bag, it *was* in the shed at Dr Johnson's home address.'

Due to seniority, the officer directed the message at DCI Vickers, but Adam replied.

'What was inside the box?'

'It's in the evidence room sir, I think it might be better if you take a closer look, at both what was in the box, and the bag.'

'You go and take a look Adam; I'll pick up a sandwich and see you in your office.'

'Thanks sir, I won't be too long.'

Adam made his way to the evidence room, signed himself in and opened the door to the storage locker where Peter Johnson's black box and bag contents had been neatly laid out on a table, which was covered with a light grey plastic sheet.

He put on a pair of blue latex gloves and quietly began examining all the items on the table.

The gold signet ring from the burnt finger of Arthur Richardson, the hand, skilfully removed from Patricia Locke.

He opened the white envelope and let the hair fragments from Ross Sullivan fall onto the table. The face mask is designed to frighten the victims. Finally, the bloodied teeth of Steven Andrew's all four of them.

Studying the items in detail, he began to consider in his mind what drove Peter Johnson to murder his victims, selectively hunting them down, one by one.

During his time at Chaffinch House, he clearly must have endured pain and humiliation from his victims. Later in life, they saw what they did to him as a twisted form of entertainment for themselves.

They were seen as superior to the boys in their control, abusing them at every opportunity, believing that they'd never be found out, or have to pay for their actions.

On the surface, Peter Johnson led a normal and fulfilling life, whilst keeping his violent tendencies hidden from those who knew him best.

He glanced over to the right-hand side of the table, observing a pair of black leather gloves, what looked like sturdy flex, several lengths of wire, four knives of different lengths, a wooden handled hammer, and a pair of electrical pliers, the pliers still had remnants of blood on the jaws.

There was also a larger brown envelope on the table, Adam opened the top flap and pulled out a photograph, although it was well worn, it was the same photograph that DS Frank Bailey had taken at Patricia Locke's property.

He now knew this was Chaffinch House, it showed four images, marked through with a red cross, on the top row was a final image, marked with a black circle, which he believed must have been Walter Heathcote.

DCI Vickers was looking out the window of Adam's office as he returned, sandwiches and a Diet Coke on the desk.

'I've just called the Chief Superintendent and updated her on the current position. She doesn't know Peter Johnson, but like all of us, she's having trouble taking it in.'

Adam checked his watch as he sat down at his desk. 'We're due back in soon, is there anything that you believe we're missing? The interview is being recorded and you're taking notes in the logbook, so we're interviewing by the book, and in the correct way.'

Tom Vickers didn't reply, he knew what Adam was referring to, Daniel Ashby.

An innocent young man, a flawed investigation, found guilty of the wrong murder, spending fourteen years in prison.

If only Mary Ashby had spoken up earlier, and told Peter about his son, then maybe, just maybe the other brutal killings could have been avoided.

They were about to go back downstairs when Adam's mobile rang, an unexpected name came up.

It was Frank Bailey.

Ninety-eight

ADAM PRESSED THE GREEN icon on his mobile phone, 'Frank is that you, are you okay?'

'Hi boss, yeah, it's me and I'm doing fine, should be home, maybe even tomorrow. Have you arrested Peter Johnson, is he opening up about murdering Wilfred Heathcote?'

'Yes, he's at police headquarters, both DCI Vickers and I are questioning him currently. He's admitted to murdering Walter Heathcote and the other killings we've been investigating, starting with Arthur Richardson all those years ago. He killed Patricia Locke, Ross Sullivan and finally, the brutal killing of Steven Andrews. He will also be charged with the attempted murder of an acting police officer. I'll brief you further when I see you, including all the motives for the vicious actions he's taken.'

'Well, at least the stitches in my stomach were worth it then.'

'Don't joke, Frank, you could have died.'

'You don't get rid of me as easily as that boss… I know what you mean, but if I think about it too seriously, I'm not sure I'd ever return to active duty.'

Not pausing, Adam quickly replied.

'Oh yes you will, you're my right-hand man, you're going nowhere.'

Adam waited for a reply, but it didn't come.

'Listen, Frank, we've got to head back downstairs, can I call you tomorrow and we can fix a time for me to come over?'

'Okay boss, oh and by the way, thanks for looking after Julie, much appreciated.'

The line went dead.

Peter Johnson still sat alone as both DCI Vickers and DI Fox entered the interview room, he didn't look at either of them until they sat down opposite.

'Before we go any further Peter, I need to ask you if you've reconsidered and now want to be represented by a solicitor,?, if you don't have one, we can arrange a duty solicitor to represent you.'

'Thanks, Detective Inspector Fox, but as I mentioned earlier, I don't require any legal assistance, all they'd tell me to say is. No comment.'

'Can we discuss the attack and subsequent killing of Wilfred Heathcote, I understand he was the headmaster at Chaffinch House, is that correct?'

'Yes, he was, at least whilst I was there. I'm sure he knew what was taking place at the boarding school, after all, he was the headmaster, supposedly the person in charge. But he did nothing to protect the very boys he was responsible for, so like the others, he had to be punished. I still remember the day he announced to everyone about the sudden death of my friend Toby. He almost made out it was *his* fault for drowning, I couldn't ever prove it, but I'm sure he knew that some of the other boys were to blame.'

'How did you know he was at the nursing home?'

'Oh, that was easy, I've got… sorry, had several patients on my list that resided at the home. It wasn't too difficult to check that he was being cared for there. I booked a couple of days away from the medical centre, a pharmaceutical conference I was supposed to be attending. Drove over to the home, managed to check which room he was in and made my way up the stairs, bag in hand. He was just sitting there, looking out of the window, I'm not sure he knew anyone had entered the room. I unzipped the bag, took out one of the knives and slit his throat. I was going to mark his forehead, just like the others, but then your officer came in.'

'What about our colleague, DS Bailey?'

'That was a mistake which I'm deeply sorry for. I shouldn't have attacked him like that. As a doctor, I should have stayed with him, stabilised him, and made sure he was out of danger. But as I've mentioned, I panicked, just wanted to get away.'

Tom Vickers looked up from taking notes, 'You left one of my officers for dead, if it hadn't been for the quick thinking of staff at the nursing home, you'd have a further murder on your hands.'

He put his pen down firmly on the table and turned to face Adam. 'I think we're done here, I'll write up all the notes and we'll do the paperwork tomorrow. I need some fresh air.'

'Before we finish the interview sir, I want to ask one more question, a question that's baffled me and the team right from the very beginning of the investigation.'

'Why leave petals at every killing apart from the last one?'

Adam noticed for the very first time during the whole interview process that Peter had a slight smile on his face.

'When my father died unexpectedly I took on the responsibility of taking care of my mother. She never really got over the death of her husband and unbeknown to me, and I should have known, she had the start of pancreatic cancer. During her final months, she'd ask me to pick some roses from the garden, she loved to smell them in her bedroom. It was only a matter of a few weeks before she died, I never forgave myself for not doing more whilst she was alive. Leaving those petals after I'd finished punishing the victims brought some form of release, letting them drift around the bodies, it seemed to help… Her name was Rosemary, but everyone knew her as Rose.

It was late evening before Adam left Central Derbyshire HQ, thankfully the traffic was light, and he drove home in silence, no Spotify tonight.

Viv's Skoda was on the drive when he pulled up, the lounge curtains still open, glancing through the window, he noticed she was sitting on the settee, working on her computer.

He knew it was going to be a difficult conversation, Viv was very fond of Peter, and he'd given her the opportunity of a partnership, something he guessed she'd never forget. Opening the front door, unlike most other evenings there was no smell of food wafting from the kitchen, just stillness.

'Hi sweetheart, he was going to ask 'How are you feeling? But decided against it.

'Sorry, I'm a bit late, as you can imagine, it's been a tough day.'

Adam hadn't seen Viv wear her prescription glasses for weeks, the PC screen reflecting in the glass. The sadness he saw in her eyes pulled at his heartstrings, that look like she'd had before when they'd been talking about Scarlett.

She turned to him.

'I need to get some work done tonight, take my mind off what's gone off. The medical centre is going to have to take priority from now on, the patients, the staff, they must come first.'

He took off his jacket and sat down at the side of her, noticing tracks of tear marks down her face.

Reaching over, he closed her laptop, 'Work can wait, Viv, we need to talk about what's happened with Peter.'

'Is he all right?' I still don't understand what's happened. How could he have killed all those people?'

'He's admitted and been charged with the murder of five people, the first one from several years ago. He's also been charged with the attempted murder of Frank; he'll be back home soon too. I'm not going into detail at this point, you'll appreciate that, except to say, it all goes back to a traumatized period spent at boarding school, a period he's never been able to forget. We'll work through a process for the medical centre, don't worry about that. The important thing is that I take care of you, I've always done that, and I always will.'

Ninety-nine

ADAM HAD SET HIS MOBILE ALARM for 6:30 a.m.

Viv lay at the side of him as he turned over in bed, her face looked pale, and her eyes looked sore from crying well into the night.

He was going to suggest that she take the day off, but then he realised that she was now the most senior partner at the practice, so didn't say a word.

He'd agreed with DCI Vickers that he would visit Frank Bailey before coming into the office, Frank deserved to know what the full situation was with Peter Johnson.

Showered and dressed, he made his way to the kitchen, making a fresh pot of filtered coffee, and taking a mug up to Viv.

She'd just opened her eyes as he entered the bedroom, placing the mug of coffee on the bedside table, she moved towards the centre of the bed, giving him room to sit next to her.

'Good morning, I brought you a coffee, your favourite mug, the ones we bought when we went to the DENBY shop.'

She held his hand, squeezing it tightly.

'Thank you... Do you remember when we first met in that pub in Sheffield, you walked over to me, and we spent the rest of the night just chatting. By the end of that evening, I knew I wanted to spend the rest of my life with you. So, you could bring me fresh coffee every morning.'

The disappearance of Scarlett would have placed huge pressure on most marriages, but Viv always managed to rise above the challenges that life threw at her. Adam often wondered if it was her family background, having that financial security, or the fact that being a GP she had to have a positive view on life, either way, she seemed to have an inbuilt ability to absorb and deal with challenging news.

Adam had only been to Frank's house once, so he'd asked him to text the details. Putting the postcode into the sat nav system gave direction to the village of Wymevale, a thirty-five-minute drive towards Ashbourne, then taking the A523.

He turned on Spotify and selected The Beatles, track one played, I Feel Fine, and he began to sing the lyrics.

'Baby's good to me.'

'You know, she's happy as can be.'

'You know, she said so.'

'I'm in love with her and I feel fine.'

'Baby says she's mine.'

'You know, she tells me all the time.'

As he started to sing the second verse, his mobile rang, checking the caller's name, it was Craig Slater.

'Adam Fox Good morning.'

'Adam, it's Craig Slater, are you free to talk?'

'Morning sir, can I call you back?' I'm driving at the moment, give me five minutes.'

'That's fine, thanks a lot.'

About a mile ahead was a pub, it was still early in the morning, so ample parking spaces, he pulled in and switched off the engine.

DCS Slater answered his mobile immediately.

'Hi Adam, thanks for returning my call. I've just been speaking with Tom Vickers; he suggested I contact you directly. Firstly, how is Frank Bailey?, I understand he's out of hospital.'

'Yes sir, that's where I'm going now, see how he's doing, bring him up to speed with the case.'

'Okay, well, give him my regards. I also wanted to have a quick word with you about your daughter, and if it's appropriate to talk on the phone. Scarlett, I think her name is.'

His heart missed a beat as he heard the name of his daughter. 'Yes sir, her name *is* Scarlett, what did you want to discuss?'

Craig Slater didn't answer immediately, then replied.

'Well, if you recall when we last met, we chatted about the possibility that Scarlett's disappearance could be linked to local drug gangs, some form of retaliation for trying to bring down their business empire. I've spoken with a DS Sarah Ward; she's updated me on her progress too. Adam, we now believe this may have been an inside job, someone was passing on information about your investigation when you were at Sheffield, that's how they knew where you lived.'

Adam sat there in silence, struggling to take in what DCS Slater had just told him.

'Are you sure about this, how did you find out?'

'I knew you were going to ask me that, and it's a very interesting question. One of the gang members you put away is squealing like a banshee, giving us details of some of the main ringleaders running the gangs, and how it's organised. Including the fact that someone inside the force is also involved. Unfortunately, he doesn't have a name or rank, but at least we now know how details could be getting out, and that includes your home location. He's done a deal with us. With a reduced sentence and a new identity, we might get more from him as time goes on. That's not all, he's also convinced, with the amount of time that's gone by since your daughter's disappearance… I'm going to level with you here Adam. He believes she could have been sent abroad, or sadly… she may have been killed by one of the gang associates, as an example of their pledge of loyalty to the hierarchy.

A surge of pain flashed across Adam's forehead, his hands felt damp, his eyes filled with tears, blurring his vision, and his stomach began to churn, he had to get out the car, get out the car, get out the car.

'Adam are you there?, I'm sorry to bring you this news, I wanted to tell you face to face, but I'm supposed to be on annual leave as of today, so I thought this was the best option. I didn't want to wait until I returned, you needed to know.'

He leaned against the car bonnet, seeing his reflection in the paintwork, his legs felt like lead, unable to move, his body was in shock, but his mind was clear. He'd find out where the leak was coming from, and whoever was responsible, make them pay for their actions, and bring them down, bad decisions have consequences.

'Adam, are you still with me?'

'Yes sir, thanks for bringing me up to speed. I was always mindful that news like this was possible, it's been so long since she went missing, it was only a matter of time before the truth would emerge.'

'Listen, Adam, we'll get together when I get back, but for now, I'm sorry for the terrible news.'

DCS Slater hung up.

He got back in his car, his throbbing head beginning to ease, but personal heartache kicking in 'What should I do next,' he said to himself.

Travelling to Frank's house, going back to the station, or going home and waiting for Vivian to come from work, he decided Frank's was still the best option.

Julie Bailey opened the front door, greeting Adam with a friendly smile, she'd brushed her hair into a ponytail, which revealed a sharp oval-shaped face.

'Hi Adam, come on in, he's in the lounge, watching the morning news.'

Frank sat in what looked like his favourite chair, switching off the TV as Adam entered the room.

'Morning boss, thanks for coming over, how are things at the station?'

'Hi Frank, all's okay. But first things first, how are you feeling?'

'I'm doing fine, a bit sore around the wound, but the stitches should be out in the next few days, then it'll fully heal, and I'll be back at work. I was incredibly lucky, the doctor explained, if the stab wound had been a couple of inches higher, it could have been a completely different outcome, so oddly, Peter Johnson did me a favour, not killing me too.'

'Peter Johnson did you no favours, you got in the way of a mass murderer, frankly, a serial killer. He wasn't bothered if you lived or died, he just wanted to get away, leaving you there, bleeding to death.'

A serious look came over Frank's face.

'Doesn't it come with the job, every day that we're at work, aren't we exposed to personal danger, trying to protect the very people who want to injure us, and getting attacked in the process.'

Adam knew only too well about danger and the effect it can have on your personal life, the call from DCS Slater earlier that morning had brought that well and truly back into focus.

'Listen, Frank, Peter Johnson won't be able to murder anyone else anymore. I've talked with Tom Vickers this morning; Johnson has been charged with five murders and one attempted murder. He's currently been remanded in custody until the trial date.'

'That's great news, finally, we can bring the investigation to a close… You know Adam, they're always found out in the end, violent criminals, murders, rapists, drug gangs, eventually we bring them to justice, that's what makes the job so worthwhile.'

The lounge door opened, and Julie came in with a pot of tea, cakes and three cups and saucers, placing the tray on a side table. 'I thought it was time we had a drink, I've made a lemon drizzle cake, you're going to try some aren't you Adam?'

'You try and stop me,' he replied.

'This is the man who's a bit of a fitness fanatic' Frank responded. 'Black coffee, diet coke, then eats' drizzle cake, and KitKats at work.'

'Careful Frank, what goes on at work, stays at work.'

Julie put her cup on the tray, placing a second slice of cake on Adam's plate.

'How has Vivian taken the news about Dr Peter Johnson? It must have come as a great shock to her, they were quite close weren't they.'

'They were Julie she was struggling to take it all in, although he was the senior partner, he was a good friend and a great GP, or so she thought. It'll take her some time to understand why he did what he did, maybe we'll never really know. Speaking of Vivian, I need to take my leave, I promised to be home early today, and I've got to get back to the station, quick update from Tom Vickers.'

Frank shuffled up the chair and stood to his feet.

'Thanks for coming over boss, I'm hoping to be back at work soonest, I've got a visit with occupational health next week, so I'll keep you posted.'

'Don't worry about that, just look after yourself and don't think about returning to work until you're one hundred percent fit… and that's an order.'

One hundred

DCI VICKERS GOT UP FROM BEHIND his desk as Adam entered his office. He was going over the notes he'd taken during the interview with Peter Johnson.

'Morning Adam, how's Frank doing, hope he's recovering well?'

'He's doing fine sir, meeting with occupational health next week I understand, and if he passes, then he can return to light duties. But I've told him not to come back until he's ready.'

'Good, I hope you gave him my good wishes.'

'Yes sir,' although he hadn't.

'I've given a full briefing to the chief super on Peter Johnson, I also confirmed that the whole interview was conducted under PACE guidelines, no more errors this time. He's been remanded in custody, no date as yet for the court appearance, hopefully, it shouldn't take too long.'

'Finally, it brings this case to a close sir. I know you won't mind me saying this, but if we'd have been more thorough in the initial murder of Arthur Richarson, all that followed, well, it could have been prevented.'

CDI Vickers walked back to his desk, his leather chair creaking again under his heavy frame, a frustrated look on his face.

'I know exactly what you're saying Adam, but it's now finished with, you've got your killer and that's the end of it. We've far more important things to discuss if you don't mind.'

Adam pulled back one of the two chairs in front of the desk and sat down, linking his fingers together.

'Have you spoken to DCS Slater today, he was going to contact you about your daughter?'

'I took the call this morning, he explained what he understands to be the circumstances behind the disappearance of Scarlett.' His fingers tightened like a vice just mentioning her name.

'I'm sorry sir, but if DCS Slater is right, I'm struggling to understand why anyone inside the force would be involved with drug gangs. Passing on sensitive and personal details, what do *they* get out of it? Yes, it's correct, when I was in South Yorkshire we infiltrated what we understood to be organised crime, but other officers were involved. Some senior to me, so why single out my family?'

'That's what you and DCS Slater have to find out Adam. Craig Slater is an exceptionally experienced officer, operating at a senior level. If he believes it's an inside job, a corrupt officer, I'd stake my pension that he's on the right track. Work with him, see how he operates, and share information, he'll be good for your career, you can't trust everyone, but you can trust him.

Adam had already made his mind up, if Craig Slater wanted to work with him on Scarlett's disappearance, he'd welcome it with open arms.

'And that brings me to my next point. After careful consideration, I've decided to take early retirement. I've already discussed this with the Chief Superintendent. After nearly thirty years, it's time someone with fresh thinking and new ideas took on the role… and the wife wants more holidays together.'

The look of frustration had eased as Adam replied.

'That's a complete surprise, Tom, are you sure about this?'

'Absolutely, you know when the time is right, and this is the right time Adam.'

Seconds turned to minutes before either of them spoke.

'The chief super wants *you* to consider the position. She's impressed with how you've handled this case, and firmly believes you'd make a great DCI. And as a matter of fact, so do Craig Slater and me, you're the right man for the job Adam.'

He left the office at 4:25 p.m. the conversation he'd had with Tom Vickers swirling around in his mind. Who was passing on information to the drug gang leaders, and apart from DCS Slater, who could he trust now and in the future?'

Viv hadn't arrived as he pulled onto the drive. He unlocked the front door and shot straight upstairs for a shower.

Towelled dry, he headed back down and into the kitchen, picking up his mobile, he called Viv's number, and she answered immediately.

'Hello you, what time will you be home? I thought I'd do the cooking tonight.'

'Wow, that makes a change. Err, sorry, I'm just about to leave now, it's been a tricky day, can we not discuss it when I get home? I want to put the whole thing to the back of my mind for now, see what happens further down the line.'

'Yep, that's fine, I'll have a white wine waiting when you get back.'

'I'll just have sparkling water,' replied Viv.

He grilled some chicken, made a fresh salad with French dressing, and placed two wine glasses on the breakfast bar.

Car lights shone through the lounge window, confirming Viv had arrived. Opening the front door she placed her laptop on the floor as usual and made her way to the kitchen.

'Dinner is served,' Adam announced, finally enjoying an evening meal together.

He decided that he wasn't going to tell Viv about the conversation with Craig Slater, nothing would be gained by telling her something that was at this point, just a theory, he needed more time.

'I've had an interesting conversation with Tom Vickers earlier today, nothing to do with Peter, we're not talking about that.'

'Thank you, so what did DCI Vickers have to say, and did he ask about Frank?'

'He *did* ask about him, he's doing fine, and could be back at work in a couple of weeks if he behaves himself.'

'That's good news, I like Frank, he's a good man. So, what else did he have to say?'

'He's retiring, hanging up his truncheon, or whatever coppers say when they finally finish. The chief super wants me to consider the position, to take over from Tom as Detective Chief Inspector. I'm sure there'll be other candidates to be considered, but according to Tom, I'm their first choice.'

'Adam, that's fantastic news, you deserve promotion, what's *your* thoughts?'

'I'm going to go for it, what can I lose, if the Chief Superintendent has confidence in me, and I *know* I could do the job, then yes, if it's offered, I'm going to accept.'

Viv turned to him, and picked up her glass of sparkling water, replying. 'Detective Chief Inspector Adam Fox. You're the man.'

THREE MONTHS LATER

SURPRISINGLY, ONLY A HANDFUL of people were queuing outside Nottingham Crown Court, waiting to take their seats in the public gallery.

It *was* a cold, damp morning, and the tram system had gone down, this may have put some individuals off attending.

The case against Dr Peter Johnson hadn't received the coverage from the local press that others of a similar nature might have created, both editors in charge sticking to their previous agreement with DCS Craig Slater.

Walking up the concrete steps accompanied by two prison officers and taking his seat facing the opulent wooden-panelled courtroom, Peter already knew his fate.

Thankfully he hadn't got to face twelve members of a jury as he had already pleaded guilty to all five murders and one attempted murder, so in his mind, this was just a formality.

Everyone stands as the judge enters and takes his seat overlooking the whole courtroom. He opens the laptop and removes his glasses, placing them on the bench.

Before passing the sentence, the judge intentionally looks over to his left noticing both Detective Inspector Fox and Detective Sergeant Bailey in attendance.

'Peter Alexander Johnson, you have pleaded guilty to the murder of Arthur Richardson, Patricia Locke, Ross Sullivan, Steven Andrews, and Wilfred Heathcote, and also the attempted murder of Detective Sergeant Frank Bailey during the course of his duties. This was a heinous and shocking crime, planned and fulfilled atrociously and shockingly. Whilst you have continually accepted full responsibility for your actions, and considering this, I have no alternative but to sentence you to an indeterminate term in prison, with a minimum period of twenty-five years. Take him down.'

Peter looked at the prison officer on his left and then directly over at the judge and replied. 'Thank you.'

As he began to make his way down the steps, he stopped and looked towards the gallery, scanning the rows of chairs. Tears began to form in his eyes as he caught sight of Mary and Daniel Ashby, and sitting right behind, Dr Vivian Flemming.

***

'I know they're keeping this under wraps until it's officially announced, but congratulations on your promotion, Detective Chief Inspector Fox.'

Craig Slater had agreed to meet with Adam at Central Derbyshire Headquarters. Several months had passed since their first conversation about Scarlett's disappearance, and several leads had surfaced.

They'd met in Adam's current office, which if he was allowed, he'd want to stay there following his promotion, it had a better view outside.

'The team at EMSCO have uncovered a network of drug organisations operating between Leeds and the East Midlands. Several high-profile raids have taken place, but they always seem to be one step ahead of us.'

'So, by the sounds of it, the person or people passing on confidential details about our operations, *they do* work within the police force, and at a fairly high level. I don't think this is the work of a police constable, day to day they're not exposed to classified information like we are.'

'I think that's right,' said Craig Slater. They're not, but we're no closer to finding out who they are, it's going to take time.'

'I've waited over four years to find out what happened to our daughter, dead or alive. Even if I have to continue to investigate this myself, I will find out who the perpetrator is. No matter *what* level they're at, they won't be protected, and I will bring them to justice. That's guaranteed.'

***

It was Saturday morning; the sun was desperately trying to break through the curtains of Kate and Adams' bedroom window, although it was throwing it down with rain.

They're both used to waking up early, but today was special, it was Viv's birthday.

Adam went downstairs, checked the water in the kettle and switched it on. Normally, it was a rushed job, but this morning was different, breakfast was going to be served in bed, fresh fruit salad topped with non-fat yoghurt, coffee and as a treat, warm croissants with strawberry jam.

Making his way back, Adam checked to see if any mail had been pushed through the front door letterbox, probably a bit too early, he thought.

He pushed the bedroom door open with his foot, placing the breakfast tray at the bottom of the bed.

'Here we go sweetheart, birthday breakfast for the birthday girl, no full English here, just a healthy start to the day.'

'What time is everyone arriving?, not too early I hope, I've got to get myself together.'

'Well, your parents are going to arrive around eleven thirty, I thought we'd just have a sandwich for lunch, then everyone will start to arrive around four o'clock for the birthday celebrations to start.'

'Has the post arrived yet?'

'No, I've checked, but it's a little bit early for the postwoman, just enjoy your breakfast, take a shower, or even a bath if you want.'

'When was the last time I had a bath… No, a long hot shower will be fine thanks.'

Adam moved over the bed and held Viv's hand, 'It's been a tough few weeks. Let's celebrate your birthday with family and friends and have a wonderful time. Also, are we going to announce the good news? Your decision entirely.'

Viv smiled back at him, 'I think we should, you're the man.'

A large Happy Birthday banner swung over the lounge fireplace, and the kitchen was arranged with glasses, plates, and serviettes.

Adam had ordered platters of party food from a local shop in the village, and a birthday cake, all scheduled to arrive around one thirty to two o'clock.

He'd called at the supermarket a couple of days previous, picking up sufficient alcohol for around fifty people, although only about twenty couples were invited.

Around forty minutes later, Viv made her way down the stairs, breakfast tray in hand, making her way into the kitchen, Adam did a second take; she looked stunning.

Wearing the red dress he'd bought for her birthday, loose fitting with a belt around the waist, tied in a knot, with two tassels hanging down at the front.

She almost came up to Adam's shoulders, wearing the light grey high-heel shoes she'd purchased recently, looking more like a movie star than a GP.

'You look fantastic, the shoes, the dress, nearly as good as the uniform you wear at the medical centre.'

She lightly punched him in the stomach, 'You cheeky sod… Looks good, yeah?'

'Great,' he replied.

Adam checked out the kitchen clock, as a knock came at the front door, eleven-thirty, right on time, Viv's mum and dad had arrived.

Minutes later a second knock, this time it was the post woman, she had a handful of mail, too much to push through the letterbox without tearing some, she explained.

Adam sorted them into two piles, birthday cards taking priority, stacked neatly on the granite work surface.

By four-thirty everyone had arrived, including staff from the medical centre, this was a last-minute suggestion from Adam.

Some of Viv's friends, neighbours from next door and the two houses opposite.

Then some of Adam's work colleagues, whom Viv also knew. Frank and Julie Bailey, he was well on the way to full recovery. Close friends Chris and Fiona Mitchel. Tom Vickers, and his wife, which was Viv's idea, and finally, Dr Rachel Munroe and her female partner.

Adam tapped the side of his wine glass; an announcement was underway.

He looked over towards Viv, standing there in her beautiful red dress. 'Ladies and gentlemen, a big thank you from Vivian and me for making this birthday incredibly special. And from Viv, thank you for all the lovely presents. This is a double celebration, firstly, it's my wife's birthday, so Happy Birthday Vivian.

We also have a second celebration. We're both delighted to announce that we're going to be parents again, my darling wife is having another baby.'

Sounds of applause, laughter and congratulations filled the lounge and kitchen, Viv's parents giving her a hug and a congratulatory kiss.

Looking around, Adam hoped everyone was enjoying the party, even Tom Vickers and his wife.

As he looked at the birthday guests, he began to wonder if the informer was in this house right now. He'd known and worked with these people, and yet, did he know them at all?

Could one of them be passing on classified information to the ringleaders of the gangs, and how would he be able to prove it?

He knew he'd have to work closely with Craig Slater, however taking a second glance at Viv, he decided this wasn't the time or place to be thinking this through, and yet he was.

Adam picked up all the birthday envelopes, placing them in size order, noticing, but paying little attention to one from The Netherlands.

One by one, Viv opened the cards, thanking people at the party for their kind wishes, halfway through, she too noticed the typed home address franked, The Netherlands.

'I have no idea who this is from?. Possibly from Dirk Classen of FRODEN Pharmaceuticals, he's Dutch.'

As she ripped open the envelope a small Polaroid photograph dropped by Adam's feet, he ignored it momentarily, as he witnessed the blood drain from Viv's face.

'What is it sweetheart, are you all right?'

She handed him the birthday card. On the front was a teddy bear with the words. Happy Birthday, Mummy. He opened it up, and it read. Miss you mummy, love from Scarlett xxx.

He bent down and picked up the photograph. It showed a young girl sitting on a chair. She was around the age of four, with long blond hair, and a small mole on her left cheek. In the background, hanging on a door hook was a black and white striped baseball cap.

Could Scarlett Fox still be alive?

ACKNOWLEDGEMENTS

Acknowledgements are due to everyone who's encouraged me to write this book, friends and family. Also, my close buddy Glyn Hughes. Who tirelessly reads my books and offers genuine, constructive feedback.

A special thanks must go to retired Police Officer Richard Henson for all his patience, professional guidance and advice, and to my old friend Anthony Hubbard for the introduction.

Finally, a special mention must go to Keith Abbott and everyone at Michael Terrence Publishing for their leadership and direction in bringing this book to life.

– Thomas Heald

TH

THOMAS HEALD

WWW.THOMASHEALD.COM

Printed in Great Britain
by Amazon

63203080R00194